P9-ELD-512

The Rendition

The Rendition

A Novel

Albert Ashforth

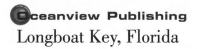
Longboat Key, Florida

ISBN: 978-1-60809-059-4

Published in the United States of America by Oceanview Publishing
Longboat Key, Florida
www.oceanviewpub.com

2 4 6 8 10 9 7 5 3 1

Printed in the United States of America

To Erika,
who is always there

Acknowledgments

In writing this book, I received help at every stage and of every kind. I am especially indebted to Pat and Bob Gussin, not only for their professional expertise, but also for their extraordinary encouragement and support. Susan Hayes edited the manuscript in a manner that was outstanding in every respect. Manuscript suggestions were also provided by many Mystery Writers of America colleagues and particularly by Pat Carlson, Stacy Kaplan, Bob Knightly, David Linzee, Theasa Touhy, and Kay Williams. Andy Ruch of the Munich Police and Otto Brüstle provided information I could not have found elsewhere. Among the many people I worked for overseas, I want to express my particular gratitude to Monika Zwink, Rosemary Hoffmann, E. M. Huschka, the late Bob Speckhard, and Paul Lovello. To the many military and civilian men and women I have worked with over the years, I want to say how proud I am for having served with you, and how grateful I am for having known you.

Rendition: The practice of sending a foreign criminal or terrorist suspect covertly to be interrogated in a country with less rigorous regulations for the humane treatment of prisoners.

– Shorter Oxford English Dictionary, Sixth Edition

Military terminology is not always understood by civilians, although over time many phrases make their way into the everyday language. Acronyms like GI and KP are used without a second thought. Intelligence agencies, however, are often so super secret, they not only do not want to advertise their activities, they don't want to admit they even exist. As a result, much intelligence terminology remains obscure to civilians. The term "rendition" is a case in point. Its use to signify the illegal abduction of a person from one country to another was coined after the practice came to be an accepted response for combating global terrorism. Rendition has now seeped into the language, but it has only been used in the intelligence sense for the past few years.

Please see the explanations at the end of the book for further insight into military and intelligence terms and acronyms.

The Rendition

Chapter 1

Monday, March 19, 2007

It was just before 2400 hours, and it was the kind of chilly night you get in the Balkans in late March. Scattered patches of snow on the forest floor and a few small drifts were the last remnants of winter. After nearly three hours, my jacket had become caked with mud, and the muscles in my shoulders and upper arms no longer just ached —but were now numb. I was in a slight depression in the ground, in a grove of scrub pine and 150 feet from the house, peering through my night-vision goggles, which transformed everything I could see into an eerie shade of green. I was becoming more restless with each passing minute.

I had the feeling we could use more backup. One more guy would make a difference. Two would make one helluva difference. There were just three of us, all dressed in field jackets and black coveralls for the occasion—Larry Scott on the far side of the building, and Angel in the woods about thirty yards away. Angel and I were covering the door we expected them to use when they heard the big bang and came tumbling out of the house. But things were taking longer than planned. Or maybe I just had the jitters and wasn't all that good at this sort of thing anymore. No way could I admit that, of course—not even to myself.

When Buck asked me, I could have said, "No. Absolutely not. Find someone else." If I had, I'd be back in the States, and whatever I'd be doing would beat chasing around in the woods and playing soldier the way I'd been doing for the last two days. And if it had been anyone but Buck Romero, my old partner, who'd asked me, I would have said just that. "No. N-O. Absolutely not. Find someone else."

That's the worst of owing people favors. They usually expect you to repay them.

I took another slug from my bottle of water and continued to peer toward the house. There was faint light inside, maybe from some candles, but thick curtains were drawn across the two windows in my line of sight. Scott should have gotten things rolling before this. If the people running this rendition had thought to provide us with some Semtex or C-4 along with the weapons, it wouldn't be necessary to improvise a Molotov cocktail. Still, how long does it take to light a Molotov cocktail and toss it under a car in the garage?

Making sure the volume was down, I decided to break the radio squelch. "What's going on?"

Scott's voice responded, "It's gonna happen. There's a padlock on the garage. I gotta get it open."

Angel was impatient too. "How long does it take to pick a goddamn padlock? The car should have gone bang at least ten minutes ago."

"You guys hold your water."

Angel said, "I been pissing in my pants five minutes already."

After the explosion, our plan called for them to charge out of the house in this direction—and into the sights of our automatic weapons. I had an M49 machine gun set up on its bipod, and my left hand firmly around the magazine, but the position was becoming more uncomfortable with each passing minute. Again the thought occurred to me that I hadn't fired one of these babies since I last qualified on the range at Fort Bragg. How long ago was that? Ten years? Longer. Time flies.

Hopefully, I wouldn't have to fire it now.

We'd had these people under surveillance for nearly twenty-four hours, watching them come and go. Just three of them were in the building now, doing what I had no idea. Sleeping, probably. What we were aiming to do was execute a quick flushing operation, the kind of thing we had drilled into us at some point during our urban-warfare training. When people are surprised, their responses tend to be pretty predictable.

Duck! Look for the nearest exit! Shout and scream! Start shooting!

I've even known people to pray.

We were interested in only one of the people inside, an individual named Ramush Nadaj. It was never explained to us just why someone somewhere wanted Nadaj so badly that they were willing to pay us a bundle to bring him in. In fact, we didn't have even the slightest idea who it was who wanted him. But when you work in intelligence, you get used to things being "compartmentalized," which is another way of saying the left hand doesn't know what the right hand is doing. During the flight over, we kicked the subject around a bit, but we'd each learned a long time ago that's mostly how it is in this business. Which, of course, doesn't mean we weren't curious as all hell.

The house, which sat on a wooded hill a couple of miles from Pristina, Kosovo's capital, was rectangular, had maybe six rooms and, like most buildings in Kosovo, was built from bulky red cinder blocks. The roof was red slate. An outhouse was in back and the wooden garage with the Opel in it was on the far side. Houses in this part of the world are built for utilitarian purposes. The utilitarian purpose this house was serving was as a hideout for Ramush Nadaj.

Kosovo is probably Europe's poorest country. Although it's technically still a province of Serbia, that situation is due to change if the Kosovo Liberation Army has anything to say about things. From what I could see, with undocumented Albanians streaming in by the busloads and joining the ranks of the unemployed, Kosovo was becoming poorer by the day. Despite its eagerness to break free from Serbia, I doubt that a declaration of independence will have any effect on the province's poverty problem—or its crime problem.

We had a VW van sitting off the road a quarter of a mile away. Once we got our man, we'd give him a stiff shot of Thorazine, shove him beneath the floorboards, and hustle him back in the direction of Camp Bondsteel, the U.S. Army installation in Kosovo. But in the same way nature abhors a vacuum, the American government also abhors this kind of extraordinary rendition—or at least says it does. And because there couldn't be any official recognition of what was going down here in the Balkans, military facilities were off limits.

"Completely and totally black," is the way Buck described the operation for us just before we flew out of Dulles last week.

We'd bring Ramush Nadaj to a helicopter pad located less than a mile from the installation, where a Black Hawk chopper would be waiting to carry him away into the wild blue yonder—and eventually to Jordan, Romania, Bulgaria or perhaps to "the salt pit," the less than cozy prison our government runs just outside of Kabul in Afghanistan. Before the helicopter ride, they'd exchange his clothes for a jumpsuit in the event he might have a weapon concealed somewhere, stick some more Thorazine into his arm to help him relax, and jam an enema and some Pampers into his ass to keep him occupied after he wakes up— and after all that happened, he wouldn't be our worry anymore.

It was a variation of the operation we ran some years back out of Tuzla, in Bosnia, when we extracted Slobodan Milosevic from the friendly confines of his Belgrade apartment. At the time, he was watching the tube, drinking *raki* and, as he angrily complained in accented English, "not bothering anybody." That was an undertaking I was also involved in, but in a slightly more peripheral way than I was in this one.

I don't know which I heard first—the twig snapping or our Molotov cocktail exploding.

I must have heard the twig first because I was already moving when the big bang came from the garage. And then I felt a gun barrel thrust so hard into the small of my back that I let out a loud shout. Even as I rolled over and was trying to get my KA-BAR out of the sheath on my hip, I knew it was too late. Someone crunched my arm with a boot, picked up the KA-BAR and barked something at me in guttural Albanian. At that moment, two of the three occupants of the house came scrambling down the stone steps and began running in this direction.

When the barrel of an automatic weapon smashed into my face, I realized that things weren't going down exactly as we'd planned.

Still on the ground, I was able get my arms up, and the second and third hits were less direct. I vaguely remember the shouts, Albanian curses, and then I was being half dragged, half carried back into the woods. When I tried to resist, somebody aimed a boot in the neighborhood of my kidneys. Briefly, I blacked out. There was the sound of automatic weapons, but I wasn't sure who was shooting them. I thought

I heard Angel's voice, and he could have been shouting my name.

When I tried shouting back, another boot smashed into my mouth. I later discovered I had a mouthful of loose teeth.

And then they had me by the legs and were dragging me again. There was the distant sound of an automobile engine, but maybe it wasn't as distant as it sounded. Someone was using me for a punching bag, and something came down on my head. Hard. When I awoke, I hurt all over. Since my brain wasn't processing information with quite the efficiency it normally does, it took maybe thirty seconds to figure out that I was in the trunk of someone's car, which stunk of engine oil and seemed to be bouncing and bumping over a washboard dirt road. It was a safe bet we were on a dirt road since 90 percent of Kosovo's roads are still unpaved.

Although Mr. Nadaj seemed to have turned the tables very nicely, I did my best not to dwell on that fact.

It was a bumpy ride. We rode for what seemed like three hours, but when you're squashed into the pitch-black trunk of a vehicle with your knees only inches from your jaw and wondering how the hell you got into this mess, believe me, time drags. Particularly, when you're in the kind of rattletrap vehicles people drive in this part of the world, where probably four out of five cars on the road are either unregistered or stolen. For all I knew, we could have been underway for only forty-five minutes. After we stopped, I could hear people jabbering and moving around. Finally, someone pulled open the lid of the trunk and from out of the pitch darkness shone a flashlight into my eyes. Although my first impulse was to kick the two guys who reached in to grab my legs, I decided that discretion might be the better part of valor. As it turned out, I was wrong. They yanked me out of the trunk and over the bumper, then let me drop to the ground.

"For cryin' out —" I never finished the sentence.

"Shut up, asshole." I still wasn't tracking too clearly, but it sounded like someone was familiar with the English vernacular. It also sounded like the voice of a woman.

Before I had a chance to look around, a bearded guy wearing a green jacket and brown work pants and with a white rag on his head, whose breath stank of garlic, dragged me to my feet and sent me stumbling into a pitch-dark shack. When I said "Keep your goddamned hands to yourself," he responded by jamming his weapon into my back and shouting something in Albanian. I figured him for the individual who'd come up behind me and smashed my face with the butt of his weapon. Naturally, I also figured I owed him one, more than one. All right, so I'm vindictive.

After someone got the room's one lightbulb turned on, he motioned to me to remove my field jacket. First, he patted me down, looking for a weapon. Then he went through the jacket pockets. I watched silently as he carefully placed what he found onto the room's one table. There wasn't much: besides the KA-BAR, I had a couple of hundred euros, a handkerchief, a Leatherman, a bottle of liquid soap, a pocket comb, my passport. He told me to remove my G-Shock wristwatch, which he tossed to the guy who seemed to be in charge. That was Ramush Nadaj himself. I knew that because before we left we were given an array of his pictures, full-face and both profiles, which we'd committed to memory.

When you're running a rendition, you don't want to bring back the wrong guy. It has happened. More than once.

After he'd examined it, Nadaj tossed the watch on the floor and started pounding it with his rifle butt and then with the heel of his boot. I knew what he was doing—making sure the watch, in case it contained a transmitter, wouldn't be sending a signal to a satellite and giving away our location. With the watch in pieces, he held up a tiny component attached to a wire and flashed a triumphant smile. When he heaved it in my direction, I ducked, and then he barked something that seemed to mean I should put my hands on my head and sit down on the floor. I guess I didn't react quick enough to please his majesty because he immediately swung the barrel of his weapon at my head. Again I ducked, but when I tried to grab the gun, he was too fast for me. He swung it again, opening a gash on my left cheek, which immediately began to drip blood.

He smiled when he saw the blood, said something I couldn't understand, and swung his weapon in front of my nose. His smile was kind of goofy, reminding me of a couple of the individuals I encountered during a visit I once made to a facility for the criminally insane. Then he jammed the weapon against the side of my neck. I froze. As he held a brief conversation with the woman, I steeled myself, waiting for the inevitable. With the safety off, he didn't have to do anything more than squeeze the trigger.

Then I heard her say, *"Mos shti'ni."* Don't shoot.

After half a minute, he relaxed the pressure on the gun—and I started breathing again.

It was my passport that interested them most, and they all gathered around to take a look. I wasn't surprised when the guy with the droopy mustache tossed away the soap since, in Kosovo, they haven't yet heard that cleanliness is next to godliness. The individual who'd clobbered me—the one with the white do-rag around his head and garlicky breath—sat down on a cot and began playing with the Leatherman, an all-purpose utility tool, as though he'd never seen one before, which he probably hadn't.

When I saw Nadaj jam the wad of euros into the pocket of his field uniform, I had no doubt who was the boss here.

As they spoke, I looked around. The building wasn't much more than a small shack, sparsely furnished with a couple of cots, a wooden chest, a table, and some rickety chairs. It had two small windows, one of which had a broken pane, a flat ceiling, and a wooden floor. I could hear a humming sound from the generator supplying current for the single lightbulb.

After removing her fatigue cap, the woman turned her attention to me. With the cap off, her dark hair hung to her shoulders. She had very blue eyes, a thin straight nose, and a long pale face. Like Nadaj, she was dressed in black "cammies"—camouflage fatigues—which fit so loosely it was hard to tell what kind of figure she had. In other circumstances, I might have thought of her as mildly attractive.

With my passport in her hand, she said, "All right, Alex Klear, tell us why you're here. Who sent you?" Her English was accented but fluent. "Are you with KFOR?" KFOR is the designation for the NATO stabilization force occupying Kosovo, the army with the thankless mission of keeping Serbs and Albanians from one another's throats—peacekeepers, so-called.

I gave her the standard jive. "I'd like to speak with someone from the American Embassy."

"Tell us what we want to know. Then you can speak with your embassy."

"I'd like to—"

"UNMIK? Are you with UNMIK?" UNMIK is the United Nations Mission in Kosovo, which is headquartered in Pristina, the capital. UNMIK has the next-to-impossible task of trying to administrate the lawless province.

I said, "I can only give you my name, rank—"

"Cut the crap, asshole! I don't want this name, rank, and serial number bullshit."

She looked at Nadaj, said something in Albanian, obviously letting him know I wasn't being cooperative enough. Nadaj pointed toward me, made an upward movement with his fist. When she turned back to me, she had a strange smile on her face. "You don't answer our questions, we can make you wish you did." She stepped forward and aimed a kick with a muddy boot that struck against the inside of my thigh. "Next time I don't miss. And then I cut them off. You won't be able to get it up after that. It'll just hang there." She sneered. "No matter who the bitch is, it'll just hang there. You fuckin' understand me?"

I did understand her—well enough to know I was in a very bad situation. I made an enormous mental effort not to think about just how bad it was.

"Do you understand me?"

"I understand, but I don't see why I can't speak with the American Embassy."

Ignoring my comment, she said, "You can't be with UNMIK. They all wear blue uniforms and those stupid blue helmets. They're all cowards. They let Muslim people die in Srebrenica." She seemed to be working herself into a frenzy. "Thousands of people, men and boys, some just twelve years old, slaughtered like cattle. We'll never forget that!"

I knew what she was talking about. When I was in Bosnia, I'd gone to Srebrenica, an old mining city, where I helped keep the lid on a memorial celebration for slain Muslims that some of our people thought might get out of hand. Before that, the government had given me a ten-day course in Albanian and Serbo-Croatian, but that was a while ago, and I could only guess at what these people were saying. The last thing I could admit was that we were here on our own. There was a possibility, however slight, that they might think twice before killing a military member of KFOR. If they tumbled to the real situation, I figured I'd be dead before sunup.

"Are you with KFOR? Working for someone else? Answer!"

Definitely the excitable type. When I again mentioned the American Embassy, she spoke loudly to Nadaj, who shook his head.

Then the guy with the garlicky breath and the white do-rag on his head made a fist and shouted something at me. He seemed to have solved the Leatherman, and was acting as if he'd just invented the telephone or the internal combustion engine. If the Albanian language has the equivalent of "Eureka!" he was shouting it. He stood up from the cot, held up the Leatherman, then snapped out the knife blade and made a sawing motion. When the woman said something, they all started laughing.

Turning to me, she said, "Quemal is called by the people in his village 'Vrasës.' Do you know what that means?"

I frowned, recalling only that the word had something to do with killing.

When I shrugged, she said, "Killer or assassin." She smiled. "Quemal is known as 'The Assassin' because he killed the mayor of his village when the mayor insulted his sister."

Before I could reply, Quemal started jabbering again. When the woman said something, they again laughed.

"Quemal says in the village when they cut off someone's balls, he then has to eat them. I told him, with you no problem. Americans will eat anything that has ketchup on it."

"How would you know?" I said.

She smirked. "That's right, isn't it?"

"You speak good English." I figured some flattery couldn't hurt. And for understandable reasons, I was doing my best to change the subject.

The three guys were staring at me intently, trying to pick up what we were saying. There was a rickety wooden table at the center of the room, and Nadaj sat down at it, leaned forward, and said something to the woman. "Ramush says the people of Kosovo are fighting for their independence. He says in this country people die for what they believe. Not like America, where all the people want is to wear jeans and listen to pop music. He says one more person in a grave in Kosovo won't matter to anyone."

Although I assumed I was the "one more person" Ramush had in mind, I pushed that thought out of my mind. My left shoulder felt like it was dislocated. My mouth was full of blood. My head was pounding. I wondered what she'd say if I asked her for some Tylenol. Probably become even more hysterical.

"I'm asking again. Tell us who sent you." When I didn't respond, she said, "You think Quemal isn't serious?" She shouted at the guy on the bed, who stood up, pounded his chest, and shouted "Quemal Vrasës." Then he stepped forward, again snapped open the Leatherman, and began the sawing motion. I felt a wave of nausea, as though I might have to heave then and there.

Placing her hand on his shoulder, the woman pulled him back, then, turning back to me, she spoke quietly. "Listen, Alex Klear. You don't belong in the Balkans. Being an American won't help you here. Your only hope is you tell us who sent you here, and why."

I could agree with her that I didn't belong in the Balkans, and I couldn't help questioning the series of events that had landed me in this situation. The irony was, I couldn't answer her question. I didn't know who wanted Nadaj. Or why they wanted him. I was as curious about that as they were.

Still trying to change the subject, I asked how she'd learned English.

"You know where Bridgeport is? I lived there for three years, almost." When she again smirked, I saw she was missing a couple of teeth, a fact that definitely made her less attractive, and another reminder of how far behind the rest of Europe this country is. "My name is Viktoria. In the States they called me Vickie."

Ramush said something, and Vickie nodded. "How did you know where to find us?"

When I didn't answer, Vickie said, "You people aren't as smart as you think you are. We knew you were watching us."

That at least explained how they were able to grab me. I wondered about Angel and Scott, my two partners in this undertaking. I felt a sinking sensation as I realized that if they were dead I was as good as dead too. Buck was our contact, but none of us knew where he was. At the CIA station in Skopje? At Camp Bondsteel? Quite possibly, he was still back in D.C. Even if Angel and Scott were alive, they wouldn't know where I was. And with the van so far away, they couldn't have followed us.

I watched warily as the four of them talked. Quemal stood up from the cot, crossed the room, pushed back the table, and pulled open a heavy trapdoor in the floor. From where I was sitting, I could see wooden steps leading down to a small crawl space.

Vickie told me to stand up. Then Nadaj motioned to me to put my hands back behind my head.

When I again didn't react fast enough to suit him, he aimed his fist at my gut. I was ready this time. I sidestepped and swung, catching him solidly on the side of the head, hitting him hard enough to stagger him. He looked surprised, then angry. He barked something at the other two guys, who came at me in a rush. I got in a couple of good shots before they got hold of me, each of them hanging on to an arm. With Nadaj pounding me, I doubled up. Then something came crashing down hard on the back of my neck. When I was down on my knees, I got a kick in the face from Quemal, 'The Assassin.'" A couple of them dragged me toward the open trapdoor.

Vickie's laughter was more like a cackle, and over the ringing in my ears I heard her voice. "That's where you're spending the rest of the night, Alex. The rats and spiders will be good company."

I went down into the hole headfirst, tumbling down the wooden steps, my arms landing hard in a pile of junk, everything from broken glass to orange rinds and coffee grounds. When I tried moving my hands, I found myself with a fistful of human excrement. Someone dropped the door with a loud bang, a sound that made me think of a coffin lid being slammed shut. The earth beneath the house was damp and cold and stank as badly as anything I've ever smelled in my life. Someone had done a half-baked job of shoring up the dirt walls, which were crumbling and crumbled a little more every time I moved, and made me think that a too-sudden move might result in me burying myself alive. Except for a slant of light coming through a crack in the floor, it was pitch black. I felt pains shooting through my arms and back. There was hardly any room to move.

Above me in the room, the woman said something to her friends and they all laughed. Mixed in with the Albanian, I thought I heard the word "ketchup."

Chapter 2

Tuesday, March 20, 2007

I may have dozed during the night, but I never really slept. The lack of circulation and the dampness had caused all my joints to ache. Maybe the worst pain was in my head, where one of them, probably Quemal, had caught me with a boot. I could taste blood in my mouth. I suppose I spent four or five hours in the hole before I heard the tinny sound of a cheap radio, someone playing pop music, Albanian-style. After a while, the music was interrupted by a guy chattering excitedly, some kind of Albanian language newscast. In Kosovo, what passes for news is such transparent propaganda no one even pretends to believe it.

For maybe the third or fourth time, I threw up.

After they'd been moving around and talking for about an hour, things became quiet. Without my watch, I found it hard to gauge time. I heard a car engine turn over. A short while later, Nadaj pulled open the trapdoor. As I looked up, he pointed an automatic pistol at me and shouted something. He had a bandolier over his shoulder. As I staggered up out of the hole, he kept his weapon pointed in my direction. He needn't have bothered. I wasn't in shape to make any sudden moves.

But the weapon in his hand definitely caught my eye—a 9mm machine pistol, an MP5. So far as I knew, these were used exclusively by Special Forces, and were favored by "special ops" people in Afghanistan. I wondered how these characters could have gotten their hands on one of those babies.

I was aware how filthy my coveralls were, caked with mud and smeared with every kind of filth. I felt lightheaded, and not sure of what to do, I just stood there. Finally, the woman told me to sit down at the table with my hands out in front of me. In the center of the table was a partially filled bottle of water and a wormy-looking apple. She took out my passport, flipped through it, then smiled, obviously enjoying her little power trip.

"We know why you're here, Alex Klear." When she nodded in the direction of Nadaj, something told me the two of them were lovers. If they were, they deserved one another. "You people wanted Ramush. You wanted to grab him and take him back. Right?"

Still playing dumb, I frowned. "Ramush?"

"We don't think you're with KFOR. You're not military. Is that right?"

I was thirsty and tried not to look at the water. This character with the bandolier slung over his shoulder sitting opposite me at the table was definitely the individual in the pictures we'd been shown, all of which were in the glove compartment of our van. I told myself that this was going to have a good ending. I also told myself I'd gotten out of other scrapes, some of them worse than this one. I told myself I'd get out of here one way or another.

But while I'd been in some tight scrapes, I'd never before been so dumb as to let myself become a prisoner.

I was close to the point where I was running short on optimism. The danger in black operations of this kind is that you don't have fallback. For all we knew, Buck Romero, the guy who'd organized the Nadaj rendition, was still in the States. He'd given us a number to call in case of an emergency, but I had to wonder whether KFOR, even assuming Angel and Scott reached someone in Camp Bondsteel, would lift a finger to get me out. The military would only regard us as a bunch of bounty hunters, and now that I thought about it, who could blame them?

Nadaj fixed me with a stare, and just having to look at him up close was enough to shake my confidence a little more. Behind his unkempt curly hair, deep-set brown eyes, and black beard, there was a crafty, malicious look, the look of someone who can smell weakness and will always go for your jugular. I already knew Nadaj was good at sucker punches. The truth was, I was surprised that I was still alive.

"If not Ramush, what then? You tell us, you get something to eat and drink." Vickie tossed my passport onto the table.

I said, "Give me something to eat first, Vickie. Then we can talk." My voice sounded strange. The throbbing ache in my head was making me dizzy, and the room was beginning to spin.

She shook her head. "We know you're not with KFOR. You'd have ID."

"I want to speak with someone at the American embassy."

"You'd have one of those badges. Am I right?"

"I'm thirsty." I tried not to sound as tired as I felt.

She hesitated, glanced at Nadaj, then pushed the water and the apple in my direction. Drinking the water in Kosovo can be a ticket to a case of dysentery, but I was thirsty and I took a couple of sips anyway. When I started gnawing on the apple, I became aware of my loose teeth.

"Fadilj and Quemal will be back in an hour. You're going to wish you talked with me, Alex."

"Sure, Vickie." I took another bite out of the apple. Despite the worms, it was sweet, tasted good. I said, "Did you like America?"

Vickie looked at Nadaj and said something. When he laughed, she looked back at me. "Bridgeport's a shithole. I worked in a furniture factory. All day long I glued pieces of wood together. I wore a mask. I got less than fifty dollars every day to take home."

"That's more than you can make in a month in Kosovo, Vickie. And you don't have to give half to a warlord."

"I gave it to a landlord, asshole. My apartment was six hundred dollars, more. The landlord was a son of a bitch, and he kept the heat turned off. And your goddamned supermarkets charged for food like—"

"You should've gotten a green card. You could've earned more."

"I had a goddamned green card, asshole. You people and your stupid green cards. I hate your fuckin' goddamned country!"

Before I could say how much we Americans love our country, Nadaj said something and she nodded. "Ramush wants to know if you know about Afghanistan."

"What about it?"

"About what happened there." When I shrugged, she said, "Answer! Do you know what happened there?"

I shook my head, and Nadaj started talking excitedly, gesturing with his left hand, the hand without the gun. He shouted something at me, leaning over the table, sticking his dumb face in front of mine. I wondered what had gotten him so excited. Vickie started talking to him, as though she was trying to quiet him down.

"Ramush is unhappy with you, Alex Klear. He wants to know who sent you. He wants to know how many of you were back there. He thinks you know about Afghanistan. He knows you were after him."

Like I say, I couldn't have told Ramush exactly who sent me since I didn't quite know myself. I had no idea why they were asking about Afghanistan. This operation had been shrouded in mystery from the beginning.

Nadaj was still talking, but now he had his knife out. I became aware of my pounding heart. The knife had a curved black handle, a shiny steel blade, and I couldn't take my eyes off it. He stuck it in front of my face and kept it there for maybe a minute. The room started spinning again. As Vickie continued to talk with Nadaj, he calmed down. When he finally put the knife away, I breathed a shade easier.

"You just had a close call, Alex. Ramush says in his village the custom is to punish an uncooperative person by cutting off his nose. Ramush says without a nose you would be willing to talk. He says then you would tell the truth. He still wants to know who sent you." She paused, looked at Nadaj, who was smiling and nodding like the village idiot.

How could I have been so dumb as to fall into the clutches of people like this?

"I think you should tell us," she said. She picked up my passport. "Why is there no entry stamp? How did you get into this country?"

I tried not to look at Nadaj, who I'd decided was a total creep. I could have told her that I got the passport, my wristwatch, and the Leatherman from Buck Romero, the guy who sent us off on this little expedition. I could have said that we flew into Skopje, in Macedonia, and bypassed the customs officials at the border by paying them money. It was somebody's thinking that there shouldn't be any official record of our having been in Kosovo.

Since I couldn't say any of these things, I continued to play dumb. While Vickie turned the pages of my passport and spoke with Nadaj, I heard the sound of a car. The driver was gunning the motor, and it was working hard to get up the hill. In Kosovo, it's not generally understood that you have to keep a car's engine tuned for it to run efficiently. Even when it is understood, there aren't any tools or timing lights around to do the job. A civil affairs officer, a woman with a lot of experience in these parts, once told me that in Kosovo the people are obsessed by only one thing—their struggle for independence. When they talk about politics, they always end up discussing some battle they fought with the Serbs in the 1300s. Efficient engines are way down the list in importance.

Kosovo ain't America. Believe me.

A few minutes later, Quemal and Fadilj pushed their way in through the narrow door, both of them talking a blue streak. Fadilj had a basketful of food, which he set down on the table and which Nadaj immediately began examining. Within seconds, he had a box of cookies open and was stuffing the contents into his mouth, indifferent to the crumbs falling into his beard. Quemal, I noticed, was carrying a camcorder.

Fadilj pointed at me and laughed.

The worst of it was, it was probably my euros that had bought the camcorder. I had an idea I knew what it was for. And I now knew why Vickie had been able to talk Nadaj out of cutting up my face. They wanted me to look pretty. I also had an idea that I'd remain alive only for as long as I was useful to them.

While I sat at the table wondering if I should make a break for it right there, the four of them talked among themselves. Then Vickie said, "How do you like the idea of becoming a television star, Alex Klear?"

The Assassin said something, and Vickie nodded. "Quemal says he's going to make you famous. You'll be on television all over the world, Alex."

Behind me, Fadilj and Nadaj stood in front of the bare wooden wall holding their weapons. Both had scarves wrapped around their faces. Nadaj now had a bandolier slung over each shoulder, his fatigue cap covering most of his face. Very macho. They'd moved the table, and I was on my knees in front of Fadilj, who was seated on a chair. I guess I was the star because they had the camcorder pointed directly at me.

Vickie was standing off to the side sucking on a bottle of soda pop. She'd spent fifteen minutes explaining what they wanted me to say. She motioned to Fadilj to begin rolling the film.

"You can start now, Alex," she said, smiling.

With the camcorder rolling, I looked into it. "Mr. President. I'm in Kosovo. Through my own fault, I've been captured by freedom fighters. That's what they call themselves. My only hope to be freed by these morons is if you take our troops out of Afghanistan and demobilize the army. Before you do, I hope you will send an air strike and completely exterminate these creeps and their—"

Suddenly, Vickie started waving her hands and shouting, obviously telling Fadilj to stop filming. As she continued to talk, Nadaj, looking puzzled, asked what was going on. A second later, I felt what could have been a rifle butt against the back of my head. Two of them dragged me to my feet, and Nadaj drove his fist into my stomach. I wasn't too aware of whatever else he did because at some point I passed out.

Sprawled on the floor, I could hear voices, which grew loud and then faded. After a time, I could hear Vickie. Since she was speaking English, I knew she was talking to me. But it sounded as though she was in a tunnel. Then she was shouting my name. When I didn't respond, someone kicked me. Then I got some water thrown on me.

Then I was sitting up with everyone looking at me.

"We want to try it again. It's important to us. We'll keep doing it until you do it right." She again told me what they wanted me to say.

"It's your only hope. You want to live, don't you?" She grinned. "Even though you won't have a nose?"

Behind her, Quemal was smirking and making a sawing motion with the Leatherman.

A few minutes later, we started in again. "Mr. President. I'm in Kosovo. Captured. There are people here who want to set me free. But they prevaricate. They say they are freedom fighters. Enemies of America and lowlifes is what they really are. Vickie was in Bridgeport. Find out who the hell she—"

This time Vickie slugged me.

After a while, we tried it again, but for some reason it didn't go any better. I guess we didn't get a wrap. I felt myself smiling. That's what they say in Hollywood. "It's a wrap." I wanted to say that even after they'd beaten me up and while they were dragging me across the floor.

Even while Vickie was telling me I was going back in the hole, I wanted to say, "I guess we didn't get a wrap." I wanted to say something funny, let them know I thought they were a bunch of goofballs and nothing they could do would ever change that. But I was finding it difficult forming the words.

"You better talk tomorrow. Ramush is becoming very unhappy with you."

There were other voices, then a loud noise, something slamming shut—the lid of a coffin that I feared would never again be opened.

I'm having trouble breathing. Face down in a pile of filth. No idea of time. Smell makes me want to throw up. Like it was in Ranger School, eating mud on the obstacle course, DIs shouting and screaming. Vickie said I was stubborn. Who was it who always said that? It was Irmie— long time since we've seen one another.

Irmie, I still think about you.

Can hear the dogs. Keep stumbling. And those stupid Vopos, the East German Army, one dumber than the other. Buck, you remember that day? They were yelling. "Halt! Halt!" I fell. Really took a header. Hard ground. Frozen. Shots. I'm swerving one side to the other—don't want to give them a target, but that slows me down even more and, Buck, you're already in the chopper.

Expected to see you guys lift off, can't scrap the mission because of one dumb guy who can't get out of his own way.

I always worried that things would end badly if I stayed with the agency too long.

Buck, you and I go back a long way together. I couldn't say no when you needed a favor.

It's still so clear how they recruited me that day—Fayetteville, North Carolina, next to Fort Bragg, Cumberland County Sheriff's office. It's all flooding back. Me in my Class As, and Sergeant Aubrey, big, black, and hard as nails in his starched fatigues. Desk sergeant to our left behind the Plexiglas barrier, walk down the corridor, McDaniel leading the way, says why not hold the meeting in the sheriff's office, so we go down there. Sergeant Aubrey, Sheriff Wilson, Detective Solomon, and McDaniel. I don't know what's going on, and the way they're talking—leaving me out of it—makes it hard to understand.

Get a grip! You're in a hole underneath the hut. Stop dreaming! Hard to stay focused, have this awful stomach pain, probably from that water.

If I'd told McDaniel "no" that day, I wouldn't be here in this hole, would I? Do you know who McDaniel was, Irmie? He recruited me to become an intelligence officer. I was only nineteen.

Irmie's not here! Stay awake. Buck's not here either.

Sheriff knew what it was all about, but I didn't. They wanted Sergeant Aubrey in on it, so he stayed. I remember Detective Solomon saying "I'm from the Sixty-Seventh Precinct, gentlemen. That's Brooklyn, New York, Corporal Klear's hometown." Solomon points at me, and everyone nods. I can feel McDaniel's eyes on me. I didn't know he was from an intelligence agency. His eyes—like they're boring into me, making little holes.

Remember how I used to complain, Buck?

You're alone! Buck's not here.

Now I laugh at that stuff. Remember that one-star had us kicked off the installation when we wanted to interview his son about drug trafficking, and how mad I was? You said the guy had problems enough, give him a break.

I'm real surprised Detective Solomon knows about the muggings even though Mom never told anyone. They must've gotten it from the junkie, from Kraus. Kraus knew I was in the army. Mom all alone. He thought I was still overseas, which is where I was before I got temporary duty orders for the 82nd Airborne, which meant I was on my way back to Fort Bragg.

According to the detective, Kraus picked on older women. They were afraid, so they'd give him what he asked for—fifty, a hundred bucks. He mugged some too, not just Mom. Had to feed his habit. He knew who had money, who got Social Security checks. Mom told him no, speaking her broken English. I can imagine that scene. Made him feel like the worm he was. Good for her. So he waited a week, then mugged her in the vestibule. She didn't tell me about that, or about the second time. She only told me after the third time. On the telephone. Crying.

Weekend pass. It's Saturday night, I go to his apartment, my heart pumping, mad as all hell, ring the bell, wait. When he opens the door, I hit him, push my way in. He's big, but I'm still able to mop up the place with him. "Never do it again," I say. He's on his couch, a handkerchief up to his face, blood on it, staring at me with his little pig eyes.

He left Mom alone for two weeks, then he took her pocketbook while he held a knife to her throat. Knocked her down, left her lying in the gutter, and told her not to say anything to me or he'd have his friends take care of us both.

The pistol's a .38, got it in a hockshop, in Wilmington, North Carolina. Never told Mom I was home that weekend. Saturday night, waiting on the landing just above Kraus's floor. He doesn't show. But he comes in Sunday night, and I fire twice, miss once, get him with the second slug. His left knee.

He never saw who shot him. I figured he'd find it hard to mug people from a wheelchair, figured it'd be okay to go back overseas once I got my silver wings. Said goodbye to you, Mom. You baked challah bread, remember? Proud as all hell when I finally got those wings.

"Kraus is a piece of shit," Solomon says. "But he's filed a complaint that Corporal Klear was the one who shot him. He got a witness to say he saw Corporal Klear in the hallway."

When McDaniel finally speaks, that's when I figure I'm heading off to the military stockade for a good long stretch. "I'd like to point out that Detective Solomon's remark about this Kraus is irrelevant," he says. "Citizens can't take the law into their own hands like this here trooper did."

Looking at me, "Klear? Is that your name?"

"Yes, sir."

"Whoever put Kraus out of commission," Solomon says, "did everyone a favor."

"That's not the way we do things in this country," McDaniel says.

I knew Sergeant Aubrey liked me, and he's just staring, can't believe it, I guess. Knows I'd made it into Special Forces, knows how this would mean the end of everything.

"You have a warrant for Corporal Klear's arrest?" the sheriff asks, breaking the silence.

Detective Solomon nods. "I do."

McDaniel stands up then, checks his watch. I still don't know who he is and I find it funny how he's giving orders to everyone. He suggests we take a break for lunch even though it's only eleven thirty. Out in the hall, he says there's a cafeteria around the corner, and he and I can go there.

Couldn't know in that cafeteria I'd make a decision that would change my life, and finally end with me buying the Big Farm here in Kosovo, the one with the falling-down barn and broken machinery. That farm. Most Americans never heard of Kosovo. *If I'd've said no to McDaniel, I never would have met you, Irmie. Or you either, Buck.*

Stop talking to people. You're in a hole under the damned house.

"We can get all the bright people we want," McDaniel tells me.

"And the bad-asses are a dime a dozen. Like the man says, it's easy to be hard, but hard to be smart. But what we're really looking for are people with smarts who aren't afraid to make tough decisions. In this kind of business you have to do that sometimes, you know?" "Yes," I say, like I know what he's talking about. But I don't, not really. Don't have any idea of the tough decisions I'll make over the years.

By then, he'd already told me he was a recruiter for an intelligence agency, says maybe you never heard of us, but we're active, real active. We don't have so many people looking over our shoulders.

"That was a difficult problem you had, son. I'm not saying you did exactly the right thing, but the way you handled it—not too many people woulda done what you did and that tells me something about you. You got real high scores on your aptitude tests, Corporal. But also interesting is this language ability you have. How come you know two languages besides English, and you never left the country?"

"My mother's parents were refugees, sir. They lived in England, went back to Germany. My mother married a GI, moved to the States. He died young." I shrugged. "She never really adjusted. We spoke mostly German at home. Spanish I learned in school and on the streets."

When he asked if I was interested in becoming an intelligence officer, I asked for time to think. Didn't really know what the job was, but after ten minutes, I said yes. I guess I could've said I'd already been accepted into Special Forces, but with the criminal complaint against me, I couldn't be sure what might happen there. *Looking back, I didn't have much choice, did I? But I wouldn't be in this mess if I'd said no. And Irmie, if you'd only waited.*

My head's splitting apart, I have this awful stomach pain and the world's spinning, spinning around something awful. I'm trying to breathe but can't get any air.

Rat-a-tat-tat. Rat-a-tat-tat. Sounds like someone shooting, far away. Clump, clump. Noise, lots of noise. If my head didn't hurt so much, I could think better. Too much noise.

It was the chopper pilot, Buck, he told me the story. They wanted to lift off, but you kept your gun on them until I made it across that field with the dogs and Vopos hot on my trail. They were shooting. Rat-a-tat-tat. You made them wait.

"Thanks, Buck."

Clump, clump. Clump, clump, clump. People running?

"Alex?"

Rat-a-tat-tat. Louder now. Can't breathe, can't think. I shouldn't be here—never should have come. Too late now for regrets. More rat-a-tat. Everything spinning around. No more shooting, thank God. Silence. No more noises. But I wish my stomach didn't hurt so much.

My head is clear, but I think it's coming apart.

"Alex Klear?"

Quiet again.

"Alex?"

I'm Alex. Someone moving around. Clump, clump. I don't know where I am. What's up or what's down.

"Alex Klear, you in here?"

I'm somewhere, not exactly sure where. I think there's someone calling my name.

"Answer if you're in here, Alex."

Too tired to talk. Can hardly move.

"He ain't in here, Buck."

"In the back?"

All I can think about is my head hurts—bad—

"Nothin'. I looked all over."

I'm here. Maybe I can move my foot—maybe then—

"Keep looking. You too, Scotty. Is that a closet? Shine your flash over there."

"I looked in there, Buck. It's empty."

"Alex! Damn it all! You gotta be in here! Answer!"

My foot. If I kick the floor with my foot, maybe then they'll know. In this hole—

"Alex! Alex Klear! Answer me, goddamn it! You gotta be somewhere."

I can't reach the floor with my foot. It's too high to reach.

"There's nowhere else to look, Buck. They musta—"

One more time—

"What was that?"

"What?"

"Shine your flash over here, Angel. I heard something. Not there, over here under the table."

"I didn't hear— Shit, you're right, Buck. It looks like a trapdoor."

"Push this table back. Get it open. Not like that, the other way. Do I have to tell you every goddamn thing?"

"I got it. Holy shit! Scotty, shine the flash down there. My god! Someone's down here. A guy down here. A body. Wait a second while I— It's him, guys. It's Alex. Hey, buddy, it's us. We been lookin' for you. Geez Buck, he's in bad shape."

"Is he breathin'?"

"Lemme feel. Yeah. Yeah, he's got a pulse. We gotta get him out. Ain't no air here."

"Easy. Lift him. Easy, I said. Okay, I got his legs. Geez, what a mess down there. A goddamned latrine is what that is. They had him in there?"

I wanted to say, "Yeah." But I couldn't.

"Look at his face. Blood all over. Geez, what'd they do to him? Ol' Alex is in bad shape, Buck. What do we do?"

"Only one thing to do. We take him to Bondsteel. To the military hospital. Grab his legs, Scotty."

"You think they'll take him in over there? Only KFOR people stationed at Bondsteel. This operation is strictly black—"

"If they think we're just some bounty hunters they'll never—"

"They'll take him! It's an American hospital, isn't it? What's it there for?"

"I don't know, Buck. You sure?"

"One way or the other, guys, they'll take him. I'll think of something."

Chapter 3

Wednesday, March 21, 2007

"You're awake. Finally." I was looking up at an attractive black woman with a wide smile and her hair in a bun. She was wearing a silver leaf on the collar of her white smock, the insignia of a lieutenant colonel. The stethoscope around her neck indicated she was a doctor. Her nametag said "Raymond."

I mumbled something. I was flat on my back, in bed, and surrounded by clean white sheets.

"How do you feel, Captain?" she asked in a quiet voice.

I struggled to form a sentence. "Not too bad. Still a little tired." When I attempted to pull myself into a sitting position, I realized I hurt pretty much all over. I felt a shooting pain in my left shoulder.

She nodded, smiled again. "Your vital signs are good. All your passages are open. We still need to do some tests." She looked down at a clipboard, sighed. "You really got banged up. A concussion. A few other things."

"You must see a lot of banged-up people."

"Unfortunately. In Iraq, I saw more than I see here. I was at Balad, the 21st Combat Support Hospital, for fourteen months. Do you feel well enough to travel?"

"I'm not sure." My left arm felt stiff. I was hooked up to a machine, a needle on it jumping back and forth. I wondered what she meant by travel.

She said, "We're feeding you intravenously. Along with everything else, you seem to have a case of dysentery. Not good."

"The water in Kosovo doesn't agree with me, ma'am." I could have added that there were a few other things in Kosovo that didn't agree with me. I was feeling tired. "I have an awful headache."

"There's a flight out in an hour, Captain, but I'm going to recommend we keep you here another day."

"Can I ask where I am, ma'am?"

"In the army hospital on Camp Bondsteel. We'll be moving you up to the military hospital in Germany, at Landstuhl. They'll give you some tests we can't give here."

"How long have I been here?"

"Not so long. They brought you in early this morning. You were unconscious. We burned your clothes. I hope you don't mind."

"Who brought me in?"

"I'm not sure. Civilians, from what I understand." She frowned. "Colleagues? Friends? I wasn't on duty at the time. Colonel Brooks approved your admission." She nodded to a corpsman, who had just entered the room.

She said, "From what I understand, there was quite a row at the main gate. We'd received some intelligence about a possible terrorist attack, and they increased the Force Protection Condition from Bravo to Charlie. The beefed-up security people wouldn't let you on post. At first they thought you were one of the locals. You didn't have KFOR ID, not even a passport. The people with you were insistent, really insistent. Force Protection finally called out Colonel Brooks. He was the only one who could override the response procedures. Then someone had him call a government number in Washington. They had to wake up some people over there—"

"Everything worked out, I guess. I'm really grateful."

She frowned. "You are military."

"Of course. I was—"

"Things would have been easier if you'd had ID, Captain. Or your KFOR badge. I guess you know that. I won't ask what happened to it." She looked at me sternly. "One of your colleagues signed you in. You're Captain Sanchez?" When I nodded, she said, "George Sanchez?" When I again nodded, she consulted her clipboard. "I mean Gerald Sanchez."

"That's correct."

"Why did you nod when I said George?"

"I didn't hear you, ma'am. I've still got a headache."

"And Geraldo is with an 'o'?"

"It's pronounced 'Heraldo,' ma'am."

Then she read off an Army serial number. When I nodded my head, she jotted something down on the clipboard.

"Someone in the Pentagon vouched for you, Captain Sanchez. Told Colonel Brooks you were to be admitted immediately and with the highest priority. You're in a private room. We've been treating you like a VIP." She nodded, seemingly satisfied. "Call me if you need anything."

With Colonel Raymond gone, I looked around. As far as hospital rooms go, it was nice. Next to my bed was a table. On the far wall was a washbasin and next to the basin was a large window, sunshine coming through some curtains. A corpsman came in, got the tube off my arm, hooked me up to another one. Another corpsman said he was there to change my bandages. Even lying in bed watching people work was tiring. After a while, I dozed off.

Early in the evening, Colonel Raymond returned. When I asked her again about the people who brought me in, she said, "There were three of them, Captain. All Americans. That's all I can tell you."

"Are they still around?"

"I don't believe so. Colonel Brooks said they left in a hurry. They didn't say where they were going. But we've cut a set of orders for you."

"For Geraldo Sanchez?"

"For Geraldo Sanchez, Captain, U.S. Army. You'll be leaving tomorrow, Captain. For Landstuhl. You can maybe catch up with those people up in Germany, Captain."

"Maybe," I said, although I was pretty sure that whoever brought me in was long gone. I assumed it was Angel and Scott, and I wondered how they'd found me. And I had a dreamy recollection of a voice that sounded like Buck's.

The last thing I could remember was being tossed back into the hole that I'd come to think of as a kind of coffin, a place from which I never thought I'd get out of alive. The third person must have been Buck. But how could he have known who to call in the State Department? Or in the Pentagon? Or wherever? And who could have rustled me up a military identity on such short notice?

Afterward, a nurse came in with a tablet and said I'd sleep better if I took it. Before falling asleep I had more time to think. The mission to get Ramush Nadaj had really gone off the rails. We were shorthanded from the start. It was a totally black operation, freelance, and only three of us had gone in. We didn't have fallback, no Plan B. And not much of a Plan A, now that I think of it.

The worst of it was, I'd let myself become a prisoner. That's not supposed to happen.

That was my last thought before falling asleep.

Early the following morning, I drank a liquid breakfast, had a bath, got my bandages changed. Nurses came by at regular intervals. Colonel Raymond was right. I was being treated like a VIP. As he was drawing blood, the corpsman told me I'd be flying from Pristina to Ramstein in Germany, at 1500 hours. I couldn't help thinking about the mission. Whenever I caught up with Buck, I'd have a lot of questions. I'd let him know how close I came to not making it out of there, although I was pretty sure he knew that already. Give him a piece of my mind, anyway. For the first time in a while, I felt myself smiling. At two hours before flight time, Colonel Raymond came in to give me a folder containing my medical records and flight orders.

"Have a safe trip, Captain." She emphasized the "Captain."

Minutes later, I was wheeled out of the hospital and placed in an ambulance that took me out to an airport where I was rolled up the cargo ramp of a gray aircraft that I recognized as a C-130—which had an American flag painted on the tail fin and U.S. Air Force in block letters on the fuselage. When we were airborne, a corpsman made his way through the mountain of cargo every so often to ask how I was doing and if I wanted anything.

Although I did my best to stay awake, I fell asleep halfway through the flight. When I awoke, two corpsmen were wheeling my cot down the ramp and across the tarmac into a waiting ambulance. Soon afterward, I was in another hospital bed. As she fluffed out a pillow, a nurse with a soft voice told me it was 2230 and said I should get some sleep. Too tired to open my eyes, I nodded and drifted off into dreamland.

Chapter 4

Monday, March 26, 2007

"How do you feel?" a nurse asked. She was tall, blonde, and attractive. I guess I was beginning to notice things like that again. It was early afternoon, and I was propped up on a couple of pillows in my hospital room watching a TV game show on Armed Forces Network. I'd already been in the big military hospital at Landstuhl, Germany, for five days.

"Never better," I said, exaggerating ever so slightly. I was still suffering the symptoms of dysentery. And from occasional headaches. And my shoulder sometimes ached so bad I wondered if it would ever get better. The only exercise I'd been getting was short walks around the corridors and daily trips downstairs to the hospital PX for soap, toothpaste, and magazines.

My face was so banged up I hated to look in the mirror. I was scheduled for a nose operation sometime the following week.

"Are you well enough to have a visitor, Captain?" When I nodded, she said, "A female visitor?"

I sat up, wondering who it might be.

"She says if you're not feeling up to it, she can stop by tomorrow. She's waiting for you in the dayroom. She says she only arrived from the States a few hours ago. Would you prefer to take a wheelchair or to walk?"

"I'll walk," I said, climbing out of bed and grabbing my bathrobe from a peg next to the door. As I navigated the wide corridor, I ran a comb through my hair. It's second nature for me to want to look my best when women are around.

In the hospital dayroom, a bright room with chairs, tables, and a gigantic TV in the corner, a female bird colonel stood by the window gazing out on the parking lot. I looked around. Since the other people in the room were all male GIs, I decided she must be my visitor. I walked over.

"Good afternoon, ma'am."

Turning, she said, "Alex Klear? I'm delighted to meet you. I'm Colonel Sylvia Frost."

She knew my name. I found that interesting as all hell. After we'd shaken hands, I said, "People here know me as Captain Geraldo Sanchez."

"I'm afraid you'll have to continue to be Captain Sanchez until you get back to the States. You'll go back on a military aircraft when you're up to it. We'll handle all that." She looked around at the dozen or so occupants scattered across the big room—GIs in hospital gowns either reading or talking quietly with one another. Then she pointed the way toward a sofa in the corner and tossed her briefcase down on the adjoining table. "I hope being Captain Sanchez isn't too much of an inconvenience." She smiled. "It's the best we could come up with on short notice."

Pointing to my face, I said, "The real inconvenience was having a bunch of fanatics beating up on me for two days."

Colonel Frost nodded sympathetically. "One of the nurses said you've made significant progress in the time you've been here. I'm happy to hear that."

"I'm assuming you had something to do with the planning of this operation, Colonel. Am I correct on that?"

"I could use some coffee. Can I get you one?"

I waved off the offer and watched as Colonel Frost, whom I judged to be in her early thirties, made her way to the coffee urn. She had auburn hair, cut short, wide blue eyes, a high forehead, a long face, a gloss over her delicately shaped lips. She wore her fruit salad very well, and since a military uniform can't conceal everything, I concluded that Colonel Frost had a very nice figure. When she eased herself down on the sofa, I thought she might have cheated just a bit on the army regulation that requires female officers to wear skirts no shorter than knee-length.

I wasn't going to let myself be distracted by the sight of Colonel Frost's thighs.

"I know you had a rough couple of days, Mr. Klear—"

"'Rough' isn't the word, ma'am."

"Let's take a step back, shall we? Getting banged around a bit comes with the territory. And you made it back. That's the important thing. We won't try to determine whose fault it was that you became a prisoner."

"Why not? The fault lies with whoever did the planning. We never had enough people. With five or even four guys, we could have handled this."

"Well, that's not exactly what I heard. I heard that they made you. Couldn't you people even carry out a simple surveillance?"

"I've done a lot of surveillance and never been made before, Colonel Frost. And something else. What kind of fallback did we have?"

"You're way out of line, mister. You shouldn't be asking a question like that. You wouldn't be here if there hadn't been adequate fallback. I can't see what you're complaining about. A simple rendition, and you messed it up. You people had what you needed to carry out a successful operation."

I thought about that. It's true our source had pinpointed Nadaj's hideout. They'd supplied our weapons. We'd leased the van. All in all, it was a pretty straightforward job. But the fact was, rightly or wrongly, I was still steaming because of what had happened.

"I'm only alive because they wanted to use me for some kind of propaganda campaign. After they got me to say what they wanted, I would have been dead."

"Wrong again, my friend. You let yourself become a prisoner— captured by a bunch of amateurs, if you ask me. You're only alive because after you messed things up so royally we were able to locate you. You'd been given a watch and a Leatherman, both of which had GPS transmitters inside. They had you in a shack outside an abandoned mine—in a pretty remote area, I might add. We had people over there just as quickly as we could."

"It was over two days—"

"Something else you might consider. We could have let you end up in a civilian hospital. How long do you think you would have lasted there? Treated by an Albanian doctor with a beef against Americans? Someone who's mad because Kosovo's still part of Serbia?" She paused. "Well?"

I knew better than to try and answer that question. I said, "You say you located Nadaj and his people. Is he in custody?"

"Ramush Nadaj is still on the loose. Unfortunately."

"If he's so important, you could have gone in in force. How many thousand troops do we have in Kosovo?"

"Our troops in Kosovo are peacekeepers, Mr. Klear. They're not here for special ops. No one over here knows anything about this operation. And we want to keep it that way. That's why we called on you people to extract Nadaj—because we couldn't do it any other way."

"What's so important? What's going down?"

Ignoring the question, she removed a small tape recorder from her briefcase and placed it on an adjacent table. All of a sudden, I knew I was in for a grilling, or as it's known in the military, "a post-op debriefing."

Pointing to the tape recorder, she said, "Do you mind?"

"Yes, I do, as a matter of fact."

"Are you objecting to being debriefed, Mr. Klear?"

"Hold on a second, Colonel."

"No, no. You hold on, mister. If you're objecting to being debriefed—"

I shook my head, waved my hand. "Not at all. I'm objecting to being bugged. I'll answer your questions. My suggestion is you take notes. By hand."

"Some people said you can be difficult. My feeling is you enjoy being difficult."

"Suit yourself, ma'am."

We began with my arrival in Skopje a week and a half earlier and moved into the reason for my coming to Kosovo. After identifying my two partners, I said that all I knew about the mission was that we were to run a rendition.

"Who was the target of the rendition?"

"Someone named Ramush Nadaj. We were provided pictures of him before we left."

"What do you know about him?"

"Very little. Only that he was a Kosovo national and tied up with the KLA, the Kosovo Liberation Army, which is considered to be a terrorist organization. At least by some people."

"You were taken prisoner by Ramush Nadaj and his KLA people. Is that correct?" When I nodded, she asked, "How did that come about?"

"Unknown to us, they'd made us during the surveillance. They knew someone was watching them. They had someone outside the house." I explained that, because we only had three men, we needed to wait for precisely the right moment to try and roust Nadaj. "Things didn't go exactly as we planned." Talk about an understatement.

"How long were you in their custody?"

"Although it seemed longer, it was two days."

"How were you treated?"

"Not well, ma'am."

"Can you be more specific?"

I pointed to a crease in my forehead and a long gash under my left eye. "I didn't always have these dents in my face, ma'am." Since I assumed Colonel Frost had spoken with the medical people at Landstuhl, I kept the description as brief as possible. I described being beaten up by Nadaj and his crew. I also described the two nights I spent in the pit beneath the house. As I spoke, Colonel Frost wrote rapidly in her notebook.

"Was there anything else?" When I said that, among other things, they threatened to castrate me, Colonel Frost frowned.

I shrugged. "I figured they wanted to scare me. I tried not to let it get to me."

"Why didn't they kill you?"

"I've thought about that. First, they wanted to find out who I was and who sent us. They knew we were after Nadaj. Second, they wanted to film me telling the world how wonderful they are."

"Are you sure?"

"Pretty sure. When they brought in the video camera, I realized what they were doing. They wanted to use me as part of a propaganda campaign—"

Colonel Frost suddenly looked very alert. "Did they indicate exactly what they wanted you to say?"

"They told me a bunch of things to say. To be honest, I can't remember exactly."

"Can you make an effort? It's important."

"Well, they said I should criticize the government, the president, that sort of thing."

"Try to discredit America, in other words?" When I nodded, she said, "Is that all? Was there any mention of weaponry?"

"I was supposed to say we don't fight fair. We commit atrocities. We didn't get too far with it, probably because I wasn't that cooperative. I figured that once they got me to say what they wanted, I'd become expendable."

She asked how I was able to escape, and I said, "I was rescued by three men, who were able to determine where I was being held. I heard automatic weapons. I assume they had to shoot their way in."

Colonel Frost said, "Do you know how they were able to determine where you were?"

"Before leaving, we were each provided a passport, a watch, some small tools. As you've just indicated, Colonel Frost, the watch and one of the tools each had a GPS transmitter." I paused. "Was Buck Romero involved at all in rescuing me?"

"You can make your own surmise about who was or was not involved. Your partners radioed in what had happened. Another question: Who was with Ramush Nadaj?"

"Two men and a woman. The men were called Fadilj and Quemal. Quemal was also known as 'The Assassin.'"

"Why? What did he do?"

"According to the woman, he got the name back in his village when he killed the mayor. He may have earned it in other ways too."

Colonel Frost looked at me questioningly. "Killed the mayor?"

"That's what the woman said."

"Was he some kind of hit man?"

"Possibly. Or someone who just liked killing people. Everyone needs a hobby."

Needless to say, Colonel Frost ignored the last remark. "What can you tell me about the woman?"

"Her name was Viktoria. She said she had lived in the States for a time. Her English was fluent. She said she'd lived in Bridgeport and had worked in a furniture factory there. You might want to make her."

"Was she legal?"

"She said she had a green card."

Colonel Frost nodded, seemingly impressed by this information. "Did you speak with them at all?"

"Only with the woman. Among themselves they spoke Albanian. I don't understand that language."

She said, "You were once given a ten-day course in Albanian. It says right here that—"

"The course was Albanian and Serbo-Croatian, ma'am, and it was over five years ago. We were in Bosnia, where everyone spoke Serbo-Croatian. Except for a few phrases, I've forgotten most of the Albanian." I'd taken the course while we were planning the Milosevic rendition. My impatience with this grilling was beginning to show.

"Was there anything noteworthy that you overheard? You say the woman spoke to you in English."

After trying to recall what I heard, I said, "She spoke about Afghanistan. She asked if I knew anything about Afghanistan."

"Is that all she said? I have to ask again: was there anything about weaponry?"

"Not that I can recall."

"You're sure? It's important if there was."

"Nadaj became very excited at one point. It had something to do with Afghanistan. But I don't know anything more than that." I decided not to mention that he threatened to cut off my nose. "One other thing. I noticed that Nadaj was carrying an MP5 machine pistol. That surprised me."

"Why?"

"As far as I know, that weapon is only cleared for special ops people in Afghanistan."

She nodded. "I guess we can assume that's where he got it."

When she crossed her legs, her skirt climbed higher. When she became aware I was having a difficult time keeping my eyes away from her legs, she gave her skirt a quick tug. Her eyes flashed. Then she uncrossed her legs.

She said, "Do you have any questions?" She closed her notebook, began fussing with her briefcase.

"Sure? Why is Ramush Nadaj so important? No one ever told us that."

"I can't reveal that. Is there anything else?"

"Only one more thing, ma'am. And that is, I am completely through with working for the United States government. When I am back in the States, I guarantee—guarantee—that I will never ever say yes to another contract. Be sure to write that in your report. I don't want anyone calling me, writing me, e-mailing me, or visiting me. After nearly twenty-five years of this stuff, I have had it—up to here."

Acting as if she hadn't heard me, Colonel Frost continued fussing with her briefcase.

Chapter 5

Wednesday, May 2, 2007

"Let's put it this way," Buck Romero said. "It was the one thing that under no circumstances was supposed to happen."

My old partner was referring to the fact that in the course of the Ramush Nadaj rendition, I ended up a prisoner of the very guy we were looking to extract. It was worse than embarrassing. It was disastrous. He was explaining to me in unwelcome detail just what were the consequences of my little screw-up.

Buck and I were talking for the first time since my return to the States three weeks before. Because I'd been ordered to report to Walter Reed and would be in D.C. for a couple of days, I suggested we meet at Arlington Cemetery, where my father is buried. Buck had known where to find me.

"They did a nice job," Buck had said by way of greeting. He was referring to my face, which the military doctors in Landstuhl and Walter Reed had patched up. "Considering you weren't exactly a matinee idol to start with."

Buck was right. Except for a hardly noticeable scar on my left cheek, an indentation in my forehead and the fact that my nose now leaned just slightly to the starboard, my face wasn't any different from the way it had looked before my arrival in Kosovo.

Earlier we'd stopped by the recently dedicated memorial to the 184 victims of the Pentagon attack. It was a beautiful May day—blue sky and a bright sun making the white headstones seem even whiter and the grass even greener. Now we were wandering through the big cemetery, looking at names and inscriptions and wondering about guys and gals we'd known through the years, both of us in a reflective mood. My close call in Kosovo had the effect, however fleeting, of making me reflect a little more than I normally do on my own mortality.

As we strolled, I said, "Things would have gone down differently if we'd had some backup." I wasn't happy about the fact that I seemed to be catching most of the heat because things hadn't worked out. "Who put the operation together anyway?"

"I'm guilty, but I had an accessory."

"Colonel Frost?"

"From what I understand, you and she have spoken."

"I gave her—shall we say, my views of the situation."

"Not to mention a piece of your mind. By the way, what are your views?"

"That there was too little margin for error. And that it wasn't that well thought out."

We nodded hello to two women—one in her twenties, the other somewhat older—who were out here with two youngsters, a boy and a girl, neither of them older than six and both carrying a bunch of flowers. I didn't want to think about the reason for their visit.

"One of the characters who was in that shack is dead." When I asked which one, Buck said, "He had on a red bandana, a field jacket, green corduroy pants over boots. On the way in there was a brief firefight, and he made the mistake of getting in Angel's way."

"His name was Fadilj." I recalled Fadilj waving his automatic weapon in front of my nose and pounding me with it while I was flat on the floor. "He wasn't one of my favorite people. Tell Angel that's another lunch I owe him."

"Angel and Scotty send their best. Angel's out in Vegas." We both grinned. Angel had a weakness for casinos, where he generally blew the money he made on his government jobs. Larry Scott's weakness was the opposite sex. Well, none of us are perfect.

I said, "I told Colonel Frost that I'd worked on my last contract."

Buck nodded. "You did the right thing. By the way, how did it go out at the hospital? You get your chit punched?" He was referring to my visit that morning to the psychiatric section of Walter Reed Medical Center in D.C. One of the military doctors, having mentioned something called post-traumatic stress, had ordered me to see a government shrink. It's the kind of thing people in our business don't usually do, except under orders.

I said that my visit had consisted only of an hour-long interview with a female psychiatrist, an attractive blonde woman behind a large desk piled with papers.

"You didn't hit on her, I hope."

"I might have, but she had a picture of a guy and two young girls on her desk."

"I'm impressed by your discretion. By the way, how does it feel to be a civilian again?"

"I enjoyed being Captain Sanchez. All those nice nurses. I don't think I've ever been so spoiled."

I'd arrived back in the States on a military flight from Ramstein, Germany, to McGuire Air Base. Although I didn't quite kiss the tarmac, I can say it felt great to be back on American soil. I spent nearly three weeks as an outpatient at Walter Reed, where the military doctors and dentists got me squared away. It was now six weeks since Buck, Angel, and Larry had hauled me out of the hole in which Ramush Nadaj and his buddies had me stashed. The last time Buck and I had spoken was back in March at Dulles, just hours before I'd left for the Balkans, when we'd made the final arrangements for the Kosovo rendition. At that meeting he'd given me some currency, the watch and Leatherman with the GPS transmitters, and a few other knickknacks.

It was the transmitter in the Leatherman that had made it possible to locate us. I'm not sure Buck planned it exactly that way, but I couldn't complain about how things had worked out.

Like me, Buck had been in the military—until someone decided that his talents might be put to more effective use working covertly rather than overtly, with the result that he went from being a captain in Special Forces to being an operations officer in our agency. In the mid-nineties, when things quieted down on the intelligence front, he went to work for a D.C. legal firm which represents the defense industry. His colleagues include a number of former two- and three-star generals and well-connected legal people. The job gives him a certain amount of access and keeps him in touch with old friends. He knows what's going on, and if he doesn't know he's usually in a good position to find things out.

As we walked, I asked Buck about Colonel Cranley.

"Frank's retired. He spends most of his time fishing and playing golf."

It was Cranley, an MI officer on a listening post in the Alps, who had first introduced us. That evening Buck and I had traveled up to Munich and had dinner—and learned that we had at least two things in common: we'd both started off in Special Forces and we liked to drink beer.

Although we would subsequently determine that we worked well together, it was a while before we found that out.

Buck has a mildly forbidding air about him, giving the impression that he disapproves of just about everything and everybody. He's a broad-shouldered, six two, has dark hair, brown eyes, and a square jaw. He isn't that easy a guy to get to know, which might be the result of his having grown up in a hardscrabble mining town in Pennsylvania, a place where he once told me people spend all their time "either working, watching football, drinking, or fighting."

As we wandered through Arlington National Cemetery we were both thinking the same thing, recalling the seven hectic years we'd worked together. Our beat was central Europe, during the Cold War years before the Berlin Wall came tumbling down. Those seem like innocent times now, with none of us aware of the vast array of enemies our country has in the world.

Among the people Buck and I recruited were quite a few who turned into wellsprings of information. After a time, we had it down to a science. When the NSA analysts, usually working with electronic intercepts and tidbits of information, identified and built a file on someone in the Soviet bloc hierarchy who could be persuaded to work for us—usually a military officer or a politician—Buck and I would get the file. After figuring our approach, we'd head into the East and close the deal. At some point, I lost track of the number of times I'd gone through the Iron Curtain and the number of different passports I'd carried. Mostly, we went to East Germany, where our cover usually was that we were businessmen traveling to one of the trade fairs or factories. We carried business cards and I had a nice line of patter—usually along the lines of "our firm's" need for heavy machinery of one kind or another. Besides East Germany, there were forays into Czechoslovakia, Hungary, and even into Russia.

If we could turn the guy, we'd run the agent for as long as possible, which usually meant until he was experiencing psychological meltdown from the stress of leading a double life. When the agent finally came out, he'd have a substantial bank account, a brand new identity—and the opportunity to lead a comfortable life in the United States, usually a far more comfortable life than those of the American taxpayers who were footing the bills for his room, board and, quite often, the payments on his sports car. Mostly, the taste of former Russian officers tended, in cars, toward Porsches and, in women, toward leggy blondes, both of which would get heavy use before being traded in for newer models. When we weren't reading files or recruiting, Buck and I worked out of the white building near the Tivoli Bridge in Munich's English Garden and posed as journalists. That cover was always good for a laugh since neither Buck nor I could have typed out a news story if our lives depended on it. Fortunately, they never did.

We had some close calls. One time I had to exit the Workers' Paradise by way of the Baltic Sea, on a small boat that someone had thoughtfully stashed for me on a beach called Warnemünde and which I only found after a three-hour search. On that occasion, I reasoned that drowning was preferable to five years in an East German slammer, both of which I figured for total career killers. Fortunately, I encountered a Danish trawler before meeting up with a Communist patrol boat.

Another time Buck and I were bringing out a Russian general, a guy who'd given us more information about Warsaw Pact battle plans than even we wanted to know, but who was close to a nervous breakdown and who'd outlived his value as a source. It was a Sunday night in the dead of winter, and we were supposed to rendezvous with a Black Hawk helicopter on a farm northeast of Berlin. First, we got lost. Then someone caught wise to the helicopter parked on the field and alerted the *Volkspolizei*, who normally weren't the world's most efficient police force but who, this time, arrived in short order. As things turned out, I was bringing up the rear and, after taking a header, was a hundred yards behind Buck and the general as they scrambled onto the chopper.

I didn't know how far the Vopos were behind me, but the shots and the barking dogs sounded awfully close.

As I zigzagged back and forth across the field, I expected to see the chopper go sailing off into the sky. But that's not what happened. I later learned why they waited. With his weapon trained on the impatient pilots, Buck was shouting over the engine noise, shaking his head and pointing out to the field where I was stumbling and dodging with a platoon of East German soldiers in hot pursuit. Somehow I made it, with lots of hands hauling me up into the chopper with nothing to spare. With the three of us sprawled on the deck of the Black Hawk and holding on for dear life, we made it out of East German air space by flying under the radar at a speed upward of 140 knots.

Buck and I still laugh when we recall that wild chopper ride, careening around and over smokestacks, communications towers and apartment buildings, and the deathly pale expression on the face of the Russian general. "Welcome to life in the West, Yuri!"

We got the "Gold Dust Twins" moniker because we worked so well together and chalked up a few successes along the way.

Looking around at one point, I paused and said, "There are times when I pinch myself just to make sure I'm not imagining things. That I'm still here to take this all in."

Buck didn't answer but he knew what I meant.

After leaving the cemetery, we rode out on I-95 in the direction of Alexandria, and Buck suggested a restaurant he knew not far from Fort Belvoir, a place with dark paneled walls, subdued lighting, and what appeared to be a largely government and military clientele, men and women who kept their voices low and hardly ever smiled. Just observing these people was enough to remind me of how happy I was not to be a part of their world anymore.

It wasn't until after we'd knocked off a couple of steaks and were on our third or fourth beer that we began to kick around what happened in Kosovo. From talking with Angel and Larry, Buck knew the story up until the time Nadaj and his gang grabbed me.

I gave him the rest of the story.

"Who's this Vickie?" Buck asked when I'd finished.

"We should be able to find out," I said. "She said she had a green card."

Buck nodded. "Anything else?"

"I did my best to listen in, but they were talking Albanian all the time, so I couldn't pick up that much." I paused, trying to recall the events of those two days, most of which I'd repressed, or tried to. "One thing: Nadaj got very excited about Afghanistan. They kept asking if I knew what happened in Afghanistan."

Buck looked thoughtful. "So we can assume something happened in Afghanistan that has a lot of people very jumpy, including people on the National Security Council and in the DOD. Something else I know is that Nadaj was the leader of a KLA outfit that went out to Afghanistan. They were in the mountains and fighting with the Taliban. According to what I could pick up, Nadaj's people were well disciplined and well armed, and they caused our guys lots of problems."

I said, "How did you get involved?"

Buck shrugged. "I don't know much more than you do. It began when I got a call to meet a guy out at Rock Creek Park."

"Anyone I know?"

"Yeah, as a matter of fact. Jerry Shenlee. You remember Jerry?"

"Of course. Berlin, way back when."

Both Buck and I had worked for a time with Jerry Shenlee, who was then attached to the 766th Military Intelligence Detachment, helping out with security investigations and whatever else needed to be done. But the big investigation was the one that followed the 1986 bomb blast in the La Belle discotheque in West Berlin. In fact it was Jerry who, in a frantic telephone call that afternoon, first alerted me to the fact that British intelligence had intercepted a message to Tripoli in which the Libyan embassy in East Berlin was predicting a "joyous event."

"'Joyous' for them means anything but joyous for us, Klear," Jerry had shouted into the phone, and I knew immediately what he meant. When Jerry said we needed to find out what was going down, I told him I'd do my best.

I spent the twelve hectic hours that followed Jerry's call racing around the city, checking out bars for suspicious characters, talking to people, and trying to figure out what was likely to happen. It was agonizing having prior notice of some kind of attack but not knowing anything beyond that. Because the intercepted message said something about "maximum victims," we figured it would be in some public place and was going to be bad—and as we later learned, two MPs were on their way to warn the La Belle patrons and were just three hundred yards away from the disco when the blast went off. The bomb, which had been in a suitcase in the club's washroom, killed two American GIs, a Turkish woman, and with flying nails doing tremendous damage, injured over two hundred others.

Almost immediately, we zeroed in on the employees of the Libyan Embassy in East Berlin. Because the bomb had been put together with plastic explosive mixed with nails, we were quickly able to ID it as the handiwork of Yasir Shraydi, a Palestinian who we already suspected of terrorist activities. I remember a case officer, one of the first people on the scene, later telling me he could have strangled Shraydi with his bare hands and enjoyed every minute of it.

Moammar Kadafi badly miscalculated when, a few days later, he praised the bomb blast and described its perpetrators as "glorious revolutionaries." President Reagan ordered Kadafi's personal compound in Tripoli to be bombed, an action that showed the world that Colonel Kadafi's enthusiasm for bomb blasts rapidly diminished the closer they came to his home and person. The American government has a long memory, and whether Colonel Kadafi knows it yet or not, his name is on a short list of dictators to be toppled.

I asked, "What's Jerry up to?"

"Jerry is a National Security Coucil staffer, and I get the impression some important people have a lot of confidence in him, one of them being the deputy secretary of defense. Jerry said they needed to run a rendition, and the person they wanted was this Nadaj. He said the chief of station in Skopje had a reliable informant, who knew Nadaj's precise location. But he also said the source would only talk to someone on the ground, and only after he got paid."

Remembering a sullen looking character with tousled hair and a slight limp, I said, "That was the guy we met in the hotel."

"Shenlee insisted we act fast. The other thing, there couldn't be any way to trace this operation back to the DOD or to any government agency. You know how persistent some of these reporters can be."

"And Jerry was just dumping all this into your lap?"

"He was also dumping a great deal of money into my lap—which was when I knew this had to be a high-priority operation. There couldn't be any signed contracts—which meant it had to be freelance and totally black. I had to see that you guys got weapons, and I had to arrange to run the operation. Something else was there couldn't be any screw-ups."

I winced when Buck said that. By getting myself captured, I'd screwed things up very badly.

"My only contacts turned out to be you, Angel, and Larry. I couldn't get anyone else on such short notice. Under other circumstances, we would have had five people, and I could have run it out of Camp Bondsteel. Since it was freelance, absolutely and totally black, I had to run you guys out of a tiny apartment in Pristina, with the electricity going on and off and the lights not working half the time. I had a couple of cell phones, a secure laptop, a flashlight, and a bunch of telephone numbers, but not much else. Now and then, I'd try for a catnap. You can imagine how it was, sitting there day after day with earphones and a couple of monitors, wondering what was going on, and feeling pretty helpless." When I nodded, Buck said, "I was able to keep track of you guys off the satellite. When Angel called and told me you were a prisoner, I got over there as quick as I could. You know the rest."

Recalling my debriefing in the military hospital, I asked Buck about Colonel Sylvia Frost.

"Colonel Frost works for the deputy secretary of defense. In fact she's the deputy secretary's special emissary, and when she's involved in something you can bet that he's also involved in a significant way."

I said, "That's more evidence that this Ramush Nadaj rendition was a high-priority operation."

"Very high, Alex." Buck looked at me over the top of his beer mug. "You should also know that it was Colonel Frost who pulled the strings to get you onto Camp Bondsteel. When the Force Protection people wouldn't let us on the base, I had them phone Shenlee back in D.C. for me. I got through, but he didn't have any answers. He gave me Colonel Frost's number. She came up with the Captain Sanchez identity on the spot. Then she personally called Colonel Brooks."

"He's the CO of Bondsteel?"

"Yes, and one very tough hombre. But like everyone else, he knows better than to mix it up with Colonel Frost. That was how you got admitted to the military hospital so fast. If it was anyone else on the phone, it wouldn't have happened."

Buck didn't say it, but we both knew it was the medical people on Camp Bondsteel who pulled me through. I wouldn't have survived twenty-four hours in a Kosovo hospital, assuming that Kosovo has hospitals. Maybe I'd been obnoxious during the debriefing, but considering what I went through in Kosovo, I didn't see where I owed anybody anything.

"By the way, Colonel Frost graduated numero uno in her class at West Point. I thought you should know."

"That's very impressive. She's also very attractive, if I'm allowed to say that."

"I'm glad to see you still notice those things."

"Ha ha."

"Here's a nugget of gossip. When she was out in Afghanistan, she supposedly got the hots for another officer. The word is they spent a lot of time in each other's room in the Ariana Hotel in Kabul."

"Boys will be boys, and girls will be girls."

Buck lowered his voice. "People often find her difficult. Around the office she's known as Colonel BOW." When I frowned, Buck said. "Colonel Bitch-on-Wheels."

"So she's a tough boss. What do her people think they're getting paid for?"

As the waiter set down two more mugs of beer, I watched Buck smear some Stilton cheese on a slab of dark bread. "You're not suggesting I owe Colonel Frost an apology."

Between bites, he said, "Like I say, Alex, Colonel Frost has forgotten you and your obnoxious behavior."

Recalling the debriefing, I said, "I did an awful lot of kvetching." Courtesy of my mother, I command an extensive vocabulary of Yiddish expressions, spoken with a Bavarian lilt.

Buck nodded. "I heard. She definitely showed superhuman restraint. As have many of your friends and colleagues on occasion."

After a minute, I said, "If the Nadaj rendition goes back to Colonel Frost, then—"

"Then it goes back to the deputy secretary of defense."

I said, "And from him to the secretary of defense."

"We're both thinking the same thing, Alex. The government is eager to get its mitts on Nadaj."

"What the hell did he do?"

Buck shook his head. "No idea."

Chapter 6

Friday, January 18, 2008

"My friends would hate me if they knew some of the things I've done to make a living," I said.

Eight months had elapsed since my meeting with Buck at Arlington Cemetery.

Jerry Shenlee touched a finger to his rimless glasses and gazed at me across the table with a noncommittal expression. "I'm surprised you still have friends. Most of us don't."

Shenlee is clean shaven, has a square, mildly flushed face, and wears his red-blond hair cut short, in the military style. He retains a kind of flinty look, a characteristic he acquired growing up on the plains of North Dakota and that he's never quite been able to shake. But the important thing is, he fits in at the Pentagon, which is where I understand he now spends a good deal of his time.

It was just after eight, and Jerry and I were having breakfast in AP Smith's Restaurant on Main Street in Saranac, a town in the northern foothills of the Adirondack Mountains—and a place in which I've come to feel very much at home.

As Jerry and I spoke, I began to feel a growing sense of alarm. "What's up?"

"When you hear what it is, you'll know what's up."

When I first met Jerry, he was a newly minted Annapolis grad, a spiffy-looking young guy attached to the 766th MI Detachment, with a windowless basement office located in one of the detachment's sections at Tempelhof in West Berlin. Like a lot of us, Jerry Shenlee's come a long way since the days of the Cold War.

Something else about Shenlee: I've never seen him smile. On this day, he appeared particularly grim. He was wearing a gray sports jacket, open collar, khaki-colored pants, and, on his wrist, a G-Shock digital watch. As I silently watched, he pushed aside his cup of cold tea, reached down and pulled some colored folders out of his briefcase, a couple of which had "CONFIDENTIAL" stamped across the top. The folders were filled with forms, letters, printouts, and who knew what else. I assumed that Shenlee had my 201 personnel jacket, evaluations, and detailed reports on some of the "special projects" I've been involved with over the years.

When they say "special projects," think "special ops."

As he leafed through his folders, he shook his head. "If our government is good at anything, Klear, it's creating paper and keeping tabs on people."

"Tell me about it," I said as I poured out some more coffee, resigned to the fact that this was Shenlee's little party and he was calling the shots.

It was Friday, already a nice day, and the sun was slanting through the restaurant's big front window. Since it was mid-January, Smith's was close to full, jammed with skiers eager to get out on the slopes. I live in Saranac and with my business partner occasionally drop into Smith's for lunch, almost never for breakfast.

"When did you get in?" I asked.

Without looking up, he said, "Yesterday, late afternoon. Flew up from McGuire on a Cessna 35A, real comfortable. Stayed the night in the Saranac Inn. Nice place."

"I was surprised to hear from you." When Shenlee asked why, I said, "I'm retired."

"Who told you that, Klear? Who ever said you were retired?"

"I decided to retire. Bought into a business. It was a personal decision. Anything wrong with that?"

Ignoring my question, he went back to reading for a minute, then said, "You were in the Balkans. That wasn't so long ago." He fixed me with an accusing stare.

"Sure. I was there—let's see—five times in all. The first time, as I recall, I was on vacation—saw the sights, went to the beach, that sort of thing."

"Where in the Balkans? If I may ask."

"Croatia, mostly."

"Split's in Croatia, right?" When I nodded, he said, "I hear they have quite a few nude beaches there, with nice lookin' babes strollin' around."

"I wouldn't know."

"I'll bet. And you were involved in the Milosevic rendition. The best renditions are the ones that no one knows are renditions. What did you do on that one?"

As Shenlee polished his glasses with a napkin, I said, "I was part of an eight-man team. We waited around in Bosnia till Special Ops got things organized."

"Where in Bosnia?"

"On Eagle Base. You know it?"

Shenlee put his glasses back on. "Sure. Near Tuzla. Okay, what I'm most interested in is this other thing—this Kosovo rendition last year. March, am I correct?" When I nodded, he said, "From what I'm reading here, things didn't go so well on that one."

"They could have gone better," I said, taking a last bite from my plate of toast and trying to be noncommittal.

Shenlee pointed to something in one of his folders. "It says here your partners in Kosovo were Angel and Scott."

"We could've used another guy over there."

Shenlee looked irritated. "How's Scotty doing? Has he settled down?"

"He's doing fine, Jerry. He's married again and he says he's never been happier."

"I'm sure." At that moment Jerry and I were thinking the same thing. One of my two partners on the Kosovo operation, Larry Scott, had been fired from the Company years before when the details of his private life became fodder for a supermarket tabloid. He'd had two girlfriends, one of them a fellow Company employee, both of whom he'd made pregnant, a circumstance that didn't go down well with his wife, who at the time was also pregnant.

But the fact was, Larry had been a fine and dependable operations officer, the kind of low-maintenance operative who's hard to replace. Once the smoke from the tabloid affair cleared, he found he was still in demand, which I suppose was fine with Larry since by that time he had so many mouths to feed.

Shenlee said, "So what happened? That op sounded like a piece of cake."

"We flew into Skopje, stayed the first night at the Alexander. We originally thought Nadaj was down in Macedonia, somewhere in the hills in the Albanian sector. Scotty had arranged for a van in Skopje and for Nadaj to be extracted with a chopper out of Kosovo."

Shenlee nodded. "What went wrong?"

I resisted the urge to say "Everything." Instead I said, "I landed in the military hospital in Camp Bondsteel, Jerry. From there I was medevaced to the military hospital in Landstuhl. It was nearly three weeks before I was well enough to fly back to the States. I spent nearly three weeks as an outpatient at Walter Reed."

"From what I understand, Klear, Nadaj's still on the loose. If you guys had done that job right, he'd be in The Hague now, on trial. Or else in jail." Shenlee took another sip of tea. "Talk about your screw-ups—"

"What did he do that deserves a trial in The Hague?"

Like I said, we'd taken Slobodan Milosevic out of circulation. That one had gone down without a hitch, and I knew Jerry had the account of that operation in his folders. But the Ramush Nadaj rendition turned out to be a greater challenge than the Milosevic rendition.

Anyway, the truth was we'd blown the Nadaj mission—and that in combination with the fact that I hadn't heard anything from anyone in the last half year, led me to think I was out of the picture, and that I was retired.

Maybe I wasn't yet a candidate for a psychiatrist's couch, but a couple more experiences like the one in Kosovo and I definitely would be.

I'd concluded that I wouldn't be hearing from anyone anymore. In one of my evaluations, an Air Force colonel who didn't appreciate my original way of thinking had referred to me as a "loose cannon to end all loose cannons." The way the intelligence brass thinks, that kind of remark can be a career killer. Anyway, after the First Gulf War I decided it would be a wiser career move to submit my resignation and, like Larry Scott and a bunch of other guys and gals, move over to working on a contract basis. I thought I would like the idea of being able to say yes or no to a job.

Mostly I said no, not that there were that many offers. Things were pretty quiet on the special ops front for a while, at least until some explosive-laden trucks destroyed our embassies in Nairobi and Kenya. I only began receiving calls after the civil war heated up in Bosnia and the UN decided to intervene. I would have said no to the Kosovo operation if it hadn't been Buck Romero who'd asked me.

But now I definitely wasn't going to accept any more contracts. My experience with so-called special operations, which had begun with a long-ago interview in a Fayetteville, North Carolina, cafeteria, was officially over. "So long, guys. It was nice knowing you."

"What's this business you've got?" Shenlee asked suddenly.

"I supply ice to restaurants and hotels."

He made a wry face, showing he was unimpressed. "Klear, I'll be candid. You're going to have to put your ice business on hold. Someone very high up picked out your name for this assignment."

"I'm retired, Jerry."

As he studied the check, Shenlee said, "You look okay. You work out regularly?"

"Sure. I haul a lot of ice. What do you people want me to do anyway, climb the Matterhorn?"

On the way to the door, I thanked him for breakfast.

"Thank the American taxpayer, Klear." Out on Main Street we made room on the sidewalk for a young couple, each with skis on their shoulders, and an attractive young mother, slim and brunette. As she pushed a stroller with one hand and led a youngster eating an apple with the other, she smiled a "Good morning." I smiled back.

At that moment, a husky blond guy wearing a blue pullover over a flannel shirt, jeans, and brown work boots tossed down his newspaper, gave us a wave, a loud hello, and climbed down from the cab of a refrigerator truck parked at the curb. It was my partner, Gary Lawson, and the truck was one of the two we owned. I'd told Gary to pick me up at Smith's after breakfast.

After I'd introduced Gary to Shenlee, Gary looked at me. "I just got a call. The country club's lookin' to throw a party tomorrow night, Alex. All kinds of food deliveries will be coming in, and they'll be wantin' a full load, three o'clock at the latest."

Shenlee's mouth was set in a grim line. When I glanced toward him, he frowned, shook his head, then drifted up the sidewalk to where he was out of earshot.

At that moment I was reminded of a long-ago barroom conversation with a veteran spook, a guy we called Bud, who was already well into his cups. "Once you're in," Bud said, slurring his words ever so slightly and raising his bourbon glass, "you'll never again be out." Bud's observation was based on experience, his own no doubt. When he put down his glass, he grimaced. You were so right, Bud.

Quietly, I said, "I have a feeling I'm going to be tied up for a day or two, Gary. Can you get Ross to help out on the delivery?" Ross is one of the more dependable locals, a retired New York City cop who we call whenever things get busy.

Looking puzzled, Gary glanced toward Shenlee, who was now standing with his back to us and gazing off in the direction of Haystack Mountain, which was silhouetted against the bright sky. Shenlee's greeting to Gary had been true to form, a polite nod, and I had a feeling Gary hadn't exactly taken a shine to my old friend. Who could blame him?

"I don't get it, Alex," Gary said after a second. "Why pay Ross? What's up that's so goddamned important?" Before I could answer, he shrugged. Maybe he saw an impatient glint in my eye. "Sure, Alex," he said before I could answer. "No problem. I'll call Ross."

Gary was too considerate to ask questions, and I was grateful to him for that. Gary is a good guy, hardworking and anxious to succeed, and Saranac is a friendly town. As I watched Gary climb into the cab and slam the door, I took a deep breath. When I saw him pick up his cell phone, I knew he was punching in Ross's number. He loudly gunned the engine, and a couple of seconds later with the phone at his ear, he had the truck out in traffic and was gone.

I felt a pang of frustration somewhere in the pit of my stomach as I realized I wished I was with him. We'd get our machines working, load up our trucks, haul the ice out to the club, and while the members partied in the club's big ballroom, Gary and I would end the day drinking beer and laughing it up with the club's crew. I didn't like the idea of having to spend time with Shenlee—and discussing the topics I suspected he wanted to talk about. That stuff was all part of my past, and I wanted to keep it there—in the past. But I didn't see that I had a choice.

As we walked down the sidewalk in the direction of Sears, Shenlee said, "Pack an overnight bag. Be at the airport at noon. We'll be taking a ride in that Cessna I mentioned."

"I have a date tonight. I told my girlfriend we'd—"

"I'm sure your girlfriend has a telephone. Call her. Tell her you're tied up."

"Suppose I say I'd rather not go? Suppose I say I'm through with special operations?"

Shenlee flashed a disgusted look. "C'mon, Klear, don't play games. You're going. Get packed!"

I felt as if a mule had given me a hard kick in the solar plexus. Shenlee was right. I would be going. There are certain people in our government you don't want to get mad at you, people who you just don't say no to—and Jerry Shenlee was now one of them. He knew that and I knew that.

Chapter 7

Friday, January 18, 2008

"I could never get used to living in New York City," Shenlee said. "Look at this traffic."

"Is D.C. any better during rush hour?" I asked. "You said you don't like the Beltway."

We were in a rented Caddy, and headed south on the Van Wyck Expressway, a six-lane highway running through the borough of Queens. Our plane had landed at LaGuardia Airport, and almost immediately after driving out of the airport we found ourselves in a traffic jam.

"Look at this!" Shenlee screamed suddenly while honking his horn at a driver in a blue Lexus who had managed to force her way into our lane. Once the Lexus driver had completed her little maneuver, she grinned, gave Shenlee an unfriendly salute, gunned her engine for emphasis while again changing lanes.

"I oughta—"

"Where are we going?" I asked for maybe the fifth time.

"Like I said, Klear, you're going to be talking to a very important individual. You'd better be on your best behavior."

When I said, "I always am," Shenlee said, "Yeah, sure."

After a while traffic eased up, and we exited onto another highway, this one somewhat less crowded than the expressway. We seemed to be driving in the direction of New York City.

"We're looking for exit eleven," Shenlee said. "We wanna go south."

"Where will that take us?"

"We're headed to Floyd Bennett Field. You ever heard of it?"

"Vaguely."

Shenlee shook his head. "If you knew a little more history, Klear, you'd know Floyd Bennett was New York City's first municipal airport. Famous people took off from there."

"Like who?"

"Like Amelia Earhart. You've heard of her, I'm sure. How about 'Wrong-Way' Corrigan?"

"What did he do?"

"Flew to Ireland. I think it was Ireland. Thought he was going to California."

"Did he forget his compass? Didn't he ever look down? C'mon, Jerry. No one could be that dumb."

"Maybe he thought his oil-pressure gauge was his compass. How the hell should I know?" With one hand on the steering wheel, Shenlee gestured impatiently with the other. "Anyway, Floyd Bennett was a naval air station. But it's been decommissioned. It sits right on the water, just west of Kennedy. But it still belongs to the government and—"

"And it continues to have its uses."

"It's out of the way. That's always a plus for people in our business."

I could have told Shenlee that I wasn't in his business anymore, but then I wasn't really sure whether I was or whether I wasn't.

I also could have told Shenlee that he was throwing a very large monkey wrench into my life, but I knew that wouldn't do any good either.

I was thinking of my girlfriend, Vanessa, an attractive and lively schoolteacher whom I'd met four months ago in the taproom of the Saranac Inn. With her engaging personality and off-the-wall comments, she'd quickly made me forget the TV baseball game to which I had my eyes glued while knocking down a hamburger and my third or fourth Sam Adams.

When someone legged out a ground ball, causing the crew at the bar to let out a spontaneous cheer, Vanessa turned on her stool and innocently asked, "Did your team score a goal?"

"No," I said. "The tight end just kicked a home run."

"How did the end get tight?"

"Let me buy you a drink and I'll show you."

We were on a stretch of highway that had a garbage landfill on one side and fields full of cattails on the other.

"Are you enjoying the scenery, Klear?"

I assumed Jerry meant the remark ironically and didn't reply.

Vanessa was fun, but whenever I thought about settling down with her, I'd begin thinking again about Irmie. As we drove, I shoved all thoughts of Vanessa from my mind. I didn't even want to think what her reaction might be to the news of a sudden departure on my part.

Farther on, we passed a ball field and some ancient hangars, and Shenlee said that was the airport. On the other side of the road was a marina and dunes full of swamp grass. In the distance, I could see water and what looked like a bridge. Even though we weren't that far from New York City, there didn't seem to be much going on out here, certainly not on a cloudy January afternoon.

Shenlee slowed, we hung a left, drove through a patch of scrub pines and weeds until we reached a barrier. When Shenlee flashed some ID, the guard raised the barrier and we drove maybe another quarter of a mile before arriving at a small complex of cinder block buildings. In front of the largest building was a guard who seemed to know Shenlee and who nodded as we headed inside.

Shenlee did some talking with a guy at a metal desk and we passed through a metal detector, went down a short corridor, and entered a room furnished with a wooden desk, some chairs, a couch, a table with a computer on it. On the wall behind the desk was a map of the East Coast of the United States and next to it stood an American flag.

A few minutes later, the door opened and a woman entered. She was carrying a thin briefcase, which she immediately tossed on the desk. Not only did I recognize the briefcase; I also recognized its owner.

"Hello, ma'am," I said, trying not to appear too surprised.

"Good afternoon, gentlemen." Colonel Frost extended her hand. "Nice to see you again, Alex."

"Can I get anyone anything?" Shenlee asked.

"I'd like coffee," Colonel Frost said. "Alex?" When I said the same would be fine with me, Shenlee went trotting off.

On this occasion, Colonel Frost was out of uniform. She was dressed in a gray suit, the jacket of which she removed and placed on a coat peg beside the door. Much as she'd done in the hospital dayroom overseas, she pointed me toward the couch. Seated in a chair opposite me, she said, "You're looking fine, Alex. Much better than last time, if you don't mind my saying so."

I suppose surprise was still written all over my face. I recovered enough to say, "I certainly feel better, ma'am." I knew I looked flustered. I couldn't help recalling how boorish I'd been during the debriefing overseas. Although Buck had said that it was Colonel Frost's clout and quick thinking that had saved my life, it was also Colonel Frost's patched-together operation that had landed me in the clutches of Ramush Nadaj and his gang.

"I don't know how much Jerry has told you—"

"Jerry is nothing if not discreet."

Colonel Frost allowed herself a thin smile. "Good, Alex. I'll start at the beginning." Shenlee had said I'd be talking with someone from D.C., but hadn't said with whom. They'd set this up very nicely.

But at some point I wanted to get across the fact that I wasn't interested in taking part in any special ops.

As with our first meeting, Colonel Frost made a point of being all business. I couldn't help recalling Buck's nuggets of gossip—that she'd had an affair with another officer in Afghanistan and that her subordinates referred to her as "Colonel Bitch-on-Wheels." Except for the fact she was now in civilian clothes, she looked much the same as she had last time. She still had her chestnut hair in a kind of military bob. She was wearing a white blouse and her gray skirt was not quite knee length, a little detail I couldn't help but notice. I made an effort to avert my eyes but wasn't completely successful. She also had on tiny silver earrings. Although she had a ring on her left hand, it wasn't a wedding ring. No question that Colonel Frost projected a quiet intensity. I've always liked intense women. Of course I've also liked quite a few who weren't all that intense.

Although I'd already decided that I wasn't going to take part in whatever these people had in mind, I was having trouble getting a word in edgewise. I realized now I'd made a mistake when I let Jerry drag me down here.

Before she could begin, we were joined again by Shenlee, who was carrying coffee and crullers on a plastic tray. With the coffee and cream ritual out of the way, Shenlee found a seat next to me on the sofa.

"As you've probably already guessed, Alex, we don't have a lot of time. Once you hear the story, I think you'll know where you fit in." I couldn't help noticing that everybody just assumed I'd be accepting this assignment.

"I see." I said the words unenthusiastically, but neither Jerry nor Colonel Frost took any notice.

"A woman named Ursula Vogt was murdered, stabbed to death. The murder took place in Miss Vogt's home late on a Friday afternoon, three weeks ago. Miss Vogt lived in Munich."

"And she was a journalist," Shenlee said. "Worked for that big news magazine, *Welt-Bericht*."

Colonel Frost put down her cup. I had an idea she didn't like being interrupted. "*Welt-Bericht* means 'World Report' in German, as I'm sure you know. It belongs to the Mehling Group, and the proprietor, Kurt Mehling, is not exactly pro-American."

Colonel Frost pulled a couple of magazines from the pile of paper on the coffee table and passed them over. I recognized the familiar blue masthead of the magazine with the words "Welt-Bericht" splashed in large block letters on the cover. I leafed quickly through the copies, saw nothing much had changed since I'd last seen the magazine.

"I assume you're familiar with the publication, Alex."

I nodded. "I used to look at it occasionally." I didn't mention that I found the magazine too predictable to be very interesting.

"Anyway, the person arrested for the murder is an American named

Douglas Brinkman. Brinkman is a former major in Special Forces, who has been living in Munich. He was involved with Special Ops in Afghanistan. Brinkman and Miss Vogt had been seeing one another. We want to know what happened and why."

"We're assuming they knew one another pretty well," Shenlee said. "We know they met in Afghanistan. Brinkman did three tours there, one for about thirteen months."

"We're hoping you can find out who killed Miss Vogt, Alex," Colonel Frost said.

It was now obvious where I fit in. They wanted me to go back to Europe. I'd worked in Munich for over seven years, during which time I'd gotten to know how the people over there think and how the German legal system works. I'd become comfortable with the dialect people speak in that part of the world, a small skill but a useful one when you're trying to make friends or just maintain a low profile.

"I have no intention of going back to Europe."

Colonel Frost's jaw tightened.

"And I have no intention of taking part in any special ops, assuming that's what you people have in mind." I stood up from my chair.

"Siddown, Klear!"

"I don't want to hear any more. Find someone else. I have a business to run."

I'd become untangled from the special ops stuff, and I wanted to stay untangled.

"What's the problem, Alex?" Colonel Frost asked.

"The problem is, I didn't like the way the last operation turned out. I'm surprised you even ask a question like that."

Shenlee said, "They got to you, Klear. Is that what you're saying?"

Shenlee is as subtle as a kick in the teeth, and I ignored his obvious attempt to needle me. "There are plenty of people around who'd be happy to go over."

Colonel Frost said, "You're perfectly qualified for this kind of assignment."

"So are dozens of other people, ma'am."

"You've got contacts over there, people you can call," Colonel Frost said. "We don't have a lot of time."

I didn't say anything. I wondered how many of the people I knew I could still call. I could imagine some hanging up the minute they heard my voice on the telephone. In the kind of job I had, it was impossible not to antagonize people.

"I think he's gun-shy," Shenlee said, gazing at Colonel Frost. "It happens, even to the best of them, guys who—"

When Colonel Frost glared, Shenlee shut up. Then she pointed toward the door and said she wanted to speak to me alone. With Shenlee gone, I sat back down.

"Alex, listen, the Munich police had Major Brinkman in *U Haft*— in other words, under interrogation—at the big prison, Stadelheim. He's out of the interrogation section, but still in jail. Once they get a case prepared, he'll go on trial." Colonel Frost consulted a pad on the table. "The only person who's been able to speak with Brinkman is a man named Owen. He's supposedly from the consulate."

"Supposedly?"

"The FBI's legal attaché, actually. But the Germans don't know that."

"Don't be too sure they don't know it," I said.

Colonel Frost nodded. "Right, it would be a mistake to underestimate . . . an ally. In any case, we want you to work around American officials. You can play things by ear, but we don't want you to advertise your presence."

I shook my head. "I'm just not interested. Find someone else."

"We're assuming you know people over there. They owe you favors. They'll be happy to see you again."

"You're making some unwarranted assumptions, ma'am."

She removed her reading glasses. "Jerry's right, isn't he? You're gun-shy." When I didn't reply, she said quietly, "I'll go even further. I think you're scared."

I smiled, shook my head. "Believe what you want to believe, ma'am."

"Afraid of what might happen. Afraid someone will toss you back in that hole? Is that it? Scared shitless?" She lowered her voice. "I'm right, aren't I?"

I supposed it was remarks like that which earned her the "Colonel Bitch" moniker among her subordinates, but I wasn't going to let Colonel Frost get to me.

When I didn't comment, she said, "Brinkman maintains his innocence. We believe him."

"Why? Does he have an alibi?"

"That's maybe part of the problem," Colonel Frost said. "He doesn't have an alibi, but we still believe him." She paused. When I didn't say anything, she said, "Brinkman has a fine military record. He was one of the best. All the people who served with him had nothing but the highest praise. Doesn't that mean anything to you? The fact that a good soldier is getting a raw deal?"

"Of course. But I don't see that I can do anything about it."

"People like Major Brinkman don't just go over the edge."

I could feel myself frowning. The truth is, people do go over the edge, and I doubt there are many special ops people who haven't felt close to the edge at some point in their careers. I knew that, and I had a feeling Colonel Frost knew that. Although I didn't say anything, I made a point of looking at my watch.

For a long minute, Colonel Frost went through her papers. I took a sip of cold coffee. The silence was oppressive. Because I had an idea that was how Colonel Frost wanted it to be, I didn't say anything. When she looked up, I fixed her with a cold stare, letting her know I didn't intend to budge.

Finally, she said, "You drive a hard bargain."

"What do you mean, ma'am?"

After a brief pause, she said, "I picked you for this assignment, and now I'm going to tell you why. Your ability to get around in Europe is useful, but you're right. We have plenty of people who can handle that end of things. There's another reason I chose you. Are you still listening?"

"I'm curious."

"This operation ties in with the Kosovo rendition. Not only are the two operations connected, they're closely connected. I can't give you all the details up front, but you can believe me when I say that."

"That may be true but—"

"The same people are involved. I'm offering you a golden opportunity, Alex, the kind of opportunity that very few people in our business ever receive."

"What would that be?"

"You're going to have a chance to get back at the people who tossed you into that hole. The woman, what was her name?"

"Vickie."

"Thanks to you, we were able to ID her. You said she'd been in the States, in Connecticut somewhere."

"She said Bridgeport."

"Which isn't that far from Stamford. When a well-heeled businessman in that city stopped making his annual quarter-of-a-million dollar contribution to Yale's Alumni Fund in favor of sending the money to a front organization for the Kosovo Liberation Army, his bank became suspicious. They passed the information on to us. You provided the answer. We discovered he'd been tangled up with a woman from that part of the world who fit your description to a T. She used another name over here, but if she is who we think she is, she's a major player. And she plays very rough."

"Rough?"

"The businessman eventually took his own life." For a brief second, Colonel Frost's expression was a twisted grimace. "If we land her, we won't have any mercy. As far as I'm concerned, you can rape her until your dick falls off."

I said, "The person I'd most like to get back at is Nadaj." I didn't add that I'm reminded of Nadaj every time I look in the mirror and see the two large dents in my face.

"Are you just a little bit interested?"

"Why are we after him? No one ever told me that."

"You'll find out—after you've signed on."

The memory of Kosovo returned in a rush. All of a sudden, I was interested—and it was more than just a little bit. I could feel my heart pounding. I suppose there was nothing I wanted more than to get back at the people who banged me around in Kosovo.

"It's going to be payback time, Alex, and you can be part of it. The gloves will be off, I promise you. We don't play by any set of rules. But you're going to have to make up your mind here and now."

"I'm vindictive, it's true."

Colonel Frost smiled wickedly. "There's nothing wrong with that. You can be as vindictive as you want to be, but along with everything else, you'll be doing a service for your country."

I considered the matter for maybe another minute. I knew that if I didn't say yes, Shenlee and Colonel Frost would spread the word that I was not just burned out—but that Nadaj and his crew had turned me into someone afraid of his own shadow.

I could imagine Shenlee retelling the story at length in the bar of the Army-Navy Club in D.C., and he'd make a point of telling it to people I knew and with whom I'd served. He'd make sure Felix, the gossipy bartender, heard it and would pass it on. People would listen and shake their heads and refer to me as "poor Alex."

After a minute, I said, "I'm game."

"You made the right decision, Alex, believe me. We can handle your in-processing right here," Colonel Frost said, getting to her feet. "Jerry knows the drill."

We shook hands, and before I could say I'd enjoyed seeing her again—or anything else, for that matter—she'd hauled out her cell phone and was punching in some numbers. Interview over, she nodded, smiled politely, and pointed me toward the door. Outside, in the hall, I looked around for Shenlee, and found him in an adjoining corridor chatting with an attractive female in the uniform of a Marine captain.

When he saw me, he straightened up, quietly told the Marine he'd see her later, then pointed me in the direction of a neighboring office. "You won't be freelancing this time around, Klear. You're going to be working for the U.S. government. On a contract basis. How does that grab you?"

I gave Shenlee a stony stare.

"You ain't retiring, and you know it. In fact you're anxious to get back. I can see it in your eyes."

"Sure, Jerry. You could always read my mind."

"I wonder why."

"I wear my heart on my sleeve."

Shenlee nudged me toward an adjoining office. "You're gonna need some paperwork. Your security clearances are in order, I assume."

"I've resisted the urge to join the Communist Party, if that's what you mean. And to burn my draft card out on Main Street."

"Maybe if you'd resisted the urge to keep opening that big trap of yours all the time, you would have gotten a little further in the world."

"Maybe, Jerry, but I'm not sure it would have been worth it."

At one of the two desks, the operator punched my name into a computer and, from a government database, called up a lot of personal information on me, again reminding me that the government may know more about me than I know myself. Since I'd been through all this before, I only needed to update a few facts. They even had my thumbprint on file.

At another desk, someone took my picture, and I had my medical coverage reactivated and again signed on for my government annuity. Then I signed two copies of an agreement that stipulated the terms of my new assignment. I was to be employed by a contractor called Security Assets, which was no doubt some kind of government front. When I looked at the money I would be paid, I was reminded of one reason why, despite its many inconveniences, I'd been in this business for so long.

"I'll hold both copies, Klear," Shenlee said. And when my ID card emerged from the laminating machine, he grabbed it from the operator. "I'll take this too." He almost smiled. "For safekeeping. Use your passport to get around. It's good for three more years. I checked. You're a tourist."

"Terrific." In a roundabout way Shenlee was saying I'd be covert. He'd taken my ID card because I wouldn't, under any circumstances, be identifying myself as an employee of the government. We were being careful. In some situations having it in your possession can backfire.

But this meant I was totally on my own. If I got myself into hot water, I couldn't look to the government to bail me out.

When we were back in the corridor, I said, "Will I be carrying?" I only asked Jerry the question to needle him. I knew I wouldn't be armed, unless I decided to arm myself.

"You're going to Germany, Klear. The Krauts don't look kindly on people carrying firearms, as you well know."

Of course, no one would have to know if I was to provide my own artillery. When I started in this business, things were less complicated. The difficulty these days is getting a weapon by the security people at the airlines. I'd have to decide myself how I would approach this particular problem.

When I asked him when I'd be leaving, he said, "We've purchased your plane ticket. You fly day after tomorrow."

"That's kind of short notice, isn't it?"

"How long does it take to pack a damn suitcase?"

"I have to make arrangements with Gary. He'll need—"

"You and your partner can work something out, I'm sure." Shenlee wasn't much interested in the fact that I'd be putting my business and personal affairs on hold. "You'll be flying direct to Munich. You'll be staying at one of the safe houses we've got there, a nice place. I checked it out." Shenlee gave me two manila envelopes and two smaller envelopes. "Don't lose this stuff." He took a sheet of paper out of one of the envelopes and said, "I suggest committing this one to memory."

"And then burning it?"

"Ha ha. Stay in touch."

I said, "With who? Who's my contact? Who's running this?"

"Relax, Klear. We trust you to get the job done. A guy like you doesn't need someone to hold his hand."

"You expect me to play it by ear?"

"Someone will contact you." When I again asked "who?" Shenlee said, "You'll find out when you need to find out." He gave me a pat on the back that, I assume, was supposed to be reassuring. "Oh, yeah, you'll find a bunch of cell phones in the apartment. They're all disposable. The Krauts call them *Handys*. I guess you know that, right? Also some telephone cards. They can be useful. And a set of car keys and a registration. They call it a *Zulassung*, right? Don't worry. The vehicle's untraceable, registered to a nonexistent business. Car's in the adjacent garage. Try not to get anyone mad at you. That's it." Shenlee stuck out his hand. "Good luck."

I decided to let Shenlee have the last word. I began to sense that this operation wasn't completely kosher—and for a brief second, I felt myself wondering whether I wasn't going to need more than luck to come back in one piece.

Chapter 8

Sunday, January 20, 2008

"You've got a goddamn death wish. Is that it?"

Buck Romero isn't the type to mince words or to pull punches. It was two days after my meeting with Shenlee and Colonel Frost in Brooklyn, and Buck and I were at a corner table in the bar of the Holiday Inn adjacent to Kennedy Airport. I'd spent much of the weekend making last-minute arrangements—with Gary to run the business, with the postman to hold the mail, with a neighbor to watch the house, and with a kid to tend my lawn.

"They're using me because I was involved in the Nadaj rendition."

"You believe that?" Buck took a swallow from the green bottle of Heineken in his big mitt.

My own flight was still six hours away. I was scheduled to arrive in Munich early Monday morning.

"Why shouldn't I believe it?"

"Because it doesn't ring true, that's why. Do you think the colonel gives a damn whether or not you get back at the people in Kosovo? Get real."

I hated to have to admit that Buck was right. In the two days that had elapsed, I'd come to realize that Shenlee and Colonel Frost had manipulated the situation very nicely. But in the last analysis, it was Colonel Frost who'd known precisely which buttons to press.

The bar was a dark room with a couple of TVs playing. Most of the patrons were on their second or third drink. Their conversation was unpleasantly shrill and their laughter annoyingly forced. I had a headache, but I didn't know if it was from the noise or the fact that I knew Buck was right—and that I never should have said yes to this assignment.

When I'd spoken with Buck on the telephone two days before and told him about Jerry Shenlee's reappearance in my life, he said he'd fly up to see me off. He also said he'd call around and try to find out what might be going on.

"Sometimes it takes a braver man to back out," Buck said. He was only half kidding.

I nodded, recalling some operations I would have been well advised to back out of before they got off the ground. The Ramush Nadaj rendition was high on the list.

Buck shook his head. "You said last year you were through with this stuff."

I hadn't seen Buck in nearly eight months—since the day back in May when we'd met at Arlington. It had been nearly a year since my Kosovo adventure, and I was still dreaming about Nadaj and Vickie in glorious living color—and still pounding against the lid of a closed coffin before waking up drenched in sweat.

"From the way they described it," I said, "it sounds pretty straightforward. An unobtrusive murder investigation. A former Green Beret got himself into some hot water. They figure I know my way around that part of the world."

Buck grimaced. "The FBI has people to look into situations like this. I don't see why they'd need you. I called someone. The bureau has a legal attaché in Munich, a guy named Owen, and he's the only person who's seen Brinkman."

"Anything else?"

"If Colonel Frost has an interest in this, Alex, you can be sure it's of interest to the deputy secretary of defense and to some highly placed officials in the Pentagon."

"And the National Security Council if Jerry Shenlee's involved."

Buck nodded. "Maybe that's why they've decided not to use the bureau. It has too many blabbermouths."

"I almost fell over when I heard Shenlee's voice on the telephone. He was the last person on earth I ever expected would call me."

"For some reason," Buck said, "they seem to want you."

"For my good looks?"

"Possible, but not likely."

One Sunday morning, I'd seen the deputy secretary of defense on a news show, and when he'd referred, in a vague way, to "disappointments" in the Balkans I almost felt he was referring to the Nadaj rendition. Not only hadn't we gotten our man, I'd been nabbed by the very guys we were trying to extract.

The news of that episode must have gone over big back at the Pentagon's command center.

Buck said, "I guess you know that one or two details concerning the Kosovo rendition nearly leaked." When I said I thought that something like that might have happened, he said, "A reporter from one of the magazines in New York kept calling around. He'd heard a rumor about a Yank being captured and then being let go after a day or two."

"Nice of them to let the guy go. Who should I thank?"

"He was trying to make sense of what he'd heard, but he hasn't come up with enough to work with—no names, no places. But he's still calling around."

"I'll take my phone off the hook."

When I asked Buck if he'd been able to find out anything about Brinkman, he said, "I was able to talk with a couple of people who served with him. They said he was a good guy, very capable. He served in the First Gulf War, was stationed briefly in Germany. He went into Afghanistan with the first wave, spent time in the mountains shooting up the Taliban whenever they could find them. He did a second and then a third tour. And he got the Distinguished Service Cross for breaking up a riot at a prison out there."

"The dead woman, Ursula Vogt, was a journalist who covered the war in Afghanistan. She worked for *Welt-Bericht*. Brinkman seems to have met her in Afghanistan."

"Then he followed her back to Munich?"

"I got the impression Colonel Frost doesn't want a European court to convict Brinkman, or even to try him."

Buck said, "A trial of a Green Beret would bring reporters from the States on the run, that's for sure."

"They want to keep it beneath the media's radar. There's stuff there they don't want to come out."

"Why? What could be so important?"

"Good question."

The waitress brought two more beers, and when I mentioned that she had a friendly smile and a nice figure, Buck asked me about Vanessa. I shrugged. "Vanessa is very unhappy with me. I have a feeling she won't be sitting alone at home while I'm gone."

"Can you blame her?"

The chemistry between Vanessa and me had been apparent from the moment of our first meeting in the Saranac Inn, and her breaking up with me was another reason I now felt signing on for this job was a big mistake. When I called her, Vanessa had said something about "breaking commitments," announced that she'd have to "reevaluate" our relationship, then made a hard-to-understand comment about "easy come, easy fucking go"—and slammed down the telephone.

Vanessa normally never used profanity. Our goodbye could have been worse, but not much.

Buck took a swallow of beer, and when he asked who was running the operation, I told him I still didn't know. "Shenlee said someone would be contacting me."

"Probably, it'll be Shenlee himself. They like him in D.C." Buck frowned. "But why wouldn't he tell you?"

I shrugged. "Jerry and I have never quite been on the same page."

"They figure you don't need to know yet."

"'Need to know.' I've heard that often enough."

Buck was too considerate to say it, but the truth was Shenlee and Colonel Frost considered me expendable. Why not? I'd screwed up the Nadaj rendition. I'd nearly spilled my Sunday morning cup of coffee when I realized the deputy secretary of defense's vague comments to the interviewer were connected to our Kosovo rendition. Buck looked unusually thoughtful, and I had an idea he felt I was in way over my head with this assignment. As with the Kosovo operation, there seemed to be too many unanswered questions.

"I gave Max Peters a call," I said after a moment. "I filled him in a little. He knows the case, says it's been in the papers over there." Max was a German cop Buck and I had worked with way back when, in the years before the Berlin Wall came down. But we knew that things were very different now in Europe from the way they were then.

"How's Max doing?"

"He sounded fine on the telephone. He's retired now."

"Is there anyone else over there you're planning to talk to?" Buck, I knew, was referring to Irmie.

"Maybe," I said. "I don't know."

After paying our bill and saying goodbye to the waitress, we drifted out into the lobby, where people were coming and going, most of them with luggage, all of them in a hurry. In the distance, as we watched, a 747, its flaps down, eased its way down toward a runway.

What really bothered me was the thought that the people in charge didn't have complete confidence in me. I was rusty, that was true. But if they didn't have all that much confidence, why pick me? Again I came back to the same reason: I was expendable.

When I asked Buck if I was being too paranoid, I got the answer I expected. "C'mon, Alex, in this business, there's no such thing as 'too paranoid.' Remember how it was on the other side of the Wall? Waking up in the middle of the night thinking there were Stasi agents under the bed?"

"Or KGB agents outside the door? Remember Yalta?" Buck grimaced. Yalta, where we vainly tried to recruit a vacationing staff officer in the KGB's First Directorate, was another city from which we had to make a hurried departure by boat. Now that I think of it, I doubt that even one percent of the stuff that went on during the Cold War ever got into the papers. By the time the historians get around to writing things down, there won't be anyone around to tell these stories, and everything will be pretty much forgotten. Maybe it's just as well.

Buck said he'd continue to nose around on his end, and we said goodbye in front of the hotel. He definitely left me with the thought that I never should have accepted this assignment.

As Buck's taxi receded in the distance, I thought again about Jerry Shenlee, a guy I'd known for twenty years, from the time we were both stationed in West Berlin and making the two-mile trip from Tempelhof to the intelligence gathering facility out at Teufelsberg. Tempelhof was the big Berlin airport that, as the Cold War began to heat up, became our headquarters for running agents and carrying on covert activities of every conceivable description. From the out-of-the-way installation at Teufelsberg, which was adjacent to the Grunewald, Berlin's big city park, the National Security Agency conducted electronic eavesdropping on microwave transmissions all over Eastern Europe. The resulting process was very much like putting together a big jigsaw puzzle from an array of tiny, strangely shaped pieces. With the tidbits of information we got—mostly from recon photographs, snatches of gossip, and overheard telephone conversations—the analysts targeted potential agents. While people like Jerry manned the desks and made the decisions—and, incidentally, seemed to get most of the promotions— it was guys like me and Buck who, using a combination of blackmail and enticement, went into the East and did the actual recruiting. Because I felt I was doing an important job that very few other people could do, or that anyone in his right mind would want to do, I still think of those years as a great time in my life.

And, of course, they were made even greater by the fact that I survived them.

But that was then—and now the need is for people who can operate in another part of the world and who can speak languages like Farsi, Pashto, and Arabic. Or maybe they speak Albanian, which would have been useful while I was in Kosovo and tangled up with Nadaj and his crew.

From my hotel room, I called Max Peters, my one good contact in Munich. Max didn't answer, and I left a message telling him when I'd be arriving.

While doing the last of my packing, I ordered two more bottles of beer to add to the three or four I'd already knocked down.

Chapter 9

Monday, January 21, 2008

After my reassignment from South America in the 1980s, Buck and I
spent three months at an NSA station in the Alps before being posted
as "journalists" to Radio Free Europe, which at the time occupied a
compound located in a secluded corner of Munich's English Garden.
It took a while to adjust to the new situation. Germany—West and
East—was the battlefield on which the Cold War was largely fought,
and the way things were done in Europe was different from the way
they were done in South America. But knowing the language the way
my mother spoke it made life much easier—and permitted me to
quickly make contacts and establish relationships that would hardly
have been possible otherwise.

While I was working at RFE, Max Peters was one of the people I
got to know well.

Unfortunately, my personal life took a turn for the worse toward the
end of my tour in that part of the world—and I get a headache whenever I think about that. And the truth is I still think of it a great deal.
But that's another story. Max and Irmie had been colleagues and, naturally enough I guess, it was the personal stuff to which he immediately
referred when I met him a couple of hours after my arrival.

"You don't look happy, Alex," Max said only minutes after we'd
shaken hands and plunked ourselves down on a bench in the English
Garden, Munich's big city park that, with its broad paths and rectangular shape, always put me in mind of New York City's Central Park.

"Does it show, Max?" I said, as I watched a teenager dribble a soccer ball across the broad expanse of grass.

"I'm afraid so," Max said. "You're wishing you were somewhere else. I can see it in your eyes."

Max was right, of course. The city held too many painful memories. Despite the piles of snow and slush-covered paths, the skaters and bike riders were zooming back and forth. As I looked around, I remembered the many hand-in-hand strolls that Irmie and I used to take here, often in the evenings after work. I'd left at the wrong time and under the wrong circumstances, and that thought depressed me even further. Nevertheless, now that I was back and shooting the breeze with Max in the Bavarian-accented German that I'd learned from my mom and later picked up in these parts, I unexpectedly found myself thinking about Irmie again and wondering how she'd weathered the passing years.

Trying to get away from the personal stuff, I asked Max about Douglas Brinkman.

"I don't know if I can be of much help to you on this one, Alex," Max said. That was about what I figured Max would say.

Max has wavy gray hair, bright blue eyes, a silvery mustache, a slightly flushed face, and a noticeable beer gut. During the Cold War, he was a Munich police detective, who spent a number of years as liaison between the city's police force and American intelligence, and that's how we met.

After my arrival that morning at nine a.m., I took a quick look around the new Franz Josef Strauss Airport, then took a taxi to the address Shenlee had given me. The city seemed to have changed considerably since my last visit nine years before. One improvement was a three-lane highway that I didn't remember having existed when I left, and in the distance I could see that the city's skyline exhibited a number of new buildings.

The apartment—or safe house—had a good location, on a quiet side street not far from the Hirschgarten, and I was relieved to find the keys Shenlee had given me all fit. It's anybody's guess how many of these setups our intelligence services have at their disposal around the world. From my experience in staying in quite a few of them, I can say they vary greatly as far as comfort and convenience go. In a couple I recall having no running water and having to sack out in a sleeping bag on a concrete floor. After looking this one over and deciding it would be more than adequate, I tossed my gear into one of the two bedrooms and tried out one of the cell phones I found on the dining room table. I called Max, then took a taxi out to the English Garden.

When Max said that he couldn't be of much help, I asked him what the problem was.

"I have an uncomfortable feeling, Alex. The Vogt woman was a journalist. I don't want to be dragged into this case if it has political implications." Max looked somber, more somber than I remembered him. He seemed to be at loose ends. His wife, Anna, had died two years before, and I had the idea that he hadn't gotten over losing her.

"Whatever you can do, Max, I'd appreciate it." I hadn't been encouraged by the fact that when I called Max and told him what I wanted he suggested we meet on a bench in the English Garden rather than in a downtown restaurant. Or rather than in the noisy canteen in Munich's downtown police headquarters in the Ettstrasse, a place where, in the old days, we discussed a lot of business and drank a lot of coffee.

And had plenty of laughs. I already had the feeling that on this trip there wouldn't be too much to laugh about.

"Things aren't like they once were, Alex." Max was referring to the fact that German-American relations had noticeably cooled in the years since the Wall came down and the Cold War ended. Germany, these days, seemed to be cozying up to Russia, its former enemy, while distancing itself from the United States, its former friend and protector. Because of quite a few harrowing East Bloc experiences, I knew I would always have problems thinking of Stasi and KGB types as dependable friends.

I wondered whether this might be a matter on which Max and I did not exactly see eye to eye—quite possibly, one of many such matters.

"Sure, Max. I read the papers too."

"We don't need you to protect us from those big, bad Russians anymore. And we're still mad about the way your GIs were constantly taking our women back to America."

"Could it be possible that we treat women better in the States? And maybe us Yanks deserve some credit for pumping up the German economy for all those years."

Max smiled, then nodded in the direction of the restaurant adjacent to the Chinese Tower, one of the English Garden's landmarks. "I'll buy you a beer. Then we'll be even."

With the weather having turned cool, I was glad to go indoors.

After we'd found a table, Max said, "You're looking good, Alex. You haven't changed much since the last time I saw you."

Max was being kind. My face still showed some signs from the banging around I got in Kosovo. There were a couple of small scars, one long scar, quite a large indentation in my forehead, and my nose now leaned slightly to the starboard. The emotional scars were invisible, at least I hoped they were.

I lowered my voice. "Like I said, Max, anything you can tell me about Brinkman would be helpful."

"Do you have any kind of official status, Alex?"

I made a sour face. Jerry Shenlee had made a point of saying I'd be traveling as a tourist. As we watched the waitress set down two half-liter glasses of beer, I said, "I'm a concerned citizen. Isn't that enough?"

"Concerned citizen? What are you concerned about?" It was Max's turn to look serious.

"Cheers, Max. Prosit."

"Prosit." Max put down his glass, wiped his lips. "After you called, I talked to one of the homicide detectives who handled the case."

"A good cop? Dependable?"

"He's not one of my favorite people. But that's neither here nor there. I got along better with his partner, but he's left the force." Max's face clouded over. "Dropped out of sight, actually. He might be dead. No one knows for sure."

"What did the detective say?"

"According to him, Brinkman and Miss Vogt were friendly, and spending a lot of time together. He's a former member of Special Forces, and he met her in Afghanistan, where he was stationed and where she was working as a correspondent for *Welt-Bericht*. According to the guy I spoke with, Brinkman's a violent guy with a short fuse."

"How do you know?"

"I looked up his arrest record."

"Brinkman was a Green Beret. Is that what you're talking about?"

"He was arrested some years back for fighting in a bar."

I didn't say anything, recalling a few of the restaurants I'd broken up before I'd become at least partially socialized. Max saw that I was far from convinced.

Gazing at me over the beer glass with his cold blue eyes, he said, "Maybe Miss Vogt was about to give him the gate. He blew his stack." He paused. "From what I understand, she was a looker."

"You think that's the way it happened, Max? That sounds a little too pat." I'm sensitive to the way the police, no matter what country they belong to, like to make the facts and circumstances of a situation fit whatever case they're trying to make.

"Alex, the woman had a dozen knife wounds in her. Then she was shot. Someone was very mad about something. Who else would it be but Brinkman? And there were other things."

"Like what?"

"There was lining from an army field jacket under her fingernails. She was trying to defend herself. She must have ripped whatever the guy was wearing."

Max got to his feet and came back a couple of minutes later with a pair of sausages on rolls. After smearing mine with mustard, I said, "There are a lot of military field jackets around. From a lot of countries."

"Yes, but they're made out of different material. This kind of lining is from an American military field jacket. Granted there are plenty of people walking around the city wearing field jackets, but there aren't too many wearing American field jackets. Not anymore." It's true that the U.S. military, which except for bases in Vilseck and Grafenwöhr, has pretty much pulled out of Bavaria.

Before Max could buy a second beer, I suggested we ride out to the house. I needed to see it for myself.

Max's face clouded over and he looked at his watch. Finally, he nodded. Maybe I was overreacting, but I had the feeling he wasn't too

anxious to see me again or to give me any kind of help in this case. But
we'd worked together for a lot of years, and in the course of that time
done each other more favors than either of us could count. At Christ-
mastime, the German cops threw great parties to which we were always invited, the fanciest being the annual shindig on one of the upper
floors of the Police Presidium and hosted by the police president himself. I had met Irmie at one of those Christmas parties. For our part, we
saw that Max and his crew got invites to our blasts, and I always made
sure Max went home with an American turkey from the PX and a large
bottle of bourbon, the kind of things that, because of EU tariffs and
trade barriers, you just can't get in Europe.

We took the Ring, the highway that circles Munich, and as I looked
at the passing sights, I found it difficult to believe that, after all these
years, I was really back in this city. In the distance on the right was the
Funkturm, the tower from which television and radio signals are broadcast and one of Munich's landmarks. On the left we went by the
Olympic Stadium, the massive hanging Plexiglas roof that no one
thought would last a year still very much intact. The fact that every car
on the road seemed to be a snazzy new model served to remind me that
Germany, like the other countries of the EU, is enjoying a period of
mild prosperity.

As we drove, Max said, "I have to admit, I'm surprised to see you,
Alex. I mean, I just never thought you'd come back."

I knew what Max was talking about. "That makes two of us, Max."

"Have you been in contact with Irmie at all?"

"Not for a while."

The truth was, I'd written one letter while she was in the hospital.
When she didn't respond, there wasn't any more contact between us.
That was a long time ago.

I was curious about Irmie, but I decided not to ask any more questions.

Ursula Vogt's house was in Munich's northwest corner, a neighborhood called Obermenzing, a place of upper-middle-class respectabil-
ity. Max turned off the Verdistrasse, the main drag leading out to the
autobahn going west, then on to a curving street along a narrow side-

walk. Driving slowly, we went a few blocks until we reached a wider street called Karwinskistrasse. We then made a left onto a tree-shaded street of comfortable looking homes, all with well-kept gardens, many with secure fences. We parked in front of a house that was behind a high hedge. "That's it, Alex, that's where Ursula Vogt lived."

It was a nice piece of property, but all that was visible was a thick eight-foot-high hedge, at one end of which was a steel gate. When I tried the gate, it was locked.

"I guess she liked privacy," I said.

"I guess so," Max agreed.

Peering through the gate, I could barely glimpse a two-story building with white walls set back fifty feet from the sidewalk.

After we'd spent a couple of minutes looking things over, I said, "I'd like to go inside, Max. Take a look around."

"Sure you would, Alex, but I don't think that can be arranged."

"Maybe you can talk with someone downtown." When he shook his head, I said, "You sure, Max?"

Years ago, Max hadn't been above carrying out a "black-bag" entry when the circumstances called for it, and when the interests of our respective governments harmonized, we'd even collaborated on a couple. To be honest, I never thought of those illegal entries as a very big deal. We always had good reasons for the break-ins, and we were always careful to make sure no one was any the wiser. On one of them, we found and photographed evidence used in a case against a member of the Bundestag, an elected representative who was being paid to funnel information to East Berlin. On another, while I was installing a bug in a suspected agent's telephone receiver, I heard a key being inserted in the downstairs door—and to avoid detection, Max and I ended up spending a below-freezing night on the guy's terrace. But that was then, and this was now. Our personal relationship had changed—"cooled" might be a better word. As I stood looking things over, I concluded that this house might be a tough nut to crack.

A mildly overweight neighbor who'd been raking the lawn of the adjoining property took our arrival as an excuse to take a breather. He paused, wiped his face with a handkerchief, and stood watching. When

Max walked over and flashed some ID left over from his years as a cop, the guy said, "My name is Thiemann, Ludwig Thiemann. My God, it was a terrible thing. I still can't believe it. She was a nice woman."

Thiemann's dialect was thick, and because Bavarians sometimes exhibit a bunker mentality, dealing with the locals on this kind of assignment can be a challenge. Along with talking like them, you need to think like them. Looking at Thiemann, I figured he enjoyed his quota of sausage and beer.

"How well did you know her?" I asked.

"Pretty well. But she did a lot of traveling. She'd be gone sometimes for weeks or even months." He sighed, wiped more perspiration from his face. "I guess that's the way it is when you work for a newspaper."

Max pushed open his gate. A path of flagstones wound around a flower bed and ran alongside the hedge separating his property from Ursula Vogt's. With his practiced cop's eye, Max gave the property a quick once-over.

"Anything else you can tell us?" he asked.

"Not really. I spoke with the detectives the day after it happened. They were all over the neighborhood, asking questions. It was a Friday afternoon. Funny, I was home at the time." He shook his head. "I didn't hear anything. Whoever did it came and went without anybody seeing them."

While Max talked, I took a stroll. At a point some fifty feet back from the sidewalk, the hedge gave way to a five-foot metal fence. From this point, I could see the rear of Ursula Vogt's home. There were two glass doors looking onto a stone veranda with some garden furniture strewn chaotically and a grill lying on its side. It looked as if the Munich police hadn't picked up after themselves.

Which, I suppose, made them no different from the police everywhere.

I strolled back. "I guess you know they arrested a guy for the murder."

He nodded. "The American. I've been following it in the newspapers."

"Did you know him at all?" I asked.

"Sure. I used to see him. Tall, broad-shouldered. Spoke with him a few times. He knew some German. Said at one time he'd been stationed down in Bad Tölz. That was the Green Beret headquarters. He told me about the training, skiing around in the mountains and all. That was before they closed the base." When I asked if there was anything special about Brinkman, Thiemann said, "Not really. He seemed friendly enough."

"How often would he come around?"

"I couldn't say. My wife would know. She keeps track of things like that." When I wondered whether he could ask her, Thiemann said, "Sorry. She's up in Frankfurt, visiting her mother. You know, the guy I would have looked at was the other guy who used to come around."

"Who was that?" Max asked.

"The handyman."

"What can you tell us about him?"

"Not much. To be honest, he always seemed suspicious to me. I think he repaired stuff for her and did some gardening. He wasn't around all that long. If I was her, I wouldn't have let him in the house. Cops questioned him. But they let him go." He paused. "But there was something about him I never liked. Couldn't put my finger on it exactly."

I said, "Could you try?"

"He'd say he was going to come but he wouldn't show. A lousy work ethic."

"How would you know that?" I asked.

"She told me."

"That doesn't mean he'd kill someone," Max said. "Just because he has a lousy work ethic." When Thiemann agreed, Max threw me an impatient glance. It was obvious we weren't going to get much more out of this guy, and he wanted to get moving.

"A lot of these Balkan people are like that, I guess," Thiemann said.

I halted when he said that. "Where in the Balkans was he from? Do you know?"

"Bosnia, Macedonia, Croatia. Who knows? All those countries are the same to me." After wiping away some more perspiration, he jammed the handkerchief in his back pocket.

"You ever been down there?" I said.

"We were planning to go to Sarajevo back eleven or twelve years ago, but then the civil war started. I told my wife to forget about it."

Max said, "Thanks for your help."

The neighbor pointed to his lawn. "My wife's coming back tomorrow. I need to have everything shipshape or she'll raise hell."

We said we understood his problem.

"Nice meeting you guys," Thiemann said before returning to his raking.

Before climbing back into the car, I took another look at Ursula Vogt's home. "I need to take a look inside." I knew I was pushing it.

Max didn't say anything for about a minute, then he shook his head. "I have to draw the line somewhere, Alex, and I'm drawing it here." He turned over the engine. "I'll drive you back to wherever it is you're staying."

Chapter 10

Monday, January 21, 2008

Whoever had decided on the location for the safe house had a good feel for the city and had chosen wisely. The apartment was on the top floor of a four-story building located between the Hirschgarten, a beer garden where in the old days I'd spent many a summer evening, and the park surrounding the Nymphenburg Palace. I remembered reading that, in 1972, some of the Olympic horse riding competitions were held on the palace grounds. It was a low-profile neighborhood, and my comings and goings weren't likely to attract much attention. Since I figured it might be wise not to let the police know exactly where I was holed up, I had Max let me off at the Romanplatz and walked the rest of the way.

Max diplomatically didn't ask where I was staying, and I didn't volunteer the information.

It was a quiet street, and as I walked I passed only a woman with a dog and an elderly man carrying packages, neither of whom gave me a second glance. Using one of my keys, I let myself into the building, which had two apartments to every floor. What I found mildly intriguing was that the apartment, which was alone on the top floor, wasn't listed on the bell register in the lobby. A nice touch, I thought, for a place meant to house only intelligence people. Guys like Shenlee were well paid for dreaming up this kind of dodge.

Maybe I got into the wrong end of the business.

Although it was late afternoon, I'd slept on the plane and still didn't feel tired. As one of my former bosses used to say to people looking for some extra time off, "Jet lag is only in your mind." But just as I was about to insert the key in the door, I stopped. Inside the apartment I could hear a voice, the excited sound of a newscaster describing some disaster or other. Someone had the TV on.

At one point in my career, I simply would have drawn my Beretta automatic, kicked open the door, and barged in. But now that I've mellowed, I try to handle things with more, shall we say, finesse.

Or maybe my hesitation was due to the fact I wasn't carrying a handgun on my person—out of consideration, naturally, for the German government's extreme dislike of anyone in their country packing a weapon. When the Frankfurt cops during a routine traffic stop found one of our case officers with a sidearm in his glove compartment, they tossed the guy into the local cooler for three weeks, which was the amount of time that elapsed before he decided to sing. Even then, it was a while before he told his story to the cops' satisfaction. With his cover blown, he returned to the States, resigned, and hasn't been heard from since.

In this business, the smallest blunder can be career ending. Or life ending.

With this thought in mind, I stood in the hallway considering things. I decided that if someone was looking to surprise me, they wouldn't be playing the TV at this volume.

As soon as I rang, I heard movement inside, and seconds later the door was opened.

"Hello, Alex," Colonel Sylvia Frost said, and motioned me into the apartment.

"Well, this is a surprise. I rang because I heard the TV."

"I didn't want to surprise you when you got back." She closed the door. "You are surprised?" She crossed the room and turned off the television.

"Yes, of course. For some reason I assumed I'd be the only person—"

"With a key to this apartment?"

With Colonel Frost just behind me, I walked through the apartment and checked out both bedrooms. Colonel Frost had made herself at home. She'd tossed her gear into the bedroom I'd originally selected and put my gear in the other bedroom—which meant she was now oc-cupying the bedroom with the double bed and large closet. Needless to say, she'd also laid claim to one of the apartment's two bathrooms. I didn't know whether to be happy or unhappy about all this.

I felt I was being pushed around, so I decided to be unhappy. In my new bedroom, I took a quick look through my stuff. The three shirts I'd hung up in the other closet were now lying on the bed.

By the time I returned to the living room, she was seated on the sofa, her briefcase open, her laptop on the coffee table, and papers spread out on the sofa and on the floor. She had a pair of reading glasses perched on her nose. She was wearing a white blouse and gray slacks and some kind of house slippers with fur on them. Colonel Frost had trim, nice looking ankles. She looked up from what she was read-ing and indicated I should sit down.

"We're going to be working together, Alex."

"Couldn't you have mentioned that back in the States?"

"I thought you'd assume that. You didn't think you'd be totally on your own, did you?"

"I kind of thought Jerry Shenlee might be showing up at some point." I recalled Jerry's and my last conversation. When I explicitly asked about control and contacts, he left the question unanswered.

"Jerry isn't perfect for this job," Colonel Frost said.

"Why not? He's worked in Germany before. He knows his way around. I knew him in Berlin back in the eighties. We worked the La Belle disco investigation together."

"Jerry doesn't like Germany. He doesn't get along with German people. He doesn't have your contacts."

"And he doesn't like sauerkraut."

"No, it's red cabbage he doesn't like."

"I can see where that might be a problem."

"Besides, he doesn't know the language."

I knew Shenlee had been at the army language school in Monterey. "Sure he does. He just won't admit it."

"Well, all right, but he's not as fluent as you are."

"I'm glad to hear that."

"We recognize your capabilities, Alex."

"I'm glad to hear that too."

She gazed up at me, her expression betraying nothing. "That's why we're going with you, not Jerry."

"I still think I could have been more thoroughly briefed, ma'am."

"Please, call me Sylvia. Like I said, we'll be working together. Is there anything else on your mind?"

I said, "I'm not sure about the living arrangements."

She frowned. "What's wrong?"

"Maybe I should move into a hotel." I didn't say that maybe Colonel Frost should move into a hotel. I was here first.

"There's room enough for us both. There are two bedrooms, two baths. I don't see where there's any kind of problem. Does having a female in your living space make you uncomfortable?"

I could have said that it depends on the female, but I had an idea she wouldn't take kindly to that answer either. Seeing her again, though, I couldn't help being impressed by her sexy good looks—particularly by her smooth pale skin and her wide round eyes. I made an effort not to steal a glance at her legs or to imagine moving my hand along the smoothness of her thighs. When I didn't respond, she said, "Or are you one of those delicate people who has to have their own undisturbed personal space?"

"I'm thinking of you. I snore."

"I'll keep my door closed."

"Very loudly, from what I've been told."

"Who told you?"

"Quite a large number of people, now that I think of it."

"I'm assuming they were female people. How many?"

"I don't keep track of those kinds of numbers."

"Well, I'm glad of that. But I have to go back to my original statement. I think the living quarters are adequate, more than adequate. And because we'll be working together in this investigation, I think there's a decided advantage in our remaining together." She paused. "I hope that settles that matter." She paused again. "Where were you before?"

"I was on the job."

"What were you doing?"

I told Sylvia about my meeting with Max Peters. I also mentioned the fact that Max, one of my best contacts in this country, didn't seem too eager to be of help.

"Why is that, do you think?"

"Offhand, I can think of three reasons. Germany and the United States aren't as friendly as they once were. This case is politically sensitive. Or maybe he's mad at me."

"Does he have any reason to be mad at you?"

"Everyone seems to have a reason to be mad at me."

"I wonder why."

I figured that Max might be remembering Irmie, but I wasn't going to mention Irmie to Colonel Frost—or should I say Sylvia. I was still having difficulty calling my new roommate by her first name.

"Okay. Whatever problems develop, we'll try to work around them. Anything else?"

I said, "I'd like to have a look around inside Miss Vogt's place." I told Sylvia how, when I made the suggestion, Max had vetoed the idea.

"Is it important?"

"It could be. I'll only know when I'm inside."

"What would you expect to find?"

"Maybe some proof that Brinkman is innocent of the murder—that is, assuming he is innocent."

Sylvia looked thoughtful. "Could we go in on our own? And if so, how would we do it?"

I paused, recalling the house and its layout. "It's an interesting challenge."

"You don't sound all that confident."

After a second, I said, "There are two glass doors leading off a veranda in the rear. The house is enclosed by hedges, so going in at the rear should mean we'll be out of sight of the neighbors' prying eyes. That's a plus."

"But can you get over the hedges?"

Recalling the stretch of low fence between the two houses, I said, "I think so."

"Alarm system?"

"Always a possibility."

"There could be some very unpleasant consequences if this doesn't work out."

"In that case, we'll have to make sure that it does work out."

"I don't think that—"

"Are you always so negative?"

Having read through my file, Sylvia was no doubt familiar with the numerous black bag operations I'd carried out over the years. She gave me a searching look. "I'm assuming you're still good at this sort of stuff."

"Isn't that why you got me over here? Because I'm good at this sort of stuff?"

Sylvia hesitated, then nodded. "That's one of the reasons."

"What are the other reasons?"

Ignoring my question, she said, "If you think you can handle it, I'll take your word for it."

"There's only one way to find out."

She nodded, then checked her watch. "We go at eleven o'clock. People will be falling asleep by then."

I reached for my jacket. When she asked where I was going, I told her the local hardware store. I had my lock picks in my luggage. But I was going to need a glasscutter, rubber gloves, a jimmy and some rope. And some plastic bags.

Chapter 11

Monday, January 21, 2008

Dressed in black and wearing running shoes, I was standing in the pitch-dark garden behind the home of the late Ursula Vogt. I'd been able to get this far by entering onto the property of the next-door neighbor, the loquacious Herr Thiemann. Going over the five-foot-high metal fence had required about twenty seconds. The problem now was to gain entry to the house itself. I had a number of choices, all of which looked extremely uninviting. I had already decided against going in through the glass doors. Whispering, I got Sylvia on my cell phone. "All systems go."

"Quiet on this end." Sylvia was in the BMW, parked on the next street. In this area of the city, we figured the police, if they showed, would most likely have to approach from the Verdistrasse, which was the neighborhood's main drag, and would have to go by the point where Sylvia was parked.

Although the two glass doors on the veranda looked easiest, I couldn't see beyond the heavy curtains drawn across them, and decided they might be alarmed. A better choice would be an upstairs window. I tossed the rope over the branch of an oak tree adjacent to the house, used it to haul myself up the trunk, which brought me within precarious reach of a second-story dormer window. Unfastening the rope from the tree branch, I looped it around the chimney, then wound it around my waist and drew it tight. With the rope secure, I was able to balance myself on angled eaves on the side wall. I needed to cut a hole through two panes of window glass, not an easy feat. Aware that a false move here could lead to a severed vein or artery, I again tested the rope and made sure of my footing. Looking around, I decided no one could see me. The loudest sound was my own breathing.

Holding tight to the rope, I began to cut the glass very, very slowly, making sure, as I worked, that the opening was wide enough for my arm. When I'd traced a sufficiently large circle, I had no choice but to punch the glass inward and let it fall between the two windowpanes. Cutting the second pane was trickier. When I pushed it, I did so very gently, hoping that it wouldn't break. The sound of breaking glass is something that we second-story men take great pains to avoid. Fortunately, it fell with a soft thud against the windowsill. It was the kind of tilt window common in Europe. Reaching inside, I eased the handle up to horizontal and very carefully withdrew my arm, first through the inner and then the outer pane. The window swung outward. I didn't like the idea of leaving the rope, but there was no way to get it down from around the chimney without climbing onto the roof, and I couldn't see myself doing that at this moment. Maybe later. I swung myself over the window ledge and dropped silently inside.

After a brief look around and making sure no one was in the house, I called Sylvia. "I'm inside."

"Very good. No problems?"

"I didn't realize I was so good at this stuff. I may have missed my calling."

"What do you see?"

"A corridor. Bedrooms. It's a nice place she had. Looks like an antique mahogany chest on the landing. Persian rugs. I'd like to have this rug in my own place."

"Stop admiring the furniture."

"I didn't know newspaper reporters were so well paid."

"They're not. Pay attention. Do you see anything that looks like an office?"

After opening some doors, I said, "Negative."

"Still quiet out here. Keep looking."

"Yes, dear."

I peeked into the bedroom where Ursula Vogt's body had been found. The bed was a mess, although someone seemed to have changed the sheets. There was some blood on the rug. The Munich police needed a lesson in neatness.

Using my pencil flash, I went down the staircase. When you're in, the next thing to figure is how you'll get out. On the ground floor, I carefully examined the doors to the veranda looking for an alarm and saw an unobtrusive electrical contact. I opened the lock, but kept the door closed. Looking around, I found the living room, dining room, kitchen —but nothing that looked like an office. Leading from the kitchen was a stairway to the basement.

Downstairs, just beyond the gas furnace, I found a room with a desk, a computer, a bed, and some metal filing cabinets. More mess.

The cops, or someone, had been through the files. Papers were strewn all over, on the desktop, on the chair, on the floor. Old copies of *Welt-Bericht* were piled on the floor. On the wall was a map—Uzbekistan, Pakistan, Afghanistan, Iran. In the drawers of the room's one desk were some folders jammed with paper, old newspaper and magazine clippings mostly, but nothing that looked too interesting. I tossed a few of them into the black plastic bag anyway. Otherwise, there didn't seem to be anything that would be very helpful, certainly not the kind of thing I was hoping to find.

I was beginning to think that this expedition was turning out to be one large waste of time.

It's always darkest before the dawn. I decided to keep looking.

I went through the closet but couldn't find anything but clothes. There were two banks of filing cabinets. Both were heavy, but I moved them anyway, thinking they might be concealing a compartment in the floor. They weren't.

Flat on my stomach, I crawled under the bed, ran my hand across the dusty floor but didn't feel anything. Pushing my way farther under, I could feel the molding at the base of the wall. There was a break in the molding, and when I got my fingers into the break, a two-foot long piece of the molding swung open. That was interesting. I shone the flash at the wall and saw a section of the paneling that was separate from the rest of the wall.

Getting back to my feet and brushing off the dust, I moved the bed.

It was a simple arrangement. I only had to slide the wall panel upward. A small compartment was situated inside the space in the wall. It was filled with all kinds of stuff that I assumed Ursula Vogt preferred the world, without her permission, didn't see.

There were neatly tied together notebooks, folders full of typed sheets. I jammed them into the plastic bag. Some boxes full of photographs looked interesting. I took them too. I found some folders full of computer disks, put them in.

Telephone!

"Alex! A police car just went by, moving fast, no lights. Get out. Move."

I grabbed a last batch of papers, tossed in another folder, then went out of the office and up the stairs and through the dining room. It was good that I'd thought to unlock the veranda door. I dodged the veranda furniture and ran forty feet across the lawn and a flower bed to the six-foot fence. I'd just made it over when I heard voices from the street, no doubt the arriving cops. With my one escape route cut off, I moved farther back into the garden.

I recognized one voice—Thiemann, the neighbor, again being helpful. Now he was telling the cops he'd been on his back porch having a smoke when, through the basement window of the Vogt house, he saw a flashlight moving around in the Vogt place.

"My wife doesn't like it when I smoke in the house. She says I—"

"You sure it was a flashlight?" one of the policemen asked.

"At first I wasn't sure, so I waited. When I didn't see it anymore, I thought it must be my imagination. But then I saw it again."

"The front gate's locked," another policeman said. "How would anyone get in?"

"He'd maybe go in through the back," Thiemann explained. A minute later, he was leading the police into the garden and showing them the fence. I was squatting twenty feet away, shielded only by a large hedge.

"Hell, yes. You're right." One of the cops shined his flashlight into the other yard. "Someone went over this fence. It's bent. And it looks like a footprint there in the flower bed."

"There's no other way out," Thiemann said. "There's barbed wire in the hedges. Whoever it is, he's probably still in the house."

Out in front I could see a flashing blue light, which meant more cops. The fence at the rear of the neighbor's property loomed up twenty feet, much too high to climb. It was only a matter of time before a cop thought to shine a flashlight back in this direction.

"Hey," one of the policemen shouted, "we're back here." When they turned their attention to the arriving cops, I remembered something Thiemann had said when Max and I were talking with him—his wife was away.

I had maybe five seconds to decide, no longer. Doing something, no matter how dumb it is, always beats doing nothing.

That's one of the unforgettable insights I acquired while attending Leadership School.

Still carrying the bag, I scooted silently across the garden, up the steps of the porch, and quietly pushed open the door into the Thiemann kitchen. After scraping dirt off my shoes on an already muddy mat, I made my way through the house. There wasn't anywhere to hide in the living room. And nowhere in the dining room. On the far side of the dining room was a short corridor at the end of which was a utility room—furnace, washing machine, dryer, some shelves with boxes of detergent and a few tools. The door was ajar.

After slipping inside, I had no choice but to leave the door ajar, which meant anyone in the corridor had a view of most of the room. In order to keep from being seen, I had to squeeze myself down into a corner behind the electric dryer, a space so narrow I couldn't move anything except my hands. The plastic bag I jammed behind the door.

I probably would have been better off staying in the garden. I was a sitting duck here.

Outside, I heard cops talking and an occasional radio squawk. Through the small window, I could see bright lights. They told the dispatcher they had the house surrounded and were beginning a search. There was a lot of activity. Someone said they'd found rope looped around the chimney and the veranda doors wide open. It sounded like at least a dozen cops out there.

This was not good. My hands became sweaty and my heart began pounding so loud I thought someone might hear it.

My watch said 12:45. There was no way out. I was stuck—all a cop had to do was stick his head through the door, and I'd be on my way into a German jail. This was a really lousy way to have to end this operation, by getting busted on my second day in-country. It was also a lousy way to end my illustrious career as an intelligence officer. I thought back on all the black bag stuff I'd done—all of which went off without a hitch. Maybe I was rusty. When I told Shenlee I was retired, I should have stuck to my guns—and stayed retired. It took the cops outside twenty minutes to determine the Vogt house was empty and another half hour to determine the guy they were now calling a *raffinierter Einbrecher*—"break-in artist"—wasn't anywhere on the property. But it seemed they were still searching very diligently.

Just outside the utility room window I could hear two policemen talking. "How the hell did he make it out anyway?" one asked.

"These characters are full of tricks. I doubt we'll nab him now."

Thanks for the compliment, guys. I definitely hope you're right.

Twenty minutes later, Thiemann and what sounded like three policemen came clumping into the house. One went clumping upstairs. The other two I could hear moving around, going from the kitchen into the dining room, opening closets. Just as one of the cops was about to glance into the utility room, his radio emitted a loud squawk. I wiped away the beads of sweat that had formed on my forehead—and waited for the axe to fall.

"Hey, Hans!" someone shouted.

"I'm here," the cop said. From the sound of his voice he was ten feet from where I was squashed. I couldn't believe he hadn't seen me—or heard the beating of my heart.

After announcing into his radio that they hadn't found anyone in the house, Hans clicked the utility room door shut. The other cop asked Thiemann where his bathroom was. After a few more minutes clumping around the house, they left.

Later, two more cops came in to use the bathroom. They were so close I could overhear their conversations. One of them said he'd just met a really hot-looking chick at a night spot in Schwabing and was looking forward to getting laid on the weekend. The other cop said he wished he was single again.

After they left, things became quiet. Thiemann bustled around the kitchen for a while, then got on the telephone.

"Hello, sweetheart. I know it's late, but I thought you'd be interested. Someone broke into the Vogt place. I saw a flashlight, moving around in there, I called the police. Lots of excitement. The place was crawling with police. I don't know how the creep could have gotten away."

Well, I haven't gotten away yet. And I don't like being called a "creep."

"It was like maybe two minutes from the time I saw the light until I made the call. The cops were here within minutes. They've got a car out on the street now, just in case he's still in the neighborhood. Sure, I'm safe. The house is locked up tight. Right. I miss you too. How's your mother? Okay, let's see. I'll leave here at seven, so I should be up there just after noon. Okay. Love you. Tschüss."

After that, he bustled around a little more, humming something that sounded strangely like a German version of "On the Street Where You Live," then headed upstairs. I gave him time to undress, relax, and fall asleep. Hoping he slept soundly, I called Sylvia at a few minutes before four a.m.

"Alex! My God! I thought—"

Keeping my voice low, I told Sylvia where I was and said I wasn't anywhere near out of the woods yet. From experience, I knew the German police to be very thorough and I wasn't surprised that they'd still have some people out on the street. I told Sylvia what she should do.

Thiemann was awake at six and I could hear him moving around in the kitchen, which was so close to where I was huddled in the utility room I could smell the coffee. My biggest worry was that he'd come in here for some reason. Five minutes went by, ten, fifteen. I thought I heard him humming to himself, a song about "roses in the mountains." And then the sound of the dishwasher. Finally, at around seven a.m. I heard a door slam, and a few minutes later a car engine turned over. The cops, of course, would observe him leaving, and that complicated things a little more. As he backed out of his garage and onto the street, the engine sound grew faint—and then faded altogether.

With Thiemann gone and the house quiet, I climbed out from behind the dryer, stood and stretched, doing my best to get some circulation into my arms and legs. I walked through the kitchen and dining area to the front room to peer out the front window. I was able to make out the police patrol car, which was still parked diagonally across the street, only about twenty yards from Thiemann's front gate.

Not good. With the police this close, I couldn't take a chance. My black sweater and dark slacks would be a giveaway for any reasonably alert cop. Until now, Thiemann had been helpful, and I decided to give him a chance to help out a little more.

Upstairs, I picked out a freshly laundered white shirt from my host's drawer, and in his closet I found a pair of shoes a size too big. I found a checkered gray jacket that matched my dark pants. I grabbed a dark blue tie off his rack. On the dresser was a small stack of business cards people had given him, one of which read: "Lorenz Schmidt, Lloyd Shipping." Lying on the bed was a trim official-looking briefcase with decals of the initials LST—Ludwig Thiemann's initials—prominently in gold over the lock. Using my all-purpose Leatherman, I gently pried off the T, leaving the other two letters. I emptied out the papers, laid them neatly on the bed.

Decked out in the uniform of a briefcase-carrying businessman on his way to the office, I again called Sylvia. I retrieved the black plastic bag from the utility room, stepped out of the front door and waited. Across the street, I saw the patrol car, parked inconspicuously between two trees. It was just becoming light when Sylvia arrived, halting in front of the house and leaving her motor running. There were two cops in the patrol car.

After taking a deep breath, I exited the house, slamming the door shut behind me.

I stepped out onto the sidewalk and brazenly deposited the plastic bag in the garbage can standing in front of the house, then nodded to Sylvia. One of the policemen got out of the squad car and, as he stifled a yawn, gave me the once-over. He was plump, in his mid-twenties, and wasn't wearing his tunic. With a questioning look on his face, he walked toward me. I waved, crossed the street to meet him, said a cheerful "Good morning."

When he only nodded, I said, "You fellows have had a long night. Any sign of him?"

"Who are you and where are you going?" the cop asked.

I was holding the briefcase so he could hardly keep from noticing the initials "LS." "My name is Lorenz Schmidt. I occupy the basement apartment." I handed him the business card I'd found in Thiemann's bedroom.

"Who was the guy who just left?"

I figured the cops knew who had just left. "That's Mr. Thiemann. He owns the house. I'm his tenant. I'm on my way into work." I tapped the briefcase.

"Where's that?"

"The transportation office at Lloyd."

"That's the ship company? In the Landsbergerstrasse?"

"Right. The place with all the warehouses. I have to get in early. This is our busy season and we've got more orders than we—"

Pointing at the car, the cop frowned. "Who's this?"

"Sylvia's a colleague." When he continued to stare, I said, "I figure the two of us can get the bills of lading out of the way. Then we'll do the invoices. After that we should—"

Tuning me out, he stepped toward the car, gave it a quick once-over. When Sylvia smiled, he smiled back. Then he took another look at the card, stuck it in his pocket.

"You can call me at the office if you want and—"

"You can go," he said.

"Have a good day, guys," I said pulling open the passenger-side door.

Visibly more relaxed, he said, "Yeah, buddy, you too." After rubbing some sleep from his eyes, he ambled back toward the patrol car.

As Sylvia and I drove slowly up the street, I hoped neither of the cops would have the presence of mind to write down our plate number. I also hoped there wouldn't be a garbage pickup before noon, which was when I figured it would be safe to retrieve the plastic bag. It would be a shame to think that we'd gone to all that trouble for nothing.

Chapter 12

Tuesday, January 22, 2008

Looking across at Sylvia, who was dressed in a loose-fitting white blouse with short sleeves and a tight pair of jeans, I said, "Ursula Vogt was an attractive woman."

It was early afternoon, and Sylvia and I were seated at the big round dining room table. Sylvia, a pair of reading glasses perched on her thin nose, looked up as I tossed a photograph across the table in her direction.

The picture showed Ursula Vogt naked. She was facing the camera with a comb in her hand. Her hair was a wild tangle, and she wasn't smiling.

After retrieving the plastic bag full of CDs and paper, we'd divided up the contents and begun the tedious job of looking for anything that might give some indication why Ursula Vogt had been killed and who might have done it. On the table in front of us was a pile of paper, some manila folders, envelopes, computer discs—all the stuff I'd found in her place and tossed into the bag. I'd been looking through a small box of photographs, mostly pictures of Ursula Vogt herself taken informally, in a variety of places, with a variety of people—and in a variety of poses.

Some of the poses were extremely revealing, and they were interesting to look at—and I could readily see why she would have wanted to keep them under lock and key. They gave an insight into some of the methods she might have used to gather information.

Along with being attractive, she was sexy—tall, with curly blonde hair, and delicate features. She had long legs and nicely shaped breasts, conclusions for which I had plenty of evidence. A number of the photos showed her either half dressed or totally undressed. In one of them, she was seated on a cot, wearing only a pair of jeans and eating from a paper plate. In another, she had her arm around a loopy looking individual with a dark beard who was dressed like a muja-hedeen soldier. In another, a half-dressed man was on top of a nearly naked woman who was lying on a cot in a barren-looking room. Although the woman's head was half buried in a pillow, she had curly blonde hair and I assumed she was Ursula Vogt. I wondered who took that picture. Two or three other photos were equally revealing. Naturally, I went through them all.

I didn't want to jump to conclusions, but I was reminded of stories I'd heard concerning some successful female war correspondents—and the methods they sometimes used to get stories that their male counterparts couldn't get. One woman, a reporter for one of the wire services, was widely known for having dispensed favors generously, particularly because she detailed them in her autobiography. Like the wire service correspondent, Ursula Vogt seemed to be good at combining business and pleasure.

A couple of photos showed her putting on a gas mask. Another photo showed her standing in front of a small building with a gas mask in her hand and wearing what looked like a chemical-warfare uniform. I wondered what that was all about. Other photos showed people in chemical-warfare uniforms looking at a pile of dead bodies. I had an idea one of the group was Ursula Vogt.

But what had really grabbed my attention was a picture of her taken with a bunch of ragtag characters who were all dressed like soldiers and were holding automatic weapons—one of whom looked familiar. It was Ramush Nadaj.

Silently, Sylvia reached across the table and picked up the photograph.

"How did Ramush Nadaj and the Vogt woman become friends?"

She looked at the picture, then began gazing at the other pictures in the collection. Finally, she said, "Is this the only one of him?" She looked thoughtful, then began toying absentmindedly with the top button of her blouse.

I said, "I haven't looked through all of them." After a second, I said, "You still haven't answered the question. How did they become friends?"

"It was in Afghanistan. Up in the mountains." As she began going through the photos, Sylvia said, "It certainly looks as if they were friends. Maybe more than friends." She paused. "We assumed they knew one another."

"We did?"

"We assumed they'd met one another once or twice, maybe more. I figure she interviewed Nadaj."

"Is that important?"

"It could be. One of the things we're trying to do is trace the Vogt woman's movements."

I said, "Nadaj kept asking me if I knew what happened in Afghanistan. What did happen in Afghanistan?"

Sylvia ignored the question. "You've been told what you need to know."

I stood up.

"You told me that this assignment connects to the Nadaj rendition. I'd like to know how it connects."

Acting as though she hadn't heard me, Sylvia said, "I wonder when this was taken. She made a number of trips out there. She got to know Nadaj and Brinkman, both of whom she met in Afghanistan."

"I'm still wondering what happened in Afghanistan—and to be honest, I'm wondering about a few other things as well."

"What kind of things?"

The truth was, I'd been thinking about what Buck had said at the airport. Considering the way I'd screwed up the rendition down in Kosovo, it just wasn't logical that Sylvia and Shenlee would select me for this assignment. More logical was the thought that I was expendable. Buck had been blunt, saying it looked as if I had a death wish. I was also bothered by the fact that Sylvia was withholding information that I felt I should know.

"I still feel—"

"Alex, you're becoming very tedious."

Still standing next to the table, I said, "I feel I'm being sensible. I was dumb to let myself be talked into this operation. I should know better than to—"

Sylvia stood up, and we were only a foot apart. "What do you mean?"

"I should know better than to trust you people."

"Which people?"

"You and Shenlee. And the whole gang at the National Security Council, or whoever it is you work for."

"Cool off, Alex."

"Not to mention the deputy secretary. Even worse is the fact that you're pretending that nothing's wrong."

"You'll have to do a better job of explaining yourself."

"What's wrong is you haven't told me what this operation is all about." I took a deep breath. "From the way you described it, I assumed this was a straightforward murder investigation. You said that Brinkman was getting a raw deal. The idea was, I was supposed to use my contacts with the Munich police, assuming I still have any, to see what's going on."

"You're overreacting."

"Something else I've never been told: Why it is that everyone's so interested in Nadaj? Why did we make him the target of a rendition?"

"Is that all that's bothering you?"

"What's bothering me is that I haven't been told why I'm over here. That's why I'm leaving."

"Do you know what I think, Alex?" When I didn't respond, she said, "I think the same things I did at Floyd Bennett. You're afraid. You're afraid of Nadaj because of what happened in Kosovo. Maybe Jerry's right. You're afraid Nadaj'll capture you and throw you back into that hole you told me about." She turned, headed toward the kitchen. "I'm going to make myself a cup of tea. Would you like one?"

"That's ridiculous."

"I think I'm right."

I said, "No, Sylvia, you're wrong. Nadaj has nothing to do with it." I followed her into the small kitchen, where she retrieved a box of tea from the pantry. "What I don't like is that you and Shenlee haven't leveled with me." I watched as she measured out the tea and poured in the boiling water into a teapot and pulled cups and saucers down from the cabinet. From a drawer, she took out a small strainer. She'd all at once become very prim and was clearly making a point of ignoring me.

If she'd again said that I was afraid of Nadaj, I would have thrown her out the window. Fortunately, she didn't.

"It's very simple. I'm leaving because you haven't been honest with me."

"Oh, really?" The top button of her blouse was undone, and I couldn't help noticing that her jeans were very tight. Sylvia had not only nice legs but a nice rear end. She poured the tea from the teapot out into two cups, gave me one of the cups.

Back in the living room, I said, "Yes, really."

"You have a contract. You break it and leave me stranded here, I'll see you never work again."

"I have my own business. I'm independent."

"I'll get laws passed in that town—what's the name again?"

"Saranac."

"Right. Saranac. You'll be in violation of every local ordinance. Your ice business will go under."

"The iceman cometh—and goeth."

"You're an idiot. You're going to go bankrupt, and all you can do is crack unfunny jokes."

"I never let my ice melt."

"Your ice will melt and you'll be bankrupt."

"You'll freeze my assets."

"You won't have any assets to freeze."

Sylvia was right, of course. There was no way I could break the contract at this point. But when I saw alarm in Sylvia's hooded blue eyes, I had the feeling she thought I was about to go out and buy a plane ticket.

But there was a serious side to this little squabble. I like to think I can depend on the people I'm working with, and I wasn't at all sure I could depend on Sylvia or Shenlee, both of whom were super ambitious and had their own personal agendas. In the pressure-filled environment in which they worked, you needed ambition and toughness to survive.

"You know," I said finally, "I think I'd like to see Nadaj again."

"Good. You may have the opportunity."

Badly in need of some time to do some thinking, I grabbed my jacket. "I feel like some fresh air." Standing with her hands on her hips, Sylvia watched with an uncertain look on her face. "I've decided to go for a walk."

Out on the sidewalk, I felt the effect of the fresh air and began to relax. As I walked, I tried to figure out what was going on. If this case connected to Nadaj or led us back to Nadaj, I'd have an opportunity to pay back a few people for what happened last March. According to Sylvia, she was actually doing me a big favor by getting me over here, but Buck laughed when I mentioned that to him.

I enjoy walking, and once I got started, I didn't feel like stopping. In at least one way, it was good being back. As I thought about Irmie, I had the feeling someone had turned the clock back eight or nine years. I stopped at a café for a cup of coffee, then angled over to the Nymphenburgerstrasse, a wide street with a lot of apartment buildings and the courthouse at the far end. I lived for a couple of weeks in an apartment in one of the buildings, but I no longer remembered which one. Back then, I had a lot on my mind.

When I got back to the building two hours later, I said hello to a young married couple who were leaving.

Inside the apartment, I could smell chicken frying. Standing at the counter in her stocking feet and wearing an orange apron, Sylvia was cutting up a tomato and making a salad. I hadn't known she was domestic.

"While you were gone, I went food shopping. Are you hungry?"

"I'm starved."

"Would you mind taking a look in the pantry? I need some salt."

I said, "We've had our first argument."

She fixed me with a stern expression. "Uh-uh. You're forgetting the hospital. That was our first argument. This was our second. And I've won them both. That's something you should keep in mind. You might also want to keep in mind that I'm running this operation, and you don't so much as take a shit without asking my permission. Understood?"

"Understood."

"And when I give you permission, then you squat and ask, 'What color?'"

"If you say so." I was impressed by Sylvia's familiarity with the vernacular of the U.S. Army's drill instructors.

"I say so," she said quietly. "Now would you mind bringing me the salt?"

Chapter 13

Thursday, January 24, 2008

Douglas Brinkman eyed me suspiciously, then asked, "Just who are you anyway?"

We were sitting opposite one another in one of the small interview rooms of Munich's Stadelheim Prison, a thick plate of glass between us. There were two other inmates in the room, both of them talking guardedly to people who could have been family members or lawyers. A guard was stationed at the door, and another was seated on a chair at a point against the wall that gave him a view of everybody's hands.

It was two days after the break-in, a cloudy Thursday. I'd called the prison the previous day, and Sylvia had spoken with someone at the consulate. She'd arranged for an attaché to provide me with a letter on consulate letterhead that said I was speaking to Brinkman on behalf of the American government in connection with his legal representation.

Even at that, getting into Stadelheim had taken time. I'd had to jawbone with guards at the entrance, fill out forms, submit to a search, then spend a half hour in a waiting room with a bunch of other visitors, all of whom were women. Before leaving, when I'd asked Sylvia what I should be looking for, she said that she'd lost contact with Brinkman after his arrest and wanted me to see how he was holding up.

When Brinkman asked who I was, I didn't see I had any choice but to keep my answer vague. I said, "I'm here at the request of someone in our government."

"Who in our government?"

Brinkman was over six feet, had a square face, a broad mouth, and thin lips. Despite his size, he seemed to move gracefully, almost like a big cat. Like the other inmates, he was wearing a blue shirt with an open collar and blue work pants. He had brown hair cut short. In German prisons, everything is regulated—from the size of your calorie intake to the length of your hair.

Something else about German lockups—no weight rooms or TV. In German jails you only do hard time. Although they don't have capital punishment, prisoners have been known to die from boredom.

"Someone who wants to get you out of here."

"Well, tell them they sure as hell better get me out of here," Douglas Brinkman said. "Tell your boss that."

I nodded. The overall game plan called for me to find out what was happening in Brinkman's life—and if possible keep him from ever having to appear in a German court. Exactly how I was going to manage all that was anybody's guess, and I was, as usual, flying by the seat of my pants.

"How are you handling all this?"

"I'm fine. It's just that I don't want to spend the next twenty-five years in this place."

"How's the food?"

"Lousy, and they don't give you enough. I've lost weight in here. I'd rather eat MREs." MREs are Meals Ready to Eat, which soldiers are issued on maneuvers and in battle. At Fort Bragg we gave them the politically incorrect name of "Meals Rejected by Ethiopians."

Brinkman paused briefly as one of the guards ambled over, gazed at us curiously, then strolled away. I said, "We intend to get you out of this mess, one way or the other." I hoped I sounded more confident than I felt. The walls to this room were awfully thick, and beyond the building there was a forty-foot-high wall with guard posts every few yards. A jailbreak was out of the question.

"Yeah, yeah. Of course you will. You're here to help me, is that it?" When I nodded, he took a deep breath, then ran his fingers over the edge of the table.

"How are you gonna do that?"

"I'll need some information first."

"Like what?"

"You could maybe begin by telling me how you got into this situation."

"I got into it because I knew Ursula." He paused. "I've told Owen, the guy from the consulate, all this stuff."

"You knew Miss Vogt pretty well?" When he nodded, I asked, "How well?" Now that I knew what he looked like, I knew that there weren't any pictures of Brinkman in the photo collection of Ursula Vogt. It seemed she'd mostly hung out with the Taliban people. "How did you come to meet her?"

"I'm not sure I should be answering these questions."

"Why? What do you have to hide? If you're innocent—"

"I'm still not sure who you are."

"I can't help you otherwise."

"How's this all going to help? I'm tired of telling the story. Your people should know all this."

"I don't know how it will help. We'll see."

After a brief pause, he said, "I met her in Afghanistan. Have you ever heard of Mazar-e-Sharif? It's northwest of Tora Bora. We had a prison there, and there had been an attempted breakout. She got wind of it and turned up, had a photographer with her."

"Then what?"

"She told me she was a correspondent for *Welt-Bericht*. I thought she was pretty gutsy. She spoke good English. I know some German. I was stationed over here for a while, down in Tölz."

"Flint Kaserne?"

When I said that, Brinkman looked surprised. Bad Tölz at one time was European headquarters for Special Forces 10th Group, before the command closed down the post and moved to a location near Stuttgart. Flint Kaserne was the name of the former installation.

"You know it?"

I nodded. "I was there too." I figured he might warm up to me a little if he knew I'd been with Special Forces, even if my stay hadn't been all that long.

Brinkman didn't say anything, but it was clear he liked the idea that he was talking to a former member of the brotherhood. I asked him what it was he and Ursula Vogt found to talk about.

"Well, she was a reporter, so she wanted to pick up whatever she could about the American invasion. We'd only been in country about two months then."

"That's all it was? Just business?"

"Boy meets girl. You know how it is. Afterward, we talked about all kinds of things."

"Politics, you mean? The world situation?"

"She wanted to know what was going on with us. With the Americans. The Germans call us Amis."

I said, "Not as bad as some of the things we call them."

"She was very interested in the American military. How things ran, all that kind of stuff."

"How much did you tell her?" When he shrugged, I figured he knew she'd been pumping him. I said, "Did you two spend a lot of time together?"

He nodded. "Afterward, yeah. I ran into her in Kabul, in the Ariana Hotel."

"How often?"

"I was part of the Special Operations force. After Tora Bora, I spent time in Kabul. We'd be going on missions all the time. But we talked, sure. I'd get back. A few times she was out there. With us."

"Out where?"

"Out in the mountains. She had a lot of freedom. Her paper let her go pretty much where she wanted."

"So you saw quite a bit of one another?" I had visions of the two of them sharing a sleeping bag, à la Hemingway.

He frowned. I could see he didn't like the questions.

I said, "Did you think Afghanistan was going to be your last tour?"

"I guess. But everything changed later. But, yeah, I was thinking of getting out at that time. I'd put in close to twenty years. It was time to do something else. I couldn't see the sense in going back to Bragg again. All that training gets old after a while." He shook his head. "Fighting the war wasn't as bad as training for it."

I nodded sympathetically. I knew what he meant. At Bad Tölz reveille was at 0345 hours and we woke up by swimming a couple of laps in an ice-cold swimming pool. "Is that the reason you wanted out? Because you didn't want to go back to Fort Bragg?"

He looked at me suspiciously, then he nodded. "Like I say, everything changed later. I went back to Afghanistan in 2003."

I turned the conversation back to Ursula Vogt. "How come you came to Munich?"

"What do you mean?"

"Why didn't you go back to the States? That's what most guys do."

"I'm not most guys."

I had the feeling I was losing him. I could see I'd said something that was bothering him. After being surrounded by foreigners for so long, he liked the idea of talking English with someone, and maybe that was the main reason he was willing to see me. But he didn't like all the questions. "Munich's a nice city. I'd been stationed down in Tölz. I knew my way around."

I thought about what Max had told me—that he'd broken up a bar. Although I wondered what might have brought that on, I decided not to mention it. A little alcohol, together with a lot of frustration, once led me to do something like that. Fortunately, First Sergeant Aubrey kept the lid on, and I got off with an Article 15 and by paying damages to the bar owner. By this time, Brinkman was frowning. I decided not to push matters. I had an idea he'd maybe be more open about things if I came around again. I'd broken the ice, or at least I hoped I had.

When I told him I was about to leave, he said, "So what's going to happen? The Krauts wanna try me for murder."

I said, "We'll see."

"Mr. Owen says they're arranging for another lawyer. The first one they had got sick or something."

I didn't say anything. I had an idea the lawyer might have sensed there were more angles to this case than he wanted to handle. Or he might have been disqualified by people back in D.C.

I said, "You're innocent, and we may be able to get you off before things get that far."

"How far?"

"To a trial." Then I recalled my visit to Ursula Vogt's house. "One more thing." The guard had come over and was pointing at his watch. I told him I needed another minute. He frowned, then nodded. "Did you know the handyman that worked for Miss Vogt?"

"Oh, you mean Quemal? Yeah, he came around twice when I was there. Ursula didn't like him."

"Was that his name? Quemal?" When Brinkman nodded, I wondered whether it was the same Quemal who was with Nadaj in Kosovo. If so, he was definitely on the short list of people I hoped to one day encounter in my travels.

Brinkman thought for a moment, then said, "Ursula said her publisher arranged for the guy to come around. She said he gave her the creeps." When I asked him what else he knew about him, he said, "Not much. I know he hung around this club—"

"Club? What kind of club?"

"An Albanian club."

"Was this Quemal Albanian?"

"Not exactly. He spoke Albanian, but he said he came from Kosovo."

"What was the name of the club?"

"The Kalashni Klub," Brinkman said. "The club was called the Kalashni Klub, short for Kalashnikov, the assault rifle. There's a little sign with a picture of the weapon in front." He smiled. "Bang, bang— if you know what I mean."

"Where is this place?"

"On the road toward Ingolstadt. You know where that is?" I nodded, recalling that I once made a trip to Ingolstadt to pick up a new car from the Audi factory.

"You're sure of this?"

"I gave him a lift one time. We went inside. I had a schnapps, and left." He grinned. "Lots of chicks hanging around, if you know what I mean."

As I pushed back my chair and stood up, he looked at me but didn't say anything.

"I'll try to get back to you." I wasn't sure when I could get in again.

"Mr. Owen said he'd come tomorrow. Can I mention I talked with you?"

"I think it'll be okay." I knew that Owen, coming from the consulate, would have an easier time getting into the prison than I just had.

As I was leaving, I said, "*De Oppresso Liber.*" It's the Special Forces motto, and means "to free the oppressed."

"Yeah, sure," Brinkman said without enthusiasm. If he was thinking of himself as one of the oppressed, I couldn't blame him for that.

When I was out of the prison and driving home, I punched in Max's number on my cell phone.

"The Kalashni Klub, Max, you know it? Some kind of Albanian hangout?"

"Every cop in Munich knows the K Klub, Alex. Steer clear of the place."

"I want to take a look, Max. And I'd like some backup. Someone who has some authority in this city."

"No. Absolutely not. I'm retired, and I'm not accompanying you to that place." Before I could say anything more, Max said, "I know how you operate, and I'm not getting mixed up in one of your schemes. Those days are over."

"I don't have to go in right away. I can wait a few days—"

"Listen, Alex, and listen carefully. Things aren't like they used to be. It's not ten years ago."

"Come off it, Max."

"You know what I'm talking about. There are no more American Army installations here in Munich—which means no more American military people throwing their weight around." I knew what Max was referring to. When the situation called for it, we'd bent the rules and pulled some wild over-the-top stuff, with black bag operations being the least of our stunts—things that, admittedly, I never would have dreamed of trying back in the States. I thought that some of the resentment that might have been building up inside Max over the years was finally spilling over.

"Do you understand me, Alex?"

"No, not really. I thought we were friends."

Max made a point of not commenting. After a brief pause, he said, "I'll give you a call in a day or two. Until then, take some friendly advice—and stay away from the Kalashni Klub!"

As I drove back to the apartment, I wondered what Max might have in mind, if anything. At one time, he'd been a great guy to work with, but time had changed things.

Chapter 14

Thursday, January 24, 2008

After reporting to Sylvia on my visit to Brinkman, I found a beer in the fridge and poured out a half liter into a glass. Then I collapsed onto a chair. For some reason, I'd found the conversation with Brinkman emotionally draining. "I think I broke the ice. He trusts me, a little bit at least."

As I took a long swallow, Sylvia eyed me with what could have been mild distaste. "Has anyone ever told you that you drink too much?"

"No," I said, taking a long swallow and very nearly emptying the glass. The truth was, I had begun to drink too much. I'd been away from the special ops stuff for a while, maybe for too long. My nerves were drawn tight, and I needed a quick way to relax.

"Has anyone ever told you you're hard to get along with?"

"Most people say I'm very friendly and cooperative."

"Has anyone ever called you a loose cannon?"

I didn't respond. It sounded as if Sylvia had been reading through my personnel file.

"Has anyone ever called you 'a loose cannon to end all loose cannons'?" When she quoted the Air Force colonel, I knew she'd been reading through my personnel file.

Since we were getting personal, I could have said, "Has anyone ever referred to you as Colonel Bitch-on-Wheels?" I wisely refrained from putting any additional strain on our already strained relationship.

She crossed the room and stood at the window for a long minute, her arms folded, her back facing me. "What's he like?" she asked finally.

Much of the stuff I'd brought back from Ursula Vogt's place—folders, photos, paper—was still stacked up and spread out on the table. Sylvia had said she wanted to handle that end of things, and she'd gone through most of it.

"He's tough. He's smart. I guess you could say he's like most Green Berets."

"How's he handling the prison situation?" She was facing me again.

"Like I say, he's in Special Forces. He's probably handled situations that were a lot worse."

"If he's so smart, why did he become involved with Ursula?"

I said, "That's probably not so hard to figure. You've seen the pictures."

"Did he know about her other boyfriends?" Sylvia asked.

Something occurred to me then. I sensed that Sylvia knew Brinkman personally. I remembered what Buck had said about a relationship between Sylvia and another officer while she was in Afghanistan.

"Maybe not at first," I said. "Maybe what happened was, he tumbled to the fact that he had competition—quite a lot of competition."

"And then he killed her? We don't like that idea."

"But maybe it happened that way. He has a short fuse."

"So? A lot of people have short fuses. I have one myself, but I haven't killed anyone—not yet anyway."

"You've shown admirable restraint."

"I'm glad you've noticed. As I said, we don't like that idea. We're here to prove Brinkman innocent, to get him out of jail."

After a second, I said, "According to Max Peters, the German cops are positive he killed her."

"Have the German cops ever been wrong before?"

"They're like cops everywhere. They're wrong as often as they're right."

"You're awfully cynical."

"When you've had as much to do with cops as I have, you'd be cynical too."

"I doubt that, but let's not argue the point. I've been going through some more of Ursula Vogt's stuff. She wrote a lot of notes. She also kept a diary. But one article is of particular interest." Sylvia held up a CD.

"What is it?"

"She was writing a long article explaining her reporting in Afghanistan. She was reporting a story about a battle in the mountains—and how she'd come to change her mind about what had happened there."

"What happened?"

Ignoring my question, Sylvia said, "I also found some notes regarding interviews with some American officers in Afghanistan that tie into this article." Sylvia began hunting through the pile of paper on the table. Finally, she found a small notebook. Sylvia held up a small notepad. "This seems to be a record of some conversations she had with Brinkman." After quickly leafing through it, she passed it over to me. "She used a kind of shorthand, and this slanted German writing is difficult to read."

Sylvia was right. The notebook was nearly indecipherable.

Sylvia said, "If you look at the first page, you see Brinkman's name and some dates. I don't think she interviewed him exactly. It looks as if these notes were put down after she'd spoken with him a number of times. But they're probably a fairly accurate record of what he might have said."

Sylvia was also right on the fact that the notebook seemed to hold a record of a number of meetings and conversations. Between the various meetings there were usually some dates and one or two blank pages. "What do you make of it?" I asked. I couldn't decipher much of it and tossed it back on the table.

"She was pumping him. Asking questions and putting down the answers afterward." Sylvia picked up something else that was on the table, a tape cartridge. She held it up, then inserted it into a small tape player on the table. As the tape began to play, she turned up the volume.

For a couple of minutes, there wasn't much beside some sighing and sounds that were somewhere between a groan and a cough. There was a good bit of external noise, which made the voices difficult to understand, and some more gasps and comments. Finally, a woman said,

"What are you doing?" and then there was some giggling. Sylvia politely cleared her throat. "I'm going to fast-forward a little."

I thought it might be a good idea, but didn't say anything.

A woman's voice speaking accented English: "Where are the cigarettes?"

"You smoke too much." I recognized Brinkman's voice.

"So I have a weakness."

"That's not your only weakness."

"How about you? Don't you have any weaknesses?"

"No. I'm perfect."

"Ha. That's a laugh." When I glanced at Sylvia, I saw she was listening intently.

"Name a weakness I have."

"You're addicted to sex," the woman said. "Stop that."

"Sex ain't a weakness." They both began to laugh. "Should I stop?"

"No," the woman said.

When I raised my hand and flashed Sylvia a questioning look, she said, "I'll fast-forward again." Her face was beet red. I couldn't tell if she was embarrassed or angry.

"—and we had three Delta operators with us." It was the man's voice.

"How many were you altogether?" Woman's voice.

"With the Delta people and the Air Force guy and the intel guy and me, we were six people."

"And just what were you trying to do?"

"We were trying to break up this supply line the Taliban had. They were getting regular fuel shipments. One time we found these two drivers on the side of the road, fast asleep."

"When was this?"

"Oh, like the second week in December. Like I say, we snuck up on these two drivers. I jammed my M4 up against—"

"M4?"

"My sidearm, an automatic pistol. I jammed it up against his head, told him to start talking or else. He did, but it was hard to figure out what he was saying. One of our guys knew some Pashto. They gave us some song and dance about selling the gas to farmers."

"Maybe it was true." Woman's voice.

The man laughed. "Maybe. But whether it was or wasn't, we called in a couple of choppers and they sent a bunch of rockets flying into the trucks. That was some fireball, believe me."

"How were you people traveling?" the woman asked.

"We were just a couple of pickup trucks—no headlights. I was driving, using my NVGs."

"Who was commanding this operation?"

"We were part of Task Force Dagger. But altogether we weren't more than twelve A-Teams. That's why we needed the Northern Alliance."

Woman's voice. "But I'm more interested in the other battle—"

"I told you. I wasn't up there."

Sylvia fast-forwarded again.

"They were burning up the telephone lines," the man said. He laughed again. "They didn't realize we were intercepting all their calls off the satellite, so we knew that they were heading back into the mountains, toward Pakistan."

Sylvia turned off the tape player. "Do you recognize the voice?" When I said the male voice was Brinkman's, she nodded. "What else do you think?"

"He was talking about Tora Bora. The heavy bombing started right around the end of November. Part of the problem was, we didn't have that many people in-country at that time. We had to depend on the Afghans. There was a lot of heavy fighting. We know that things didn't work out exactly as we wanted them to."

"Anything else?"

"You're right about Ursula. I think she was pumping him without him knowing it. Right after speaking with him, she'd write down what he said."

"And sometimes she'd use a tape recorder. That was pillow talk. What else does this tell you?"

"That the female of the species isn't to be trusted. But that's not exactly news."

"You are the most obnoxious male chauvinist I've ever encountered."

"Do I have any redeeming features?"

"None at all." Sylvia paused, a thoughtful look on her face. "Ursula Vogt made a number of trips into Afghanistan. She always went into the east, into the mountains. She got to know her way around out there. There was an attack on a company of Taliban, most of them holed up in some caves. They all died. She went there, saw what happened."

"The Taliban also killed some of our people. Quite a number, mostly special ops." I recalled that I had at one time been a member of Special Forces. I can't help wondering from time to time how my life would have turned out if I'd remained a Green Beret.

I said, "What may have happened: Brinkman discovered that he was the source for a lot of the stuff in her stories, realized he'd been used, followed her here to Munich—and then killed her."

I figured Sylvia would shoot down that surmise, and she quickly did. "Alex, I said Brinkman did not kill Ursula Vogt. I know what I'm talking about. Would you kindly get that through your thick skull?"

"Yes, ma'am."

"My name is Sylvia."

I said, "We have another lead we should be working on."

It was just over two hours later, somewhere after seven. I'd banged together a meal of soup and sandwiches, and at the moment I was munching on an apple. I was observing Sylvia, who was sitting across from me in the dinette, as she worked on her laptop and drank the last of a cup of tea.

She looked up and said, "Does it have to do with Doug?"

Sylvia had changed into a light-blue blouse that was not quite transparent, and I was doing my best not to stare at her tits. Living at close range with an attractive woman tends to dilute your ability to stay focused, at least if you're a male. I wondered if we'd end up in bed together.

Is that what she wanted? Is that what I wanted? Unfortunately, I had an idea that I was in a situation where what I wanted wasn't important.

"Doug?"

"Doug Brinkman. Does it have to do with him?"

"It has to do with something that Brinkman mentioned."

When Sylvia asked what it was, I told her about Ursula Vogt's handyman, Quemal. Then I explained that one of the two soldiers in Nadaj's crew had been named Quemal. "Maybe it's only a coincidence, but we have two people with the same name."

She said, "Is Quemal a common name in Albania?"

"I don't know."

"Why don't you know? The government gave you a course in Albanian. I remember reading that in your file."

"The government gave me a ten-day course in Serbo-Croatian and Albanian, and that was in 2000. Then they sent me into Bosnia. I spent time on Eagle Base. During the run-up to us extracting Slobodan Milosevic, I was on the ground in Belgrade, learning the streets, attending demonstrations, formulating a Plan B in the event we needed a Plan B. Fortunately, we didn't."

"So you're saying there's a possibility that Quemal, the handyman, might be the same individual you encountered in Kosovo—and that he actually murdered the Vogt woman."

Recalling my conversation with Thiemann, Ursula Vogt's neighbor, I said, "He certainly had the opportunity."

"Keep going."

"Nadaj knew Ursula. The picture showed them together. Maybe Nadaj got mad at Ursula for some reason and sent Quemal to Munich to kill her."

Sylvia didn't say anything for a long moment, and I had an idea she was considering the possibility of what I'd just told her. Finally, she said, "You and I could drop by this club. Check the place out."

"I don't think so. I spoke to Max about the place. He says something like that wouldn't be advisable."

"What do you suggest?"

I said, "Let me think about it for a day."

"All right, you have twenty-four hours." Sylvia crossed the room, and took a VCR tape out of a box of stuff she had placed next to a lamp. She said, "I want you to see this."

After she'd jammed the tape into the TV set, we both moved over to the sofa.

"What are we going to do? Watch *Wheel of Fortune?*"

She shook her head, and when I put my arm around her shoulder, she said, "We're not at a drive-in. Please remove your arm."

I said, "I spent the happiest days of my life going to drive-ins."

"You may be older than I thought." She hit the switch and the TV screen lit up. There was some music, then in bold letters: *"Das Erste Programm Sendet: Politiker Antworten."* Sylvia said, "The name of the show is 'Politicians Answer.' This was broadcast last week. One good thing about television over here—no commercials. I was given the tape just before I left."

When I said something about the commercials being the best part of most programs, Sylvia, naturally, ignored the remark.

The TV program was a political interview—a guest being questioned by an interviewer doing her best to pry out a juicy political quote or two. In other words, it was the kind of show that at home I would do my best to avoid.

Then we saw a desk. On one side was the interviewer, a serious-looking blonde woman wearing a gray suit, with not one strand of hair out of place. Opposite her was the guest.

The guest had medium gray hair, a high forehead, a prominent beak, and a square jaw. He didn't look handsome, exactly, but he appeared distinguished, and was probably in his early or middle fifties.

Sylvia nudged me. "That's Kurt Mehling."

"He looks okay."

"Don't be fooled by his suit and tie."

"I'm a sucker for custom-made clothing."

"What else are you a sucker for?"

"A good-looking woman."

After a brief introduction and some softball questions, the interviewer asked Mehling why he was so against the United States. This brought forth a lengthy answer.

"I was an exchange student back in the late seventies. At Yale. At first, I liked living in America. After I graduated, I got myself a green card and a visa. But after a while I became disenchanted."

I said, "His voice is very cultivated."

Before the interviewer could ask another question, Mehling was talking again.

"It was the emphasis on money that disturbed me. All that's important to Americans is the size of their bank accounts." I recalled what Nadaj had said to me in Kosovo—that all Americans care about is listening to pop music and wearing jeans. At times, talking to people from other countries about one's own land can be instructive. I remember a Russian general once asking me whether Americans ever ate anything but fast food—and then not believing me when I said yes.

It was quickly apparent that Mehling liked to talk.

"America doesn't have the influence in Germany it once had. That's because we no longer need America to protect us from the big, bad Russian bear."

"What stories are you working on now? There's a rumor *Welt-Bericht* will be running a series critical of America."

"I can't give you details." He smiled again.

I asked, "What's this critical story he's going to publish?"

"Ursula Vogt's story, of course," Sylvia said, turning her head to look at me.

"You're on record," the interviewer said, "as saying your magazines have been pressured by the American government. Is that true, Herr Mehling?"

Mehling said, "The American government admits it has spent millions—hundreds of millions, probably—in its propaganda efforts. Our magazine presents a different point of view."

I didn't say anything. It wasn't exactly news that our government threw its weight around in a variety of ways. But who can blame us for that? While Buck and I were in Munich, one of our covers was that we

were journalists, working for Radio Free Europe. In Berlin, I'd been involved for a time with employees of RIAS, short for Radio in the American Sector, agents who doubled as broadcasters—or was it vice versa?
I'm not sure anyone knew. I certainly didn't.

I do know that during the years of the Cold War lots of East Germans tuned into RIAS to learn about the outside world, for the kind of
news and information they couldn't get anywhere else.

When the interviewer asked about Ursula Vogt, Mehling said,
"Miss Vogt was a truly fine reporter. Her death was a tragedy. We know
who murdered her."

The interviewer seemed surprised. "I hope you're not saying that
Miss Vogt was murdered by this Green Beret? There hasn't been a
trial—"

"Of course, I'm saying that!" He waved his arm dramatically.
"What's his name? Brinkman? Everyone knows he was acting on orders
from CIA or other intelligence people. As far as I'm concerned, they
can find him guilty and throw the key away."

Talking to the tube, I said, "He hasn't been convicted yet."

"No," Sylvia said as she turned off the TV, "but I'm afraid he will
be."

"What got Mehling so excited?"

"What makes you think I know?"

Sylvia went into the kitchen, removed a bottle of Riesling from the
refrigerator and handed it to me to open.

"Well? What did you learn from Mr. Mehling?" Her voice had soft-
ened, and now sounded almost sultry.

After she'd rinsed a couple of glasses, I poured out the wine.

"Not much that I didn't know already. Cheers."

As she took a sip of wine, Sylvia gazed at me over the top of her
glass. We were standing next to one another at the kitchen counter, her
lips perhaps ten inches from mine. I wondered what she would do if I
tried to kiss her. When I placed my hand over hers, she didn't remove
her hand, at least not right away. I wondered what I might be getting
myself into, if anything. Sylvia was wearing eye shadow that made her

eyes appear mysterious and full of promise. Except that I didn't know what they might be promising.

Do other people find themselves in situations like this? Or is it only me?

She said softly, "We're going to have to spring him."

"Spring who?" Unfortunately, I knew who.

"Brinkman. Who else? You just heard Mehling. Brinkman's a dead man otherwise."

"How much power does this guy have?"

"He swings a great deal of weight, Alex. Believe me. He's got money and he's the publisher of a news magazine. People fear him. He can publish an article and destroy a politician's reputation. He's got people in the government under his thumb."

"Like who?"

"Cabinet ministers, for starters."

Cabinet ministers? How did I get into this situation?

"Our job is to see that Doug Brinkman doesn't get convicted. I told you that back in New York. We're pulling out all the stops. That's why we're going to have to spring him."

"You and me?" What she'd just said sounded ridiculous. "You have a great sense of humor, Sylvia."

Sylvia looked at me unsmilingly, letting me know she was dead serious. It was the same look that Sergeant Robinson, one of our DIs at Fort Bragg, had on his face when in basic training he'd assigned me to a week of KP for having my hair a quarter inch too long.

Chapter 15

Friday, January 25, 2008

I'm not a big fan of early-morning telephone calls, so when my cell phone went off at 0700 the following day I expected the worst. Adding to my irritation was the fact I'd left the phone in the living room, and I had to leave a warm bed to go answer it.

Since only Max had this number, I said, "What's up?"

"I hope I'm not calling too early."

"I'm fine. Still a little sleepy." Standing half-naked in the middle of the room with a draft sending a chill through me, I was thinking of my warm bed, and wondering why Max was calling at such an ungodly hour. Through the slightly ajar bedroom door I could see my room-mate's skirt and brassiere lying on a chair next to the bed.

"I'm wide awake. When you're my age," Max said, "you'll be wide awake at this time every day too. I promise."

"I'm sensitive to your sleeping problems, Max. I hope you appreciate that. I also hope you didn't call just to tell me about them."

"You remember where I live?" When I said I did, Max said, "Drop by. Right now I'm going out to the baker. How many *Semmeln* can you eat?"

Before leaving, I knocked on the door of Sylvia's bedroom, said I was on my way out. When I heard a muffled response, I pushed open the door. She was sitting upright on the bed rubbing sleep from her eyes with one hand and struggling to hold up the blanket with the other. So Sylvia slept topless.

"Max called," I said. "He wants to see me."

"About what? Why are you staring?"

"I'm not staring." I could have told Sylvia that when you're living at close quarters with another person you have to get used to being seen in a state of dishabille.

"You're gawking like a sixteen-year-old who's never seen a woman's breasts. I don't like being stared at."

I was staring, of course. I was also wondering whether she slept naked. "He didn't say. When I see him, I'll ask him."

"You're still staring. You're making me self-conscious."

"I was about to say—"

"Don't tell me I have nice tits. Just pay attention. It sounds like you may be talking with the German cops." When I said I didn't know who I'd be talking with, she tossed off the blanket, flung two great legs over the side of the bed and stood up. "Let me think." She slept topless, but not bottomless. Her eyes were red, and strands of chestnut-colored hair were going off in every direction. When she asked, "Where's my robe?" I pointed to a chair next to the bureau. "Alex, listen."

"I'm listening."

As she slipped on her robe, she said, "Keep your lip buttoned, if that's possible. Those people aren't your friends."

"Who are my friends?"

"You don't have any."

"Anything else I need to be reminded of?"

Our early-morning exchange only served to remind me that I was sharing these quarters with an extremely attractive woman. I was doing my best not to forget that she not only outranked me, but that she was also my boss. Again, I reminded myself to keep things businesslike and impersonal.

But the truth was, this job and this living setup were making me very nervous.

Twenty minutes later, Max and I were standing at the marble-topped counter in his kitchen, sipping coffee and smearing jam on warm Bavarian rolls. I had just poured my second cup of coffee. The kitchen was as cozy as I remembered it, with a round mahogany dinette in the alcove, light-blue cotton curtains tied back in front of the large window.

With Max's wife, Anna, doing the honors, I'd had many a weekend breakfast here. I recall particularly one sunny New Year's Day—being here with a dozen other people, one of whom was Irmie, and welcoming in the New Year with a champagne brunch. That was another memory that I was better off without. Who knows how my life would have worked out if I hadn't left this city so suddenly?

But now I was wondering why Max had rousted me out of a sound sleep to get me over here. I knew it wasn't just to eat rolls, kick around the latest political scandal, and speculate on the chances of FC Bayern, Munich's soccer team, winning another championship—which is what we did for fifteen minutes. One thing I knew: Max would only tell me what he wanted to tell me when he felt like telling me.

Finally, after checking his watch, he said, "It's this Albanian club, Alex. The Kalashni Klub. That is, if you want to call it a club." He looked at me. "I guess you didn't go in there the other night."

"You're right—but how did you know?"

"I figure you wouldn't be up and around this morning if you had. I know you too well. You'd have antagonized someone in there and bought yourself some big trouble. You might even be at the bottom of the Isar." The Isar is the river that runs down from the Alps and bisects Munich. The first warm spring days bring out bevies of young women to the English Garden, where they swim nude in the Isar, sunbathe on its shores, and wave saucily at overly curious passersby. It's an annual ritual to which the tabloids never fail to give full pictorial coverage.

"You're right. I followed your advice, Max. I didn't go out there. But I'm still curious."

"Can I ask why?"

I didn't like telling the Kosovo story to anyone. I think you're better off burying experiences like that as deep in your subconscious as you can possibly get them. In fact, I know you are, regardless of what Dr. Freud may think. I hadn't mentioned Kosovo to the female shrink in D.C. either, at least not in any kind of detail. But I had an idea Max had gotten me over to his place for a reason, so I said the Vogt case could connect to Kosovo, but I left it at that.

"How did you get onto this Albanian club?" Max asked. He was being persistent, one of the qualities of a good cop.

I remembered what Sylvia had said, then decided I could tell him that much. "I spoke with Brinkman out at Stadelheim. He mentioned that the handyman hung out there."

Max nodded, seemingly satisfied with that answer.

Max was silent for a long moment during which he drank the last of his cup of coffee and began washing up the dishes. Then he said, "Quemal is probably a common name down in Kosovo. Like Jim or George in America."

"Or like Fritz over here. Or Adolph."

"Why is it that I knew you were going to say that?"

"Because you know what a pain in the ass I am."

"All right. It's a common name, but maybe we should check it out anyway." When he'd finished rinsing, he looked at me and said, "Thanks, Alex. I appreciate your telling me why you're over here. At least a little bit."

"Sure, Max. No secrets." Not too many anyway.

"You think there's some kind of connection, is that it?"

Thinking of how Sylvia seemed to be keeping certain things to herself, I said, "I haven't been told everything. I'm working in the dark. I'm not particularly happy about it."

"Lighting a candle is always better than cursing the darkness."

"Sure, but cursing the darkness is much more fun."

As the former cop liaison to military intelligence, Max knew how things worked. Without saying anything more, he grabbed the receiver from the wall phone and headed into the next room. Still wondering what he had in mind, I stepped toward the door, but couldn't make out what he was saying. But there was something in his tone that made me think he might be talking to a woman. While he was gone, I busied myself leafing through a copy of the *Süddeutsche*, Munich's big newspaper.

When Max returned to the kitchen, he was zipping up his jacket. "C'mon, we're going downtown." By "downtown" Max meant the Ettstrasse, and the green fortresslike building located not far from the Marienplatz—Munich police headquarters.

After arriving at the Police Presidium, we got buzzed in and headed upstairs. Max led me to a room at the end of the third-floor corridor. Except for us, the room was empty, and we sat down across from one another at a long wooden table. The only window was barred. In the far corner were a small basin and a water faucet. This was the kind of place you could use for everything from hatching conspiracies to conducting searching interviews with uncooperative prisoners. The walls were cement blocks painted green, obviously soundproof, and although I didn't see any bloodstains, I could imagine police detectives using the basin to rinse their hands after a tough interrogation. In Germany, suspects in criminal investigations don't enjoy quite as many rights as they do in the United States.

"We'd like to close the Kalashni Klub," Max said. "It's a *Poof*—"

"A brothel, in other words. Why don't you?"

"They've got clout with the right people, people in the government."

I frowned. "The city government?"

Max shook his head. "Someone way up." I wondered whether he was talking about the federal government, in Berlin. That would mean that whoever was running the Kalashni Klub would have to be very well connected.

Max looked at his watch. "We're waiting for someone." When I nodded and said "Okay," Max paused, let a couple of seconds go by. "It's someone you know, Alex."

I frowned, wondering who else in Munich I still knew—and who I knew that would be likely to turn up here in police headquarters. And then it hit me.

Max nodded, shrugged. "Irmie. She's a detective now."

"Irmie? Irmie knows I'm here?"

"I told her."

"Irmie's a detective?" I don't know why I should have been surprised, but for some reason I was.

"She's with the *Mordkommission*." The *Mordkommission* is Munich's homicide squad.

I didn't know whether I should be happy or unhappy. I do know I suddenly became nervous. I could feel my stomach beginning to churn, my face beginning to burn. Although I made an effort to remain calm, I was aware of a drop of perspiration on my forehead.

"She's gone to get the file concerning that club. There was a murder there not too long ago. She's been involved in the investigation. We want to talk to you about that."

"To me?" When Max nodded, I recalled what Sylvia had said that morning—that I didn't have any friends.

A minute later the door opened, and there she was.

Chapter 16

Friday, January 25, 2008

Irmie handled the moment much better than I did. Both Max and I got to our feet. I stammered a greeting, and Max said, "You two remember one another, I'm sure."

"Of course," Irmie said. She smiled and we shook hands.

As she stood there, I noticed that beneath her dark-blue pantsuit all Irmie's curves were still in the right places.

She had some colored folders with a lot of paper in them, printouts and official-looking forms mostly. When she put on a pair of reading glasses, they made her appear older. Was it really nearly nine years since we'd seen one another?

Except that she seemed a shade more mature than the young policewoman I remembered and at least in this situation not quite as bubbly, Irmie didn't look much different—medium length blonde hair, blue-green eyes, round face, just the shade of a smile in her expression. She still wore eye shadow and she had a pink gloss on her lips.

How many hundreds of times had I kissed those lips? Or thousands of times? I made a determined effort to return my thoughts to the present.

"Max tells me you're here back in Munich on a case, Mr. Klear."

I didn't like the "Mr. Klear" mode of address particularly, but I didn't see that there was much I could do about it. Not at the moment anyway. When I said that was right, she said, "Can you give me some of the background?"

I thought for a second before speaking. Irmie might be the perfect person to provide some help. "Some of our military people in Kosovo ran into some trouble with some members of the Kosovo Liberation Army. We got word that one of those KLA people, an individual named Quemal, has come to Munich. I'm here to check that information out. We'd like to ask him some questions." I decided not to mention that I suspected Quemal of having murdered Ursula Vogt.

"Is Quemal his first name or family name?" When I said I wasn't sure, and that it could even be a nickname, she said, "Who exactly would like to ask him some questions? Would that be you?"

As she leaned forward, I saw the softness of her breasts. I thought her silk blouse might be buttoned a shade too low, and I wondered if there was a police regulation governing things like that. Well, why not? In Germany there's a regulation to govern just about everything else.

The truth was, I'd never been able to keep my eyes off Irmie. I was fascinated by her every movement. I could spend hours just gazing at her, observing every small detail, from the way she blinked her eyes to the way she moved her hands. And I had an idea she was aware of it.

I shook my head. "Some people back in the States. People in Washington, D.C."

"Can you be more specific?"

"To be honest, I don't know myself." As far as I knew, our people in D.C. only wanted to ask Ramush Nadaj questions, but I didn't say that. And as far as the Nadaj rendition went, I knew just about nothing.

"Are you here in an official status, Al...Mr. Klear?"

"No, not really." When she said "I see," I assumed that Max had told her that I was checking out the death of Ursula Vogt.

"Do you have a visitor's visa?" When I said I'd had my passport stamped, she asked to see it. I watched as Irmie noted something down on a pad. I knew what she was looking for—an SOF stamp or any of the other markings that indicate an individual is carrying out official government business. I recalled Jerry Shenlee's instructions to the effect that I'd be traveling in a purely unofficial capacity. If either Irmie or Max felt that I was doing anything I shouldn't be doing, they didn't indicate it.

Irmie said, "From what I understand, Kosovo is planning to declare its independence."

I said, "There are all kinds of behind-the-scenes deals being worked out. The success of Kosovo's struggle for independence depends on whether other countries recognize it as independent."

Irmie looked at me with her round eyes. "I'm investigating the murder of a Kosovo national. It seems that the murder might have some political implications."

Max said, "I told... Mr. Klear... about the Kalashni Klub."

I didn't say anything. I wondered how much Max might have passed on to Irmie, or for that matter to any of the police. I knew I might be talking too much and maybe to the wrong people, and that I might soon be finding myself in some very hot water. But in spite of Sylvia's warning, I figured I had no choice. At the start, Sylvia had said they wanted me over here because of my contacts.

Irmie said, "One of our homicide cases seems like it might connect to the Kalashni Klub." She fished out a sheet of green paper from one of the folders and started reading it. "An Albanian man was found murdered a while back, almost a month ago." She hesitated briefly. "He was found— Well, I'll come back to that."

Looking at me, Max said, "Didn't you mention that this Quemal had been in Afghanistan?" Then he glanced toward Irmie. I had the feeling they were communicating with one another with nods and glances.

"This is one of the things we wanted to know, Mr. Klear. The murder victim seems also to have spent time out there."

I asked, "In Afghanistan?"

Irmie nodded. "He'd been in Afghanistan earlier. But he came to Munich from Kosovo."

After referring to the report, she said, "We have no idea what he was doing in Afghanistan. His name was Muzaci, Nicola Muzaci. He had a visitor's visa, good for three months. He wasn't working, just hanging around. He was staying in a warehouse, just a bunch of beds in a big room. He had some money, a few hundred euros. From what we've heard, he spent time at the Kalashni Klub."

Max said, "And he got himself killed."

"It might have been someone he met at that place who killed him. Muzaci seemed to have it in for someone, some other Albanians."

"People from the club?" I asked.

"Maybe." Irmie again glanced down at some of the papers. "I'm getting this from Detective Schneider's report. He's a colleague. He interviewed some of the people out there. Muzaci started spending time at the bar, coming in every evening, drinking, talking."

Max looked at me. "Just the rotgut they serve there could have killed him."

Irmie said, "He talked a lot about Afghanistan."

I frowned. "Afghanistan? What was he saying?"

"That's what we've been trying to find out," she said, "but it's been difficult. You know how these people are. They keep to themselves. If you're not Albanian, well, you don't count." She paused to take another look at one of the papers in front of her.

Max said, "You know what the *Kanun* is?"

I nodded. "The code of law."

Irmie said, "The *Kanun* governs their lives. They really stick by it. We couldn't get anyone to open up about anything. And we questioned quite a few people. We've asked them all to remain in Munich." She pointed to the paper. "I have the names here. Muzaci seems to have served with some guerrillas down there—"

Max interrupted. "Fighting with the Taliban?"

"How they came to join up with the Taliban is still unclear. According to Muzaci, someone sold them out. At least that's what he seemed to be saying—or something along those lines. We're not really sure."

"Sounds like Muzaci was asking for trouble," I said.

"Well, he certainly found it. Something else he said had to do with the Kosovo Liberation Army."

I said, "What was that?"

"He seems to have said something about someone breaking the *besa*, his word of honor. He said that someone had betrayed the KLA and Kosovo. His body was found in this raunchy warehouse where he was crashing—on his bed in the corner of this big unheated room. Lots of blood. Someone had cut up his face. One of our detectives said he'd never seen anything quite like it before." Irmie removed a pair of photos from the dossier and slid them across the table.

Max made a sour face. "What happened? It looks as if—"

"You can see for yourself, Max."

Shaking his head, Max said, "It looks like someone stuffed something in his mouth. He shook his head. "Bad."

When I saw the pictures, I was glad I hadn't given Max any of the details of my Kosovo stay. The recollection of my two days in the company of Ramush, Quemal, Fadilj, and Vickie served to speed up my heart rate just a shade. These pictures were pretty much the kind of nightmares that had me waking up shouting for the past eight months. In one of the recurring dreams, I was on my back in a coffin. When a grinning figure closes the lid and everything goes dark, I wake up, soaked in sweat, naturally.

I pushed them back across the table toward Irmie, made a noncommittal nod.

As she returned the pictures to the folder, Irmie made a point of ignoring our comments. I continued to glance at her out of the corner of my eye. She'd always known how to keep me in my place.

But what I was thinking of at that moment was Ramush Nadaj's references back in Kosovo to something having happened in Afghanistan. I also recalled the weapon he was carrying, an MP5 machine pistol, an automatic weapon that was cleared only for American Special Operations people in Afghanistan. If Muzaci had been in Afghanistan, he might have been involved in some way with Ramush Nadaj, the guy our government wanted to talk with so badly.

I looked across the table at Irmie. "What do you figure to do?"

"What you've said about this Quemal could be important. I had no idea he was also in Afghanistan. Detective Schneider, my colleague, will want to talk with him."

I said, "I'd appreciate it if you let me know what he finds out."

Irmie looked directly into my eyes, but her expression gave away nothing. As she began gathering up her folders and stood up, I wondered what she might be thinking. I had the urge to say something,

something personal—to ask how she was feeling or ask to see her after work.

Again we shook hands, and she said it was nice seeing me again. Very businesslike.

When she was gone, I looked at Max. "You could have at least given me some warning."

Downstairs, Max suggested a cup of coffee, and we headed across the Marienplatz, pushing our way through knots of shoppers and tourists until we arrived at a small café next to the Viktualienmarkt. After getting coffees, Max said, "It makes sense."

"What makes sense?" For some reason, my mind was wandering.

"What we were talking about up there. The handyman working for the Vogt woman might connect with this murdered Albanian guy in some way. It's worth looking into."

But at the moment I didn't feel like discussing the case. "Irmie looks good. She hasn't changed."

Max looked at me, nodded. "What did you expect?"

"I don't know. I still remember that story of how she landed in the hospital."

"She had a close call and was in the hospital for nearly two months." When I didn't say anything, Max said, "When she returned to the job, they gave her a commendation."

I recalled the story well enough. A pair of armed robbers had become trapped in a bank at the southern end of the city, not far from Irmie's assigned precinct. They'd taken some hostages and were threatening to kill two young children unless the police gave them safe passage out of the country. Hearing that, Irmie didn't hesitate. But when she entered the bank, one of the robbers sent a hail of fire in her direction, hitting her on the left side of her body, one round piercing her body armor and two striking her in the left thigh.

But by diverting the robbers, she gave another cop the chance to roll a tear gas grenade into the bank, an action that made it possible to disable the thugs and rescue the children.

For some strange reason I felt responsible, and I couldn't sleep for weeks after hearing the story.

We lost something, Irmie and I, when she stormed the bank on that hot summer day—and it still hurts me to think about it. Although I used to wonder if we could ever get back what we lost, I never wanted to risk finding out whether what was lost was irretrievable—and I suppose it was that fear that kept me from ever wanting to return to this city.

At times I wondered what would happen if I bought a ticket, jumped on a plane, and telephoned Irmie from the airport—but I never did it. It was a daydream and nothing more. Deep down I knew I never would have come back to Munich if circumstances hadn't brought me back.

As Max munched on a cruller, and I gazed at the people drifting back and forth, some of them looking for things to buy, some just gawking, I thought about Irmie as a police detective and working homicide. Although I'd never precisely imagined her doing that kind of work, I remembered how quick and capable she was, with an ability to make difficult decisions and take things in stride—and to combine an inborn scrappiness with a sparkling, bubbly, very feminine personality. Irmie could handle the police job. She'd discern things that her male counterparts would completely miss. In the end, I could see her being a valuable addition to the city's police.

I've known any number of capable and attractive women, but for me Irmie was special—and the minute I saw her again, I knew I'd never meet anyone who could replace her.

I said quietly, "I lost touch. I wrote, but she never wrote back."

Max said, "Do you blame her? She liked you, Alex. You know that." When I didn't respond, Max said, "Very few guys ever have a woman feel about them the way Irmie felt about you, and certainly never a woman like Irmie." Max paused. "Do you know what I used to wonder, Alex?"

"What?"

"I used to wonder what it was that made her so crazy about you."

"Smoke and mirrors, Max, nothing more."

Max took a sip of coffee, gazed at me unsympathetically, his blue eyes suddenly seeming very cold. "That's what I thought."

Thinking back, I couldn't blame Max for thinking I was a fool for leaving Irmie and never writing. Everything that happened was the result of a series of misunderstandings—and while I hated to admit it, most of them were my fault. Maybe all of them were. Back then, I was working a dangerous, stress-filled job, in a foreign country, living from week to week and month to month and unsure about the future—and frankly fearful that every time I went behind the Wall I would never come back. Then a woman fell in love with me. It had all happened too suddenly. I needed time, to think and to sort things out.

Maybe I felt I was responsible for Irmie landing in the hospital. During my home leave, which coincided with the intelligence drawdown, I was reassigned to the States. The following year, I decided to do what some other people were also doing—resign in favor of contracting. Afterward, I'd let myself be distracted by other activities—and, I suppose, other women.

But that's all those activities and women were. Just distractions. For better or worse, I knew that now.

"I kind of thought she'd be married by now."

Max shrugged. "She was friendly with a guy in the construction business for a while. I don't know what happened."

Max looked at me thoughtfully, but didn't say anything. He'd said what he thought needed to be said, and we sat in silence for a minute.

After I got up and brought back two more coffees, Max said, "Things are different in Munich from the way you remember them, Alex. The Albanian mob has pretty much taken control of the drug trade and the trafficking of women. They're well organized. It's an international network, tangled up with Kosovo and even with the Taliban in Afghanistan. They're into other stuff, but they've got the trafficking end of the market cornered."

I said, "I suppose that's what the Kalashni Klub is all about."

"Yeah, pretty much," Max said. "And they must be paying off the right people. We can't close the place."

"You know, sometimes I wish the Cold War hadn't ended. Things were simpler then."

"Remember how we used to complain?" Max said. "We didn't know how good we had it. I never thought that I could ever be nostalgic for Checkpoint Charlie."

We sat there silently for a minute thinking fondly of the Berlin Wall. "Amen," I said after a while.

Back at the safe house, Sylvia had the heat turned up and was seated at the table frowning over her laptop—and was quite possibly communicating with someone back in D.C., maybe even someone in the National Security Council. Or for that matter, in the White House. Even POTUS, which is the Secret Service designation for the president, wasn't beyond the realm of possibility.

When I stepped around behind her in order to get a look at what she had on her computer screen, she shooed me away.

I didn't say anything. I'd come to realize that, where Sylvia was concerned, anything was possible. The Pentagon has its own intelligence agency, and in the years since 9/11, I've sometimes gotten the feeling that the spooks and people like Sylvia are running our government.

Sylvia was wearing a pair of ripped blue jeans and a man's white shirt that looked two sizes too large and no bra. She had the sleeves rolled up and the top two buttons were undone. When she turned to face me, I said, "How long since you combed your hair?"

"The last time a man made a saucy remark to me, I shot him."

"If I'm going to die at the hands of an attractive woman, I'd prefer a lingering death." When Sylvia said "Really?" I said, "What I'd like you to do is first—"

"Spare me your lingering death fantasies. What happened at police headquarters?"

When I looked at Sylvia, I couldn't keep from comparing her with Irmie. Gazing at her brown, not quite rust-colored hair, blue eyes, and delicate features, I was reminded that I was living at close quarters with a remarkably attractive and very capable woman.

After I'd told her the story of my interview with the police, she said,

"I don't like it. You talk too much. The German cops are smart. They pick up on everything."

"I was careful."

"I didn't think you knew the meaning of the word."

"That's because you underestimate my vocabulary."

"But you say you told them you were in Munich in a semiofficial capacity. That doesn't sound too bright. The police could throw you out of the country for that."

"My passport was in order. No identifying stamps or notations. Nothing to raise suspicions."

She threw me a skeptical glance, again making me feel she was able to read my mind. Sylvia's disheveled sexiness almost certainly would have been more of a distraction if I hadn't just seen Irmie again. I was still thinking about her and only half paying attention to this conversation. Although I'd told Sylvia that Max and I had spoken with a female police detective about Quemal, I diplomatically failed to mention that I'd known Irmie way back when. "Not too many people have been to Afghanistan," I said. "It's worth checking out."

"You didn't tell the detective how Quemal connects to the Vogt case?" When I shook my head, she said, "You're sure?"

I said, "They should make the connection, but I agree—better later than sooner."

"I know you've known some of these people for a while, Alex, but we can't trust the German cops."

"I never trust any cops. All they care about is themselves and their pensions. They don't have the honesty and integrity of us intelligence types."

"They're not patriotic like we are." Sylvia turned off the computer, stood up from the table, reached up, placed her hand on my shoulder, pulled me to her. I had no choice but to give her a brief kiss. "Not patriotic like you and me." Her voice was a throaty whisper. "What do you have in mind, Alex?"

"Quemal could be our man," I said, resisting the urge to put down the beer bottle, slip off her shirt, place my hand on her naked breast, and tell her what I really had in mind. I fought against that urge. No one knows me better than Buck, and he says women are my big weakness.

Although Sylvia still had her hand on my shoulder and her lips were inches from mine, I continued to talk. "Quemal could have killed Ursula Vogt. He could be the character I encountered in Kosovo. He could have murdered this KLA soldier who was complaining about what happened in Afghanistan. Nadaj and his crew were all in Afghanistan. It seems to add up."

"So what do we do?" Her voice was still a throaty whisper, more sultry than before. Naturally, I could have said that what we do first is go into the bedroom and spend the night in bed together—but I was already thinking about the Kalashni Klub.

"Do you have any plans for Sunday evening?"

Chapter 17

Sunday, January 27, 2008

"I hope you know what you're doing," Sylvia said. "Check that. I mean, I hope you know what we're doing."

"It doesn't sound as if you have much confidence in me."

"No comment."

Sylvia was dressed in a navy-blue turtleneck sweater, dark slacks tucked into black motorcycle boots. On her head she had a knitted cap, and to complete the package, she wore black gloves. When I told her she looked sexy, she told me not to be "facetious."

I told her to speak English.

I was dressed more appropriately for an evening on the town, in a dark-green golf jacket, beneath which I had a blue flannel shirt, jeans, and the kind of peaked cap that's popular in Europe. Beneath my shirt, I had my KA-BAR in a sheath at my waist.

"Do you know where this place is?"

I said, "I drove by it today. If they haven't moved it in the last eight hours, I know."

Sylvia was referring to the Kalashni Klub, where Doug Brinkman said Quemal hung out. If you knew it was there and knew what you were looking for, it wasn't that difficult to find. A small, lighted sign with an assault rifle fashioned to look like an arrow pointed you in the right direction.

If you weren't looking for anything, you'd ignore the sign and go on about your business.

When Sylvia asked if we were ready to go, I said, "Almost."

I went into my bedroom and returned a minute later with a 9mm

Beretta pistol. I said, "I'm assuming you know how to handle one of these."

I knew Sylvia was familiar with the weapon because the military had adopted the Beretta after concluding that the .45 Colt automatic was too bulky and, for most situations, not all that practical.

"I pick my teeth with these babies."

"Oh, wonderful. A woman after my own heart."

"What I'm wondering is, whose is it and where did it come from?"

"It's mine, and it's very dependable. I brought it with me." I snapped an ammunition clip into the handle. Unlike the .45, which requires you to first slide a round into the chamber, the Beretta is ready to fire when you release the safety. That's a small wrinkle but, for some situations, a critical one.

"No problems at the airport?"

I'd placed the pistol in a glassine bag, then packed the bag in a mixture of epoxy and graphite. There are numerous ways to circumvent the most thorough baggage checks, and Sylvia knew them as well as I did.

I said, "As you know, I'd rather leave home without my credit card than a weapon of some kind."

Although Jerry Shenlee had kept a straight face when he warned me against having a weapon in Germany, I figured he didn't mean for me to take the advice too literally. What he'd meant was, just be careful and don't let the authorities know you're carting around artillery.

Sylvia frowned. "I'm assuming you think this might come in handy." When I nodded, she looked at me skeptically. "Are you sure we want to go out to this place?"

"I intend to be very careful."

Sylvia watched as I sat down and strapped a holster to my left ankle. After slipping the weapon into the holster, I pulled my trouser leg back down and stood up. I pulled up my shirt and showed her the KA-BAR knife I had at my waist.

When her expression darkened, I said, "Don't worry. I don't expect to have to use any of this stuff."

On the drive through Munich, I told Sylvia for the final time what

I had in mind. Although Max had warned me about the Kalashni Klub, I thought the risk was worth taking. If this Quemal was Quemal the Assassin, I could pick him up, and we'd get him to confess to the murder of Ursula Vogt. And we'd force the authorities to drop the charges against Doug Brinkman. The fact that he'd been in Afghanistan and had a connection with Ursula Vogt led me to think it could be the same guy.

If it wasn't, we were back at square one.

When we were within a half mile of the place and waiting at a traffic signal near the Münchner Freiheit, I removed a bottle of brandy from the glove compartment, and figuring I didn't fit the profile of the average K Klub customer, I'd splashed some of the liquor on my jacket, and rolled some around in my mouth.

A questioning look on her face, Sylvia shook her head, but didn't say anything.

It was after ten when we turned off the Ingolstädterstrasse and drove past the lighted Kalashni sign. Cars were scattered around, parked haphazardly on both sides of the road. Two hundred feet farther on I made a U-turn, then halted on the shoulder.

As Sylvia climbed out, she said, "How long will you need?"

"Are you nervous?"

"Of course not. Are you?"

"Yes, actually." It was true. I didn't exactly have cold feet, but I was wondering if this was a wise undertaking.

Sylvia all at once looked troubled. "Maybe we should abort this mission, Alex. It's not too late."

Although I had the feeling she wasn't as concerned for my safety as she was for the success of the operation, I was curious about this place. I shook my head. "I only want to have a look around, and maybe ask some questions. It's probably all a false alarm anyway. I'll try not to be obvious about it. If I'm not out in ninety minutes, call Max. Don't come looking on your own."

I eased the car into gear, then drove slowly up the road. When I reached the lighted sign with the picture of the assault weapon, I made a right turn. Although it called itself a club, the German word *Poof,* or brothel, would be more accurate. For some reason, Albanian gangsters have an international stranglehold on this business. They have strong stomachs.

It was a two-story building located thirty yards down a narrow street in an area of warehouses, factories, and old buildings, some with broken windows and an abandoned look. The K Klub's two front windows were covered by thick drapes. I found the sight depressing, maybe because during my two tours in Bosnia I'd been inside places like the Kalashni Klub, in Tuzla and Banja Luka, and hadn't liked what I found. I'd had a few encounters with some of the gangster types operating these businesses, from the Mafia chiefs to the pimps—and learned how quickly they like to reach for their knives. In fact, as a souvenir of a disagreement in Tuzla with one of those characters—a guy whose specialty was turning young girls into drug addicts—I have a small scar above my right hip.

Some steps led me up to a small concrete porch on which were a couple of chairs and a table. A guy seated on one of the chairs was bent over and smoking a joint and didn't bother to look up as I went by. I pushed open the heavy wooden door and closed it behind me.

I was inside the K Klub, the place Max told me I should stay out of.

Inside, it looked unruly, but I'd been in my share of unruly places before. It didn't look dangerous—at least not if you didn't antagonize the wrong person. From the ceiling hung a bunch of red fixtures through which shone the light, and in between two of the fixtures was an opening in the ceiling, which might have housed a security camera. The red light mixed with the clouds of blue cigarette smoke hanging over everything and caused the room to be bathed in a weird pink-blue glow. A girl with a great rack and wearing a tiny halter was on a small stage doing some bumping and grinding to the accompaniment of music blaring from a loudspeaker. Although it was amateurish, it was amusing to watch—which might have been why most of the males on hand were paying close attention.

The tables were round, made of wood, had cigarette burns all over them, and were pretty well banged up. They were squashed so close together I had to step around them as I crossed the room. Some were occupied by women in groups of two or three, the others by men—from unpleasant looking Slavic types to unpleasant-looking European types, most of them talking to one another and sizing things up. At one table four heavily made-up women showed off generous amounts of thigh. Maybe I ogled. As I went by, one made a comment.

I said, *"Mirëmbrë'ma!"* Albanian for "Good evening," one of the greetings I recalled from the course I took in Bosnia. When I smiled and blew her a kiss, she looked away.

All the women seemed to be smoking and staring at nothing in particular, almost as if they were all stoned. Despite their empty expressions, I thought a few of them looked kind of nice. They were probably new to the business—and might have been wondering how they'd landed in this place.

Who could blame them? I'd only been here a couple of minutes and was already wondering how I'd landed in this place.

At the bar, the bartender, who had a chrome dome and probably did double-duty as a bouncer, looked me over, perhaps sizing me up, wondering if I fit the profile of a K Klub customer. If I didn't, I'd take that as a compliment.

"'nen Korn!" I slurred the whiskey order, staggered against the bar, ran my fingers through my hair, fumbled a roll of euros from my jacket, and tossed down a couple of tens. After pouring me a clear whiskey and removing one of the bills, the bartender, seemingly satisfied that I was just another male desperate for female company, moved off and began talking with two women seated a couple of bar stools away. Next to me two men were speaking quietly in Dutch and eyeing the women at the tables.

When I turned around, I saw him, and when I recognized him, my heart went into double time. My hunch had been on the money, but I hadn't expected it to pan out so quickly.

At the far end of the room and standing with his back partially toward me was Quemal the Assassin himself, my friend from Kosovo, the star performer in my worst nightmares. ·

He was talking with half a dozen guys seated at one of the corner tables.

There was no question it was Quemal. He had the same hawk nose, hooded eyes, stringy black hair hanging over his ears, and for anyone close enough to notice, probably the same garlicky breath. I hadn't seen him right away because he'd been smart enough to shuck the white do-rag he'd had on his head in Kosovo. And he'd replaced the green jacket and brown pants with a formless gray jacket over a red shirt. In place of the beard, he was sporting a large, slightly droopy mustache.

Although I wasn't close enough to see, I assumed he had the same glint in his eye. Once a psychopath, always a psychopath. I wondered whether I might have made a mistake coming to this place alone. Too late for that now.

The Assassin seemed to be in the middle of some kind of argument. He was exchanging comments with a woman at the next table. When she replied, the men all stopped talking.

I'd found out that this Quemal and Quemal the Assassin were one and the same—which was all I wanted to know. Now I was going to have to get out of this place. But how? If I turned around now and headed for the door, I might be calling unwelcome attention to myself.

I'd definitely walked right into it.

The Assassin stepped forward, reached over and slapped the woman.

There was a low rumble among his buddies. I assumed she'd insulted him, maybe questioned his manhood. Or told him the name Quemal the Assassin sounded more dumb than dangerous. Something else I'd learned during my tours in the Balkans was that people take offense very easily. In Kosovo, when I'd once made the mistake of addressing an Albanian Muslim in Serbo-Croatian, a couple of our GIs had to hold him down to prevent him from carving me into tiny pieces with his pigsticker.

After that altercation, I was known as "the guy who nearly started a third world war."

Even from across the room I could smell the wariness. The way I figured, he'd murdered at least two people within the last couple of months—and most of the people around here would know that.

With The Assassin and me now within spitting distance of each other, I was reminded that Sylvia, at the airport in Brooklyn, had promised me an opportunity to retaliate for the shellacking in Kosovo. Well, she'd been right. I might get that opportunity. But now all I was thinking about was Max's warning to stay out of this place—and how I could get away in one piece. But as long as Quemal remained occupied with his friends and I kept my back to him, the chances were good he wouldn't make me.

I'd stay cool, and when the opportunity presented itself, I'd quietly head for the door. No heroic stuff—like strolling over to Quemal and saying, "Remember me?" Or asking for my Leatherman back.

A minute later, the dancer ended her performance, removed her halter, jiggled two very nice tits at the audience, and flashed a smile. As the men yelled and pounded the tables, I wondered whether this might be the right moment to leave.

But the place suddenly went silent.

Someone had kicked open the door and, now, two men were clumping in. One of the newcomers stood at least six five, weighed three hundred pounds, had an enormous head of dark curly hair, was sporting a large gold earring, and wearing a knee-length white coat—and for obvious reasons was immediately the center of attention. He shouted something in Albanian. Then he picked up a chair and tossed it across one of the tables. After some more shouting, he grabbed a table and upended that.

This was definitely an individual who liked being in the spotlight—and who was unhappy about something.

One of the Dutch guys next to me uttered the Dutch equivalent of "What the fuck!"

The bartender headed out from behind the bar in the direction of the hubbub.

As the newcomer weaved through the big room toward the stage, he shoved aside some men who'd made the mistake of sitting at tables that were in his way. When one of them said something, the big guy turned around, pulled him up by his collar, then with his hand against the guy's face, shoved him into a tableful of women.

After that, everyone kept their distance.

A tall, skinny individual with blond curly hair, clearly the boss pimp, materialized from somewhere, and he and the newcomer began arguing. A minute later, the pimp was joined by Quemal and the bartender, and they began arguing with the big guy's partner. It was a real donnybrook. Everybody was shouting at everybody else.

When the newcomer kept pointing at the table with the four women at it, the boss would become even more excited. It didn't take a genius to know they were arguing about possession of one of the women, seemingly the same one Quemal had slapped around a moment before. She had brown hair to her shoulders, was wearing a low-cut dress, had a round face, and smooth olive skin. She had an innocent attractiveness that the other women in the place lacked. I had a feeling she wouldn't have it very long.

The first person to reach for a weapon was Quemal, who all of a sudden had a knife in his hand. He grabbed the arm of the woman and ripped her dress. A second later, he had her by her hair and was holding the blade to her throat.

The disagreement had escalated very quickly—and Quemal was behaving true to form.

The big man stopped talking in mid-sentence, believing like everyone else in the place that the woman's throat was about to be slit. He hadn't expected that, and suddenly, he and his buddy appeared to be outgunned by Quemal, the boss pimp, and the bartender. Then the pimp gave the word, and Quemal cut through the woman's bra, exposing her breasts. When the newcomer stepped forward and threw a punch at Quemal, he responded by slashing him with a rapid movement of his blade.

Suddenly, there was blood all over, and the big guy was holding his blood-soaked right arm and screaming in pain. I doubted he'd be wearing the white coat again.

When the bartender pushed the woman to the floor and held her down, she didn't try to get up.

For a long minute, the big man stood holding his arm, making threats and pointing toward the woman. Although he wanted her to come with him, it was clear that with the bartender holding her down she wasn't moving.

Then with Quemal's knife only inches from his face, he took a couple of steps backward—you could sense it was all over. Although the newcomer kept talking, blood was dripping from his arm, and it was obvious he'd be wiser going to see a doctor than mixing it up any further—at least not at this moment.

At the door, when he shouted something, I had an idea this battle was going to be continued at some future time, and that's what he was telling Quemal.

With the big guy and his buddy gone, the bartender hauled the woman to her feet and, as she tried to keep her breasts covered with what was left of her dress, he dragged her behind him toward the rear. I had an idea she'd made the mistake of expressing a preference for working somewhere else and was in for a beating, very likely from Quemal.

I assumed that would keep him busy for a while.

Chapter 18

Sunday, January 27, 2008

Within minutes, the place was humming again, and something approximating music was blaring from the loudspeaker. A blonde in a bikini took her place on the stage and was bending over and displaying her very round rear end. It was as if nothing had happened.

With Quemal the Assassin occupied with other matters, I decided this might be a good moment to have a quick look around. I drifted over to the table occupied by the four women. I'd become curious, wondering what the argument was about.

"Guten Abend."

The only one to respond was a tall brunette. In a Slavic accent, she asked me how I was feeling. I told her "amorous," and she said that was how she was feeling too. When I suggested we spend some time together, she pointed toward a hard-looking individual two tables away who'd been watching us out of the corner of his eye while pretending to talk with his friends.

Since the brunette spoke reasonably good German, I'd be able to pump her. When I asked her name, she said, "I'm Tania."

Her boss said *"bëj dashuri,"* which I recalled as Albanian for "make love," and he said it was going to cost me 250 euros for a half hour of Tania's time. After forking over the money, I walked upstairs with Tania to a room that was furnished with a chest of drawers, a night table, a chair, and a bed. Although the bed was made, the bedclothes didn't appear to have been recently laundered.

After drawing the curtain across the room's one window, Tania immediately began unbuttoning her blouse. In her business, time is money. As she unself-consciously peeled off her clothes, I asked where she was from.

"From Kosovo." When I asked which city, she said, "Dakovica." I nodded, recalling a small, impoverished place with muddy streets that I'd once driven through and was glad to leave.

Tania had jet-black, shoulder-length hair, smooth white skin, a narrow face, and high forehead. As she removed her brassiere, I saw her tits were on the small side, but round and firm—and I couldn't help wondering how long she'd been in this business. Under other circumstances, I might have become interested.

As she stepped out of her skirt and I slowly undid a couple of my own buttons, I asked casually, "Who was the man who caused all the fuss?"

"Oh, that's Sedfrit. He says that Adem owes him money. He was here yesterday too." She shrugged, continued to undress.

When I said "Sedfrit?" she nodded. "Sedfrit Sulja."

I assumed Sedfrit Sulja ran his own brothel. "Sedfrit sold the girl to Adem? Is that it? The nice-looking girl? And now he wants his money for her?"

When Tania nodded to me to remove some clothes, I slowly began unlacing my shoes. Still trying to be casual, I asked about the men who chased Sedfrit out of the club.

"Adem is in charge. The man with the bleached hair. He comes from Pristina."

That figured. Pristina is the capital of Kosovo. Adem would be connected to the trafficking ring. It was likely that money from an operation like this would find its way back to Kosovo, first to one of the front organizations, and then to the KLA. Max had said the Munich police had wanted to close this place, but couldn't. The K Klub was being protected by someone in the German government. Interesting.

Tania frowned. I'd only unbuttoned my shirt. "Why are you not undressing?"

"And the others?"

I watched as, wearing only her panties, she carefully folded her skirt over the back of the room's one chair. She had long athletic legs, the kind of legs I always find sexy. "Quemal and Iaon. Iaon is the bartender."

When I removed my shirt, Tania seemed to relax. She smiled, placed her arms around my neck, and we sat down together on the bed. I was able to keep my knife out of sight. Reminding myself that I was here on business, I fought against an urge to give her a squeeze.

"And where does Iaon come from?"

"He's from Romania. No more questions. Aren't you ready? Are you shy?"

Raising her legs, she slipped off her panties, placed her hands on my shoulders and knelt on the bed. Below her navel was a small spray of brown curls. How do I get into these situations?

The German word for shy is s*chüchtern.* I shrugged, said that shyness has never been a problem.

The truth was, I had other things on my mind. "Is Quemal from Kosovo?" I asked.

"Some men"—Tania smiled—"*schüchtern.* They like to do it with clothes on."

I could have told Tania I wasn't interested in other men's hang-ups.

With Tania's arms still around my neck and her lips only inches from mine, I continued to ask questions, I said, "Is Quemal with the Kosovo Liberation Army?"

Tania looked alarmed when I asked that question—and I realized I'd pushed the envelope a little too hard. Then her hand felt the KA-BAR. Her eyes widened.

"Why you have knife? Why asking so many questions?" She slid away. This place was definitely connected to the KLA in some way. I'd rung some alarm bells and made her suspicious.

"Are you policeman?"

I held her next to me on the bed. Her nakedness increased her sense of vulnerability, and I decided to make the most of that. Maybe I wasn't behaving like a perfect gentleman, but I had to get something back for my 250 euros—even if it was only information.

When she said, "I don't understand," I said, "Maybe we can talk
for a while."

"What about?"

Tania was just one of the thousands of naïve young women who
take the bait—who, believing they will find work and better lives in
western Europe, leave villages and towns in countries like Romania,
Kosovo, Bulgaria, Moldova. In most cases, they pay dearly for their
sense of enterprise and adventure. They are trafficked into brothels,
often turned into drug addicts and exploited by international rings,
many of them run by Albanian thugs—some with ties to the Kosovo
Liberation Army.

These are some of the wonderful consequences that followed from
the dissolution of the Soviet Union. Where's the Cold War now that we
need it?

"About Quemal."

"Why you want to know about Quemal?"

I said, "Who was the man who was killed?" When she frowned, I
said, "Someone was killed two weeks ago. His name was Nicola
Muzaci. Why?"

"You policeman?"

"Just tell me, Tania."

She fought to get loose, tossed a quick glance in the direction of the
chair with her clothes on it. "I must go now." When she tried to push
away and stand up, I held her down on the bed, kept her from moving.

"I want answers, Tania."

She was squirming and kicking, but it wasn't doing any good. I had
her pinned.

I said, "You won't be leaving until you answer my questions."

"What questions?"

"Muzaci, the man who was killed, had been in Afghanistan. Am I
correct?" When I squeezed her arm, she nodded. I said, "What did he
say happened in Afghanistan?" When she hesitated, I said, "What did
Muzaci say, Tania?"

She shrugged.

"What did he say, Tania?" I could see fear in her eyes.

"That it was a betrayal. I don't know anything more." Abruptly, she rolled over, and struggled to pull away. I loosened my hold, allowing her to stand up and dart across the room. "I have to go."

I followed her, moving diagonally toward the door. "I won't let you go until you tell me. How did they break the *besa*? What was the betrayal?"

"Soldiers were killed."

"Which soldiers? KLA soldiers? How were they killed?"

Within seconds, she gathered up her skirt, blouse, and bra. With her clothing in one hand and her shoes in the other, she eyed me. Clutching her clothing against her tits, she started moving slowly toward the door. I stepped forward, blocking her way. She looked terrified, like a cornered animal.

There was no point trying to stop her. She'd only scream.

Rather than grabbing her, I tried one last question. "How did they break the *besa*, Tania? What did they do?"

After scurrying to the door, Tania stood for a brief moment with her hand on the knob. Then she clicked open the door and was gone.

I grabbed my shirt, slipped it on, buckled up my pants. It took a minute to lace up my shoes. With my shirt only half buttoned, I opened the door, peered in both directions. No one was up here, at least not as far as I could see.

I couldn't tell whether anyone had noticed Tania's hasty exit. The only way back down was the staircase. Standing on the landing and looking out over the big room, I couldn't see Tania or Quemal. The place was still crowded, the noise and smoke even worse than before. But there were other rooms up on this floor, and for all I knew, she was in one of them. Quemal could also be in one of them. He was the one person who could connect me with Kosovo, and that was something I didn't need. I ducked back into the room, took a quick look out the window. There was no balcony, no way down. I should have checked this out earlier.

My heart had begun to pound. Even though no more than three minutes had elapsed since Tania's exit, a lot can happen in three minutes.

Suddenly, there was the sound of loud music. Without hesitating, I grabbed my jacket and headed back out to the landing. Another girl was on stage and shaking her God-given attributes. Although I couldn't make out anything unusual, I knew that people here were aware of my presence.

My only thought now was to get out of this building and get back to the car.

But that might not be so easy. Iaon the bartender had left the bar and, with a cell phone to his ear, was walking toward the door and looking over his shoulder in this direction. I didn't like that. Standing not far away was a man I remembered from Quemal's table, and I didn't like that either. When I saw Iaon say something and jerk his thumb in my direction, I decided that was something else not to like.

I took the stairs down two at a time.

At the bottom of the staircase, I looked around, then saw a couple of characters moving toward the front door. I had an idea they'd be preventing me from leaving. Leading toward the rear of the building was a wide, unlit corridor. I didn't know what went on back there, but I assumed there was another door out of this place. I could feel cold sweat on my forehead. I realized now I'd gone too far with Tania. I could have let it go when she stopped answering. Making her suspicious wasn't the smartest thing I've ever done.

Moving slowly down the darkened corridor, I went by a room with WC on the door, then what looked like an office—maybe belonging to the boss pimp. Quemal and Adem could be anywhere, back here, upstairs, or even outside somewhere. I tried a door at the rear, but it only opened into a small work area. I tried another door, which opened into a room with a bed and a half-dressed man and a naked woman bouncing around on top of it. "Excuse me." I tried another door and found it locked.

At the end of the broad corridor was a window. After pushing aside a heavy drape, I tried opening it, saw it too was locked. I fought against a surge of panic. I was trapped.

Through the window I could see a big lot, beyond which was another building with what looked like a loading dock at the near end. If

I could get out there, I'd be fine. I briefly considered breaking the window but decided against that. Looking to my right, I saw only darkness. I went in that direction. After I'd gone a hundred feet, I was able to make out what looked like a door. Whether it was locked or unlocked I didn't know, but no one was back there, so I headed for it. When I reached it, I tried the handle. It opened onto a small porch piled with cartons and plastic bags. There was a cement path leading alongside the building back in the direction of the road I'd driven in on and where I'd parked. But if the bartender and his buddies were waiting for me at the front door, I'd be walking right into them.

And maybe walking into Quemal too. I decided against that.

It would be safer to head back the other way, toward the big yard that I saw from the window.

There had to be a way out of there. If I had to scramble over the wall I'd seen from the window, I could manage that. Then I'd circle around and approach my car from the other direction. Not exactly a piece of cake, but definitely better than walking back toward the K Klub's front door.

I was sweating and panting, and as I went, I thought about Quemal. I'd need to pry him loose from this place, then squeeze a confession out of him. Sylvia would have some ideas about how to manage that.

Although I had to scale a wire fence to get out of the yard, it took less than ten minutes to get around to the access road.

I'd told Sylvia to give me an hour and a half. I wondered where she was.

There seemed to be even more cars now, most of them parked haphazardly on the shoulder. I'd left our car less than a hundred feet from the building, one of half a dozen parked at the edge of the narrow dirt road.

Looking in both directions, I didn't see anyone. There was no moon.

I think this was my last thought before I was surprised by the sound of footsteps on the gravel behind me.

I spun around but was a fraction of a second too late. I threw a wild punch, but didn't hit anything. He'd stayed low, then came at me hard, catching me broadside and sending me up against the side of a car. With the wind partially knocked out of me, I was still able to dodge a punch aimed at my face. He came at me again, and down we both went. Although he was on top of me and my right hand was pinned, my left wasn't, and when I swung, I caught him on the side of the head. The blow must have dazed him. I felt his grip around my neck loosen. That was the chance I needed. Throwing fifty-pound blocks of ice around builds up your forearms, and I surprised myself with the force with which I was able to shove him off me.

Suddenly, there was something in his right hand, and it didn't require a genius to know what it was. I grabbed his wrist with my left. My right hand closed around a rock, but as I was about to bang his head with it, something came down on the back of my neck.

I felt groggy. My head hurt. It took a couple of seconds to realize there was a woman there, and that it was the woman who had clobbered me from behind with something hard—and a few seconds more to realize the woman was Tania. Then I felt someone running his hands over my body—patting me down, slipping the KA-BAR out of the holster. That was Quemal.

Still woozy, I was on the ground, flat on my stomach. Quemal had his knee in the small of my back. A knot of hair in his hand, and what felt like a knife against my Adam's apple. All I could see of Tania was her shoes as she opened the rear door of a car. Then she said, "Quemal wants to talk with you. He says to climb into the car."

I was hardly on my feet when Quemal pushed me into the rear seat, shoving me hard and causing my head to bang against the other door. He was on top of me immediately. With his knife against my throat, I hardly dared breathe, no less move. His black eyes were about six inches from mine.

I could tell from his smile that he recognized me. Because of how he had me pinned, I couldn't move anything except my left leg.

Tania climbed into the car's front seat. She seemed very composed and not at all afraid of Quemal. When she looked at me and shook her head, I couldn't tell if she was expressing sympathy or disapproval.

For a while, no one said anything, and there was only the sound of Quemal's heavy breathing. When he finally spoke, his tone was eerily familiar, another happy memory of my trip to Kosovo.

My left leg was the leg on which I'd strapped the holster.

As they talked, I wondered whether they'd notice if I moved my left wrist. Despite the darkness in the car, I decided I couldn't chance it.

Tania's attention was on my face. "Quemal says he remembers you. You were in Kosovo. He says you are responsible for the death of his friend Fadilj."

"Fadilj tried to kill my friend." As I spoke, I moved my leg back about two inches.

Tania said, "Quemal says it is justice that Allah delivered you to him. But first he wants to know how you found him here."

I wondered where Sylvia was. But even if she'd seen what had happened, I didn't see that there was anything she could do.

I decided to move my leg a few more inches. I said, "Tell Quemal he will soon be arrested. His only hope is to spare my life."

When Tania had relayed my reply, Quemal laughed, then said something in guttural Albanian.

Sylvia, where are you?

With my leg bent at my knee, and neither of them paying attention to anything except my answers, I slowly moved the fingers of my left hand. I knew that anything like an obvious move would result in my throat being slashed. One small factor working in my favor was that Quemal seemed to be enjoying his moment of triumph and was drawing it out.

Moving only my fingers, I was finally able to touch the handle of the Beretta.

Tania said, "Quemal will let you live. But only if you tell him why you are here. Quemal says he is a merciful person."

"Tell him I'm happy to hear that. Tell him to take the knife from my throat." Keeping my wrist locked and moving only my fingers, I removed the weapon from the ankle holster. But I was only able to hold it awkwardly between my thumb and my index finger.

"Quemal says you no longer have friends to save you as you did in Kosovo. There is no hope for you. Tell him why you are here and how you found him."

As I pushed the safety with my thumb, I said, "Ask him if his friend Ramush Nadaj is here."

As Quemal increased the pressure of the blade against my throat, I felt blood running down the side of my neck. Another inch and I'd be gone. He was smiling the same goofy smile I remembered from the night in the shack in Kosovo when he was fooling around with the Leatherman.

Again I asked myself how I get mixed up with people like this.

Unfortunately, I knew the answer. I'd become overconfident. Max had been right. I could have handled this differently. Too late for that now. I did my best to focus on the precarious hold I had on the weapon.

Still holding the Beretta with two fingers and now fearful I might let it drop, I placed my thumb inside the trigger guard.

I was afraid that Tania might notice my hand, but then she shifted on the front seat, and climbing to her knees, she looked me in the eye. "Quemal says again, he wants to know who is with you." When I didn't reply, she shook her head. Her face was a foot from mine. She said quietly, "Quemal is losing patience. You must answer. He will kill you otherwise."

I had an idea Quemal intended to kill me no matter what.

Slowly, I pointed the barrel upward, moving it around, trying to find a point where it was aimed at Quemal's head. If I missed, there was the likelihood I would blow my own head off. In any case, I wouldn't get a second chance.

I said, "Tell Quemal that other people know I'm here."

Quemal mumbled something, and Tania said, "Which other people?"

"I can't remember—"

With only my index finger and palm supporting the weapon, my hand began to tremble ever so slightly. I continued to move the barrel, my thumb now against the trigger.

"You must tell Quemal. Otherwise—"

I realized I wasn't sure where the bullet would go. But I also realized I couldn't hold the weapon in this position for much longer. I had no other choice.

"All right, Tania. I'll—"

I squeezed back my thumb.

I wasn't prepared for what happened next.

The gunshot within the car was like an explosion. I was suddenly covered with blood and bones, Quemal's blood and bones—the result of the slug slamming into the back of Quemal's head and transforming his gray matter into gray mush. As Quemal's lifeless body sagged against me, the knife fell against my chest. Tania screamed. I pushed open the car door, shoved Quemal onto the ground and staggered out. Tania screamed again. Within seconds, someone moved out of the darkness and was standing beside me.

It was Sylvia.

"Are you all right?"

My golf jacket was covered with blood, mine and Quemal's, and I was suddenly dizzy. I picked up my knife.

I said, "Give me a second. I'll be all right." In the other hand I was still holding the gun.

Pointing at Tania, who had just climbed out of the car, Sylvia said, "Who's she?"

"One of the girls."

Grabbing the gun from my hand, Sylvia aimed it at Tania, who was no more than ten feet away. "We can't have her—"

As she was about to squeeze the trigger, I pushed Sylvia's wrist, ruining her aim. I don't know why I did it.

"She's seen everything. We can't—" Sylvia again lifted the weapon.

All I could focus on was Tania's face, her dark eyes, the smoothness of her skin, the delicacy of her thin lips—and her expression of fear and horror.

Sylvia was so close, she couldn't miss. Holding the weapon with two hands, she trained it directly at Tania. Just as she squeezed the trigger, I again jolted her arm.

Seeing her chance, Tania turned, then began running in the direction of the building. Still holding the weapon, Sylvia glared, rage spilling out of her eyes. Fortunately, no one in the building seemed to have heard the shot, which, considering the loud music inside, wasn't surprising.

Pushing me in the direction of our vehicle, Sylvia went quickly back to the car, where Quemal's body was sprawled on the rear seat. She spent a few minutes doing something, but I wasn't sure what, perhaps going through Quemal's pockets. I fished the keys out of my pocket and walked toward our car, which was parked about eighty feet away. I still felt strange, and my cheek, at the point where Quemal had slugged me, felt like I had a dozen toothaches. I used a handkerchief to stanch the bleeding from the cut on my neck.

I stepped out of my shoes, slipped off my jacket, and removed my jeans. Sylvia saw what I was doing and nodded. Slipping off her sweater, she used it to make a package out of my blood-soaked clothes, then tossed the package into the trunk. It was a small precaution, but in the event anyone thought to go over our car, there wouldn't be any trace of Quemal's blood on the upholstery.

When Sylvia asked if I could drive, I said I could. With the car on the road, I found the necessity to concentrate on driving prevented me from thinking about what had just happened.

After a second, Sylvia said, "Let me tell you something, Alex. Nobody gives a damn about a dead whore. And something else. In this business, no good deed goes unpunished. Ever." When I only shrugged, she said, "You're too goddamned soft-hearted. I don't see how you've survived this long."

I could have said that was maybe the reason I decided to retire. Instead, I said, "Dumb luck, Sylvia. Pure dumb luck."

"Well, I sure as hell hope your dumb luck holds. For my sake as well as yours."

And that was all either of us said for the remainder of the trip back to the safe house.

Chapter 19

Monday, January 28, 2008

Standing in front of the bathroom mirror, I dabbed antiseptic onto the gash on the side of my neck, then covered it with gauze and a large bandage. I was adding another small permanent souvenir to my already extensive collection of scars and gashes that I've collected over the years. Thank you, Quemal, for giving me something to remember you by.

I remember Buck once saying that it was the emotional scars guys collected in this business, not the physical ones, that did them in. Thinking back on the events of the evening, I could see the wisdom of that remark. The gash on the side of my neck would heal and be forgotten. Likewise with the bruise on my face. But my visit to the K Klub would provide the raw material for any number of nightmares.

I heard the sound of the shower running in the other bathroom. Like me, Sylvia seemed to feel a need to wash things away. I stayed in my own shower a long time, scrubbing myself with soap, letting the water run over me, and trying my best to keep my mind on other things. Twenty minutes later, wearing a shirt, a pair of slacks, and no shoes, I entered the living room where Sylvia was seated in the big armchair.

Pointing to the bandage, I said, "It's going to leave a scar. I hope it doesn't affect my sex appeal."

"I'm not in the mood for your dumb remarks."

Although she had a slightly vacant look in her eyes and looked pale, Sylvia seemed calm. All she had on was a chemise. On the coffee table in front of her was a bottle of Jim Beam and a glass. After taking a long swallow from the glass in her hand, she nodded at the bottle. "Would you like one?"

"More than one, probably."

"I'm on my second."

"Are you drunk?"

"Not yet. Soon."

The apartment somehow seemed much cozier than it had previously. I'd packed away my blood-spattered clothes in a plastic bag. I'd toss them in some distant, untraceable garbage bin the next day. The jeans and flannel shirt would be easy to replace, but I'd miss the green golf jacket, which I'd brought over from the States and that I'd always worn when I felt I needed luck. Well, if it had done its job on this occasion, it had been for the final time.

Sylvia fixed me with a stare. "Are you all right? You don't look so great."

"I'll be fine." I took a long swallow of bourbon. I felt strange, kind of empty.

After a brief pause, she said. "Tell me about Quemal. What do we know?"

"I figure he murdered two people—the Vogt woman and this Albanian who showed up and accused him of betrayal, of breaking the *besa*. There might be some others we don't know about."

Sylvia nodded. "There probably are. They used him as their hit man. When they wanted someone out of the way, they sent Quemal the Assassin."

"He did a good job of framing Brinkman for the Vogt woman's murder."

"Yes, but he had help." When I frowned, Sylvia said, "From the German cops."

That was news to me—but I clearly remembered Max's cautious reaction when I first asked him about Brinkman. That was on my first day in-country, and I wasn't yet picking up the small signals. Max knew something but hadn't let on.

Staring off into the distance, Sylvia said, "We may never find Nadaj now."

My involvement with all this had begun with our ill-fated Nadaj rendition.

"Why are we so anxious to get our hands on Nadaj?"

"The movement toward independence in Kosovo is strong. It's being spearheaded by the KLA, and it's going to happen. That's why the President visited Albania in June—to talk about Kosovo. The province is going to declare its independence from Serbia."

"When?"

"Soon, very soon. The United States is going to recognize Kosovo's declaration of independence. So will the other countries of the EU."

"The KLA are a bunch of terrorists. They're supported by drug trafficking—and by places like the Kalashni Klub. Max says the Albanian Mafia has a stranglehold on—"

"On human trafficking. I know that, Alex, but all this is political. Russia is allied with Serbia. We're allied with Albania—and with Kosovo. Our government isn't enthusiastic about the KLA, but we don't have much choice in the matter."

"If we're supporting the KLA and Nadaj is an officer, why are we—"

"Why do we want him?" She paused to take a sip of bourbon.

"You keep saying he did something." As I poured a second whiskey, I remembered what Tania had said. "What was the betrayal?"

Sylvia looked surprised when I mentioned "betrayal." Maybe I knew more than she wanted me to know.

Seated in the large chair with her legs extended onto a small footstool and her thighs completely exposed, Sylvia studied me. "You ask a lot of questions."

I couldn't keep from ogling her legs, but she didn't seem to care.

"I have to admit that I was awfully surprised when the Vogt woman was murdered. I hadn't expected that. None of us did." When she said "us," I assumed she was talking about people back in D.C. like Jerry Shenlee, perhaps even the members of the National Security Council, perhaps even the secretary of defense and his staff. "They wanted Ursula Vogt out of the picture. She'd become dangerous."

"Who's 'they'?"

Sylvia seemed to be thinking out loud, and I let her talk. "Quemal

knew what had happened in Afghanistan." She paused. "You understand what the *besa* is."

"It's a kind of pledge. I know the soldiers enlisting in the KLA give
their *besa*."

Sylvia nodded. "In the mind of Kosovars the *besa* is something spiritual. If it's a pledge, it's a pledge not just to the living but also to one's
ancestors, a pledge to live up to their ideals, to fulfill their hopes and
dreams for the future. It's an assurance to them that they did not live
their lives in vain. I don't think that we have an equivalent term in our
culture."

"Hopes and dreams for what?"

"For their homeland, for Kosovo." Sylvia paused. "I don't think
such pledges fit very well into our modern societies or have a place in
our way of thinking. We make commitments, but we permit ourselves
a certain amount of wiggle room. Certainly we don't have the same kind
of political loyalties that people from the older societies feel."

"It sounds medieval."

"It has a strong medieval component. As you say, the soldiers give
their *besa* when they enlist in the Kosovo Liberation Army. To violate
the *besa* in the minds of these people is absolutely the worst thing you
can do."

"Muzaci, the soldier who was in Afghanistan, said Nadaj had broken the *besa*."

"And he was killed for saying it. To save Nadaj's reputation." When
I didn't comment, Sylvia said, "Ursula Vogt was in Afghanistan. She
dug up the facts, most of them. You saw the pictures. She got to know
people in the Taliban. They put her on to it, obviously. The whole thing
had been carefully planned, but they would have had to find the right
individual to go along with it. That, of course, was Nadaj." She paused.
"When Kosovo declares independence, he could eventually become
their first defense minister."

"What was Nadaj going along with?"

"Right after nine-eleven, he traveled into Pakistan, where he
made contact with Bin Laden and his people. But sometime in late

2005 or early 2006, he brought a company of soldiers from the Kosovo Liberation Army to Afghanistan to fight with the Taliban. They were up in the mountains, moving through the caves, making it tough for our people to do very much."

Sylvia looked at me. Her face was drawn. I saw lines that I hadn't seen before. I wondered if she'd ever killed anyone. There was no doubt she would have killed Tania without a qualm, in cold blood.

It's not exactly news that the female of the species is deadlier than the male.

Then she was talking again. "You heard the conversations between Ursula Vogt and Doug Brinkman. She was asking leading questions, leading him along. Getting him to say things that she could use."

"Yes, I heard the conversations, but I don't think I'm following your reasoning. What was she trying to get him to say?"

"At first Ursula Vogt believed we were responsible for what happened in one of the caves. She was murdered because she began to realize what really happened wasn't the way she'd originally thought. They murdered her because they realized the damage she could do if she ever went public."

As far as I was concerned, Sylvia was talking in riddles, but I decided to let her talk. Maybe at some point I'd be able to make some sense from the bits and pieces of information.

She fixed me with a stern expression. "Alex, let me tell you what the danger is now." When I said I was listening, Sylvia said, "It's Brinkman. He's the next person they want to silence." Before I could respond, she said, "We can't let him go to trial. He'll be dead by then."

"You have to be kidding. We're supposed to get him out of jail?"

Again Sylvia glared at me. "What do you think we got you over here for? To play games? The government's paying you good money and—"

"And now I'm supposed to earn it?"

Sylvia nodded, a vacant expression in her eyes. She'd said more than she wanted to say, and I supposed I now knew things no one outside the National Security Council and the office of the secretary of defense knew. I needed something to settle my stomach. My head felt like it was splitting apart. I stood up, went into the kitchen, found some aspirin. Before going to bed, I asked if she was all right. She didn't say anything, just nodded.

As I lay awake, I thought about what Sylvia had said about Ursula Vogt—that she'd been working on some kind of story from Afghanistan for her magazine, but then had ceased to believe that the story she had reported really had happened.

I continued to wonder what it was that had or had not happened in the mountains of Afghanistan before finally drifting off into a troubled sleep.

Chapter 20

Tuesday, January 29, 2008

At nine a.m., two days after our visit to the K Klub, we were drinking coffee in the dining nook next to the kitchen. Neither of us had felt like breakfast. We were both still tense, almost as if we expected to hear the police start pounding on the door.

Sylvia said, "You never should have mentioned Quemal to the detectives. I still can't see why you volunteered that information."

I could have said I only volunteered it because Max and I had picked up the information from Ursula Vogt's neighbor—and that the detective who asked me was Irmie. Instead, I said, "I never thought I'd end up shooting the guy."

The fact I'd known Irmie years before was going to remain my little secret.

"There's something else you shouldn't have done."

Sylvia was referring to the fact that I had let Tania escape. She would have killed Tania without a second thought.

"Tania will say only what her bosses tell her to say. Since she's almost certainly without a residence permit, they won't let her talk to the police."

"That's what you hope, Alex. You fucked up. We should have killed her. No one would care about a dead whore." After a moment, Sylvia said, "What we'll do is we'll ride it out, see what happens. Maybe we'll be lucky."

"Maybe." I took a sip of coffee, but didn't say anything more. One of the things I didn't want to mention to Sylvia was that the Munich homicide cops have a 95 percent success rate in clearing cases. In other words, your chances of committing murder in this city and getting away with it were almost nil. We'd have to be really lucky to beat the odds.

Late that afternoon, while we were sorting through Ursula Vogt's stash, Sylvia slid three photographs across the table—and waited for a reaction.

She got one. After nearly choking on tea I was drinking, I said, "Where did you get these?"

"They were on one of the discs you brought back from Ursula Vogt's place. You're a gifted break-in artist."

Then, pointing at the disc, she said, "You said you just scooped this stuff up without looking at what you were taking. This is all new, Alex. But these pictures answer a lot of questions."

The pictures were of Kurt Mehling, the gentleman we'd seen on television, except now he wasn't in a television studio. Instead of a custom-tailored suit, he was wearing bloused fatigues, combat boots, a peaked cap, and wraparound sunglasses. In one of the pictures he was shaking hands with another smiling gentleman, Osama bin Laden. They were surrounded by half a dozen mujahedeen bodyguards, all of whom were armed and none of whom were smiling. In the background was a stone building of some kind.

"Where could this have been taken?" I asked.

"Probably in Pakistan. In the Pushtun country. I've sent copies back to D.C., and that's what the analysts think. You're helping our people pin down Bin Laden, Alex. You'll get a medal when we catch up with him. Anyway, that's the kind of building you'd find in that area."

"What was Mehling doing out there? Or let me put it another way: does anyone know he's been out there?"

"I doubt it," Sylvia said. "Back in D.C., they've been asking where we got this stuff."

As I continued to examine the picture, I said, "Who's been asking?"

"The chairman of the House Intelligence Committee, for one."

"I hope you told him. I hope you also told him that they should boost my GS rating."

"Take a look at the next one."

The second picture showed Mehling standing in front of the same building, this time with a smiling blonde woman. "Ursula Vogt," I said. When Sylvia nodded, I said, "Old home week in Pakistan."

"Let me tell you what I make of all this, Alex. Item number one: Mehling's firm is owned by a holding company that's incorporated in Liechtenstein. Item number two: they don't want the firm's true owners to become known. Item number three: Mehling is friends with Bin Laden."

"You're saying that *Welt-Bericht* is financially supported by Bin Laden's loot."

"Mehling's the perfect front man. He's spent time in the States. He's very good at deflecting criticism. What he gets out of it is money. He's even got a yacht. The Bin Laden people see to it that he's able to maintain his lifestyle."

"It adds up."

"*Welt-Bericht* is a propaganda outlet, pure and simple. But because they hire good reporters and editors, people regard it as a news magazine. The magazine's stories are picked up all over the world, even by American news outlets."

The third picture showed Mehling standing next to a group of mujahedeen, one of whom was Nadaj.

Sylvia said, "Mehling is almost certainly connected to the K Klub, and the K Klub is connected to Nadaj's KLA people back in Kosovo. They're connected to al-Qaeda, the Brotherhood, and whatever other terrorist organizations are out there."

I was finally beginning to see why the National Security Council had sent Colonel Frost over here. With Bin Laden backing him, Mehling could cause all kinds of problems.

I said, "It's too bad we let Bin Laden get away at Tora Bora."

"Bin Laden's days are numbered, believe me. We're close, and getting closer. And the next time he won't get away."

When I again asked what Nadaj did to break the *besa*, Sylvia didn't answer.

Instead, she said, "There's one thing that continues to worry me." When I asked what it was, she said, "The German cops. They could spoil everything."

Chapter 21

Wednesday, January 30, 2008

As I figured it would, the murder at the Kalashni Klub made Tuesday's papers. One of the city's tabloids even ran a picture of the building.

According to the story, Quemal Sheholi, a Kosovo national, was found shot to death in a vehicle in the K Klub's parking lot. The police were still looking for witnesses. However, there were suspects. Rival Albanian gangs often resorted to violence. The police investigation was described as "continuing."

Needless to say, I wondered what "continuing" meant—and I wondered what kind of role Irmie would be playing. Munich's *Mordkommission,* as I recalled, had twenty-five detectives. Although they helped one another with investigations, one detective caught the case and had the responsibility of following it up to its conclusion. I can't say I was surprised when, shortly before noon, I received a call from Max.

"Call Irmie, Alex. Posthaste."

"Do you know what it's about, Max?" I knew it was about Quemal's murder, but I didn't see where I had any choice but to play dumb.

"Have you seen the papers? There was a murder at the Kalashni Klub Sunday night."

"Who was murdered?"

"I'll tell you who. The very guy you were asking about."

"Quemal? Who killed him?"

"Who knows? All anybody knows is someone blew his brains out. And I mean that literally. Call Irmie, Alex. The detectives want to talk with you. They don't know how to contact you. You're supposed to be registered with the police. That's another little detail you've overlooked."

Max was right. It's the small stuff much more than the big stuff that trips up agents on foreign assignments. I knew that well enough.

When I told Sylvia about Max's call, she said, "The police are calling you in?" When I nodded, she said, "What do you think it is?"

"I expressed an interest in Quemal, and now he's dead. Naturally, they want to talk with me. It's not anything to worry about." I hoped I was right. I picked up the telephone and dialed police headquarters, but when I gave my name and asked for Irmie I was told she was away from her desk.

"I'm Detective Schneider. I'm running the investigation of a murder at the Kalashni Klub. Detective Nessler said she spoke with you about—"

"About the Albanian who was shot out there."

"Right. How did you know?"

"I just got a call from Max Peters."

"Okay. Can you come in today, say about three?" I said I could and put down the telephone. Sylvia still had a worried look on her face. I told her I had an appointment that afternoon at police headquarters.

Before she could say anything, I said, "You worry too much, Sylvia."

"And you don't worry enough. If the German cops tumble to what's going on, we end up in the slammer. I don't like the idea of my career going down the tubes for something like this."

If my career hadn't already gone down the tubes or up in smoke or wherever it is old careers go, I was grateful. Although I wasn't too concerned about that end of things, Sylvia was right that landing in the Kraut slammer for murder wasn't an attractive prospect.

"Tell me what Ramush Nadaj did to break the *besa*."

"I'll tell you later."

It was still early morning in the States, and on my way to police headquarters, I stopped to make a telephone call.

Buck and I had long ago worked out a mildly elaborate system for diminishing the possibility of an NSA analyst becoming an unwanted eavesdropper when one of us was calling the States from overseas.

From a public call box near the Romanplatz that could handle overseas calls, I dialed Buck at home and asked if "Josie" was there. When Buck, sounding just a little sleepy, said he didn't know "anyone named Josie," I recited the number I was supposedly calling, which was the number of the call box I wanted him to call, read backward. He was then supposed to call back from a public phone in his neighborhood.

I hung around the call box next to the Romanplatz for ten minutes before it rang.

I picked up, stuck my thumb inside my cheek, and said, "You callin' Alex he ain't here."

"I'm happy to see you haven't forgotten all your tradecraft."

"Some things you never forget, like always making your bed with military corners. You'll never guess who's running this operation."

"Isn't it Jerry?"

"Colonel Frost. She showed up only hours after I arrived over here."

"Colonel Frost reports to the deputy secretary of defense."

"I know. I'm in exalted company. You could have knocked me over with a toothpick when she showed up. Not only that. We're sharing the same quarters. A safe house near the Hirschgarten."

Buck was silent for a second, then said, "Be careful, Alex."

"Don't worry. It's not gonna happen." I wished I felt as confident as I sounded.

"Don't let it. You could end up in hot water."

"You mean in more hot water than I'm in already?"

"What else?"

"Somebody broke into Ursula Vogt's place." Buck would know who the "somebody" was. "It seems that there's a Kosovo connection to Ursula Vogt's murder. But that's not all. The same 'somebody' killed the chief suspect in the Vogt murder, who happened to be one of Nadaj's KLA lieutenants. That could lead to problems."

"Why did he do that?"

"His life was being threatened. He had no choice." I paused. "Things have to happen quickly."

"Things?"

"What I'm wondering is, do you still talk to the senator?" I was referring to one of Buck's long-time contacts, a senator who was a member of the Intelligence Committee.

"From time to time."

"I'm hoping he still owes you some favors. Colonel Frost is still very tight lipped about what happened in Afghanistan when Nadaj's people were out there. Also, anything you can dig up on Kurt Mehling."

"The name rings a bell."

"He's the publisher of *Welt-Bericht*. I have a feeling he's in this up to his eyebrows."

"That's not good. A guy like that has a lot of clout." Then, after a brief pause, Buck said, "Anything else?" He all of a sudden sounded worried.

"I saw Irmie. She's a detective now, working homicide."

"Good for her."

When I told Buck I was on my way to police headquarters, he said, "Tell Detective Nessler hello." Then he added, "Be careful, Alex." Everyone seemed to be telling me that these days. I told Buck I was grateful for whatever he could find out and that I'd get back to him.

"I suppose you know what happened," Detective Paul Schneider said. Irmie had introduced Schneider to me as one of her colleagues on the homicide squad, and he was dominating the interview. When I told Schneider Max had mentioned a murder at the K Klub, he said, "Quemal Sheholi, a visitor from Kosovo, was shot two nights ago."

"I'm sorry to hear that." I looked at Irmie. "I was hoping to be able to talk with him."

I was in the detectives' office, a long room with a window at the far end. Schneider and Irmie had desks alongside one another. The shelves on the walls were lined with the kind of sturdy plastic binders you see in offices all over the European Union. On one of the shelves was a coffee machine, next to it a package of filters. I remembered that Irmie liked her coffee strong.

I also remembered that we drank a lot of coffee together in the morning on the balcony outside her apartment as we watched the sun move higher in the sky. I wondered how often she thought of those times, if ever. Somewhere in the course of my travels I learned that women are much less sentimental than men.

I was seated on a chair facing Schneider. From behind her desk, Irmie was looking intently at me, her blue-green eyes filled with curiosity. She was wearing a pantsuit that was probably supposed to be practical but to me looked sexy. Beneath a dark-blue jacket I could see a beige blouse and, around her neck, a silver necklace. When Schneider gazed down at some papers on his desk, I stole a glance in her direction.

I was recalling a long-ago birthday when I gave Irmie a silver necklace.

"Was this a coincidence?" Schneider asked sharply. He wore rimless glasses, had a dark mustache, thinning hair, and a rugged face. He also had the kind of bull neck you see on football linemen. His white shirt was tailored to emphasize his broad chest and shoulders and to let the world know that he liked pumping iron. He'd be a tough guy in a fight. Munich cops often put me in mind of New York cops—whatever it is, you have the feeling they've seen it before. And when you're dealing with them, you want to be careful, always remembering that no matter how friendly they may be, they're never your friend.

And as with New York City cops, you're generally well advised to forget the excuses and explanations—and throw yourself on the mercy of the court. Unfortunately, in this situation that wasn't going to be possible.

"Is what a coincidence?" I was stalling, remembering Sylvia's warning to be careful what I told the police.

Schneider flashed an impatient frown, grabbed a pencil, then let it drop.

Irmie picked up Schneider's line of thought. "The fact that you asked about him only days before he got shot."

Schneider fixed me with an unfriendly stare. "You should know, Mr. Klear, I'm skeptical about coincidences."

I said, "I only wanted to talk with him. I didn't want to kill him." That was true enough—but I was glad I wasn't hooked up to a lie detector.

Irmie said, "You indicated that he had some connection with the KLA. Could this murder have been politically motivated?"

I thought for a moment, then nodded. "I knew very little about him." That, too, was true.

"But you say you wanted to talk with him," Schneider said. "About what? What would you have said?"

"I would have asked him some questions."

"About what?"

"About what he was doing in Afghanistan, for one thing. I would have asked what kind of connection the Kosovo independence movement has with the Taliban."

"Do you think he would have answered questions like that, Mr. Klear?" Irmie asked.

"I don't know." If this kind of interview were being conducted in the States, I would have refused to answer any more questions and called for a lawyer ten minutes ago. But in Germany you don't do things like that. In France, where the Napoleonic Code still applies, things are even worse. If the police deem you to be not forthcoming, you can be tossed into the cooler immediately.

"Take a guess," Schneider said.

"He might have. You never know."

"Suppose he didn't?" Schneider asked. "What would you have done then? Offered some encouragement?"

"We never got that far. Why bother to speculate?"

"The reason we're asking," Irmie said, "is that when you lived over here you were attached to the American government." When Schneider looked at her, she added, "Mr. Klear told me that." When I nodded, Schneider frowned, started tapping with his pencil. Irmie said, "We're concerned that you're not planning to do anything unlawful."

"Unlawful? That's not my—"

Schneider said, "Like planning a rendition. That's what you people call it, isn't it? When you grab someone off the street? A rendition?"

"Rendition?" I shook my head. "You've got the wrong guy."

"You could be the advance man. You say you're here as a tourist, but you could be scouting the territory." When I shook my head,

Schneider raised his hand. "You were maybe thinking of grabbing him, carting him off to an American military installation, and flying him off somewhere."

"Absolutely not."

Schneider was sharp and not that far from the truth. I couldn't help thinking that this all began with our failed attempt to grab Ramush Nadaj. I wouldn't be here in Munich police headquarters, stalling and evading, if the original rendition had gone according to plan.

"Can we be sure?" Schneider asked.

"That sounds pretty fantastic, Detective Schneider."

"I have to tell you, Klear. It's happened, more than once, and the last time wasn't that long ago."

I knew what Schneider was talking about. A German court in Berlin had tried three terrorists charged with setting off a bomb at an American military installation and found them innocent. Shortly after being released, the terrorists disappeared, and it was rumored that they'd been grabbed by an American special ops team.

In any case, I decided not to answer Schneider's question. Instead I said, "I worked in Germany for the American government for quite a while. I never did anything unlawful." Of course the truth was, I never got caught doing anything unlawful. And in those days, with Russia as a common enemy, the aims of the American and German governments pretty much harmonized. We were in close touch with the German Counter Intelligence units headquartered in Pullach as well as with the BND, the German equivalent of the FBI. The BND almost never countermanded our activities, although they expected to be thoroughly informed of what we were doing. On that score, we were always as obliging as we could be.

"Things were different back then," Schneider said.

"I think Mr. Klear's making sense." Irmie stared straight at me. "With Quemal dead, it's all pretty much beside the point."

Although Schneider continued to look skeptical, he didn't say anything. Thank you, Irmie.

There was a brief awkward silence, then Irmie said, "We have an idea that Quemal was murdered by another Albanian."

"Can I ask who?"

Irmie looked at Schneider, and when he shrugged, Irmie said, "Someone named Sulja. Sedfrit Sulja. He runs a trafficking ring, and he has close connections to some organizations back in Kosovo. He's a conduit for funneling money out of the EU back to Kosovo."

Tania said Sedfrit Sulja was the name of the individual who'd come barging into the K Klub with a beef about the K Klub boss having picked off one of his women. According to Tania, that was what had caused the fight.

Sedfrit had walked right into it.

"And there's something else," Irmie said. She looked at Schneider.

"He was castrated," Schneider said matter-of-factly.

I suppose I looked startled when I heard that. I hadn't done anything along those lines. Thinking back to what had happened right after Quemal was shot, I remembered Sylvia saying she wanted to go through Quemal's pockets. Well, she'd definitely been thinking ahead. No question that the detectives' first thought would be that this was some kind of gang killing. Sedfrit would fill the bill almost perfectly.

"It's possible someone was sending a message," Schneider said.

"They've certainly got a language all their own," I said.

"Of course, you never know." When I asked Schneider what he meant, he said, "This Sedfrit's a trafficker. He imports women by the carload for his brothels. He's been accused of kidnapping women, but he's got plenty of money and he can buy off any dame who complains. He's always been smart enough to avoid any kind of violence. I don't exactly see a guy like that doing something so stupid."

"Maybe he has a short fuse."

Irmie held up a flyer she was reading. "There's a meeting of the Kosovo Liberation Organization tomorrow evening. Sedfrit's listed as one of the officers."

Printed across the top of the flyer in bold letters were the words *Drejtësi për Kosova!* Justice for Kosovo!

Before I could comment, there was a knock at the door. Schneider got up, stepped out into the corridor, and held a brief conversation with someone. During the minute that he was gone, I scrawled a note and pushed the piece of paper across Irmie's desk. She only had time to slide it beneath a folder when Schneider reappeared.

"We've arrested Sedfrit," Schneider said. When Irmie asked where they'd found him, Schneider said, "He was at the club's headquarters. They'll be bringing him here within an hour."

Irmie was on her feet. "Will we get to talk to him today?"

Schneider said they'd be holding him overnight in the presidium's detention facility. I knew the drill. Within one day they'd decide whether or not to keep him in *U-Haft* or release him. I had an idea they'd want to keep Sedfrit around for a while.

Irmie came out from behind her desk and escorted me to the door. When I looked back, Schneider was standing alongside his desk with a telephone in his hand and punching in a number, and pretty much ignoring me. With Sedfrit as the primary suspect, I wasn't important anymore.

The question was, how long would Sedfrit remain the primary suspect?

I nodded a goodbye to Irmie. She gazed up at me for a long moment, but her expression betrayed nothing.

As I walked down the corridor away from the office on my way to the stairwell, I thought about the message I'd pushed across the desk. It had said, "Meet at the bench, tonight 7:30." Irmie would know what "the bench" was. We used to go for long walks in the English Garden, and for some reason always ended up on the same bench, which was situated in a quiet corner not far from the Tivoli Bridge, near Radio Free Europe where, pretending to be a journalist, I'd worked, on and off, for a number of years.

I spent a nervous three hours walking around the city, gazing into shop windows, drinking coffee—and wondering if Irmie would show up.

Irmie came.

She arrived ten minutes late, but she came. And I don't think I was ever so happy to see someone as I was to see her approaching up the path. A minute later we were seated next to one another. It suddenly seemed to me as if nine years hadn't gone by. "Thanks for coming," I said.

"You knew I'd come." When I shook my head, she said, "I gave you some help."

"I know." In the distance, lights from the Hilton Hotel flickered. The trees of the English Garden were a dark silhouette against a blue-black sky. The John F. Kennedy Bridge across the Isar was less than twenty-five yards away. A young woman with a small dog went by without giving us a glance.

"I know what you're thinking, Alex."

"You could always read my mind, Irmie."

"No, Alex, things would have worked out differently if I could have read your mind." She turned to look at me. "Why did you ask me to meet you here?"

"I haven't gotten over you, Irmie. I want you to know that."

"Well, I'm sorry for you then."

"I never will get over you, Irmie. Ever."

"It's over, Alex. Over between us." She looked away. "It's been over for a long time. That's why I came—to tell you that."

"I don't believe that, Irmie." I paused. "I don't think you do, either."

"Detective Schneider still thinks you may have some connection to this murder. I have to tell you, Alex, he's smart and persistent."

"I could see that."

"He won't let up until he's solved this case. He told me he's considering having you arrested."

"You've arrested someone."

"We're skeptical about whether Sulja committed the murder. Detective Schneider has more questions he wants to ask you."

I didn't want to even think about having to spend time in the *U-Haft*. It was a tough, unpleasant place, where you spent twenty-three hours a day in solitary—and where, under German law, the police could keep you pretty much indefinitely. I was on thin ice. I began to wonder whether my smartest move mightn't be to buy a ticket on the first plane back to the States.

"I talked him out of it, at least for the time being. I don't know why I did."

"You know I'm grateful, Irmie." I was doing my best to find the words for what I wanted to say. I didn't want to talk about the case. "I miss you. A day never goes by that I don't wake up thinking about you."

"Should I believe that, Alex?" She took out a tissue and began dabbing at her eyes. "I don't think I can believe it."

"Why not?"

Close to a minute passed before she answered. "I just can't, that's all. Too much happened. Too much time has gone by." She put away the tissue. Deep down, Irmie was tough. She'd gotten a grip on herself, and I sensed she wouldn't again let her emotions get the better of her.

"I know that. I wrote to you but—"

"Your words and your actions. They're two different things."

I knew, of course, what Irmie was talking about. And I knew I deserved whatever she might want to say about how badly I'd acted—although "dumb" and "selfish" might be better words to describe my actions. But Irmie didn't say anything more.

As we sat there in the darkness, I recalled that the quality that had first attracted me to Irmie was that she had a soft heart. She could have mentioned the dumb letter I'd written while I was in the airport and waiting for my flight back to the States. Of all the things I've done in my life this is the single thing that I most regret. I'd written the letter hastily, thinking of myself when I should have been thinking first of Irmie.

"Why are you over here, Alex? You didn't come to see me."

"I wanted to see you—more than anything else in the world."

"You said some kind of case brought you over, something that has to do with the government." She shook her head—expressing her bafflement?—or more likely, her disappointment?

"These jobs you have, these government jobs. Where do your loyalties lie?"

It was an impossible question to answer.

"I was going to call."

"But you didn't."

"I would have. You have to believe that, Irmie."

"Alex, let's face the truth. You're only here because this assignment brought you over. You wouldn't have come otherwise."

There are some things that are just beyond explanations, and this was one of them. How could I tell Irmie how I'd become involved in this situation?—beginning with the Nadaj rendition, getting whipsawed by Shenlee and Colonel Frost, then becoming involved with Brinkman.

"Irmie, I—"

"I have to go home."

We got to our feet and headed up the path in the direction of the Isar Ring, the bright lamps lighting our way along a path that hand in hand we'd walked along dozens of times.

"I'm going to take a taxi."

"Do you still live in the Maria-Theresestrasse?" Irmie had lived just down the street from one of Munich's landmarks, the Peace Angel.

"No, I've moved to Gröbenzell." I knew Gröbenzell. It was one of Munich's secluded western suburbs. "I have an apartment there." When she added, "With a garden," I was reminded of how much Irmie had always brightened when I arrived with flowers. These were painful memories. I had had so much and let it slip away.

I would like to have climbed into the taxi and ridden home with her. I would like to have taken her in my arms and kissed her. At the very least, I could have asked to see her on the weekend. I did none of those things. It wasn't the right moment, and I had no choice but to let her go.

When she offered me her hand, I said, "Good night, Irmie."

"Good night, Alex."

And then, wondering whether this was going to be the end between us, I stood on the sidewalk watching the cab until the red taillights finally disappeared into the Isar Ring traffic.

Chapter 22

Wednesday, January 30, 2008

It was just over two hours later, and Sylvia and I were alone in the cozy back room of Triangolo, an out-of-the-way café at the other end of the city. Sylvia had said she was in the mood for Italian food, and Triangolo wasn't the kind of place where you were likely to run into anyone you know. On the walls were large photographs of European movie stars, most of them Italian and French, and some scenes depicting a variety of European cities.

In the week she'd been in Munich, this was only the third time Sylvia had left the apartment. I wasn't exactly surprised by this—operations officers always keep their profiles low—but Sylvia was carrying things to an extreme. She was wearing dark glasses, jeans, and a nondescript sweater over a white blouse. It was as if she'd gone to extreme lengths to make herself unmemorable.

As we sat there, each of us toying with a glass of red wine, I couldn't help admiring her good looks—her angular features, thin nose, bright blue eyes. Although Sylvia seemed happy at the news that the police had arrested Sedfrit, I was having difficulty sharing her enthusiasm. I was still thinking of Irmie's comment that Schneider could be a very tough customer. I believed her.

Sylvia said she was hungry. After taking her order for a salad and a bowl of spaghetti, the waiter looked at me. I said I'd get my nourishment from wine and told him to bring me another glass.

Still thinking about my meeting with Irmie and Schneider, I said, "The detectives may still need some convincing that Sedfrit was the murderer."

"You're too pessimistic, Alex. You said Sedfrit had been in the K Klub only a short time before and had been publicly humiliated by Quemal. That certainly gives him a motive."

"There was something that the police mentioned, but I didn't tell you about."

"What's that?"

"Quemal's dead body had been mutilated." I fixed Sylvia with a stare. "How do you explain that?"

"You were there," Sylvia said. Her expression became grim. "You know what happened."

I nodded, remembering how I'd waited in our car while Sylvia fumbled with Quemal's body. When I had assumed that she was going through his pockets, she was cutting him up. I decided not to comment. She'd definitely been thinking ahead, and there was no question her ploy had thrown the police off the track—and deflected suspicion from me. Even though I now had an idea that Schneider wasn't completely buying the fact that Sedfrit had committed the murder, Sylvia's action had definitely bought us some time. The police, at least for the moment, were assuming that Quemal had been the victim of some Albanian or Kosovar rival—and Sedfrit filled that bill perfectly.

"We were lucky," Sylvia said quietly. "Lucky that Sedfrit had a public fight with Quemal an hour before. Let's leave it at that."

Then, just as Sylvia was digging into her spaghetti, her cell phone rang.

After she'd listened for a minute, she said, "Damn! I was afraid of something like that."

As I listened to her side of the conversation, I was able to determine she was talking with someone named Harry and the person they were talking about was Doug Brinkman.

"It's called Café Triangolo. I don't know exactly." She looked at me.

"It's near the Pasing station. Tell him to walk one block east from the exit."

"That was Harry Owen."

"The attaché from the consulate?"

As she pushed away her untouched plate of spaghetti, Sylvia said, "Someone tried to kill Doug Brinkman."

"The con came up from behind. Brinkman was on his hands and knees cleaning out the commode."

It was thirty minutes later, and Harry Owen, whom I was meeting for the first time, was sitting across the table from me, a glass of wine in his hand, and describing Doug Brinkman's recent narrow escape from death. While Brinkman was cleaning up a prison latrine, a fellow inmate had attempted to knife him.

"I think the assailant was a Turk," Owen said. "I don't know much more than that. We'd like to talk with him, but I don't see much chance of that happening. The prison authorities have clammed up."

Owen was African-American and had an intelligent and expressive face. He was broad shouldered, medium height, and had closely cropped hair. He was a chain smoker, one of those people who didn't seem happy without a butt in his hand. Or maybe it was only that his job was getting to him. If it was, I could understand it. He was the man in the middle, between the American and German governments, with the job of keeping both sides happy. If either side became disenchanted with him, he'd be on his way back to the States.

Officially, he was an employee of the American Consulate on the Königinstrasse, a legal attaché. Unofficially, he was an FBI agent. The important thing, as far as we were concerned, was that he had regular access to Brinkman.

"What happened was, this character had a real nice shiv, not homemade, and the question is, Where did it come from? Anyway, Brinkman heard him, dodged at the very last second. The knife came down on his shoulder, and he came up punching. He's also got a gash on his arm. He was beatin' the shit out of the guy when the guards broke it up."

"Where were the guards when this convict attacked Doug?"

I didn't say anything. I'd become used to Sylvia referring to Brinkman as "Doug."

"I figure they'd been bought off," Owen said. "According to Brinkman, they were outside the latrine taking a smoke break."

"How's he doing otherwise?" Sylvia looked very troubled.

"They moved him into a one-man cell. Supposedly, he's safer now. He probably is if he doesn't die of claustrophobia. The cell is six by twelve feet."

"Almost as small as a room I once had in a London hotel," I said.

Needless to say, Sylvia glared when I said that.

As Owen talked about Brinkman, I remembered the Stadelheim prison from some visits there years ago. After a pair of GIs had managed to get themselves sent up on drug charges, I'd been assigned to report on their living conditions. The cells were dark and depressing, with the only light coming through a high window during the day and from a weak bulb on the wall at night. As I recalled, their main complaint had to do with the food, which was usually cold by the time it arrived.

"He gets time every day to stand around in the yard," Owen said, "but now he's suspicious of everybody. There's a library, but everything's in German. Otherwise, he's got no one to talk to, nothing to do."

Sylvia shook her head. "Depressing."

I said, "He seemed to be doing all right when I spoke with him."

"That was just after he got out of the *U-Haft* and before someone tried to murder him. Now he's pretty much on edge all the time."

Looking at Owen, Sylvia said, "He knows he's a marked man. The murder attempt wasn't a random occurrence. We have to get him out." There was an urgency in her voice. "Alex?"

I said, "At least he's out of the *U-Haft*. We'd never break him out of there."

The *U-Haft* was a section of the big prison where the authorities kept prisoners isolated and locked up for twenty-three hours every day, occasionally for as long as a year. Very few stood up to the pressure. After melting down psychologically, the suspect would say just about anything the prosecutors wanted him to say—and thereby make it possible for a court to find him guilty of whatever crime the authorities wanted to hang on him.

"Now listen to this." Gazing across the table at Sylvia and lowering his voice, Owen said, "This is what I think you should know. In two weeks Brinkman's got an appointment for what's called a *Haftprü-fung*." When Sylvia frowned, Owen said, "It's a hearing before a judge, like an arraignment. The district attorney has to show the judge he's got evidence that's solid enough to keep the prisoner locked up."

"Where will this take place?" Sylvia asked.

"In the *Schwurgericht*—in other words, the criminal court. It's in the Nymphenburgerstrasse. Maybe we could—"

"Forget it," I said. "There's more security there than anywhere."

Owen looked at me doubtfully, then at Sylvia. "The only other possibility is the Police Presidium downtown. On Tuesday, he's scheduled for a hearing. He's got some papers we have to sign. The judge asks Brinkman a couple of questions, and that's it. Five to ten minutes at the most. But there's a catch."

Sylvia said, "What kind of catch?"

"Well, one of the guard captains told Brinkman they're letting him break out, and that'll be his only chance. According to the guard, someone's paid them to look the other way. When Brinkman asked who, he was told someone in our government. Brinkman's supposed to find keys in a prison van. According to the guard, two guards'll be escorting him in the hallway. They'll let him use the john, but they won't go in. When he leaves, they'll pretend they don't see him. Brinkman'll have like maybe three minutes to beat it down the stairs into the basement garage and—"

Sylvia interrupted, her voice very urgent. "Someone's paid them? Who?"

"Don't look at me," I said.

Nodding, Owen said, "That's what I thought. I didn't figure it would be you people."

"It's a setup," Sylvia said. "Only this time it won't be a prisoner who murders him. It will be one of the guards. What else did Brinkman say?"

"Brinkman's not dumb. He knows it's a setup. He told the guard to get lost."

"The hearing's on the fourth floor. I know the room."

Sylvia looked at me. "Alex, what do you think?"

I said, "Today's Wednesday. I have an appointment to see him the day after tomorrow."

"You'll need some kind of plan by then," Sylvia said. "You'll need to tell him what to do."

"That's not much time to work something out." Owen looked at me. "Plus, you'll have to persuade him to break out. Right now, he's not sure."

These people seemed to think I was a miracle worker. I let Sylvia and Owen kick the topic around a little more before deciding to call for the check. Outside, we found a cab. On the taxi ride home, neither Sylvia nor I said anything.

Back in the safe house kitchen I watched Sylvia remove a bottle of Riesling from the refrigerator and cut up two pears. She found some cheese, crackers, and cold cuts and laid them out on the table in the dinette. She seemed to be trying to get on my good side. A minute later, we were sitting opposite one another, and I was pouring out more wine.

When Sylvia said, "We have to get Brinkman out," I said, "Impossible!"

"Mehling will kill him otherwise. He's a sitting duck. Listen, Alex. You were told about Doug before you came over. I said he'd been framed. I was very up front about that."

"I wasn't told about Doug. I was told about Major Brinkman. And I wasn't told I was expected to break him out of jail."

"You're under contract and being paid a salary—a good salary, I might add—to make yourself available. I've made the decision. We break him out."

"There's no way, Sylvia."

"Owen says Doug'll be leaving the prison to go to police headquarters next Tuesday. That's our chance."

"He'll only be down there for a half hour, probably less."

"That should be long enough." Before I could respond, she said, "Alex, would you leave a wounded buddy on the battlefield?"

I felt the blood rush to my face when she said that. "Colonel Bitch" has a way of winning arguments.

"Well?"

"Of course not." After a minute, I said, "There are just too many obstacles. Brinkman has already said he's not sure about breaking out. I won't be able to convince him."

"I'll tell you how. Mention my name."

I didn't respond. The realization that Sylvia was serious about getting Doug Brinkman out of jail killed my appetite, and I pushed away the plate of half-eaten pears. If this scheme didn't work out—and I didn't see any reason why it should—our heads would be in a noose. Sylvia could get some government functionary to intercede on her behalf and save her career. But Jerry Shenlee had stressed the fact that I was over here on my own.

Without anyone putting in a good word for me, I'd be facing a minimum of five years in the German slammer. And that's only if no one died.

Chapter 23

Friday, February 1, 2008

It was early afternoon, and the only sound in the drafty interview room of the Stadelheim prison was the low buzz of conversations, mine with Brinkman and those of the two inmates next to us with their wives. One of the women I remembered from the waiting room, maybe because she had a kindly face, dark curly hair and reminded me of my mother. She'd spoken Turkish, and it was obviously her first visit to the prison. She'd come with a bunch of flowers. When one of the guards took away the flowers, she began crying.

The guard who had escorted Brinkman out said we had twenty minutes. I didn't see how we could cover everything in that space of time.

Harry Owen was right, Brinkman was much paler than he'd been at our earlier powwow. His eyes darted around in a way they hadn't previously, and from time to time he'd drum his thick fingers on the edge of the big table in front of him. He seemed to be a nailbiter, or maybe he'd only become one in the last week.

I didn't have to ask him what was wrong. I knew the answer. He rolled up his sleeve and pointed to a large white bandage on his forearm. "He nearly got me. I lost a lot of blood."

Lowering my voice, I said, "We want to break you out of here."

He looked at me as if I was crazy. "Everyone wants to break me out. A guard told me the American government will give the guards money if they let me escape. I'd be dumb to try something like that." With his sleeve back down, he grimaced. "I told him no way."

"You're right. You can't trust the guards. Still, you have to get out of here."

"I make a break, and then they shoot me. How dumb do they think I am?"

How was I going to get through to this guy?

"You're scheduled to visit police headquarters on Tuesday."

He shrugged. "Some kind of hearing."

"You'll sign a few papers in front of the judge. He only has to be sure the signature is genuine. He'll ask some questions. You answer through an interpreter. Then you sign a form." I lowered my voice to a whisper. "There's no way out of here, not out of Stadelheim." I was referring to the big prison's forty-foot walls and its well-regulated system for checking out visitors and keeping track of inmates. "Tuesday's going to be your only chance."

"How do I know you're on the level?"

"Because I'm telling you: Colonel Frost wants you out."

When I said, "Colonel Frost," his expression altered. He knew Sylvia. That was obvious. I assumed they'd become acquainted in Afghanistan, and I couldn't help wondering what had gone on between them.

Finally, he said, "I still don't believe you."

"Colonel Frost wants you out, so listen up." I glanced quickly toward the guard, who was still standing by the door and well out of earshot. "The guards will tell you one thing, but you're going to do something else." He continued to look skeptical and I paused. "This is your chance, your only chance. Get that through your head!"

"What makes you think you can manage something like that?" He gazed in the direction of the guard, who was frowning and looking down at his watch.

I said, "We learned all kinds of stuff in Fort Bragg. I know I did."

"Yeah, we did, but when the hell did we learn to bust someone out of jail?"

"Maybe you didn't, but I did." I paused again, giving him some time to think. "Tell me this: what've you got to lose?" Brinkman knew what I meant. Inside the prison, he was a marked man. Even if he lasted until his trial date, he'd be looking at twenty years minimum—

and whoever wanted him out of the way would get to him sooner or later, and most likely it would be sooner.

I let him think about it some more, for maybe a half minute. I lowered my voice to a nearly unintelligible mumble. "You've been in police headquarters, right?" When he nodded, I said, "How often?"

"Twice. After they arrested me, and one other time."

"What happens?"

"They took me down in a van. In cuffs. No way out of that sucker."

I looked toward the guard, who I sensed might be about to say time was up. "What happens then?"

Brinkman sensed it too because he began speaking quickly. "They drive into the building, into an underground garage. We get out of the van. Then we wait downstairs. On benches."

"The hearing's going to be on the fourth floor. This one's at fourteen thirty hours. It won't last long. Harry Owen, the guy from the consulate, will be there. When did the guards say they'd let you make a break?"

"I'm supposed to ask to use the latrine while they wait outside. Then I leave, supposedly without them seeing me. I'm supposed to beat it downstairs, grab a van, and drive it out."

"They can't let you out of their sight for very long."

"They're giving me three minutes to get downstairs."

"Then the alarm goes off?" When he nodded, I said, "Tell them you'll go along with the plan to let you take the van."

I figured I knew the rough location of the fourth-floor hearing room. I'd have to figure out which of the lavatories he'd be using.

"Give it to me again. Quick." The guard had begun strolling in our direction. "What did they say you should do right after the hearing?"

"There's a washroom down the corridor. I ask to use it. It's got bars on the windows, so they leave off the cuffs and don't worry about me trying anything. Then I beat it down the stairs."

"On the third floor, look for a washroom with an out-of-order sign on it. There'll be a change of clothes in there. Do you know where the main entrance is?"

He thought for a second. "The side away from the Marienplatz?"

"Not exactly, but you'll have to find it. There's a guard. I'll try to distract him. He buzzes people in and out."

I knew Munich's Police Presidium from having spent so much time there. I knew the security procedure at the entrance, but the presidium was a sprawling building, one in which you could easily get lost. My mind was racing. Brinkman would have to change and find his way down within minutes.

As I continued to talk, Brinkman's expression slowly began to come alive, and after a minute he sat up in his chair. He had big hands, and he began knotting them and unknotting them. As a member of Special Forces, there's nothing a guy learns to like as much as an all-but-impossible challenge. Doug Brinkman's eyes took on a wild glint, a glint I'd seen before in the eyes of soldiers who were on an adrenaline high. At that moment, it might have been in my own eyes. If it was, I hoped it wasn't too obvious.

After I'd explained everything, he said, "Are you sure something like that'll work?"

I wasn't sure. In fact, I found the scheme kind of crazy, but given the circumstances it was all I could come up with.

"Sure, it'll work. But you're gonna have to move fast, and it will only work if you do exactly what I tell you to do."

At that moment, the guard was walking toward me and pointing at his watch. I told him I wanted another minute. I breathed a sigh of relief when he turned his attention to one of the other visitors.

Speaking rapidly, I said, "Look for civvies in the latrine. A cell phone and an S-Bahn ticket will be in one of the pockets. And some money. There'll be a number to call. Act like somebody important. A doctor, maybe." I figured I had to give him self-confidence.

"I'm an *Artzt*?"

"Right. You have to say, '*Ich bin Artzt.*' That's if anyone asks." I paused. "Think of yourself as someone important, someone who doesn't have to show his ID."

Then the guard was there again. I continued to talk, speaking quickly and hoping Brinkman was picking it all up. "And make sure you put the tie on, and the shoes. The clodhoppers will give you away otherwise." As I stood to leave, I said, "And there'll be a wig in there. Stick that on too. And the cheaters."

Outside the prison, I noticed that the sun was no longer shining, and the city looked gray and somber, which was an almost perfect match for my mood. As I drove back to the apartment, the thought occurred to me that what Brinkman had said was true. Probably one of the few things they didn't teach us at Fort Bragg was how to bust someone out of jail.

Chapter 24

Saturday, February 2, 2008

On Saturday morning Sylvia and I went shopping for Brinkman's clothes.

Although I thought our little expedition would require maybe an hour, it lasted nearly six hours, during which time we visited department stores, boutiques, accessory shops, a haberdasher, and a shoe emporium. As I watched, Sylvia carried on endless discussions about colors, styles, combinations, and sizes.

"The idea," she told me when we stopped for a brief lunch, "is that he looks important. If he's going to walk out of police headquarters without ID he's—"

"Got to look the part."

"Exactly!"

By the time we arrived home, we had a gray sports jacket, a white shirt, a blue tie, a pair of black moccasins, glasses with gold frames, and a brown wig.

I was impressed by Sylvia's familiarity with Brinkman's shirt and shoe sizes—further proof, I suspected, that they had gotten to know one another fairly well at the Ariana Hotel in Kabul.

At supper that evening, we hardly spoke. I broke out a bottle of wine, and afterward we disposed of half a bottle of vodka. The tension was getting to us. An hour later, while I was undressing, Sylvia pushed open the bedroom door and gave me a playful shove, which landed me on the bed.

When she fell on top of me, I realized that beneath her blouse she wasn't wearing a bra. Because her blouse was already half unbuttoned, I found it easy to remove.

As I kissed her, I realized this was the moment I knew would eventually arrive.

Even with Brinkman's breakout attempt still three days away, we needed to vent the tension, and now we'd decided how to do it.

But this was also the moment Buck had warned me about.

Although Sylvia and I had been pretending there was no attraction between us, the chemistry had been there from the moment of our first meeting in the army hospital. I followed our first kiss with a second, which was long and intense. I could feel Sylvia's softness against me. Neither of us felt the need to talk, and within seconds, I was oblivious to everything except Sylvia's presence, which somehow seemed to make whatever else was going on in the world unimportant or nonexistent.

I felt myself being pulled into another existence, one where only Sylvia and I mattered and where no one else and nothing else was important.

"Alex, can I talk —"

"Should I stop kissing you?"

Sylvia began to giggle. "No."

On top of the sheets was a thick, soft feather bed, and locked in one another's arms, we were rolling around on top of it. I don't know how much time went by. As I smothered her with kisses, my lips all over her naked body, I heard Sylvia sigh. But then I also heard a voice coming from somewhere.

Is this what you really want?

Yes, yes, it is.

Really?

Irmie! Irmie, is that you?—Is this what you want, Alex? Yes, but I want it with you, Irmie.

And then what was happening in the bedroom somehow wasn't that important. My heart just wasn't in it.

Sylvia drew me to her. But when she tried to kiss me, I didn't respond.

I felt her stiffen.

"What's—what's wrong?"

Irmie, I wish I was holding you in my arms.

"Kiss me again, Alex."

Then I remembered something Buck had said—that Sylvia had been involved with another officer in Afghanistan.

"Is this how it was?" I whispered as Sylvia pressed her lips against mine.

"Was? What do you mean?" Sylvia still had her arms tightly around me. She was still trying to kiss me.

"You know. In Afghanistan. With Doug."

"How what was? What are you talking about?"

"Sure, you know. Doug Brinkman. You and he were in Afghanistan together. At the Ariana Hotel —"

Sylvia was no longer holding me. "What do you know about the Ariana?" And then she was pushing me away. As I continued to talk, she became a different person.

She struggled to sit up, then said, "How do you know that?"

"I figured it out. I know how you feel about Doug—"

"It's none of your goddamned business how I feel about Doug."

And then she was on her feet, gathering up articles of clothing. Her last words before slamming the door were, "You're jealous, aren't you? You bastard!"

Twenty minutes later, I was sprawled on my bed with a magazine when I heard the noise coming from the kitchen. It took me a half minute to figure out what it was—the sound of breaking dishes.

In between each smashed dish there was an interval of perhaps twenty seconds. People have different ways of venting their anger. One of Sylvia's, it seemed, was to throw dishes. Leaving the bedroom, I walked down the corridor and stood at the door of the kitchen. By this time, she'd smashed maybe half a dozen plates and saucers. There were shards of china on the floor and on the counter. The door to the cabinet holding the dishes was wide open.

She whirled around when she saw me, her eyes wide with anger.

I said, "I want to apologize." When a look of bafflement crossed her face, I said quietly, "It was my fault. It shouldn't have happened."

She approached me until her face was six inches in front of mine. Then she said, "You're goddamned right it was your fault." She pushed her way by me.

Keeping my voice low, I said, "You have a right to be mad."

Following her into the foyer, I watched as she grabbed her jacket from the peg next to the door. I said, "I shouldn't have let it happen."

With her hand on the doorknob, she turned to face me. Maybe it was only my imagination, but I thought there was less anger now in her expression. She left the apartment, clicking the door shut behind her.

Although I shouldn't have let things go as far as they went, my main concern now was the thought that our relationship might have permanently altered. If we were going to continue with this operation, we'd have to continue to be a team. Cleaning up the kitchen was my attempt at a peace offering.

By the time she returned an hour later, the kitchen was spotless. I hoped that she noticed it. Unless we continued working together, there was no hope of getting Brinkman out of jail—or for that matter, of staying out of jail ourselves.

Chapter 25

Sunday, February 3, 2008

"One key element is that Brinkman's guards are going to be looking the other way after he enters the fourth-floor washroom."

It was the next day, and Sylvia and I were in the dinette and discussing how we hoped to break Doug Brinkman out of jail. I was doing my best to sound confident.

I said, "The other key element is he'll be wearing civilian clothes. He'll be able to leave the building—providing the alarm hasn't sounded."

"How long will he have?"

As Sylvia refilled my coffee cup, I said, "I figure, a three-minute window that begins when he ducks out of the men's room. Maybe a shade longer than three, but that will depend on Owen. He'll be on the fourth floor, and might be able to divert the guards for a minute. Two minutes, maybe."

Sylvia looked worried. As she replaced the coffee beaker in the machine, she said, "That's not very long. Not for everything he has to do."

Neither Sylvia nor I had discussed the brief amorous interlude of the previous day, which I hoped we'd been able to put behind us.

"We have to get him out of the building during the time when the guards are waiting for him to arrive downstairs—in other words, during the time they think he's still playing ball with them. Once they realize Brinkman isn't heading toward the garage, they'll sound the alarm. And when that happens the building will be sealed up tight."

When I said that, Sylvia went white, and I couldn't blame her. I hated to think of what the consequences of a screwup would be. The way I saw things, Sylvia was making a huge error by insisting we try this stunt.

She said, "But he also has to get past the guard at the entrance and out of the building."

"I'll be holding the inner door open. He waves to the guard behind the glass—and if the alarm hasn't sounded by then, the guard buzzes him out. Brinkman takes the S-Bahn a couple of stops, gets off, and we pick him up."

"You make it sound so easy, Alex."

I spelled out the well-known acronym—KISS, which stands for "Keep It Simple, Stupid!"—and which every operations officer has had pounded into him at some point in his or her training. In devising this plan, I really had focused on making it simple.

I then showed her what I'd been working on during the morning. It was a large official-looking sign: *Ausser Betrieb. Kein Eintritt.*

Sylvia nodded. "Out of order. Stay out."

"I'll paste it up on the door of the men's washroom a few minutes before Brinkman arrives. We don't want any cops barging in while Brinkman is changing and sticking on his wig."

Sylvia asked, "Is the wig really necessary?"

"Where cops are concerned, there are two things that give away an escaped prisoner—shoes and a prison haircut. And over the last two years, because of the terror threat they've really beefed up security at the Police Presidium. In fact, from what I understand some terror suspects tried to break out just last month. That caused them to beef things up even further."

"When you talk like that, you scare me. This has to succeed."

"Brinkman's hearing is scheduled for Tuesday afternoon, fourteen thirty hours. It should only last a couple of minutes. Owen will be there. He calls me on his cell phone precisely when Brinkman exits the hearing room. And that's when I move."

After a moment of silence, Sylvia said quietly, "I see."

I had to admire Sylvia's determination—and her courage. I was aware of the highly pressurized and brutally competitive world in which she worked. I had to admit to myself that, in her position and with so much to lose, I wouldn't dream of trying anything this risky or this dangerous. The careers of people in the special ops business come to a screeching halt when this kind of operation fails to succeed.

Chapter 26

Tuesday, February 5, 2008

Munich's Police Presidium is a large, green, fortresslike building located a couple of hundred yards from the City Hall, which is itself located on the Marienplatz, the center of the city. No vehicles are permitted in downtown Munich—and as I stood in the pedestrians-only area outside the building, I was again reminded just how fortresslike the building is. The walls are thick, and thirty feet beyond the main entrance is a ten-foot high wall. When I entered, two guards in green and khaki police uniforms were on duty, each with an automatic weapon slung over his shoulder.

When they asked me the nature of my business, I said I had an appointment with Detective Schneider of the *Mordkommission*. The guards were another obstacle we had to contend with, and one that could cause problems.

But in the crowded neighborhood of downtown Munich, the automatic weapons were for show, not for shooting.

As I waited for the guard behind the glass to buzz me in, I recalled once being part of a team testing security precautions at an Air Force installation in Italy. I knew how quickly even the most carefully worked out procedures could be forgotten and even the most secure setups breached. The important thing was, as a guard, not to let yourself become distracted. Although that is easier said than done, the uniformed guards outside seemed observant and, with their automatic weapons, mildly menacing. The success or failure of our little scheme was going to depend on absolutely perfect timing. Harry Owen had his role, I had mine, and Doug Brinkman had his.

What were the chances that each of us would carry out his role perfectly? I figured about one in a thousand.

My appointment with Detective Schneider was for 1400 hours. Brinkman's meeting was scheduled for 1430, but would probably last no more than ten minutes, if that. I was assuming it would begin on time. Punctuality in Germany is more than a virtue; it's an obsession.

Before heading to Schneider's office, I walked from one end of the third-floor corridor to the other and back, preparing myself for every imaginable contingency, and I could feel the adrenalin rush. The corridor was empty. Doing my best to appear casual and trying to ignore my heart, which was beating like a jackhammer, I checked out the men's washroom where we intended for Brinkman to do his quick-change act. I hoped he could find it. A couple of uniformed cops were inside, talking about a soccer match. I washed my hands and left. The room would have to be empty for Brinkman to use it.

I headed toward the section of the building housing the homicide squad. At a few minutes after 1400 hours, I knocked on Schneider's door.

"This is a nice office you have, Detective Schneider."

"They renovated this end of the building a couple of years ago. One big difference is the lighting." Schneider pointed to a fluorescent fixture. "Much brighter than it used to be."

"Nothing but the best for the homicide squad."

Schneider nodded. "Give me a second, will you, Klear? I have something here I have to finish up."

"Kein Problem." No problem.

Irmie's desk was empty. I was glad of that. After less than five minutes, Schneider tossed down his pen and removed his glasses.

"So what's the information you want to give us, Mr. Klear?" On his face was an impatient frown.

"It has to do with the murder in the K Klub." When Schneider nodded, I said, "I'd try to find out just what happened in Afghanistan. That might give some clue to what's been going on out at that club."

"This was a while ago, wasn't it?" Schneider said. He seemed distracted, and I had the idea his mind was on something else.

"Last year sometime."

"Klear, listen. We're just the local police. We have problems just keeping up with the situation in this city. How the hell are we supposed to investigate something that happened so far away?"

"One way might be to question the people out at the Kalashni Klub. They know more than they're telling—"

At that moment the door opened, and a detective stepped into the office. He looked at me, then at Schneider.

Schneider frowned. "I've got other cases, Klear."

"I know." I got to my feet. "I understand."

When I was at the door, he said, "We'll be in touch."

It was 1420 hours—two twenty—when I left Schneider's office. But the way I figured, it was still too early to tack up the sign on the washroom door. Moving purposefully, I went from the section of the building holding the *Mordkommission* toward the older part of the presidium. Some people entered and exited the offices. Two secretaries carried on a brief conversation before heading off in different directions.

I paused to read a bulletin board. I stopped at a stone fountain, which was a memorial to fallen policemen. I checked my watch: 1425.

The room in which I assumed Brinkman's hearing would soon take place was one flight up.

After some more dawdling, I figured it was time to tack up the sign, which I was carrying in a shopping bag along with the clothing and wig. Brinkman would have to move quickly to get this stuff on in time.

I started back in the direction of the washroom and had gone only a few yards when my cell phone rang. It was Harry Owen calling from upstairs. "Brinkman just left the hearing room."

"Already? I thought—"

"We were only in there for five minutes, maybe less. No judge, just a clerk, and she was a no-nonsense type. Brinkman's got two guards with him. They're walking up the corridor. No handcuffs. Wait. Okay. They've stopped in front of the latrine. He's going inside. He'll be down in a minute. I'll start talking to these guys."

"Got it."

Within seconds, I'd tacked up the sign, which would indicate to Brinkman the washroom in which to find the clothing.

Inside were two men, one in uniform and one in civvies. After washing his hands, the cop left. The other guy then decided to run a comb through his thinning hair. I could have told him not to bother but he wanted to make every strand count. Then, just as he pushed open the door to leave, Brinkman barged in.

Brinkman was wearing his prison uniform. His eyes were wide, and the tension was written all over his face. Fortunately, the guy who was leaving was still thinking about his hair and didn't seem to notice.

I nodded, pointed toward the shopping bag, then stepped outside. I was wearing jeans and a flannel shirt, and in an effort to appear like a janitor, I slipped off my jacket and slung it over my shoulder. Just as I did, two young cops approached.

"Sorry, fellas." I pointed to the sign. "We've got a small flood inside. The urinals are all overflowing. The plumber's on his way."

"Hey man, c'mon. I'll be pissing in—"

"What can I tell you? It's a real mess in there."

"I have to get back to—"

"What's with you guys? Use the washroom at the other end!"

Still grumbling, the cops left, and I assumed Brinkman was changing. We were already running behind schedule, and I figured we didn't have much more than a minute before the guards upstairs would realize they'd lost their prisoner. I felt a sinking feeling. We'd never make it.

But there was no turning back now.

After waiting another twenty seconds and turning away another customer, I took off down the stairway on my way to the main entrance. We needed every last second, and I was hoping that Harry Owen on the fourth floor had a song and dance to distract the two guards and buy another minute.

At the entrance there were a couple of people talking to the policeman behind the glass and fumbling for some ID. As the guard continued to talk with his visitors, I waved, but he didn't seem to notice. I needed to have the door open when Brinkman arrived.

By the time the guard looked in my direction, a half minute had passed.

Where was Brinkman?

With the door open, and thinking Brinkman would show, I hesitated, then began searching through my pockets.

But at that moment I saw the policeman behind the glass holding a telephone to his ear. He frowned, said something into the phone, and nodded. Then he waved to me to close the door and step into the lobby. His alarmed expression indicated he knew there was an escaped prisoner in the building. A minute later, two armed policemen entered the lobby. They conferred with the guard behind the glass, checked my ID, and told me to leave.

Outside, I pushed through the downtown shoppers and dawdlers, and headed around the corner to Donisl, the big restaurant in which I was supposed to meet Sylvia. I found her in one of the high-backed booths along the wall. On the table in front of her were a glass of white wine and her cell phone. She looked at me questioningly.

As I slid into the booth, I shook my head.

"No sign of him."

"Damn!"

"He made it down to the washroom. I waited downstairs. He never showed at the main entrance." I shrugged. The thought occurred to me that the best battle plans last only until the battle starts. Evidently, the same rule holds true for jailbreak plans.

A waiter asked me what I wanted. Pointing at Sylvia's glass, I said, "The same."

"He had time. It was over four minutes between his arrival on the third floor and when they got the alarm downstairs." I paused. "It might have worked. He only had to—"

"But it didn't work." She gulped some wine. "What could have gone wrong? Someone caught him changing clothes?"

"I don't think so. I waited outside the washroom for over a minute. Like I say, it—"

"I know. It could have worked. Save it, Alex." Sylvia's expression was full of suppressed rage. "Save the excuses and explanations, okay?"

"Look, I'm only trying to—"

"I'm so fed up with you it's hard to describe." Maybe Sylvia was still mad about our bedroom interlude. I couldn't help thinking about how badly I'd handled that situation. And she continued to harp on the fact that I'd let the woman at the Kalashni Klub escape. Now, it appeared, I'd bungled the jail breakout.

Something else I was thinking of was how pleasant life had been back in Saranac, where the week's biggest problem was a disgruntled customer.

"All I'm trying to say is—"

"It didn't work. That's all that counts. I don't want to hear it."

When the waiter brought the wine, I took a long swallow. Sylvia looked at me silently, then directed her gaze into her own wine glass. The color had gone out of her cheeks, and the lines in her forehead were pronounced. She was, no doubt, anticipating what the fallout from our little stunt figured to be. When Jerry Shenlee got the news, he'd pass it on to the NSC, and from there it would go to the deputy secretary of defense. As far as Sylvia's career was concerned, this would be more than a bump in the road.

When the cops caught Brinkman, they'd go through his pockets. I asked myself what they'd find—an S-Bahn ticket, a cell phone, some money, the number of Sylvia's cell phone. At least her number was untraceable. Jerry Shenlee had made sure of that.

I caught the waiter's eye, and when I told him to bring me another wine, Sylvia also asked for one. When the waiter returned, I exchanged our empty glasses for two full glasses. In the last five minutes neither Sylvia nor I had said anything. All we'd done is gulp wine.

As I took another long swallow, Sylvia's cell phone began ringing. She grabbed it.

"Hello— Yes— My God! Are you—? Where?" Gazing wide-eyed across the table, she began nodding excitedly. "It's him. It's Doug." I grabbed the phone.

"This is Alex. Where are you?"

"I'm at the East Railroad station. On the platform. What do I do?"

"Grab the first train going south."

"There's an S-3. It's about to leave."

"Take it. It'll take you to Holzkirchen. Get off there." I thought quickly. "Look for a restaurant called Oberland. But don't go in. We'll meet you across the street. There's a train ticket in the pocket. Make sure it's canceled. Get going."

I threw some money down on the table. "C'mon." On the way to the door, I said, "If the cops don't grab him in the train, he'll be in Holzkirchen in forty-five minutes. Where's the car?"

"In a garage, two minutes from here," Sylvia said, pointing the way and handing me the keys.

Chapter 27

Tuesday, February 5, 2008

Holzkirchen is a small city in the northern foothills of the Alps, and I figured we'd need at least a half hour to drive down there. Since she'd be taking Brinkman somewhere and didn't know how long she'd be gone from the safe house, Sylvia had tossed all her personal stuff, a large suitcase and a small suitcase, into the trunk of the car before leaving.

As we drove, she said, "Something else, Alex. I've gotten rid of everything that you brought back from the Vogt woman's place. Whatever was worth keeping I have with me."

The autobahn heading south is a heavily traveled highway that leads toward Salzburg, and twenty miles south of Munich I turned onto a secondary highway that would take us straight into Holzkirchen.

"What do you think happened?" Sylvia asked. "How did he get out?"

"No idea." There were still a number of things that could go wrong, and I was worried that the cops would be watching all the S-Bahn lines closely. Any male traveling alone would attract their attention. It now occurred to me that I should have suggested a stop closer to Munich, but there are seven or eight different lines, and Holzkirchen was the only stop that I recalled on the S-3. The longer Brinkman was in the train, the more chance there was that he could be nailed.

I'd begun to sweat and I was conscious of clutching the steering wheel as I drove.

When we reached Holzkirchen, I drove through the narrow streets and without any difficulty found the Oberland. It was a medium-sized hotel and restaurant, a landmark not far from the railroad station that would be easy for Brinkman to find. I parked the car on the street some fifty yards beyond the hotel. When Brinkman showed, we'd spot him without any difficulty.

The problem was, he didn't show. Two trains came and went. People got off and came walking out of the station, but none of them was Brinkman. When I checked my watch, I saw that well over an hour had elapsed since he'd made the call.

"What now?" Sylvia asked after the second train left the station. "Shouldn't he have been on one of those?" When I only nodded, Sylvia said, "What now, Alex?"

I was about to say the cops could have grabbed him on the train, but there was no sense tossing in the towel—not when we'd come this far.

I said, "We wait."

Sitting in the car parked in the narrow street, we waited another twenty minutes. Beads of perspiration kept forming on my forehead. Sylvia's breathing became so labored it began to sound like gasping. I was ready to announce that it was pointless to wait any longer.

Then, in the rearview mirror, I spotted a distant figure riding uncertainly up the narrow street on a bicycle. When he reached the intersection, he stopped pedaling and looked around. He seemed to be out of breath.

The cycler caught my attention because of what he was wearing— a gray sports jacket, a jacket the same color as the one Sylvia and I had bought for Brinkman—and he had on a white shirt, blue tie, and dark-gray pants. He was dressed like Brinkman. When he started riding again and got closer, I made out his face—Doug Brinkman! I jumped out of the car and waved my arms. He saw me and started riding toward us. When he pulled up alongside, we exchanged silent high fives, and I tossed the bike into the trunk of the car.

As Brinkman climbed in, he and Sylvia exchanged glances, and if I had any doubts about them being lovers, they disappeared at that moment. I got the engine going and eased the vehicle into traffic.

"I can't believe I made it," Brinkman said. He was breathing heavily, obviously out of breath from riding fast.

"What in the world happened?" Sylvia asked, her voice a combination of panic and relief.

"What could go wrong, did go wrong," Brinkman said. "Were you guys worried?"

"Of course not," I said. "A Green Beret can do anything. Isn't that what they used to tell us at Fort Bragg?"

"Yeah, but who believed that stuff?"

Five minutes later, I pulled off the highway into a small rest area just south of the city. While we sat there, Brinkman told us the story.

"The reason I didn't make it down to the entrance was I got lost. I went the wrong way when I left the washroom and couldn't find the fire stairs. So I just decided to keep moving. A couple of women unlocked a door, and I just followed them down a flight of stairs and I ended up in the employees' canteen. I saw people leaving, but I could see they were all showing ID to some cops at the door. Then I saw a fella with a container of coffee knock on a door on the other end and someone on the other side of the door opened it. I grabbed a half-empty container off one of the tables and did what he did. When someone on the other side unlocked the door, I was in a room with a lot of chairs and a lot of people with pads and pencils standing around. A couple of cops were on a podium gathering up papers and talking."

When Sylvia looked at me, I said, "The briefing room for members of the press. It's on the first floor, next to the canteen."

"Nobody expected me to turn up there," Brinkman said.

"What did you do?" Sylvia asked.

"Some kind of meeting was breaking up and as the people started drifting out, I drifted out with them. An exit was right there. A couple of cops showed up and started checking people, but I just walked by as if I was too important to show ID."

I took a quick glance at Sylvia. I'd been skeptical, but by picking out the right clothes for Brinkman, she might very well have averted disaster. No wonder the secretary of defense had confidence in her.

Brinkman said, "I don't think they expected an escaped prisoner to be in that group. I went right by them and found myself in a street next to a museum."

I nodded. "The hunter's museum. The rear door of the police build-ing exits on the Augustinerstrasse. You weren't far from Marienplatz."

"I saw that, so I went down into the S-Bahn." The S-Bahn is the subway, Munich's answer to the London Underground and the Paris Metro.

I said, "You called us from the East Railroad Station."

Brinkman nodded. "I was on the platform. But the next train I took only went a couple of stations when it stopped—I forget the name, began with a U."

"Unterhaching?"

"I think so. Anyway, I waited a minute, then took a look around. The conductor was talking to the train operator, and I figured they ex-pected to be there a while. I didn't like that. I thought the local cops might show up and start looking through the train."

"What then?" Sylvia asked.

"I might have been right. As I left the station, four cops came marching up the steps. I stayed behind a concrete pillar, then exited the station. My problem then was getting down here. My first thought was to take a taxi, but a driver could have asked questions and maybe caused problems. I went by a bicycle shop. Since I found five hundred euros in the pocket of the jacket I decided I'd buy a bicycle. The owner was real friendly. I guess he was happy to sell a bike."

Looking at me, Brinkman said, "I still can't believe it worked. Someone deserves a lot of credit for pulling this off."

"It's what we get paid for," Sylvia said coolly. "I spoke with Harry Owen a few minutes ago on the phone. He said he kept asking the guards for directions, playing the role of the dumb American. He was able to keep them busy, and that bought us a few extra minutes."

I didn't say anything. The truth was, we weren't anywhere near out of the woods yet. We were in a car parked just off the road twenty-five miles south of Munich. We still needed to get Brinkman out of the country. I assumed Sylvia knew how to take care of that end of things.

Looking at me, she said, "You and I still have things to talk over." Still wearing his suit and tie, Brinkman looked more like a lawyer than an escaped prisoner, and I figured it was safe to leave him in the parked car for a few minutes. Sylvia told him to wait while she and I took a short stroll.

As we walked along the highway, Sylvia said, "The police might try to connect you to Doug's escape. Have your story ready."

"Yes, ma'am." I shrugged. "Whatever they think, they can't prove anything."

I was wondering when we could wind up this operation. Although Sedfrit was the primary suspect in Quemal's murder, it was still possible that the cops might determine he was innocent. If that happened, they'd look for another suspect—and that very well could be me. I wanted to be out of Munich before that happened.

I said, "Have you talked with D.C.?"

"Of course. I had approval for this operation, if that's what you're wondering. We have to keep Doug under wraps—"

"Major Brinkman, you mean."

Sylvia colored. After a second, she said, "While they're working out the details for getting Major Brinkman out of the country, he stays with me. People won't breathe easy until they know he's on a plane back to the States."

"How long do you figure?"

"Two days, maybe three. There'll be some red tape. There always is. I'll be back as soon as I can make it. If the police call you down, don't volunteer anything."

I wondered where Sylvia was headed—probably to another safe house somewhere, and then to one of our military installations. Her people in D.C. would have indicated where she and Brinkman could hole up. I assumed that she and Doug might use this opportunity to renew old acquaintances. After Brinkman had shaken himself loose from Ursula Vogt, Sylvia showed up in Afghanistan, and they'd almost certainly become lovers out there.

I wasn't jealous. The only woman I ever thought about was Irmie. And I thought about her day and night.

"Something else, Alex. See what you can find out about Nadaj."

I wondered how I was supposed to manage that.

We'd walked in a circle, and now we were back at the car where Brinkman was waiting. The only other car in the rest area contained a married couple and two small children, who were eating sandwiches. It was a miracle, but so far, the cops hadn't caught up with us. I gave her the keys and Sylvia climbed in behind the wheel.

"I'll be with Doug for a couple of days. Remember, Nadaj is still a high-value target."

"It might be easier for me if I knew why we're so interested in Nadaj." Sylvia was silent for a moment, probably figuring just how much I needed to know. In this business the rule is ironclad. You don't tell anyone anything. But we both knew I needed more of a sense of what was going on.

After a second, Sylvia nodded at Brinkman. "Tell us how you met Ursula."

Leaning forward from the back seat, Brinkman began to talk. "It was in Mazar-e-Sharif, maybe six months into my first tour. We were getting ready to move into the Shahikot Valley."

Sylvia said, "I was out there. It's just a small town, but there was a walled-in compound on the outskirts. Our people set up a prison there."

I was familiar with Mazar-e-Sharif, where the CIA lost an interrogator during the first days of the war. Looking at Brinkman, I said, "You were with the Fifth Group?" I was referring to the Special Forces Group then active in Afghanistan.

Brinkman nodded. "Headquarters Detachment, Third Battalion. We were reconnoitering, trying to figure the best way into the mountains when we got a radio alert. Something was going down back in Mazar-e-Sharif, at the prison. So I rounded up as many guys as I could, and we headed up there."

"Tell him what you found," Sylvia said.

"It was bad," Brinkman said. "Our people had taken over five hundred al-Qaeda prisoners, but we had only a dozen guys guarding them. They'd begun to riot, and they'd managed to bang a big hole in one of the walls. Just as we arrived, the prisoners started pouring through. The guards had taken cover, but they wouldn't have had a chance against those numbers."

"How'd you manage it?" I asked.

"I was driving a Toyota pickup. Drove it right up against the wall where the break was, climbed out. I know a little Pashto. I started shouting, *Wadarega yaa dee wulim!* Halt or we'll shoot! We stuck our weapons right in front of these guys' noses. I don't know how good my pronunciation was. *Zaman da amruno paerawi wukra!* Follow our orders or get shot!"

Looking at me, Sylvia said, "They got the message."

"I let go a couple of bursts right over their heads," Brinkman said. "That helped. They started backing off. When they saw how the rounds chewed up the wall, they began to quiet down."

"Doug makes it sound easy," Sylvia said. "He risked his life doing that."

Brinkman shrugged. "It took a while, but we were finally able to herd them all back inside."

"He was awarded the DSC," Sylvia said quietly.

"Right after we got things settled down, we called for reinforcements. It was around that time that Ursula Vogt showed up. She identified herself as a correspondent for a Kraut newspaper. Said she wanted to talk with me about what happened. I gave her the whole story right from the beginning." He paused, looked at Sylvia. "After that, one thing led to another."

"She began chasing you around," Sylvia said.

"I should have known better, should have known it was too good to be true, having this good-looking dame showing up all the time. When I was back in Kabul, she turned up there, and we got to know one another a little better. Then she went back home. That was January 2004."

Brinkman looked at Sylvia as though getting permission to tell the rest of the story.

"Anyway, I was reassigned to Bragg, but Ursula and I stayed in contact, mostly through e-mail. A year later, our outfit deployed again. Then Ursula showed up again."

"Only now she was with *Welt-Bericht*," Sylvia said. "Working for Kurt Mehling. And she started taping all your conversations."

Brinkman grimaced. "She called them interviews."

I recalled the X-rated tapes Sylvia had played for my benefit at the apartment. Brinkman and Ursula Vogt had seen quite a bit of one another.

Sylvia said, "What she was looking for was admissions that we'd violated the Geneva Convention."

"Hell, what she was looking for was admissions that we'd used sarin gas up in the mountains."

I perked up when I heard that. Sarin is a particularly deadly nerve gas. I knew there had been some talk of Saddam Hussein possessing sarin—and that he'd used it to put down a rebellion of his own people in the years following the First Gulf War.

Sylvia looked at me. "Ursula Vogt wanted to know if we were using sarin gas in Afghanistan."

When Brinkman nodded, I said, "What did you say?"

"At first I wasn't paying that much attention. I didn't say the right thing. I said I knew we had sarin stockpiled somewhere, but I wasn't sure where. I never said we used it. She asked if we'd brought any of it to Afghanistan. I said I didn't know. She talked constantly about sarin gas. After a time I became suspicious, and finally I tumbled to what she was after."

Sylvia said, "It was Mehling who put her up to asking these questions."

I could visualize the situation readily enough. Kurt Mehling had baited the trap with an attractive woman. Probably most of the quotes Ursula Vogt had gotten from Brinkman were pillow talk—comments that Brinkman had made in an unguarded moment. But even a handful of taped quotes could become dynamite on the printed page and in another context—and particularly if they could be attributed to a decorated officer in America's elite Special Forces. This wasn't the first time that a reporter had taken advantage of an unwitting member of the military in order to land a story, and almost certainly wouldn't be the last.

"Anyway, I knew I had to report what had been going on. It went up the line and eventually all the way back to D.C."

"I was assigned to come over and determine what had happened," Sylvia said. "After speaking with Major Brinkman, I decided to have him stay close to the Vogt woman. After that, he was working for us, trying to find out what he could about Kurt Mehling."

I said, "But they didn't print the story back then. Why not?"

After Brinkman and Sylvia exchanged glances, Sylvia said, "That was because of Ursula Vogt. Although some people might question her methods, she was an honest reporter. Mehling had hired her away from one of the big newspapers where she'd built her reputation. She was talking to other people and began to doubt whether the United States had really used sarin after all. She told Doug she felt there was something fishy in the way the magazine had insisted she write that story. By the time she was back in Munich, she no longer believed it had really happened."

I said, "That's why they killed her."

"She was ready to go public with what she knew and what she thought. You brought back her complete story, Alex. It was on one of the discs. She wrote a long article describing a conspiracy to make it appear the United States had used sarin gas.

"They moved quickly. Nadaj sent Quemal to kill the Vogt woman. Although Quemal was a logical suspect, Mehling fixed the investigation, right down to pressuring the homicide cops who were assigned to the case. They were told to concentrate the investigation on Major Brinkman."

The pieces were falling into place. When I spoke with Max shortly after arriving in Munich, he'd been wary of the case, almost as if he'd smelled a rat. And Max would have been doubly careful if he'd thought the case reflected badly on the Munich cops. Even Thiemann, Ursula Vogt's neighbor, said he thought Quemal might have been the murderer. It was an effective job of framing an innocent man—and I could now see why Sylvia was so eager to get Brinkman out of prison.

Considering that she'd personally assigned him to stay close to Ursula Vogt, Sylvia was largely responsible for Brinkman. No wonder she pulled out all the stops to break him out of prison. Mehling was worried about what Brinkman might say if the case went to trial. But with Ursula Vogt and Brinkman both dead, Mehling could have run the sarin gas story in *Welt-Bericht*—and safely speculated that Brinkman had killed Ursula Vogt as part of a cover-up by the American government.

Who knows what else they could have written.

On the S-Bahn riding back to Munich, I realized that there was a piece of the puzzle still missing, something that Sylvia still hadn't told me. She hadn't said why it was still important for us to get our hands on Ramush Nadaj. And another question was: Why did Ursula Vogt honestly believe the United States had used sarin gas if we never had?

Something had happened back in Afghanistan that might provide the answer to both those questions. Sylvia's revelations confirmed some things I'd already suspected. But I hadn't known anything about sarin gas.

When I arrived back in the apartment, I found a text message on my cell phone: Will arrive Munich in two days. Buck.

Even though I was tired, I lay awake for most of the night, probably because I couldn't get these new revelations out of my mind. Buck had planned to talk with the senator on the Intelligence Committee, and as I tossed and turned, I wondered if he might have found out anything about sarin gas.

I was still awake when, early the next morning, the first rays of sunshine peeped through a crack in the curtains.

Chapter 28

Wednesday, February 6, 2008

While I was drinking a second cup of coffee, I called Sylvia's cell phone and left a message. I figured Brinkman would be flying out of Ramstein Air Base, but using a military installation to aid an escaped prisoner would make the German government very unhappy—and would probably be the cause of a flurry of notes and protests flying back and forth across the Atlantic. It would be Sylvia's job to make sure that the German government remained none the wiser.

With Sylvia and Brinkman using the car, I decided I'd be needing wheels, and rented a black Mercedes E350 from one of the downtown agencies. But while I was on the highway that circles the city, I became aware of a blue Audi on my tail and as I went by the Olympic Stadium I speeded up, and he speeded up. When I changed lanes, he changed lanes. Whoever it was, he didn't seem concerned by the fact that I'd made him, but continued to maintain enough distance to keep me from seeing who he was. I got off the Ring and turned into Schwabing, Munich's answer to Greenwich Village. When I glanced into the mirror, I saw the Audi had reappeared, and was proceeding slowly up the narrow street.

I found a parking space twenty yards from the corner. Although the Audi went by slowly and halted a few yards beyond where I'd parked, I still couldn't get a look at the driver. I exited my car and strolled across the sidewalk to a shop window. I used the reflection to watch the other driver as he backed into an empty space. When he climbed out, I recognized Detective Paul Schneider.

I should have known. Only a cop would tail someone so obviously. I supposed the idea was to make me nervous.

Even wearing a black leather jacket and brown corduroy pants, Schneider looked like a policeman, largely from the way he walked, or swaggered—with an attitude and as if he owned the street. He waved, then with his hands in both jacket pockets and a friendly smile on his face, he came strolling up the sidewalk in my direction. As it happened, the store window I was staring into was a woman's boutique, a detail that struck him as funny.

He pointed to a dress on one of the manikins. "I think you'd look good in blue. I wonder if they have it in your size."

I said, "In the States that's a remark that even a cop couldn't get away with."

"What you people over there need is more law and order. More respect for people in authority."

"How would you know?" I said.

"I spent my vacation in the States a couple of years ago—rented a motorcycle, biked around for three weeks. Enjoyed it."

He nodded in the direction of a small café on the corner. "C'mon. You feel like a cup of coffee? I'm buying."

Inside the café were mostly middle-aged women, all seemingly talking at once. I found a table in the rear next to the big glass window. Across the street a shapely blonde emerged from a beauty salon. As I watched, she strolled up the sidewalk.

"Not a hair out of place," Schneider said grinning, as he placed two cups of coffee, two crullers, and a handful of napkins on the table. As he eased himself down on the chair, I realized how big he was. No question that he was a serious iron pumper.

Without preamble, he said, "You're good, Klear. Real good. And I mean that."

I took a sip of coffee. "Good at what?" The remark sounded mildly ominous. I knew Schneider hadn't arranged this meeting just to pay me compliments.

"Let me explain. It goes back to this murder case Detective Nessler caught. The dead Albanian in that warehouse? First, you let on to me and my partner that you've got some kind of interest in this Quemal individual because he was down in Kosovo, but you also knew that he had spent time in Afghanistan. At the same time you tell us you're here in Munich as a tourist."

"Anything wrong with that?"

"Only that we wondered why a tourist would know anything about some character from Kosovo. Kosovo? Afghanistan? I mean, what's the connection? Of course with an American passport you're permitted to spend up to three months in the Federal Republic without a visa. No problem there. You haven't committed any crimes. But naturally, my partner and I had to wonder about your interest. And to be honest, Detective Nessler and I are still wondering."

I nodded. "Sure. But I was also very up front about the fact I once worked over here."

"That's true. From what I understand, you worked for the American government's radio station in the English Garden."

"You're well informed."

He shook his head. "Not really. I only know that because Max Peters mentioned it. Max was the police liaison with you guys for a long time."

"Max was good at it too. He always knew how to smooth over the rough waters and keep everyone happy."

"Max was a good cop. But that radio operation was a cover for spies and intelligence people. Everyone knows that. Not to mention all the East bloc exiles you people had working for you. Malcontents and pests, mostly. Anyway, Detective Nessler and I were willing to cut you a little slack there. And we appreciated your information that this Quemal might have had something to do with the murder at the Albanian club."

"I was trying to help."

"Like I say, we appreciated that. I think everyone in law enforcement agrees that we should all share information and work together. Particularly these days with all this international terrorism. Right?"

"I'm not with intelligence anymore." I took another sip of coffee.

"Oh right, I forgot." He smiled. "But then, Klear, something extraordinary happened."

"What was that?"

"This Quemal, the very person you mentioned. He turns up dead, murdered by person or persons unknown."

"Unknown? I thought you'd arrested someone."

"Just because we arrest someone doesn't mean he's guilty. I'll be candid, Klear. I would have brought you in for questioning right then and there."

"But you didn't."

"It was my partner, Detective Nessler. She said she saw things differently. She thought we should concentrate the investigation on this individual who had the big public argument with Quemal just before Quemal was murdered. And, of course, there was also the matter of the murdered guy having his testicles sawed off. That made it appear as if someone was sending a message. These Balkan people will do things like that sometimes."

"It sounds to me like the pieces all fit together. Like you have your man."

"That's the way things appeared at first, all signs pointing to this Sedfrit individual as the murderer."

"So?"

"We gave him a real going over. But the more I spoke with him, the more I got another impression."

"Let me guess. He said he was innocent." When Schneider grinned, I said, "Don't they all say that?"

"That's right. They do. No criminal wants to admit he committed a crime, and was so clumsy that even the cops were able to figure out who did it."

"Bad for a lawbreaker's image."

"Very bad. But Sedfrit, I have to admit, came across as a cool character, and not dumb."

"In other words, not an individual to have a public argument with someone and then knock the person off an hour later."

"Sedfrit has no record of violence. He settles things in other ways."

"But still—"

"I know, I know. There's always the possibility that he might have blown his cool on this occasion, and I've factored that into the situation. Something else I've factored in is that he has an alibi of sorts."

"What kind of alibi?"

"He was getting his arm patched up at the doctor's." When I asked if the doctor was from Kosovo, Schneider smiled.

"If you don't think Sedfrit killed Quemal, where does that leave you?"

"It leaves us right back at square one. Because I know it's not going to do us one damn bit of good to arrest the other prime suspect."

"Who would that be?"

"You, of course. Like I say, Klear, you're real good. I just don't see us squeezing anything like a confession out of you. You're tougher than you appear, I can tell that. But then this other thing happens."

I took a swallow of coffee, gazed into Schneider's dark eyes. "What other thing?" I didn't like the direction in which this little talk was headed.

"Maybe I was a little slow in making the connections. This American Green Beret who'd been indicted for murdering the Vogt woman? He broke out of jail yesterday, walked out of the Police Presidium under the noses of the guards."

"You're kidding."

"Unfortunately, I'm not."

"Well, maybe you can recapture him before he leaves the country."

"We'll try, but I'm not optimistic. All he has to do is get onto one of the American military installations. They'll fly him back to the States. No problemo."

"Hold on, Detective. Are you saying the American government would aid a murderer to escape German justice?"

"The American government is not a bunch of angels, Klear, as you and I well know. Not only that, I'm also saying that an agent of the American government may have helped this Brinkman character to break out."

Doing my best to ignore Schneider's smirk, I said, "What happened exactly?"

"Well, there's no question that Brinkman had help. But the stories are all pretty murky. He was in the presidium to get some forms signed. Two guards who were supposed to return him back downstairs let him use the washroom, and somehow he got out of the washroom without them seeing him. Their story sounds fishy, but the captain of the guards vouches for them."

"How did he get out of the building?"

Schneider shrugged. "What's more amazing is we have our cameras over all the building entrances."

I said, "Didn't they see anyone?"

"Nothing at the time. We monitor the cameras in the *Einsatz Zentrale*, right in the presidium. But on one of the tapes we got from the transit people there was a guy who could have been Brinkman going into the S-Bahn. His hair was different, but he might have had a wig on."

"Didn't you search the trains?"

"Sure. We stopped every train he could have been on."

"No luck?"

"None. It was like he disappeared into thin air."

"Amazing. But like I say, maybe the police will catch up with Brinkman."

Schneider shook his head. "No, Klear, that's unlikely. Brinkman won't have any difficulty getting out of the country, not if the American government wants him out." Schneider glanced quickly at me, then took a last bite of cruller and wiped his mouth. "But as clever as these people obviously were, I think they may have left one loose end."

"Really? What would that be?"

"You."

"Me? What do I have to do with anything?"

"I think you were involved with the Green Beret breaking out of prison, Klear. You were in the building. In fact you were in our office."

"I only wanted to remind you and Detective Nessler about some of the details of the situation I thought you might be overlooking in your investigation."

"Sure, Klear. That was real considerate. You're a sweetheart." Schneider placed the plates, cups, and napkins on the tray and climbed to his feet. When we were back outside, I thanked him for the coffee.

"My pleasure. Oh, one more thing, Klear. We're not arresting you, but I'm going to have to ask you to surrender your passport."

"It sounds like I'm a suspect."

"Klear, if you didn't murder anyone and if you didn't take part in this jailbreak, you've got absolutely nothing to worry about, believe me. Like I said before, I'm not mad at anyone."

"You're just a cop doing his job."

"You got it." After I'd handed over my passport, Schneider glanced through it, then handed me a receipt that he'd already dated and signed. "I'll be in touch." He turned to go, but all at once stopped. "Oh, one more thing I should mention."

"What's that?"

"I guess I should have told you sooner. It slipped my mind. We asked an investigating judge to issue a *Durchsuchungsbefehl* for this apartment you're staying in. All very official. In fact there are a couple of detectives going through your place right now. How do you say *Durchsuchungsbefehl* in English?"

"Search warrant." I said the words quietly, glumly. I could feel a sudden shudder shoot through my entire body, almost as if someone had shoved me into a pool of ice water. There was something at the safe house that the police absolutely must not find.

As he headed up the street, Schneider tossed a quick wave. "I have to be getting along. Like I say, I'll be in touch."

After climbing back into the Mercedes, I sat for a while before turning over the engine. I'd wrapped the gun in a piece of cloth and taped it to the bottom of a drawer in my bedroom closet. It might elude a search—or might not. If the cops found the weapon, it would be a simple matter to determine that it was the gun that fired the slug that killed Quemal.

In that case, I'd be facing a murder charge. Since EU nations don't exact the death penalty, I'd be looking at life in a German slammer, which might well be a fate worse than death. I turned the ignition key, heard the car's engine roar to life, waited for a small van to pass, then eased the vehicle into traffic. I resisted an urge to blow my cool—to push the accelerator to the floor and drive the Mercedes at top speed into a brick wall or into some oncoming vehicle, preferably a large truck. I could feel perspiration on my forehead and a sick feeling in my stomach. As I threaded my way through Munich's narrow streets and downtown traffic, I thought about the parting words of Jerry Shenlee— that I'd be traveling overseas as a tourist. In a roundabout way, but in no uncertain terms, Jerry was saying that if I got myself into trouble, I'd have to get myself out—and shouldn't expect the American government to provide any help.

In other words, Jerry was saying, don't get tangled up in anything you can't get out of on your own.

I wondered if Sylvia might have any ideas. She hadn't called, and I wondered why. As I drove, I punched her number into my cell phone. She answered almost immediately.

"Alex, I'm sorry I didn't call. I've been busy all morning." When I asked her where she was, she said, "I have to be vague about that."

I assumed that Sylvia and Brinkman were on their way to a military installation, quite possibly Ramstein Air Base, which houses the 86th Airlift Wing, and quite a few low-profile military operations as well, stuff that foreign governments don't have to know anything about. Once they were on the base, they'd cut a set of flight orders, and Brinkman would be on his way back to the States on the first aircraft with an available seat. That would be tomorrow morning.

"How are you managing?"

I didn't see where I had a choice but to pass on the information I got from Schneider. "I'm fine, but there are some problems."

"What kind of problems?"

"Some things I think you should know about."

"Listen, Alex. This isn't the best time to talk. I'll call you this evening. Ciao."

As I drove, I could feel myself becoming more tense. I dreaded what I was going to find back at the safe house.

As soon as I opened the door, I saw that the place had been tossed. Drawers were open, tables had been moved, the carpet had been rolled back. Whoever had done the searching hadn't made much of an effort to restore order. Even the kitchen was a mess, with the food from the pantry stacked on the dinette and the cabinets emptied of whatever was in them.

When I saw how thoroughly they'd searched, I felt a shudder. I already knew—and when I checked in the bedroom I saw I was right.

The gun was gone.

All right, I told myself. It's not the end of the world. Soon maybe, but not quite yet.

"They cut Major Brinkman's orders. He'll be flying to the States Space A. Flights are heavily booked at the moment," Sylvia said. "But I'm hoping he'll be leaving tomorrow morning. It was a long day. Now what's this problem you told me about?" She sounded impatient. It was just before midnight, and we were talking on the secure phone. When she said that she was calling from her room at Ramstein, I wondered whether Brinkman mightn't be in the room with her. She was slurring her words ever so slightly, as though she might have knocked down a couple of cocktails at the Officers' Club. I couldn't blame her if she had. Sylvia was mostly unflappable, but the tension gets to everyone after a while.

"What is it? You sound worried."

"The police tossed the apartment. They found the gun."

"I thought you'd gotten rid of it."

"No. I should have, but I didn't."

"Why not?"

"With the gun I could have proved that Sedfrit didn't murder Quemal. I thought of Sedfrit as a potential source into the KLA. He could maybe locate Nadaj for us."

"Off the top of my head, Alex, my advice is, leave Germany. Get out as quickly as possible."

"That might not be so easy. Or so smart."

"Why not?"

"The police have confiscated my passport. Besides, I'm sure they're waiting for me to try something like that."

"Why? Are they watching you?"

"They don't have to. The minute I try sneaking over the border, they'll know. That's all they'll need to conclude I'm guilty of murdering Quemal. They'll throw the book at me."

"This is another operation you've fucked up. I want you to know what a mess you've made out of things. Do you know what I hate about people like you?" When I didn't respond, Sylvia said, "You're the kind of person that when you go down, you take other people with you."

I figured the "other people" Sylvia was referring to was herself. Ambitious people can at times sound very self-centered. I said, "When are you coming back to Munich?"

"I'll let you know. Is there anything else you want to tell me?"

When I said there wasn't, she slammed down the phone. I had an idea Sylvia wouldn't be wasting any time reporting what I'd told her to both her superiors at the NSC and to the deputy secretary of defense. Whoever her superiors were, they were going to be very unhappy with Alex Klear.

Chapter 29

Thursday, February 7, 2008

This wasn't the first time in my life that I'd become involved in a war of nerves. It didn't take a genius to figure out that Schneider wanted me to worry and wonder. I decided I wouldn't give him anything to hang me with, not if I could help it anyway.

Sylvia was my best hope. Although the German government has a strong dislike of American intelligence people carrying out operations in their country, she might be able to get someone in the government to intercede on my behalf. In that case, the police might be persuaded to let me go. Or would they? Relations between the United States and Germany weren't anything like the way they once were.

I wondered how long it would take the police to do a ballistics test on the weapon. Not long, probably. I decided not to think about that. Despite the cold, drizzly weather, I took a drive, and parked on Elisabethstrasse, not far from the corner of the English Garden where I'd once worked. Radio Free Europe was no longer in Munich, and I felt a brief pang of nostalgia. As I walked down the tree-shaded paths, I couldn't help recalling the countless times Irmie met me here after work.

I needed moral support, and I was counting on Sylvia to provide it. At shortly after 2200 she called.

When I asked when she expected to return to Munich, she didn't answer the question.

"Before I get to that, Alex, let me say something. You're aware that when I requested that you be given this assignment, people raised their eyebrows. I went to bat for you. Not only did I give you a chance to rehabilitate your career, but my thinking was that you would also have an opportunity to get back at Nadaj. I'm sure you remember our conversation."

"Of course."

"By letting yourself become a prisoner you threw an enormous monkey wrench into our special ops program. Some journalists became very curious about our black operations—"

"Why are you telling me what I already know?"

"Because there are certain things about which you remain very obtuse, and I think they need to be emphasized."

"When are you returning to Munich, Sylvia?"

"I won't be returning. From this point on, you're on your own. You're an American tourist in the German Federal Republic and—"

"And I'm about to be charged with murder, which I committed while I was working for you and for—"

"In your place, Alex, I would inform the consulate, and, of course, arrange for legal representation. Harry Owen, by the way, has left Munich. He's returned to the States."

"This is ridiculous. You can't just leave."

"As things now stand, I was never in Munich. I say this in case you have some notion of connecting me to this murder. Now listen."

"I'm listening."

"I was never in Munich. I never registered with the police there. I never stayed in a hotel. Because I flew to Europe by military aircraft, I never had my passport stamped or even examined. I never had any contact with the German authorities. In the event anyone says they saw me in Germany—and I don't believe anyone will—I will say they confused me with someone else. If you tell the authorities I was with you in Munich, I will deny it, and it will be your word against mine."

"Do you feel you're doing the right thing?"

"I wish I could help you, but I don't believe I can. The events you described in your earlier phone call leave me no option. We feel we have to undertake a new course of action."

"Who's 'we'?"

"The decision was made at an extremely high level of government."

"But you approved it?"

"I follow orders, Alex. Where my superiors are concerned, I don't feel it's my place to either approve or disapprove. The decision was only arrived at after giving the matter much thought. I can't rejoin you."

"You might be arrested. Is that what you and your superiors are afraid of?"

"I understand your feelings, Alex. Speak with someone from the consulate. They can assist you."

"I know what they'll say. Plead guilty, and receive a reduced sentence of twenty-five years. You can't be serious, Sylvia."

"Believe me, Alex, when I say I greatly respect you."

"Twenty-five years in the slammer? The guy had a knife at my throat—"

"Tell the authorities. Explain how he attacked you. But leave me out of it."

"They'll love that story."

"You're one of a very small number of people with some very valuable skills. The way you practice the craft is original but also effective. I think we were a good team. And you're tough, much tougher than you appear to be, if I may say that. I truly enjoyed our time together. I hope things work out for you."

"Colonel Bitch-on-Wheels" was behaving with predictable self-indulgence, covering her own ass at the expense of mine.

"You can continue to use the safe house for the foreseeable future."

"Foreseeable future? What's that supposed to mean?"

"Until whatever happens—happens."

"You mean until the cops arrest me. Sylvia, listen. We've already been able to—"

"I wish you the best." Click.

I tossed the phone across the room, where it struck the floor lamp and narrowly missed the large mirror on the living room wall. Then I went into the kitchen, popped a half liter of beer and emptied most of the bottle while standing next to the refrigerator.

"I truly enjoyed our time together." I said the words out loud in a

singsong voice. "I hope things work out for you." Then I grabbed another beer. I very nearly threw it against the wall too. Showing some
self-restraint, I took it with me into the living room where I plunked
myself down on the sofa and tried to think.

I spent ten minutes with my head in my hands and wracking my
brain, but couldn't come up with any answers.

The worst of it was, I'd been warned. Buck had told me to steer
clear of Sylvia. The word was out all over D.C. about Colonel Bitch-on-
Wheels. You don't get that reputation without having earned it. I had
only myself to blame for landing in this mess. Whenever things don't
work out, there has to be a fall guy, and this time I was elected. I should
have seen it coming right from the beginning.

According to Sylvia, I'd been incompetent when, in Kosovo, I'd
"let" myself become a prisoner.

And at the K Klub I'd acted irresponsibly when I "let" Tania escape. "You've jeopardized the entire operation for the sake of a lousy
whore," is the less than elegant way she put it on that occasion.

And I'd made the mistake of shooting Quemal when he had a knife
at my throat.

Nor did Sylvia like the fact that I'd figured out that the officer she'd
become involved with in Kabul was Brinkman. Her boss, the deputy
secretary, didn't know about that—and wouldn't like it if he found out.

Put it all together, and it was clear that Sylvia regarded me as the
ideal fall guy. The perfect time to check out would have been when
Sylvia showed up at the safe house. Ironically, I almost did.

Sprawled on the living room sofa with another bottle of beer in my
mitt, I clicked the TV on to an American cop show. A couple of detectives, a guy in a trench coat and a blonde woman, were trying to
solve the murder of a prostitute in New York City. The show couldn't
have been all that riveting because somewhere in the middle I dozed
off.

I guess the detectives solved their case because when I woke up the
screen showed a group of beautiful people gathered in a circle and
chattering excitedly about books they'd read and films they'd seen.

Because I was still a shade groggy, it took me a good fifteen seconds to realize my phone was ringing. Then I spent time looking before finding it on the rug behind the easy chair, where it had landed after I'd heaved it at the wall. Aware that I was still half asleep, I answered warily.

"Alex?"

"Yes?"

"This is Irmie."

Chapter 30

Friday, February 8, 2008

The very last person on earth that I ever expected to call me was Irmie. All I could think to say was, "I'm surprised to hear from you, Irmie."

That was truly the understatement of the century.

"I'm calling because I want to speak with you." When I mumbled a response, she said, "Can you come over now?"

The beer had made me drowsy, and I made a monumental effort to clear my mind. Why was Irmie calling me? What was going on?

"Now?"

"Yes, Alex. Now." Her voice had an edge to it. "Can you manage that?" When she gave me her address, I said, "I'll call a taxi."

"No, don't take a taxi. Do you have a car?"

"Yes." Outside, it was pouring rain. Having drunk two liters of beer, I'd almost certainly be driving over the legal alcohol limit. "Irmie, couldn't we make this—"

"No, Alex. Come now. Can you do that?"

I was wondering what I might be getting myself into. I needed time to think. "Yes," I said finally.

"Good. Make sure you aren't followed. Don't park on the street. There's a space at the rear of the building."

I was about to ask who might be following me, but then thought better of it. I wondered if it might be the police. Or someone more sinister—although at the moment I couldn't think of anyone more sinister than Detective Schneider. After giving me her address, she said, "I'll be waiting for you."

I'd driven less than a mile through the dark, deserted streets when

I saw headlights a hundred yards to my rear. Keeping my eyes on the rearview mirror, I made a number of detours as well as a few wrong turns until I was sure that the car that might have been on my tail was no longer there. By the time I arrived in Gröbenzell twenty minutes later, I was positive no one was behind me. Driving slowly, I spent more time searching for the right address. As it turned out, Irmie now had a garden apartment in a four-story brick building with a lot of lawn around it. I found a parking space behind the building where my car wouldn't be visible from the street.

After buzzing me in, she was waiting with the apartment door open and said a quiet hello.

Just the sight of her face, the wide eyes, round face, and blonde hair, sent a pang of excitement through me—and despite these strange circumstances, brought back memories.

Standing in the middle of her living room I could see black mountains, the Alps, looming in the distance. When she closed the drapes, we were briefly enveloped in a silent darkness that under other circumstances I might have thought of as romantic but that now only seemed mysterious.

I wanted to ask: why all the secrecy?

After turning on a lamp, Irmie pointed me toward the dining room, and I took a seat at the room's large table. I watched silently as she brought a pot of tea from the kitchen, but as she poured her hand shook ever so slightly. Her face looked pale, as though she hadn't slept. What was going on? When she sat down, I couldn't believe that, after all these years, I was again alone with the woman whose memory had haunted me for so long. The situation wasn't just strange, it was eerie, and it was made eerier by the tension that was so obvious in Irmie's expression and movements. The only sound was the ticking of a clock on the wall. It was a few minutes before two.

Irmie looked extremely tired, and when she spoke, her voice was soft. "You're wondering why I asked you over here."

"I have to admit I was surprised to hear from you."

"Alex, I'm going to ask some questions, and I insist that you answer all of them—and that you answer truthfully. Can you do that?" When

I hesitated, she said, "I think that you're involved in some way with American intelligence. You may not want to answer these questions."

"Will you be asking them as a police officer?"

"I am a police officer." As she took another sip of tea, she looked at me over the rim of her cup with her round blue-green eyes. Again I felt her overwhelming attractiveness, a feeling so strong I was helpless to fight against it.

I thought back to Sylvia's phone call. Not only had she tossed me to the wolves, I had the feeling she'd enjoyed doing it. And now, only hours later, I had Irmie asking me questions, the answers for which could very well land me in even more hot water. Was I being manipulated again? Was Irmie also thinking of her career?

I realized I would have to make a decision—either to trust Irmie or not to trust her.

"You must answer honestly, Alex. If you can't do that, I'm going to ask you to leave."

The clock struck two.

"Well?"

I paused. As she continued to look at me, I said, "I've always been honest with you, Irmie. Anything you want to know, just ask. I'll tell you."

Without another word, she stood up. When she returned a minute later, she was holding an object wrapped in a piece of cloth. I recognized the cloth. As she removed the cloth, her hands trembled. She was holding a gun in her hand—a 9mm Beretta automatic.

She carefully placed the weapon down on the table. "I'm sure you recognize this." When I nodded, she said, "There were two of us, another detective and I, who searched your apartment. We each took a bedroom. When I tried pulling open a drawer in the bedroom closet, it felt heavier than it should have. When I removed the drawer, I found this taped underneath." She looked at me.

"It's mine. I brought it over."

"I thought so."

"Are you saying you found the gun, but haven't told anyone yet?"

She nodded. "Only you, Alex. You're the only person who knows."

Irmie took a sip of tea, then said, "I placed it in the pocket of my jacket without saying anything." She hesitated. "But now there are things I have to know."

We both knew that if what she had done became known it would not only be the end of her career but that she could face an array of criminal charges, perhaps even be charged as an accomplice to murder. Why had she taken such a risk? I took a sip of tea and waited for the question I assumed she was about to ask.

"There was a murder committed at the Kalashni Klub. My partner, Detective Schneider, is convinced you committed it. Two days after it occurred, he wanted to arrest you."

"He told me."

"My first question is, was this gun used in the murder?"

"I shot Quemal with this weapon."

Her eyes widened. "You fired the shot?"

"It was self-defense."

Irmie poured each of us another cup of tea. Despite her nervousness, I found myself admiring the deft and graceful way she did even the smallest things.

"So many circumstances point to you, Alex. Not just the murder. There's the jailbreak and the break-in at Ursula Vogt's home. Detective Schneider hasn't arrested you only because I've intervened."

"He doesn't know about us, the way things were."

"No one knows about us. Only Max, and he won't say anything. Detective Schneider thinks the pressure will get to you and you'll panic—that you'll try to get back to America. Flight means guilt. Germany will ask for extradition. Your life will be ruined."

I knew what Schneider was thinking. Even if I managed to get away, I'd live the rest of my life as a kind of fugitive, with the knowledge there was a warrant in the EU for my arrest. I'd spend all kinds of time consulting with lawyers and fighting extradition. I would lose my self-respect. I knew I could never live like that. Irmie knew it too.

"That won't happen." Or would it? I could no longer know myself what I might do. Would I panic at some point—and bolt?

"Alex," Irmie said quietly, "I have to know the whole story." When I didn't respond, she said, "It's as important for me as it is for you."

So I did something that under normal circumstances I would never do. When you're involved in intelligence, you learn to talk as little as possible. When you have to talk, you say very little and reveal almost nothing. But in this case I tossed away half a lifetime of habits, and told Irmie everything. I gave her names, dates, information. I began with the phone call from Buck that eventually led to the trip to Kosovo, my hospital interview with Sylvia, the reappearance of Jerry Shenlee in my life, and finally my arrival in Munich. I told her about the break-in at Ursula Vogt's home, my ill-fated visit to the K Klub, and concluded with the story of how Sylvia, Harry Owen, and I were able to break Doug Brinkman out of the Police Presidium. Irmie frowned as she listened to that story. Then she asked me why we did it.

The clock on the wall showed two thirty.

"I don't believe Brinkman killed Ursula Vogt," I said. "Eventually, he would have been murdered in prison."

Irmie didn't say anything for half a minute. I was surprised when, finally, she nodded. After another pause, she said, "Other people also think he is innocent. Among the detectives, there were questions about the investigation."

I said, "Kurt Mehling arranged for Quemal to come to Munich and murder Ursula Vogt. Then he put pressure on the detectives investigating the homicide to frame Brinkman."

Irmie's eyes widened. "Kurt Mehling? This is the first time I've heard his name mentioned."

"He pressured the detectives to charge Brinkman. Max told me one of the detectives resigned. The other dropped from sight and may be dead."

Irmie looked at me searchingly. "Everyone thought the obvious suspect was the handyman from the Balkans. He was also a suspect in the Muzaci murder, the case I investigated." She shook her head. "But why murder Ursula Vogt?"

"Ursula Vogt refused to report a story from Afghanistan. Mehling needed to get her out of the way to save his own reputation. She'd discovered he was involved with al-Qaeda, and that his magazine was supported by Bin Laden's money." I nodded at the weapon. "When I shot Quemal, he had a knife at my throat. It was self-defense. I had no choice."

Irmie was a police detective, and I'd told her enough for the police to lock me up and throw away the key.

"Alex," she said after a second, "someone has been asking about you."

"Who?"

"She showed me a picture of you. It looked like it was taken by a security camera. She was vague about why she wanted to locate you."

"She? A woman?"

Irmie nodded. "She wouldn't tell me much. She spoke to me because she'd learned that Detective Schneider and I were investigating Quemal's murder." When I asked what the woman looked like, Irmie said, "On the thin side. Attractive. Brunette. She spoke with an accent."

"Was she American?"

"No. I have her name here. Viktoria Rubi."

"Vickie!" I said, "That was the woman from Kosovo. She was with Ramush Nadaj."

Irmie frowned. "Why would she be in Munich?"

And why would she be trying to locate me except to get rid of someone who's causing them too many problems? I thought about that for a second. At the same time, I was very aware of Irmie watching me, her eyes full of curiosity. Her hand was resting on the table, and I had all I could do not to reach out and take hold of it.

I said, "I have an idea that the camera over the door at the K Klub took my picture. The KLA is running that place."

By not reporting the weapon, Irmie had put her future at risk.

Did she do it because she knew Doug Brinkman was innocent?

Or did she do it for me?

Irmie didn't say anything as I picked up the weapon and put it in my pocket. We both knew it wouldn't be wise to leave it in her possession.

I suddenly felt keyed up, combative, and self-confident—and ready to take on the world if necessary. Maybe that Air Force colonel hit the nail on the head when, in a long-ago evaluation, he called me a "loose cannon to end all loose cannons" and a "danger to myself and to everyone in the vicinity." Well, the person who might want to consider me a danger now was Kurt Mehling.

I thought of Tania, the woman at the K Klub. "They know I killed Quemal. They're using the picture to find me." When Irmie didn't respond, I said, "Could you call this woman in again?" When Irmie nodded, I said, "I think it's important that I get a fix on her before she gets a fix on me. Also, let me know how I can reach Sedfrit."

Irmie stood up, and at the door I told her good night.

My last sight of her before she clicked the door shut was of her very round blue-green eyes and a few errant strands of blonde hair. On the drive home, I saw streaks of red and gold in the sky, the first signs of light in the east. I was having trouble not only believing that I'd seen Irmie again, but that, for whatever reason, she'd saved me from being charged with murder.

Chapter 31

Friday, February 8, 2008

Four hours after I'd arrived back at the apartment, the phone woke me out of an uneasy sleep. "I'm at the airport," Buck Romero said. "Just stepped off the plane, and I'm hungry."

"I'm on my way. There's a café in the arrivals terminal where you can get some breakfast."

Forty-five minutes later, at a few minutes before nine a.m., Buck and I were shaking hands. Next to the table were a small suitcase and a carry-on. My old partner travels light. I told him it was good seeing him again. Another understatement.

After a second cup of coffee and getting past the small talk, I told Buck I had a possible murder rap hanging over my head. He arched both eyebrows.

"If it wasn't for Irmie, I might be in jail right now." I explained how Irmie's partner, Paul Schneider, suspected me of having killed Quemal Sheholi at the K Klub and how Irmie had found the murder weapon but not reported it.

"What does Irmie see in you anyway?"

"I'm not sure she sees anything in me. She says she had other reasons for not turning in the gun. She suspected Brinkman was being framed."

"And she thought you were about to get the same treatment? She wanted to be sure?"

"Something like that." I got to my feet and grabbed Buck's suitcase. "Let's get out of here. You can probably use a little shut-eye."

Back at the safe house, I gave Buck the bed Sylvia had vacated. I assumed he hadn't slept on the plane because a few minutes after arriving in our place he was sound asleep.

Shortly afterward, the telephone rang.

"Alex?" Irmie's voice. "The woman is in my office."

"Keep her there for twenty minutes. I'll be waiting outside."

"That shouldn't be a problem. She likes to talk."

There was some uncertainty in Irmie's tone. I couldn't blame her if she was wondering whether she'd done the right thing by not reporting finding the gun. Even I had to wonder if that had been a smart thing to do.

With my camera in my jacket pocket, I arrived downtown well in advance of when I expected Vickie to leave police headquarters. Ten minutes went by before a snazzily dressed woman emerged from the police building.

It was Vickie, but I very nearly didn't recognize her. With her dark hair hanging to her shoulders and wearing a gabardine rain coat, she definitely looked different from the woman I'd encountered in Kosovo, where she'd been dressed in black camouflage fatigues. As she went, she pulled a cell phone from her purse and held a brief conversation.

Who was she anyway? I remembered Sylvia's story of how she'd managed to blackmail an American businessman. Not only had she pressured him into making large contributions to the Kosovo Liberation Army, she'd manipulated him past the point where he could live with himself—and he'd ended up taking his own life.

She seemed to know her way around. Without hesitation, she turned to her right on leaving the police building, then headed in the direction of the Frauenkirche, which is one of Munich's downtown tourist attractions. After a brisk five-minute walk, she arrived at the Promenadeplatz, a wide square that is the location of an array of expensive shops and boutiques. It's also the location of the Bayerischer Hof, one of Munich's most fashionable hotels. As I watched, she greeted a uniformed doorman, who smiled and rushed to open the door.

When I arrived a minute later, he let me push open the door myself.

It was a few minutes before noon, and the hotel's ornate atrium lobby that has an enormous glass roof was alive with people. Turning left at the front desk, I walked through the lobby, looked around. It took a few minutes before I again was able to locate Vickie. She'd removed her coat and found herself a seat on a sofa in one of the lobby's adjoining lounges. One thing I was able to determine, even with her fashionable boots on, was that Vickie had nice legs. She had them crossed and was leafing through a magazine.

I considered sitting down next to her on the sofa. "Oh, hi. Don't we know one another?" Resisting that urge, I positioned myself behind her and waited. It looked as if she had agreed to meet someone here and that she was early.

She only had to wait five minutes before a lanky individual with fashionably long hair and wearing a dark-blue suit materialized. He seemed familiar, but it took me a minute to place his face. Although I'd been hearing a great deal about Kurt Mehling and had seen him answering questions on television, I was seeing him in the flesh for the first time. He took Vickie's hand, gave her a chaste brush on the cheek, and they sat down. While they were chatting, I circled around and snapped a pair of pictures. After about five minutes, they stood up and, both looking very serious, walked together to the Garden Restaurant, the large Mediterranean-style eating place adjoining the hotel's lobby. From a point in the lobby outside the door of the restaurant, I watched the headwaiter lead them to a booth opposite the large green plants at the center of the room.

Through the entrance I could see the table at which they were seated. They were definitely a power couple. When the waiter arrived, Mehling pointed to the wine card and carried on a brief discussion, no doubt about vintages.

Seated in one of the lobby's comfortable armchairs, I thought things over for perhaps five minutes. The Garden was a fashionable restaurant and not a place in which I wanted to make a scene or, for that matter, a fool of myself. But the way I now saw things, this opportunity was too good to pass up. At a haberdasher's in the lobby, I acquired a gray necktie that the clerk said was a perfect match for my blue sports jacket and which set me back nearly a week's salary. As I walked through the corridor toward the restaurant, I recalled, in Leadership School, a grizzled old sergeant explaining at length the many ways in which the element of surprise can work in your favor.

Of course, he was talking about heavily fortified enemy positions and not five-star restaurants.

Entering the restaurant, I went by the headwaiter with a nod.

I approached the table so that Vickie saw me first. When I halted, pretending surprise, her eyes widened.

"Vickie!" I flashed a broad smile. "What a surprise! It's nice seeing you again."

Trying to conceal her astonishment, she frowned, then stuck a napkin in front of her mouth. She might have turned a shade paler. Mehling, who had a wine glass in his hand, looked at me, obviously puzzled.

"May I?" As I eased my way into the booth, I said in English, "Vickie, you look wonderful. Life in Munich must agree with you." I noticed that her teeth looked better than they had in Kosovo. "Shouldn't you introduce me to your associate?"

Recovering very nicely, Vickie said, "Mr. Klear, isn't it? Alex Klear?"

"You have a good memory, Vickie."

"This is Kurt Mehling, Mr. Klear."

"The publisher?" When Mehling nodded, I said, "I'm delighted. Vickie and I know one another from Kosovo."

Mehling's expression clouded.

Vickie leaned forward. "This is the individual I've been telling you about, Kurt."

"The gentleman from Kosovo?" Mehling couldn't keep the surprise out of his voice. When Vickie nodded, he looked at me. "Really?"

"Yes. Really."

I couldn't help thinking that that old sergeant was right about the element of surprise. For a few seconds, Mehling's mouth hung open and his eyes remained wide. He recovered quickly. Smiling, he said, "From what I understand, you had quite an exciting time there."

"Exciting isn't the word for it, Mr. Mehling."

"Kurt. Please call me Kurt. We're all friends here."

I said to Vickie, "How are things in Kosovo, Vickie? How is Ra-mush?" I looked at Mehling and smiled. "Ramush Nadaj. He's another friend."

Mehling told a passing waiter to bring another wine glass. He'd ef-fortlessly morphed into the perfect host.

"You do get around, Vickie," I said.

"You also seem to get around," Mehling said.

"I guess you could say that, Kurt. It's such a small world. Wouldn't you agree?"

Mehling said quickly, "It certainly is. Very small."

As the waiter poured, Mehling said, "Pinot Noir from Marlborough, New Zealand." After we'd all taken a sip, he looked at me. "What brings you to Munich? Business? Pleasure?"

"Pure pleasure. There's so much for a tourist to do here."

"There is indeed."

"Museums, galleries, castles." I nodded at Vickie. "Old friends."

Smiling, Mehling said, "Have you been doing anything besides visiting museums and galleries?"

Mehling's question was an indirect reference to my having helped break Brinkman out of jail. He wanted me to know that he knew. I was sure that Vickie had described me to Mehling in detail. He might also have guessed that I'd killed Quemal.

I decided to pop a question of my own. "I heard you lost one of your reporters a while back. Is it true she was murdered?"

Mehling nodded. "Ursula Vogt. Yes, she worked for me. Her death was a tragedy."

"Her murderer escaped jail," Vickie said.

"That's terrible," I said. "Perhaps he'll be caught."

"Perhaps," Mehling said. He looked at me questioningly.

"I heard a rumor that Miss Vogt no longer believed the story she was reporting was accurate. Is that right?"

"I wouldn't know about that."

I took another small sip of wine, glanced at my watch. "I'm afraid I have to run."

"Are you sure? We'd be delighted to have you join us for lunch."

"Perhaps another time. Thank you for the invitation and the wine."

I'd gotten Mehling interested, and that was all I wanted to do. He couldn't be sure how much I knew. Or how much support I might have. Looking at Vickie, I said, "It's been nice seeing you. I'm sure we'll run into one another again."

As I got to my feet, Mehling also stood up. As I stepped away from the table, he moved with me, then placed his hand on my shoulder. He removed a business card from his billfold. "That's my private number. I'd like to continue this conversation. Call, why don't you, Alex? This evening would be fine."

I nodded a goodbye, and he nodded back. It was impossible not to be amused by Mehling's and Vickie's continuing astonishment. The sergeant in Leadership School certainly knew what he was talking about.

"My name is Klear, and I'm a representative of the American government and was with the American president when he visited Albania last June. I want to speak with Sedfrit Sulja."

It was three hours after my meeting with Mehling and Vickie, and I was standing in the living room of our apartment, my cell phone in my hand. According to Irmie, Sedfrit Sulja was a major player in the Independence for Kosovo movement.

"What do you wish to speak with Mr. Sulja about?" The woman on the other end spoke German with an Albanian accent.

"About independence for Kosovo. My colleague and I were with the president during his visit to Albania last year."

"Mr. Sulja is not here at the moment."

I said, "When you speak with Mr. Sulja, tell him that a representative from the American government has just arrived from Washington, D.C., and wishes to speak with him about independence for Kosovo."

After I'd hung up, Buck asked, "Why speak with him?"

"It's a long shot, but I'm wondering if he might be willing to reveal the whereabouts of Ramush Nadaj."

Buck frowned. "From what the senator told me, there's talk that in the new government Nadaj will be nominated for a cabinet position."

"Did the senator say anything about sarin gas?" Buck had indicated that he'd had dinner two nights before with one of the members of the Senate Intelligence Committee.

"No one's supposed to know about sarin gas. It's too deadly."

"The first I heard about it was from Brinkman. Sylvia would never mention it."

"Probably with good reason. She might have had orders from people upstairs not to say anything about sarin. The fewer the people who know that story the better."

"What story?"

"According to the senator, forty soldiers from Kosovo died from sarin gas in Afghanistan. They were killed by their own people."

"It wasn't ours."

"No, it wasn't. Saddam Hussein had factories in Iraq. He didn't have the technology to produce nuclear weapons, but he was able to produce chemical weapons."

I said, "Like everyone else, I also know that the UN inspectors never found any evidence of Saddam manufacturing nerve gas. And when our army invaded Iraq no weapons of mass destruction were found."

Buck said, "Hussein got rid of it before the inspectors arrived. The question is: What happened to it? Our intelligence people have been scrambling all over trying to locate those canisters. Some went to Syria. One of the other places they landed was Afghanistan, where they fell into the hands of the Taliban. Their first thought was to use sarin against our troops in the east."

"I never heard of that happening."

"It never did happen, and the senator told me why. The Taliban got what they thought was a better idea. Since our guys have chemical warfare uniforms, they realized sarin gas might not do much damage. So they came up with an alternative plan."

"They decided they'd use it against their own soldiers and give us the blame."

"And ruin our country's reputation. We'd look like the worst kind of international hoodlums, a country so desperate we'd break every rule and defy every treaty."

Buck took a swallow of beer and continued to talk.

"Since the Geneva Convention outlawing the use of gas ninety years ago, no nation has used it. Hitler toyed with the notion, but the idea was shot down by his generals. If al-Qaeda had been able to persuade the world that the United States was using sarin gas, we'd look even worse than Hitler."

I said, "If the world believed the story, al-Qaeda could even justify exploding a nuclear device in the United States."

"That's where Kurt Mehling fits in. They'd have to publicize it, and get the word out. As the publisher of *Welt-Bericht*, Mehling could arrange that. Bin Laden's network had been secretly financing Mehling's magazines for years. By the way, the senator says Bin Laden's days are definitely numbered."

"Finally!"

When I asked if we knew where he was, Buck nodded. "It won't be long."

Buck knew about the photographs showing Mehling and Bin Laden together. "Since they knew we would deny the charge and that the story would get plenty of scrutiny, they needed to send a reputable reporter out to Afghanistan, someone who would honestly research the story and someone whom people would believe."

"Ursula Vogt."

"Exactly. She was honest, and she was gutsy. She'd been with a couple of good newspapers before going to work at *Welt-Bericht*. She wasn't afraid of anything. In Afghanistan, when she made contact with the Taliban, they told her that the American forces had launched a gas attack."

"Wasn't she skeptical?"

"Sure, but the Taliban brought Vogt and a photographer up to examine the site. When she reported back to the magazine, Mehling told her to verify what happened, and gather as much evidence as possible that the attack was by the American army. They knew we'd deny it, and that meant their claim had to be airtight. And that's how she came into contact with Doug Brinkman again, who at that time was out in Afghanistan. She knew him already from her first tour."

"She seems to have used every trick in the book."

Buck grimaced. "She was the Mata Hari of war correspondents. At first, Brinkman fell for it all. Maybe he really liked her. I'm not sure exactly what he said."

"He admitted to making some offhand comments. That we may have stockpiled nerve gas, just in case someone uses it against us. Brinkman never said we'd used it, but perhaps in an unguarded moment, he may have said it was always a possibility."

Buck took a swallow of beer. "Well, there may have been other unguarded moments. By this time, Brinkman had been in Afghanistan for months. Suddenly, he has an attractive woman showing all kinds of interest in him."

I pulled out my phone and punched in a number. "Speaking of Mr. Mehling, he said he wants to talk with me."

"Alex! I'm so delighted to hear from you. I found our conversation today interesting. I'm wondering if we could continue it."

"Tonight would be fine with me."

He hesitated, then said, "I have an appointment, Alex."

I said, "I have an appointment too, with the prime minister. I'll cancel it."

I heard Mehling chuckle. "I truly am busy this evening." After a pause he said, "Tomorrow evening, Alex. I could meet you at seven. Do you know the park that looks out on the Tegernsee? We could meet there."

"What time?"

"Seven. I'll be on one of the benches."

"I'll find you, Kurt."

After hanging up, I said, "Mehling calls me Alex."

"Now that you're on a first-name basis with an important citizen," Buck said, "I hope you won't forget your old friends."

"What old friends?" I went into the bedroom and returned a minute later holding the 9mm Beretta that Irmie had returned to me the previous evening.

"I don't suppose you intend to shoot him," Buck said.

When I told Buck what I intended to do, he made a sour face, and I knew why. The only other time I'd tried planting evidence was a case involving some American military contractors who were selling cocaine to jazz musicians visiting Munich. When our scheme backfired, the contractors got off and I ended up in all kinds of hot water.

It was at that time that the Air Force colonel described me as "a loose cannon to end all loose cannons." Come to think of it, maybe I deserved that evaluation. And maybe I've come to see it as a compliment more than a criticism.

I said, "Mehling's a big shot. He's untouchable." My thought was that by planting the gun in Mehling's car, we could pin Quemal's murder on him.

"Let's hope it works this time," Buck said. He didn't look happy.

Chapter 32

Saturday, February 9, 2008

Kurt Mehling, dressed in a stocking cap, blue ski jacket, and dark woolen pants, paused, took a long drag on the cigar he had just lit up, and gazed out toward the water. "Some people believe we are headed toward an Armageddon," he said. "What do you think, Alex?"

"I left my crystal ball at home this evening."

He smiled. "That's what I like about Americans—the sauciness, the endless wisecracks. The refusal to take even the most earnest matters seriously."

"It sounds like you're describing prime-time television."

We were seated next to one another on a bench overlooking Tegernsee, one of the alpine lakes just south of Munich. Two men occupied a bench diagonally across the quadrangle. They were near enough to observe but not near enough to overhear. Buck had driven me out here, and since he was somewhere behind us, I wasn't concerned about Mehling's goons.

Although Mehling had suggested this meeting, all we'd done so far was exchange small talk.

In front of us was a broad lawn that sloped for about a hundred feet toward the water. The other benches were occupied mostly by couples, young people speaking quietly.

Mehling smiled appreciatively, blew some smoke.

"The humor is what I miss living in Germany." He paused. "Life here is orderly, predictable. I lived for a while in the States, you know."

"I heard."

"Ah, my reputation precedes me."

"Such as it is, Kurt." When Mehling chuckled, I said, "I'm assuming you don't like America."

"Why do you say that?"

"Your news magazine, *Welt-Bericht*, is anti-American."

Mehling gazed down at his cigar, and didn't answer right away. Tegernsee was a pretty sight, and after a moment he returned his gaze to the inky water. The lights from distant buildings twinkled in the darkness, and a handful of stars were visible overhead. In the distance the Alps were looming black shadows silhouetted against a dark-blue sky. Bavaria, like much of Germany, is so beautiful I would sometimes wonder why the German people ever felt a necessity to acquire new territories or start a war—or organize and carry out such unmitigated horrors as the Holocaust.

"You know, Alex, I'll let you in on a little secret. This is where I come when I'm seeking relaxation. When I've had a difficult day, I drive down here, find a bench. I'll sit here in the darkness, just looking out at the water. The water, I find, has a soothing effect. Sometimes I'll sit here for hours."

"The stress of modern life. Everyone feels it."

"Some of us feel it more than others. What do you do to ease the tension?"

"Nothing, Kurt. I don't have the money to afford a therapist." I suppose I could have told Mehling that I sometimes pop a beer at the end of a long stress-filled day, but I wasn't in the mood to reveal all my secrets.

"Believe it or not, I was seeing a therapist for a while. She helped a little bit. I stopped because I didn't have the time to continue going."

"Was that the reason, lack of time?"

In a matter-of-fact tone, Mehling said, "The real reason is I got tired of sleeping with her."

"So now you come down here to Tegernsee and stare at the water."

"Precisely." Then, after a brief pause, he said quietly, "Armageddon. That's what some people think we're heading for. A clash of Islam against the West."

"Do you have a reason for telling me this, Kurt?"

"Yes, actually. Now is the time to choose sides. Wait, and it might be too late."

"I've chosen sides."

"I enjoy talking with you. When I first heard about you, I wondered what kind of person you were." After a moment, he said, "You mentioned the anti-American outlook of the magazine. Your country is the difficulty, Alex. You people are causing too many problems around the world."

It sounded as if Mehling had been reading his own magazine. It wouldn't be the first time someone began believing his own propaganda.

"Do you really think so?"

"I do. Honestly. I also believe that we are witnessing the end of an era. The Western World, our civilization, is in decline. I don't think it will survive yours or my lifetime. What we'll have is a new world order, and believe me, Alex, it's not that far off."

New world orders seemed to be coming and going at a rapid rate. With the new world order that followed the end of the Cold War, I found myself aligned with former Stasi and KGB agents, and for that reason I had some reservations about it. Recalling what Buck had said, I could have told Mehling that by the time his new world order arrived it was doubtful that his friend Osama bin Laden would be around to see it.

Strangely enough, and for reasons I wasn't too clear about myself, I hadn't taken an instant dislike to Mehling. I could see why he'd been successful. He was an opportunist, and wasn't the type to let anything stand in his way. He was ready to believe anything and ready to do a deal with anyone just as long as he came out on top. I had to wonder whether he truly believed his own interpretation of events.

"There's a lack of spiritual belief, Alex. People don't care for anything beyond the most superficial pleasures. Sex and money are the two engines that drive our world. People need a better system of beliefs and real goals."

"What do you have against sex and money?"

Mehling smiled, then took another long drag on his cigar, which had burned down considerably during the course of our conversation.

"Tell me. Where's Brinkman?"

"Brinkman?"

"Don't play dumb. Brinkman is the Green Beret who killed Ursula Vogt."

"Correction, Kurt. Brinkman is the Green Beret who was accused of killing Ursula Vogt."

"Where is he, Alex?"

"How would I know that?"

"Something you said today at the hotel intrigued me. It's one of the reasons I wanted to speak with you."

I knew what Mehling was about to say.

"You said Ursula Vogt no longer believed in one of the stories she was reporting. What story would that be? Would you know?"

"It had something to do with Afghanistan, Kurt. You would know better than I would."

"What is your source for that kind of information? You seem very well informed."

"But not as well as you. Can you tell me what the Afghanistan story was all about?"

"I don't think I need to. I think you know. The break-in at Miss Vogt's home. The late Miss Vogt." He paused. "The person made off with her notes, interviews, papers, and so forth. I think that person was you. And that's how you know what you know."

"Why me?"

"Because the person must have been a genuine professional. She'd fashioned a compartment in the wall of her basement office. These were things she didn't want anyone to find. I'm assuming, Alex, that you found those materials. Among them was an article detailing her thoughts on Afghanistan."

"Miss Vogt's story told of forty Kosovar soldiers in Afghanistan who had been betrayed by their own leaders, one of whom was Ramush Nadaj. They were led into a cave where they were exposed to sarin gas.

At first she was told that the United States was responsible. But in time she came to realize the truth—"

"Which was?"

"That it was a conspiracy to destroy America's reputation. That's what she wrote."

"The reason I wanted to talk with you, Alex, I like you. Many of my people aren't very impressive, I'm afraid. You're different. I want to offer you an opportunity."

"The last time someone offered me an opportunity I ended up as the owner of ten acres of worthless swampland in Florida."

This time Mehling didn't chuckle, or even smile. "But before I tell you what I have in mind, let me say, I'm offering it to you because I value your abilities and your intelligence. I think highly of you."

Before I could interrupt, Mehling raised his hand. "Don't say I don't know you, Alex. I have ways of finding out things. You're focused, determined. I can see that. And I've been able to piece together what I've heard and what I suspect to be true."

"I assume you know what happened in Kosovo."

"I do indeed."

"Vickie—if that's her name—told you."

"You acquitted yourself well, in fact, very well. I knew the story before you joined us at the hotel. I really did enjoy meeting you. I wished you had stayed. The sea bass was delicious."

"There are differences of opinion on how well I acquitted myself. It doesn't take a great deal of skill to get yourself captured."

Mehling smiled. "Maybe your superiors didn't appreciate that, but you shouldn't be too hard on yourself. And I have to admire the way you got out of that predicament." After a brief pause, he said, "As I indicated, I asked you out here because I want to make you an offer."

"What kind of offer?"

"You'd be using your expertise. What else? And Alex, don't play dumb. It's irritating." Mehling turned to look at me. "I know that you spent time over here working for one of the intelligence agencies."

"I'm not interested."

"First, let me tell you, Alex. I'd make you a rich man. Just give me the number of your bank account. By the end of the week, I'll have paid in a quarter million euros." After a brief pause to blow some more smoke, he said, "Does that sound interesting?"

"What would I have to do to earn this money?"

"I'd want you to tell me what you've been doing for the past ten days. And don't tell me you didn't have something to do with all this stuff that was going on."

"Stuff? Be more specific."

"About the break-in at Miss Vogt's home. About the murder at the K Klub. Were you involved with those incidents?"

"Why would you think that?"

"The victim was one of the people who held you prisoner in Kosovo. You might have tracked him down—and avenged yourself."

"This Quemal who, by the way, was also known as Quemal the Assassin, worked for Miss Vogt as a handyman and was a suspect in her murder."

"Go on."

"If he was the individual I encountered in Kosovo, I would like to know what he was doing here in Munich. My guess is he was sent up here to murder Miss Vogt."

"Why would anyone—?"

"To prevent her from publishing the story we just talked about."

"Where's the story now?"

"I don't know." That was true enough. I'd assumed that Sylvia had passed on the contents of the CD to her bosses in the NSC.

"You could be more forthcoming with your future boss, Alex."

"I haven't accepted your job."

"True, but I'm hoping that you will."

"Every man has his price, right Kurt?"

Mehling smiled. "Where money is concerned, things generally are simple." He got up from the bench. "I've made my offer, and I think we can end our discussion right here." He glanced at his watch. "We should be getting back." He sounded more than a little irritated.

He tossed away his cigar, and we walked back up the hill. Although Buck had driven me down here, I said, "I'll let you drive me back to the Peace Angel, Kurt."

"Fine. We can continue to talk." As we drove, Mehling said, "You know that when I referred to your expertise, Alex, I meant your trade-craft. That is what the people in the business call it, is it not?"

"I think you may be overvaluing me—and my tradecraft."

"Let me be the judge of that. I have a yacht in the Mediterranean. I'd like you to begin there."

"What would I be doing on your yacht? Swabbing the deck?"

Mehling was no longer chuckling at my comments. "I'd find things for you. We'll be headed for the Persian Gulf, probably within a week. That much I can tell you."

"You're still being vague, Kurt. I don't like that."

When we'd arrived at the Peace Angel, Mehling turned and looked at me. "I meant everything I said. And I also meant it when I said I could make you a rich man. It wouldn't be the first time someone has switched sides, you know. In fact it happens all the time. But I do un-derstand that it is a major decision for you. You have my card. I expect to hear from you within twenty-four hours."

I pushed the car door open and climbed out.

"However, after twenty-four hours all—What's the expression?"

"All bets are off."

"Exactly, Alex. After that time, all bets are off."

Chapter 33

Saturday, February 9, 2008

"He's self-centered and he's arrogant," I said. "But he's interesting to talk to." I was describing my meeting with Kurt Mehling to Buck.

"You would have liked him better if he'd laughed at your jokes," Buck said.

"He laughed at some of them." When Buck, who was guiding the car through the Munich traffic, tossed me a skeptical glance, I added, "He has all sorts of interesting ideas."

"Like what?"

"Well, he thinks the world is heading toward Armageddon."

"Did he say who's going to win the conflict?"

I nodded. "The forces of Islam are going to overwhelm the Western World. I doubt he believes it himself. He also offered me a job, and I told him I'd think it over. I have twenty-four hours to make up my mind."

"A job doing what?"

"He's interested in my expertise, and he said something about going to work on his yacht in the Mediterranean somewhere."

"Sounds good."

"He also offered me a quarter million euros just to sign on."

"How long would it be before they tumbled you into the drink?"

"I figure two days, maybe three. They wouldn't do it until they'd squeezed every last piece of information out of me."

"One consolation: you'd die rich."

"Assuming Mehling's check doesn't bounce."

"What else?"

"Not much. He's too cagey to give away anything. He was trying to get me to talk, and I was trying to get him to talk. Neither of us was very successful. From some of the things he said, I got the idea that the detectives gave him access to Ursula Vogt's home."

"Was he looking for something?"

"He knew she was writing a story about her experience in Afghanistan that would have blown him out of the water. He wanted it."

"But you got in there ahead of him."

"Sylvia read it, and she probably passed it on to the National Security Council, possibly to Jerry Shenlee. When I saw that someone had gone through Ursula Vogt's stuff, I figured they were looking for something. That led me to look around. The cabinet behind the bed wasn't that hard to find."

"Mehling paid off the detectives who investigated Ursula Vogt's murder, is that it?"

"Irmie suspected that. It may have been one of the reasons she didn't turn in the gun when she found it."

"Do you think that was the only reason?" Buck was referring to the possibility that she might have done it because of me.

"I don't know."

We were stopped at a light, and it had begun to rain heavily. Buck turned to look at me. "Where's the gun?"

"Under the front seat on the passenger's side." I had put the weapon in Mehling's car. Our plan was for the cops to find it there.

"We want to bring that fact to someone's attention. Is that what you're thinking?"

"Detective Schneider's attention. He's handling the investigation. We're not that far from the main railroad station. This might be the best neighborhood to look for the kind of person we need."

"Someone to drop a dime?" Buck and I had worked together for so long that, in situations like this one, only minimal communication was necessary.

On the street ahead of us, a car pulled away from the curb and Buck pulled into the space.

After checking the station and not finding anyone, we decided to try the neighborhood bars, the kind of places that offer temporary haven to the lost souls who aren't doing anything or going anywhere. Their haven lasts for as long as they can pay for their booze.

"I'll go this way," I said. Buck nodded and headed off in the other direction.

I looked into a couple of places but didn't see anyone. I found Buck at a corner table in a smoky bar in the next block. For some people, those with nowhere better to go, it was a place to come in out of the rain.

When I arrived, Buck folded up his newspaper, took a last swallow from a cup of coffee, then nodded in the direction of a moon-faced unshaven guy with hair that didn't appear to have been combed recently and who was wearing a jacket that appeared to have been slept in. He had an intelligent face, but he definitely appeared to have seen better days—and he was staring into space almost as if he was doing his best to recall them.

"He was talking to a few characters when I got here," Buck said. "Bavarian dialect. Said he'd been working construction for a while. He's switched from schnapps to beer."

"Can he read?"

"There's a newspaper on his table. He was able to put sentences together a few minutes ago, but he's half smashed now."

"Not totally smashed?" I watched as the guy took a long swallow from his beer bottle. When I nodded, Buck headed off to the bar to pick up more beer, and I headed over to our friend's table.

I said, *"Grüss Gott,"* and he looked up at me with bloodshot eyes.

He mumbled a greeting, gave me an inquiring stare. As he gazed balefully out at the teeming rain, I said something about the weather gods not favoring us lately. I told him I was Alex, and he said he was Willi. A minute later Buck arrived and shoved a bottle of beer in Willi's direction.

Willi had lost his job as a machinist and had subsequently helped out on a couple of construction sites. Somewhere along the way, his wife had left him. When he said his unemployment insurance had run out, I took out a hundred euro bill and pushed it across the table. He gazed at it longingly, but didn't pick it up.

"Would you like to earn five hundred euros?" I said. "I have four more of those."

"I don't want to go back to jail," Willi said. I thought that was a good answer.

"You don't have to do anything illegal." I took out a piece of paper. "If you can read this out loud, you can earn another four hundred euros." I handed Willi the paper, but when he only squinted at it, my heart sank. I was about to take the paper back, but Willi began to fumble around in his jacket. Finally, he pulled out a battered pair of reading glasses.

"Can't even read the newspaper anymore without these."

When I said, "It's a bitch getting old," he grumbled. Then he held up the paper to six inches in front of his nose and began reading. When he'd finished, I nodded at Buck, who nodded back.

Outside, there was a row of pay phones. "You just have to read this into that telephone, Willi."

When Willi hesitated, Buck said, "This is your chance to earn some money."

Using a disposable telephone card, I dialed Detective Schneider's number at the Police Presidium. When his machine directed me to leave a message, I handed Willi the receiver.

"Ja, Detective, it's about the shooting at the Kalashni. I should have called last week. I was in the parking lot in my car. It's a brothel. My wife would divorce me if she knew I was there. I read your name in the newspaper. It's been bothering me. These two guys—they pushed the other guy into the back of the car. Shot him, left his body. Then they drove away. A Mercedes, nice wheels. It was one shot. They killed him. I took down the plate number of the car. It's M274K75."

I reached across and broke the connection. When we were back inside the bar, Willi looked at me uncertainly.

"You did good, Willi." I handed Willi four hundreds.

"Who did I speak with?"

"No one."

Buck called to the bartender for another beer. "If we ever need you again, Willi, we'll call."

Willi continued to stare, unbelievingly, at the bills in his hand. As Buck and I headed for the door, Willi was still staring.

In the car on the way to Max's apartment, I said, "Detective Schneider will want to ask Kurt Mehling a few questions—and will want to search his vehicle."

Buck shook his head. "Do you think it will fool him? He's a smart cop."

"Nothing ventured, nothing gained."

Chapter 34

Sunday, February 10, 2008

I'd just finished passing around the pictures I'd taken that afternoon of Mehling and Vickie talking in the hotel lobby. "If there's any doubt about Mehling's involvement with Nadaj, this should remove it. Vickie is the woman who was with Ramush Nadaj and Quemal in Kosovo. Their gang held me prisoner for two days."

It was after midnight, and the four of us—Max, Irmie, Buck, and I—were clustered around Max's living room coffee table.

Irmie shook her head. "Whose idea was it to use the gas like that—against their own people?"

"Probably it was Mehling's idea," Buck said. "According to people in Washington, he's as bad as Bin Laden, and now could be more dangerous. He arranged to have his own reporter killed when she wouldn't play ball. Then he framed Brinkman."

"Brinkman they could have taken care of in prison," Max said. His expression darkened. "One of the detectives who investigated Miss Vogt's murder disappeared."

Looking at me, Irmie said, "You mentioned that there were pictures showing Mehling and Bin Laden together."

Buck said, "From what we hear, Bin Laden won't be around much longer. I spoke recently with someone from Special Operations Command in Fort Bragg. Bin Laden's enjoying the hospitality of some people in Pakistan, but he won't be enjoying it for much longer."

Max shook his head. "Mehling could turn out to be as tough to take down as Bin Laden is. People fear him, important people."

At sometime around two a.m., we called it a day. I told Irmie I'd drive her home, and Max offered to drive Buck back to the safe house.

Alone with Irmie in my car, my mood changed completely. In fact, the other stuff all at once didn't seem that important. I felt I had so much to say to her, and I wondered whether she felt the same way. I wasn't sure that she did.

"There's a question I have to ask you, Irmie." She turned to look at me. "Why did you risk your life during that bank robbery?"

"I don't know, Alex. It was a long time ago. Why do you ask?"

"Did it have anything to do with me?"

"I have a question to ask you. Why did you leave so suddenly? You went back to the States without—without even saying goodbye."

I let a minute go by before I answered. "I was under a lot of pressure. The job was getting to me. I have to admit that I wasn't thinking clearly." I paused. "I intended to come back. I only needed some time to think."

"You never did come back. You wrote a letter."

"You were in the hospital." I paused. "Then I was reassigned."

"Just because you were reassigned doesn't mean you couldn't have come back."

I thought about that. Irmie was right. But by then, I'd heard the story of how Irmie had charged into the bank. That action was nearly suicidal. Had she been trying to kill herself because she thought I'd abandoned her? I found that notion hard to confront. I suppose that was the reason I didn't want to go back.

"I knew you were under pressure, Alex. I sensed it. You never spoke much about your work. And when you did, it was usually some kind of offhand remark."

As I drove, I tried to re-create those years in my mind—what it was like and what I was thinking. What was it that led me to leave so suddenly?

Irmie's expression clouded over. "I wasn't important to you. I was just someone you met at a party."

I remembered the Christmas party hosted by the police president on one of the upper floors of the Police Presidium. Irmie was new to the Munich police force, and I'd never seen her before. After exchanging a few words at the buffet, I joined her at a table where she was sitting with a couple of girlfriends. I couldn't keep my eyes off her, and I guess that was apparent. Suddenly, the most important thing in the world was that I take her home.

And that I see her again. And that I get to know her.

Those things all happened, and our lives together went on from there.

Why did everything go so wrong?

At the door, Irmie extended her hand. "Good night, Alex," she said. There was a sparkle in her eyes and I thought just the trace of a smile at the corners of her mouth. I was holding her hand, but as I drew her toward me and tried to kiss her, she raised her hand, keeping me at a distance.

On the drive back to the apartment, I was reminded of a book I'd read for a high school English class. All I could remember of the book was that the main character, who gave fabulous parties and addressed everyone as "Old Sport," was obsessed by the idea of reclaiming the past, the years during which he'd been separated from the woman he loved. Since it was so obvious that his efforts were doomed to failure, I found the book unrealistic and hard to comprehend. But now, as I thought about Irmie and what might have been, the book took on a significance that had eluded me when I was fifteen years old.

Chapter 35

Monday, February 11, 2008

"Trafficking in women must be a good business," Buck said.

Buck was eyeing Sedfrit Sulja's house, a chalet-type building situated on the outskirts of the city of Garmisch. Just beyond the house was a small grove of trees, many of them birch. We were in the rented Mercedes, waiting for a guy to unlock the chain leading onto the concrete apron that served as a parking area.

"I still say he's not going to tell us anything." Buck was dressed in a blue blazer, white shirt, red tie, and gray trousers. He looked every inch the role he was going to play—a highly placed official of the American government who had been with the president when he visited Albania the previous June.

The truth was, I shared Buck's pessimism. That morning a woman named Fabiola had called me back to invite us to have lunch with Sedfrit at his house in Garmisch. Sedfrit had caused the stir at the K Klub by getting in a knife fight with Quemal and his friends and had briefly been a suspect in Quemal's murder. Since he was an influential figure in Kosovo's independence struggle, I was hoping he'd give us some clue to the whereabouts of Ramush Nadaj. Even if it was only a one-in-a-thousand shot, I thought it might be worth taking.

As we parked the car, Buck said, "Kosovars live and die by the *Kanun*. Whatever Sedfrit may think of Nadaj, he's not going to give up anything, not to us."

It had been a while since I'd been in Garmisch, which lies directly at the foot of the Zugspitz, one of Europe's highest peaks. When Munich hosted the Olympics in 1972, the year eleven Israeli athletes were killed by a terrorist group called Black September, the skiing events had been held in Garmisch. With its proximity to the Alps, Garmisch is one of Europe's well-known winter resorts.

After I'd parked, we made our way around the house to an enclosed terrace in the rear. Seated at a long table was a massive individual with a mop of black curly hair and a bushy beard, who I remembered from my visit to the Kalashni Klub. It was Sedfrit, who was now wearing a tan sports shirt, white pants, and around his neck, an impressive collection of gold chains. Next to Sedfrit was a young woman, who was very thin and quite attractive, and I wondered about her relationship to Sedfrit. She had brown hair cut short and wore a short-sleeved white dress.

"I'm Fabiola," she said. "This is Sedfrit Sulja."

Sedfrit stood up and stuck out his hand. "*Mirëseer'dhët!*" Welcome.

After I'd introduced Buck, Fabiola poured wine for each of us. Speaking English, Fabiola said, "Sedfrit wants to drink to independence for Kosovo." I said that was a fine idea.

I asked Fabiola if the house belonged to Sedfrit, and when she said it did, I wasn't surprised. Although he was a generous supporter of the Kosovo Liberation Army, there seemed to be plenty left over for things like an expensive home.

A minute later, a male servant dressed in an apron arrived carrying a tray and placed a large bowl of salad on the table. Sedfrit pointed at the salad and said, "*Ha!*"

Looking at Buck, I said, "*Ha* means eat."

I knew we wouldn't be able to talk until we'd polished off the food.

After the salad, we were served lamb covered with gravy. The servant also brought a fresh bottle of wine.

Afterward, he brought coffee and a bottle of slivovitz.

Translating for Sedfrit, Fabiola said, "Sedfrit says the people of Kosovo are good people."

"If the people of Kosovo are good people," I said, "why were some of them fighting against the United States in Afghanistan?"

When Fabiola said that, Sedfrit's face clouded. Fabiola said, "Sedfrit wants to know what you mean."

"Ramush Nadaj led a detachment of KLA soldiers in eastern Afghanistan." When Sedfrit shrugged, I said, "Does Sedfrit know they died?"

"In the struggle for independence people must die," Fabiola translated. She began doodling on a pad, and there was something in her expression that told me she was very troubled.

This was Buck's signal to chime in. "The United States will not support Kosovo's bid for independence if Kosovo remains united with the Taliban."

Sedfrit banged a big fist on the table and glared at Buck. I heard the word *budalla*. When I told Buck a *budalla* is a fool, he grimaced.

Raising my voice, I said, "I want to know the whereabouts of Ramush Nadaj. Where is he, Sedfrit?"

"Ramush Nadaj," Fabiola translated, "is a hero to the people of—"

Buck looked at his watch, then stood up.

I still hadn't given up and motioned to Buck to sit back down. "Ramush Nadaj broke the *besa,* Sedfrit. Tell me where he is!"

Sedfrit began mumbling and toying with the bottle. Fabiola said, "Sedfrit says he does not know the whereabouts of Ramush Nadaj."

When I said, "Tell Sedfrit the American government knows he sends money to support the Kosovo Liberation Army," Sedfrit began to laugh.

Then Fabiola said, "Sedfrit wonders who you are. He says you don't know much about what your government wants."

"This is a waste of time," Buck said angrily. "All we're getting here is a goddamned runaround." Again he stood up.

Sedfrit said something to Fabiola, who said something in return. I picked up *bu'rri inxe'hur*—which meant something along the lines of "the guy's very angry."

Sedfrit laughed and waved at Buck dismissively. Fabiola seemed upset. Quietly, she said to me, "Sedfrit does not fear you or your threats."

This conversation wasn't going the way I'd hoped.

I said, "My companion is from the State Department, and he is the specialist for Balkan policy."

Glaring at me, Sedfrit said, *"Nuk ju besoj'!"* I don't believe you! I didn't need Fabiola to translate that. Then she said, "Sedfrit says Kosovo will declare its independence—and the United States will support Kosovo's independence!"

Sedfrit poured himself another slivovitz, raised his glass and said, *"Pavarësi' per Kosova!"* Independence for Kosovo! Then he glared.

When Buck said, "Let's get out of here!" Fabiola nodded. No one said goodbye.

As Fabiola silently led us back around the house toward our car, she lost her balance and stumbled against me.

Back in the car, Buck said, "I can't say I'm surprised."

As I drove slowly back toward the gate, I glanced into the mirror. In front of the house, a lonely figure stood on the terrace. It was Fabiola. Standing alone with the wind whipping her hair and skirt, she appeared very frail. She remained unmoving, watching us as we drove.

Why was she watching us? As we waited for the gate guard to materialize, I recalled her stumbling. I reached into my left pants pocket—and found a folded piece of paper with some writing.

It read: "In two days, Nadaj arrives in village outside Pec. A house near the river. My brother died in Afghanistan."

As the guard raised the barrier, I passed the paper to Buck without comment.

After a long minute, he said quietly, "Fabiola's brother was one—"

"One of the forty Kosovar soldiers who were gassed in Afghanistan."

"Do you know Pec, Alex?"

I nodded. "I know the area. I drove through it once on the way to Plav in Montenegro. Lots of small villages, heavily wooded."

"It's in the west then. Which river would that be?"

"The Bistrica. She said he arrives in two days." I turned to look at Buck. "What time is it?"

"Almost three thirty. Are you thinking what I'm thinking?"

"It's nine thirty back in D.C. Jerry Shenlee should be in his office."

By the time I'd pulled the car into a rest stop, Buck was already punching in Jerry's number. He didn't have long to wait before he was talking to someone in Shenlee's office. Just as I killed the engine, I heard Buck say, "Hello, Jerry."

After a pause, he said, "Alex says hello too. No, he's not in jail yet. Listen, Jerry, we've got a fix on Nadaj. He's still in Kosovo and—"

Buck was silent for a good half minute while Jerry, presumably, read the riot act to him.

Finally, he said, "Jerry, I know all that. Alex knows it too. Yes, he knows he should have been more careful." Buck looked at me, shrugged, held the telephone a couple of inches from his ear. "Of course our information is reliable. We wouldn't be calling otherwise. We know the location. We don't think we have all that much time—" After listening to Jerry for a while, he said, "I'll let Alex tell you that."

Buck handed me the phone.

"Forget it, Klear," Shenlee announced. "I'm not interested."

"Why not?"

"Because I'm assuming this is just another one of your cons. You're in hot water with the Kraut cops, and now you've got your buddy over there. You've dreamed up some scheme to get yourself out of trouble, and you're looking to get some help from us. Like I say, we're onto you. Forget it."

"Are you sure you're making the right decision, Jerry?"

"Completely sure. Now let me get back to work."

"You may be the one who's going to be in hot water, Jerry."

"Whaddaya mean?"

"When the deputy secretary hears we had a chance to land Nadaj, and you didn't follow up. Instead you start blowing smoke about schemes and cons—"

"I don't trust you guys. All that Gold Dust Twins bullshit. Those days are over, ancient history. Tell your partner that. All I care about is what—"

"Is what we've done for you lately. Well, we're ready to do something for you. Right now. Something that will make you look good."

"Knock it off, Klear."

"Jerry, listen. Like Buck says, we've got solid information on the whereabouts of Nadaj, but we don't have much time to act on it."

"What's this so-called solid information? Where does it come from?" When I said, "From inside the Kosovo Liberation Movement,"

Shenlee said, "Baloney! Since when do you have a source inside? You've been over there three weeks and you've developed a source in the KLA? We've been trying to get someone in there for five years. C'mon. They have this thing, what's it called?"

"The *Kanun*."

"Right, the *Kanun*. You can never squeeze anything out of them. Klear, I am so tired of your baloney. If I—"

"Jerry, will you shut up and listen? We know where he is going to be in two days."

"We know they have a big meeting next week in Pristina. We can't grab him there. Pristina's the capital. They'll have soldiers all over the place. Reporters. Klear, you're out of your mind if you're proposing—"

"Before he goes to Pristina, he's going to be holed up in a village out in the west."

"Which village?"

"We'll need weapons and backup."

"Who's 'we'?"

"Buck and me. Who else?"

"No way! Not you two. You and your buddy totally messed up the last time. And that's putting it mildly. You can't expect—"

"Without us it's a nonstarter. Forget the last time. If we still want Nadaj, this is our chance to grab him. But Buck and I have to be in Kosovo within the next twenty-four hours."

"Our KFOR people in Kosovo are peacekeepers, Klear. Everyone gets hot and bothered whenever the story of one of these renditions leaks to the newspapers. We had a guy stashed in the jail on Bondsteel, and when it leaked out, there was hell to pay. The last I heard the guy's suing the government, if you can believe that."

"You'll have to work out the details, Jerry."

"Okay, I'll get back to you. I can't promise anything. I have to talk with some people."

After giving Jerry the number of our satellite phone, I handed it back to Buck. "Jerry says he needs time to talk with his people. I have an idea that one of them will be the national security adviser."

As I turned over the engine, Buck said, "Jerry's come a long way from those rabbit warren cubicles we all had in Berlin."

I nodded. "He certainly has."

"I hope we're doing the right thing." Shenlee sounded excited. It was ten o'clock that evening, and I had just picked up the satellite phone.

I looked across the room at Buck and nodded. In less than two seconds, Buck was off the sofa and standing next to me.

As Buck and I silently exchanged high fives, I said, "What's the deal, Jerry?"

"The arrangements are as follows. I assume you guys have wheels. You and Romero drive up to Ramstein. Let's see. What time do you have over there?"

"It's a few minutes after ten."

"Okay. It'll take you four, five hours to drive up, so I suggest you pack and leave right away. At the gate, you ask for Colonel Butts. He's in base ops. He'll have your paperwork, Klear, and he'll get you guys squared away. They're cutting your flight orders right now, and you'll both be on the way to Pristina tomorrow, the morning rotator flight. In the terminal there'll be a van. They'll handle the KFOR in-processing, take you out to Bondsteel. Out there you ask for Captain Reilly. He's special ops. It seems they've also picked up a rumor about this meeting of Kosovo government people."

I said, "It sounds important."

Shenlee sighed. "Kosovo's gonna declare its independence, Klear. I guess I can tell you that much. In June, when the president was in Albania, he let them know we'll recognize Kosovo as a sovereign nation. It's gonna cause a big reaction, believe me. China and Russia are dead set against. But Nadaj can't, under any circumstances, be a member of the new Kosovo government."

"Why not?"

"What we're looking at is Greater Albania. Albania, Kosovo, and parts of Macedonia will be de facto one country. Whatever happens, we want to cut their ties with al-Qaeda."

"We're on our way, Jerry."

"I still don't know exactly when I'll be arriving."

"You're coming over, Jerry?"

"Yeah. I can't let you guys run wild. And, Klear, I want you to know that we expect you to return to Krautland when this is over. The U.S. government has problems enough. It is not going to aid a fugitive."

"We look forward to seeing you, Jerry."

"I'm sure you do. You should know I have tickets for the Kennedy Center for this weekend, a play by Shakespeare. You've thrown another monkey wrench into my life, Klear."

"Which play is it?"

"I think it's the one with Falstaff. Is that *Hamlet*?"

"I don't think so, Jerry. *Hamlet* has the 'neither a borrower nor a lender be' guy in it."

"I'll take your word for it."

After I'd hung up, I told Buck that Shenlee wanted us to leave right away.

"I can't wait to get back to Kosovo," Buck said.

Chapter 36

Tuesday, February 12, 2008

We left for Kosovo at 1030 hours the following morning in a C-130 that flew out of Ramstein Air Base. Although we ran into some heavy weather halfway down, the sun was shining when we landed in the military airport just outside Pristina. After grabbing our carry-ons from the pile of gear and getting our KFOR paperwork inside the terminal, a van took us to Camp Bondsteel, a sprawling military installation situated not far from the city of Urosevac.

At the gate we were met by an officer who introduced himself as Major Chambers and who told us we had an appointment in the administration building that evening at 1900 hours.

Much of Camp Bondsteel, which is south of Pristina, sits on top of a broad plateau. Kosovo is a rugged country of small mountains, hills, and valleys, and Bondsteel, which is over nine hundred acres, is the largest military installation the United States has built since the days of the Vietnam War. Coming up from Skopje, I'd helicoptered onto the base some years before, but it had looked different back then, not so built up. At that time, we lived in tents and took cold showers.

After we'd stashed our gear in a SEA-hut and gotten some chow, we hiked up to the Administration Section, which is behind a high chain-link fence at the top of a hill and right across the road from the helicopter pad.

Captain Reilly, whom we found in a computer-filled room in the S-2 section, turned out to be a no-nonsense Special Forces officer with a ferocious handshake. He was my height, a shade over six, with an intelligent face and thinning brown hair. Together with Chambers and a civilian named Silvio, who spoke English with an Albanian accent, we adjourned to Chambers's office.

"We've gotten the word from D.C." Chambers said as he closed the door. "Someone from the NSC is supposed to show up over here."

Buck said that would be Jerry Shenlee.

"Normally, we take orders only from SOCOM," Reilly said. "So I take it they want this Nadaj guy real bad."

"Very bad," I said.

"Well, that's what we're here for." Reilly was referring to the fact that he commanded a Special Forces A-team, which was stationed on Camp Bondsteel but which was there for special ops—not for peace-keeping.

I said that Nadaj would be arriving in Pec the following day.

Chambers nodded. "Sometimes we hear about meetings, but we never know when or where. The KLA is good at keeping secrets." When he asked Silvio if our information sounded accurate, he shrugged. That wasn't too encouraging.

"We can't just barge in and arrest Nadaj in Pristina," Chambers said. "There'd be all kinds of diplomatic protests. The word is Kosovo may declare independence as early as next month."

"That's the problem," Buck said. "Once Nadaj is part of the new government, he'll be untouchable."

Chambers frowned. "You say he's staying out near Pec someplace?" We gathered around the map on the wall, and Chambers pointed at Pec. Then he looked at Silvio. "Do you know anyone who grew up out there? Someone you can call?"

Silvio nodded. "Maybe."

Looking at Buck and me, Chambers said, "This isn't much to go on. How much time do we have?"

"No more than a day."

"Is Nadaj as bad as they say?" Chambers asked. "From what we hear, you got to meet him firsthand."

"He could have been more hospitable," I said.

Back in the SEA-hut with a three-day-old copy of *Stars and Stripes*, I read for ten minutes. By 2230 I was sound asleep.

Chapter 37

Wednesday, February 13, 2008

At 0800 the following morning, Reilly picked us up in a van from in front of the chow hall. When I asked him if he'd heard from Silvio, he said he hadn't.

We drove to the far side of the big installation, finally arriving at an area surrounded by a ten-foot-high chain-link fence behind which were a half dozen SEA-huts. The Green Berets kept to themselves. At the gate, which was surrounded by piles of sandbags, a lone sentry saluted and raised the barrier.

"This is where we hang out," Reilly said, pointing to the compound.

After we'd been there a half hour, a van arrived, and Jerry Shenlee, wearing camouflage fatigues, came scrambling out. Shenlee seemed to know Reilly, so I assumed he'd arrived at Bondsteel sometime during the night.

A minute later, Major Chambers arrived.

"Have we decided yet how we're gonna do it?" Shenlee asked.

Reilly said, "We still haven't pinpointed Nadaj's whereabouts."

Shenlee frowned. "What's with this Silvio?"

"We're hoping to hear from him anytime now," Reilly said. "He's always been dependable."

"The deputy secretary cares about this," Shenlee said.

Reilly and Chambers exchanged glances. Jerry and I went all the way back to Berlin in the 1980s, and I was used to his micromanaging style. But I had a feeling Chambers and Reilly weren't too happy about the way he was throwing his weight around. Reilly had fixed up one of the SEA-huts as an office, and we walked over there.

Reilly got his coffee machine going, and we all sat down to wait.

A little over an hour later, Silvio came walking in the door.

"I have good news and bad news," he said. "What do you want to hear first?"

"The bad news," I said.

"No one out near Pec's heard anything about Nadaj."

"What's the good news?" Chambers said.

"The good news is that last week Agim Shala ordered an enormous amount of food from the market in Pec. From the butcher in Pec he ordered sausage and beef."

"Who is Agim Shala?" Chambers asked.

"The local Mafia chief. The butcher is a friend of my brother-in-law." When no one responded, Silvio said, "It makes sense that Nadaj would only visit the Mafia chief in the area. I should have thought of that yesterday."

Taking a seat at the room's computer, Chambers said, "Where is Agim Shala located?"

"Southeast of Pec. He has property between Gornji and Ljesane."

"We conduct daily flyovers," Chambers said. "Nadaj doesn't travel alone, I assume."

"All these guys have an entourage," Shenlee said.

We watched as Chambers slid a disc into the computer and then began calling up images and pictures taken by satellite and aircraft. "You can't light a cigarette in Kosovo that we don't know about it," he said at one point. It took a while, but he was finally able to focus on the property he was looking for. Looking over his shoulder, we could see what seemed to be some kind of compound.

"It looks as if a number of vehicles are sitting in an area to the right of the gate, which might mean Mr. Shala has visitors. They weren't there yesterday morning. On the basis of when these were taken, I'd say they arrived sometime yesterday afternoon."

When I looked at Buck, he arched his eyebrows.

Within seconds, Reilly was on his feet and headed for the door. He'd be putting the A-team on alert. If we were going to try anything this evening, they'd need to be ready.

"The house is right in here," Silvio said. He was standing in front of a large map of Kosovo on the wall of Reilly's office. "It's three miles south of Pec."

"What's the area like?" I asked.

"Hilly," Silvio said. "Lots of trees. As you can see, there are also trees on the property."

Chambers called us over to have another look at his computer screen. Pointing to the monitor, he said, "These are recon photos of the area. Low-altitude shots, from one of the drones." As he worked, he was able to enlarge an area on the screen.

What we saw was a detailed picture of a good-sized house taken from the sky. Around the perimeter was a wall. At one end, a road leading out from the city was plainly visible. Silvio pointed at the map. "Here's a gate."

"I suppose there'll be guards at the gate," Shenlee said. When Silvio nodded, Shenlee asked how high the wall was.

"I would guess eight or nine feet."

"How far from the wall to the house?" Buck asked.

"Fifty yards, maybe a little more."

"A firefight is out of the question," Reilly said. He had returned a few minutes before. "If we go in, it's to get this Nadaj character. It's not to kill anyone."

"Something else," Shenlee said. "No one can know the United States is involved. We have to make it look like a local thing. We deny involvement. We give the responsibility for Nadaj's disappearance to one of the rival factions."

"Which means we don't wear uniforms," Reilly said.

Buck asked how many guards they'd have with them.

Chambers said, "Since there are four vehicles, I'd guess at eight to ten. A few will probably have gate guard duty."

Reilly pointed to the recon photo. "We go over the wall. We've got the equipment. I'd say four guys go in. They make it to the house, grab Nadaj, hustle him back to the wall."

"How do we get him back over?" Shenlee asked.

Reilly hesitated, then said, "We blow a hole in the wall. That shouldn't be difficult. Four of our people approach the gate to keep the guards there busy. They say their car conked out. Because he knows the lingo, one of them has to be Silvio. Four other guys stake out the perimeter. Four blast open the wall."

I looked at Reilly. "I'll go over the wall—"

"No, no," Shenlee said. "Not you, Klear."

"I know what Nadaj looks like, Jerry."

Looking at Reilly, Shenlee said, "I'll go over with three guys from the A-team. I know what Nadaj looks like. I've seen his pictures."

"I know him personally," I said. "I think it'll be safer if I—"

"Come off it, Klear. You and Romero man the perimeter." Shenlee looked at Reilly. "That's the way we're gonna do it."

Shenlee outranked us all, or at least he was acting as if he did. In any case, we all knew better than to argue with someone from the NSC, who at every opportunity was throwing around his association with the deputy secretary of defense.

Our next stop was the supply shack, which quickly turned into a beehive of activity. We were joined by Reilly's A-team men drawing weapons and the equipment we'd need for our little mission. Since it looked as if Buck and I would be manning the perimeter, we were each issued an M-16 and an M-4 automatic. We checked out flashlights, compasses, gloves, and radios. Shenlee needed special shoes, a rope, some climbing hooks, and got himself an M-4.

It would have been nice to have a Humvee along, but since we were supposed to be civilians we had no choice but to ride in vans. All told, we were seventeen men. We left Camp Bondsteel in four vehicles at three-minute intervals beginning at a few minutes after 1630. Kosovo's roads are primitive, and Pec was over sixty miles distant from Bond-steel. We had a rendezvous point on a road less than two miles from the house where we hoped we'd finally find Ramush Nadaj.

Color me pessimistic, but as we rode, I couldn't help wondering whether this attempt to grab Nadaj was going to be any more success-ful than the last one—and whether it wasn't going to turn into another colossal disaster.

* * *

Jerry Shenlee shook his head. "No, Klear, you're wrong." We had reached the rendezvous point, a quiet clearing on a side road, and I had just finished telling Shenlee that I should be accompanying Captain Reilly's three A-team members and going over the wall to get Nadaj.

"I have an idea this might work out better, Jerry, if I—"

"Relax, Klear. Leave this one to the professionals. It's gonna be a piece of cake, believe me." Before I could say anything more, Shenlee said, "You're rusty. That's why you're nervous."

I wasn't nervous, but I knew there wasn't any sense arguing with Jerry. It was already dark, and Reilly called me and Buck over to the van where he had a map spread out on the seat, which he was reading with a pencil flashlight.

"From here on, we go by foot," he said. "Your job is to cover the far side of the house. Over here there's a small stream, which runs out of the big river here. You can get your bearings from that. You shouldn't have any problem finding the wall." When Buck asked Reilly where he would be, he said, "I'm going to be with the munitions team. When the people inside the wall give us the word, we set off the explosive. We have a couple of five-pound satchels. It'll be just enough to make a hole in the wall for the men to come through. When they're out, we radio you guys. We rendezvous back here."

We nodded. Although I had an idea that, like me, Buck would have liked to be with the people going over the wall, he was a good soldier and didn't say anything. Shenlee was running the show.

The Gold Dust Twins' reputation wasn't anything like it once was.

Buck and I set off in the direction of the house, going through the woods and staying off the road. After forty minutes of slogging, we reached a clearing on the far side of which I could see a ten-foot-high wall.

"That's it," Buck said. The wall was about a hundred feet away. "Whoever lives there doesn't want unannounced visitors."

Pointing to my right, I said, "The gate should be in that direction." When Buck nodded, we headed off in the other direction, moving along the perimeter of the woods and doing our best to keep out of sight.

When we'd circled the house, we kept going until we reached the stream that Reilly had mentioned. On this side, the woods were thicker and extended all the way to the wall. Buck stationed himself about sixty feet from the stream. On the far side, two more of our guys would have come from the other direction and, by now, have taken up positions on the perimeter. We had the place surrounded.

When I checked in on the radio, Reilly said, "They're over the wall. So far, so good."

"Roger." I passed the news along to Buck.

I knew Shenlee's team would be proceeding slowly, and I wondered what they'd find at the house. They had bolt cutters, a large fire axe and a hooley, which is a crowbar specially designed for prying doors open.

The next thing we expected to hear was the explosive charge going off, which would be our signal to head back toward the rendezvous point. Five minutes went by without anything happening. Six minutes. Seven minutes. From where I was, I couldn't see Buck, so when I heard something, I thought the sound might have been him moving in my direction.

It took a couple of seconds before I realized someone was scrambling over the wall at a point twenty yards beyond where I was posted. I wondered whether Buck had heard the noise. Moving quickly, I made my way quietly along the wall. Thirty feet ahead of me I saw a black silhouette. Whoever it was, he was going fast. He was already over the wall and in the woods before I reached the point where he'd climbed over.

He'd disappeared into the woods with a minimum of commotion— and I wondered whether it was someone I knew.

A minute later, Buck appeared. When he flashed me a questioning look, I shrugged my shoulders, then pointed in the direction the guy had gone.

"He came over the wall real fast. I'd like to know who it was."

Then we heard the bang, which meant that Shenlee and his team had Nadaj and were now outside the compound.

If Buck and I had any thoughts about trying to find whoever was out in the woods, they were superseded by the knowledge that we had to get back to the rendezvous point.

We headed off in the direction we came. It took a half hour to make it back to the meeting place. We were the last ones.

"It's about time," Shenlee said. "What took you so damn long?"

"You got him?" Buck asked.

"Let's get going," Shenlee said.

Reilly pointed toward the van. "We gave him something to help him sleep."

Unable to control my curiosity, I slid open the door to have a look. The prisoner's hands were shackled, and he was unconscious on the floor of the van.

"For God's sakes, Klear," Shenlee shouted. "Can we get started?"

"I think we have a slight problem." When Reilly asked what it was, I said, "This guy isn't Nadaj."

Needless to say, my announcement caused Shenlee to go ballistic. After he'd finished telling me that I didn't know what I was talking about, I said, "I know what Nadaj looks like, Jerry. That's not Nadaj."

"You're sure?" Reilly said.

"Positive." Like Nadaj, this individual had a beard, but the resemblance ended there. He had gray hair and appeared at least ten years older.

Looking at Shenlee, Reilly asked him what happened at the house. "We surprised them," Shenlee said. "We could see in from outside the house. There were three of them, two men and a woman. I figured this had to be him—"

I said, "I have an idea what might have happened. Nadaj was on the premises but, for whatever reason, was somewhere else at the moment you people arrived. When he saw what was happening, he made tracks."

I explained to Reilly and Shenlee that Buck and I saw someone going over the wall at the rear of the compound.

"What do we do now?" Reilly asked.

"Give Buck and me a van and one of the maps. If we're lucky, we might locate him before he gets back to his people."

Reilly looked uncertainly toward Shenlee.

"No way," Shenlee said. "No way I let these two out of my sight."

Ignoring Shenlee, I pointed to the van with the prisoner. "Whoever this individual is, take him back. If he's the local Mafia chief, kidnapping him will only cause problems. Buck and I'll try and locate Nadaj."

Reilly nodded, and ordered his men out of the van. Looking back at me, he said, "We're on our way back to Bondsteel. You and Romero can catch up with us there."

Ignoring Shenlee, who was still squawking to Reilly and threatening to have him busted back to E-1, I climbed into the van and turned over the engine. Thirty seconds later, with Buck in the passenger seat, we were on the road.

Chapter 38

Wednesday, February 13, 2008

The first problem was to locate a road that would take us in the general direction we wanted to go. Buck had the map spread out on his knees and was trying to read it with the help of his compass and a pencil flash that he had in his mouth. It was already close to 2200.

I said, "If it was Nadaj who went over the wall, he'll want to get back to Pristina."

After a while, Buck got a fix on where we were. "There's what looks like a road leading toward Klina. Just keep going in this direction."

But as we drove, we began to realize our chances of locating the individual, whoever he was, weren't great. If he was smart enough to keep off the roads, we could be passing him by at any time and never know it. Because of the hills and largely unpaved roads, driving in Kosovo is a lot like an extended session on top of a bucking bronc, and I had an idea that the mechanics in the vehicle maintenance shop at Camp Bondsteel spent a lot of time replacing struts and shock absorbers.

We rode up and down a lot of hills before arriving at Klina, a small city in which everything was shut up tight. The moon had disappeared, and the night was pitch black. The city had a main drag, but most of the streets were no wider than alleys and hardly wide enough for the van. I decided to circle around, looking for a primary road that might take us somewhere. We were hoping we'd encounter someone on foot on the road—and that he would turn out to be Ramush Nadaj. But as we drove, we began to realize the chances of anything like that happening were extremely remote.

Without any real knowledge of the area and without any idea of where I should be going, we continued to drive more or less in circles. I didn't want to say it, but maybe Shenlee had been right. This expedition had all the earmarks of a wild-goose chase.

At some point we halted at the side of the road and spent some time studying the map and trying to figure what direction someone on the run might go. The strain of peering through the windshield into the darkness had made me feel tired, and after nearly two hours I turned the wheel over to Buck. As he drove, I kept my eyes peeled, hoping I might see someone on the road. Eventually, there were streaks of gold light in the sky. We'd been driving for over five hours.

Still later, we encountered a farmer driving a hay wagon drawn by a lone ox. He was the first sign of life, the first indication of a new day. We stayed behind him for five minutes before reaching an intersection where we could pass. Farther on, we passed a couple of cars, both of them ancient jalopies, coming in the opposite direction. Then we turned into a narrow dirt road with a lot of rocks on it. There were trees on both sides. Buck halted the van. We were really in the boondocks.

Although I didn't say anything, I wondered what Buck had in mind. He took another look at the map. Finally, he said, "Does this area look familiar?"

I shook my head. "Should it?"

He turned over the engine. "At the top of this hill is an abandoned mine."

"How do you know?"

"There's also a shack, assuming it's still there." With the van's engine working hard, we made it to the top of the hill. My watch said 0630 hours. A weak sun was rising in the east causing the trees to cast long shadows.

For a long moment, Buck and I just sat in the van taking in the scene. Behind the shack was a rugged steep hill thick with brush and scrub pine. Off to our left was a wide rock-filled path, which I assumed led toward the abandoned mine. Some thoughtful person had placed a barrier across the path, a warning to kids and strangers to stay away.

I recognized the shack as the building in which Nadaj and his crew had held me prisoner.

"Yeah," I said after a moment, "this place is familiar. It turns up regularly in my nightmares, the really bad ones." I didn't add that in the recurring nightmare I'm looking up out of a coffin when someone slams down the lid and everything goes black.

I said, "I assume you were looking for it."

"I knew it was around here somewhere. The thought occurred to me that maybe Nadaj might come over here. Hide out for a while until his friends showed up."

"It's a thought. But if he has a phone, he's probably already let people know where he is. He could be in Pristina by now."

We climbed out of the van and split up, Buck approaching the shack from one side, me from the other. When I reached the building, I took a careful peek through the window, but didn't see anyone. The place was empty. I signaled to Buck, who came around from the other side. After I'd kicked open the door and with weapons at the ready, we entered the building together.

The interior was pretty much as I remembered it—table, chairs, a couple of cots, a wooden chest that was supposed to serve as an icebox, but was empty of food. On one side was a small closet, which I opened and found empty except for some newspapers and rags piled in the corner.

Then I noticed it: On the table was a small metal ashtray. In the ashtray were cigarette ashes and two squashed butts. In the air was a faint smell of stale tobacco. Buck had smelled it too. He pointed at the ashtray, and I nodded.

We both had the same thought.

"Let's get going," Buck said, speaking loudly.

"No sense hanging around here," I said.

We clumped out of the shack, making sure as we went that we left the door open. As Buck climbed back into the van and turned over the engine, I removed my boots, unholstered my M-4, stepped back inside, looked the room over.

Did I want to do this?

The trapdoor was adjacent to the table. When I gave Buck a wave, he gunned the engine and started back down the hill.

Just standing there and recalling my experience with Nadaj's KLA gang in this very building, I could feel my adrenalin rushing, my heart pounding, and my hands sweating. I took a couple of deep breaths, trying to get my emotions under control. I didn't like the idea of making myself vulnerable to whoever might be playing hide-and-seek with us.

Crossing the wooden floor would be the dangerous part, and I stood there for a long minute just surveying the situation, determining the points on the floor where the boards were nailed over the beams and wouldn't be likely to creak. It was twenty feet to the other side of the room. Finally, when I moved, I did so very carefully, placing one foot down, then the other. Each time I took a step, I paused, waited, and listened. Just one creaking board would be enough to give away my presence to whoever, when he heard us coming, might have squashed out his cigarette, and decided to make himself scarce by climbing down into the hole beneath the shack.

Whoever he was, he wouldn't figure that we'd know there was a hidey-hole beneath the floor.

If there was someone down there, I would be very vulnerable until I could get to a point in the room where I wouldn't be immediately seen if he pushed open the trapdoor. Both Buck and I had arrived on the military scene too late for the Vietnam War, but we'd heard plenty of stories of the damage done by Vietcong concealed in spider holes who would, without warning, leap up and announce their presence with bursts of fire at short range. In some cases, they were able to take out entire squads with these brazen tactics.

The next four or five minutes seemed like an eternity, but that's how long it took before I was able to cross the floor to a point where I was standing directly behind the trapdoor. If the door moved upward, I would no longer be visible, not immediately at least. Because I didn't want to risk easing my weight down and perhaps causing a board to creak, I remained upright. I couldn't see Buck, but I assumed he'd come back up the hill on foot and was somewhere outside the shack.

After another five minutes, I was ready to concede there was no one down there and was about to call out to Buck. For some reason,

though, I decided to give it another minute—and it was at that moment that I heard something, the sound of someone moving. It seemed
to come from somewhere beneath the wooden floor. Another couple of
minutes went by. Then the trapdoor slowly began to move upward, its
rusty hinges creaking ever so slightly. As the trapdoor continued to
rise, I saw the barrel of an automatic weapon moving from side to side,
establishing a field of fire from one wall to the other. Whoever he was,
he was good, and he was being very careful.

When he didn't see anyone, he readied himself to climb out. As he
pushed the trapdoor up a little higher, I could see his arm, then the
back of his head. I thought I recognized it. Just the sight of Nadaj together with the stink rising out of the hole was enough to send me over
the edge.

His last movement offered me the opportunity I wanted. I reached
out, grabbed the barrel of the weapon, and ripped the gun from his
hands. At the same time, I shoved the table away, which upended it,
and kicked the trapdoor open the rest of the way. Then I fastened my
hand around his arm and yanked him the rest of the way out of the
hole.

When I saw his startled look, I couldn't resist.

"Hello, Ramush."

His eyes flashed, and when I saw the beginnings of that goofy
smile, it brought back more memories. The knife he produced, seemingly from out of nowhere, was the same one he'd waved in front of my
face at our first meeting, with the dark handle and curved blade—the
one he was going to use to cut off my nose. I was ready for him. Before
he could slash me with it, I smashed the barrel of my automatic against
his face. When he made another pass at me with the blade, I clobbered
him again. Blood spurted from somewhere. I suppose the smart thing
would have been to shoot him then and there, but I decided to hit him
again, catching him just below his left eye. Although his face now
looked like hamburger, he was tough, and he still hung on to the knife.
In an effort to make him drop the blade, I hit him again. By this time
blood was all over. I grabbed his wrist and forced his arm downward,

but he still had some resistance. He stepped and dodged, and somehow got his arm loose. I anticipated his next move—and ducked as he swung and narrowly missed slashing off my ear.

With my hand squeezing his wrist, he finally had to drop the knife, but my gun hand struck the upended table, causing me to lose my grip on the automatic—and it fell to the floor. That wasn't supposed to happen.

"Goddamn!"

All I could think to do was kick the gun to keep Nadaj from grabbing it. But that didn't help much either. Down on his knees, he was closer to the weapon than I was, and scrambled after it. Just as he picked it up, Buck came crashing through the door and Nadaj fired in his direction. Blinded by his own blood and with an eye closed, he wasn't even close, and that one shot was all he got.

After I'd leaped on top of Nadaj and wrestled the gun from his hand, I said, "You tried to kill my partner." Again, I smashed him with the weapon.

I said, "And that's for Fabiola's brother!"

Holding his arm over his bloody face, Nadaj looked about the way I must have looked almost a year ago, before they tossed me into the hole. For some reason, that made me feel good. A second later, I felt Buck's hand on my upper arm, preventing me from swinging again.

I was breathing hard. As I got to my feet, Buck said, "Why didn't you just shoot the bastard?"

"I'm too softhearted."

"No, you're a vindictive son of a bitch."

I wasn't in the mood to argue the point.

As Buck kept his weapon trained on Nadaj, I put my boots back on and brought some rope back from the vehicle. We made sure that Ramush Nadaj was trussed up good and tight before we shoved him into the back of the van, and then got going.

Roughly three miles from the shack, on the road back toward Camp Bondsteel, we saw a distant cloud of dust rapidly coming our way. It was a pickup truck barreling down the center of the road with its horn blasting. As Buck swerved at the last minute, doing a good job of keeping the van out of a ditch running parallel to the road, the other driver raised his fist while the half dozen guys in the rear laughed and waved their automatic weapons.

"I wonder if that gentleman has a driver's license," Buck said when we were back in the middle of the road.

"Not necessarily," I said. "Driver's licenses in Kosovo are optional."

"Those fellows in the rear could have been soldiers. They had automatic weapons."

"I noticed that too," I said. "I wonder where they could be going."

Buck only smiled. Neither one of us said what we knew to be the case: we'd caught up with Ramush Nadaj just in time.

Chapter 39

Friday, February 15, 2008

It was a good thing I resisted the urge to shoot Nadaj when I had the chance. At least that's how Jerry Shenlee explained things at lunch the following day. According to Jerry, Nadaj was much more valuable alive than dead.

"He gassed his own men in Afghanistan," Jerry told us. "He's a goddamn war criminal. We have reasons to keep him alive."

As I poured some vinegar on my salad, I nodded. I was willing to take Jerry's word for it.

We were in a cozy semiprivate dining room in Camp Bondsteel with a large round table in the middle of it. Shenlee, Captain Reilly, Buck, and I were there shooting the breeze when, to my surprise, we were joined by Sylvia who arrived halfway through the meal. I wondered when she'd arrived in Kosovo.

Needless to say, she immediately became the center of everyone's attention.

"From what I understand," she said, "Nadaj is being detained here. Good work, gentlemen. The news will make some people in our nation's capitol very happy." She smiled, and raised a glass of orange juice. "It's taken a while."

"We found him at a meeting with one of the village Mafia people," Shenlee said while munching some spareribs. "A couple of us went in after him, but he'd already split."

That much was accurate.

"After we determined that he was gone, I ordered Klear and Romero to go after him."

Although that wasn't exactly the way things happened, Reilly, Buck, and I all remained silent. The fact that Jerry would be taking much of the credit for the capture of Ramush Nadaj wasn't something that would cause any of us to become bent out of shape. We knew that Jerry had his career to think about. Maybe at some point he'd buy Buck and me lunch.

Or maybe he'd get the government to intercede on my behalf regarding the murder rap that was hanging over my head in Germany. I was scheduled to fly back to Ramstein at 1530, and I made a mental note to catch up with Shenlee and Sylvia before I left.

Sylvia said, "If Kurt Mehling or anyone else accuses the United States of having employed sarin gas against the Taliban in Afghanistan, we'll be able to counter the charge. We'll only need to persuade Mr. Nadaj to say what really happened."

"What we really ought to do," Shenlee said, "is turn him over to the World Court in The Hague. Like we did with Milosevic. This guy violated the Geneva Convention. Let them try him for war crimes."

Nodding, Sylvia said, "That might happen. But it's a decision that some other people will have to make. Meanwhile, Mr. Nadaj stays in the jail here."

"And I don't want to read about this incident in the newspapers," Shenlee said.

"He's not our worry anymore," Buck said. "We'll forget we ever heard of the guy." It was Buck who had organized the first Nadaj rendition, and I knew he was relieved that we'd finally managed to remove Nadaj from circulation. Maybe the reputation of the Gold Dust Twins wasn't as bright and shiny as it once was, but it was at least still in tact. One thing I've learned from being involved for twenty years with special ops: be thankful for small favors.

Although she was pretending not to notice me, I could see Sylvia occasionally glancing across the table in my direction. I wondered what the significance might be of that, if any. As I returned to the table with a second cup of coffee, Captain Reilly was carrying his tray toward the exit.

We shook hands and promised to keep in touch. The truth was, I'd never completely stopped wondering how my life would have turned out if I'd stayed with Special Forces. If circumstances hadn't brought me to the attention of Jim McDaniel, the agency recruiter, I never would have ended up doing the stuff I've been doing for so long.

I caught up with Shenlee and Sylvia an hour later in one of the offices in the S-2 section. Sylvia was seated behind the desk gazing at a computer, and Shenlee was resting his rear end against the desk while reading through some files. I had a feeling they'd been talking over the promotions they were likely to receive and the good reports that would go into their personnel files.

They both knew why I was there.

"Shouldn't you be on your way, Klear?" Shenlee said, looking at his watch.

"The van's outside, Jerry. My flight's not for another two hours." I looked at Sylvia. "I'm wondering if someone in the government might want to tell the German cops that I was on duty when I shot Quemal. It would help."

Shenlee uttered a sigh, an unmistakable sign that he thought my request was an unreasonable one. "Listen, Klear. No one ordered you to shoot him."

"It was self-defense. He had a knife at my throat."

"Experienced special ops people don't let those things happen. They don't get into those situations. And they don't go around shooting citizens inside the borders of friendly countries. You know that."

"You mean I should have tried reasoning with him?"

"You should have turned that information over to the German police, Alex." Before I could respond, Sylvia said, "He was one of the KLA people who'd held you prisoner down here, wasn't he?"

"You know he was, Sylvia."

Shenlee grunted. "I can believe you had a beef against him, Klear. But the Krauts don't take kindly to people who take the law into their own hands. You can't blame them for that. We don't either."

"That's right, Alex," Sylvia said. "The Germans would maintain that you were settling a personal score, and they'd be right."

"At least you were able to resist shooting Nadaj," Shenlee said.

"Tell the authorities what happened, Alex. I've already indicated that's what you should do."

"You were there, Sylvia. You could say what happened."

"Listen, Klear. You may think we're being unreasonable, but we're not. The Krauts are difficult to deal with. Forget the diplomacy. There's a lot of tension these days between them and us. Just to give you an example: The Hamburg cops arrested a couple of terrorists last year some time, a gang with all kinds of explosives and plans to blow up an American base. Then they decided to drop the charges, so we asked them to extradite these characters. The Krauts wouldn't do it. The minute these terrorists were out of jail, what do you think happened?"

"They disappeared."

"Right. With a little more cooperation, we'd have them out of circulation by now, which would mean one less headache for us."

Sylvia nodded. "Jerry's right, Alex. There's nothing we can do for you. You clearly overstepped your authority in that instance. We'd help if we could."

"I'm sure." I don't think I was able to keep the disgust out of my voice. Colonel Bitch-on-Wheels was acting true to form.

Outside, I found the van with Buck behind the wheel. From the way he looked at me, I could see he sensed how depressed I felt.

When he asked about the meeting, I said, "They say they can't do anything. Shenlee says the Germans don't like the idea of people taking the law into their own hands."

"That's not exactly news. Doesn't he feel some responsibility? After all, he and the colonel are the ones who organized the operation. I'm sure they'll be happy to take the credit."

I said, "You and I think differently from the way they do." I resisted the urge to say "Colonel Bitch," but I had an idea Buck knew what I was thinking.

"You always said we got into the wrong end of the business." Buck turned over the engine and slammed the vehicle into gear. He wasn't happy either. As we went by the PX and gymnasium and navigated the hilly road leading toward the main gate, Buck said quietly, "Shenlee indicated that they want me to fly back to the States. But I could fly back to Munich with you and see what goes."

I thought about that for a moment. It would be nice to have Buck around. Finally, I said, "It might be wiser to do what Shenlee says. There's no sense getting him mad at you. There's always the telephone. I'll keep you posted."

Buck nodded. We'd both been a part of the small world that military and government operatives inhabit long enough to know that it didn't make sense to antagonize the wrong people. I'd be on my own in Germany.

Although I said something about things working out right in the end, I'm not sure either Buck or I really believed they would. At some point in life, everyone's luck runs out. Considering the number of times I'd gone through the Wall and into the East during the Cold War, not to mention some of the crazy stuff I'd done when I was over there, I had to concede that the law of averages probably should have caught up with me a lot sooner. It had caught up with me finally—as it eventually catches up with everyone. I don't know if I ever felt so depressed, mostly because I never thought things would end like this.

But the truth is, I've known of any number of dedicated intelligence people, guys and gals who'd had great careers, for whom things ended badly. In some respects, I guess, it's the nature of the business. If it is, it shouldn't be.

Buck hung around at the military terminal, drinking vending-machine coffee with me until they called my flight. He and I shook hands at the gate. For all either of us knew, the next time I saw him might be on visitors' day in a German jail. Then, together with a couple of dozen GIs and a handful of civilians, I began walking out to where a C-130, gassed up and ready to fly, was sitting on the tarmac.

A half hour later, we were airborne and headed back to Ramstein Air Base.

Chapter 40

Friday, February 15, 2008

It was already after 1900 by the time we touched down. A couple of GIs gave me a ride from the main Ramstein terminal to the parking area, and I set off on the trip back to Munich at about 1930. I had been away for three days, and I couldn't help wondering whether the cops had tumbled to the fact I was gone.

I assumed that they had, but I told myself I would deal with that particular bridge when it was time to cross it. In any case, I wouldn't be advertising where I'd been. One obvious difference between Germany and Kosovo is the roads—in Germany they may be the world's best, in Kosovo they are among the world's worst. I enjoy driving fast, and for most of the trip, I was in the passing lane with the Mercedes speedometer at well over eighty.

During the time I was in Kosovo I hadn't had time to think about anything beyond finding Ramush Nadaj. I had to confess to feeling some satisfaction knowing that I'd finally managed to accomplish the two objectives that I'd signed on for—nailing Nadaj and springing Brinkman. And Kurt Mehling would have to scrap whatever plans he had for publishing reports of the United States employing sarin gas in eastern Afghanistan, and thereby setting the stage for a nuclear attack on the United States. But in carrying out these two assignments, I'd gotten some people very mad at me.

The Munich cops, naturally enough, were eager to jail the individual who had shot someone in their fair city.

And then there was Kurt Mehling.

I'd brought his involvement with the murder of Ursula Vogt to the attention of the Munich police. He wouldn't like that. When I recalled that Mehling had offered me a job in his organization, I had to laugh. I figured that all he wanted to do was get me into some private place and squeeze as much information out of me as he could. After that, he'd remove me from circulation permanently.

The last stretch of the A-8 autobahn took me past the city of Augsburg, which is about fifty miles west of Munich. It was now well after midnight, close to the end of a long day. I fought the urge to close my eyes and relax as I drove since, at over eighty miles per hour, you don't want to fall asleep at the wheel. All I could think of was getting back to the place and hitting the sack. Tomorrow I'd try to speak with someone, either to Max or to Irmie, and go on from there.

There had to be a way out of this mess. If there wasn't, I was going to be out of circulation for a long time.

Feeling very tired, I reached the traffic circle on the outskirts of Munich, turned into the Menzingerstrasse, which was empty of traffic. At Romanplatz, I hung a right, rode down two blocks and hung another right. It was after midnight, and mine was the only car on the street. I found a parking space a block away from the building, climbed out, locked up the vehicle, and hauled my carry-on out of the trunk. As I started up the sidewalk, I saw a moving shadow.

My alarm bells went off. If I hadn't been so tired, I would have anticipated something like this.

Someone was behind me. Six feet in front of me I saw another large shadow, this one blocking the sidewalk.

The individual behind me came up fast, but I was already moving and received only a glancing blow against the back of my neck. Not wanting to give them a target, I kept moving. I swung my carry-on, caught the one behind me squarely in the side of the head, heard him mumble what sounded like an Albanian curse. When the other guy swung, he sent me reeling, and I wound up sprawled against a parked car. As they moved in, I broke off the automobile's antenna, jabbed it at the silhouette's face, heard him cry out. With one hand over his eye, he hesitated and yelled something at his partner. I continued to slash with the antenna, but now there was a third guy on the scene. Moving in quickly, I swung at the newcomer with my left. I staggered him, but that was all.

The first two attackers I handled well enough. One was disabled and the other half disabled, but the third guy caught me off balance. He hit me with something, probably some kind of blackjack. Feeling dazed and with my eyes smarting, I was able to deflect a couple of the punches he aimed at my head. But then he caught me solidly against my ear.

I heard a loud ringing, then felt them grabbing my arms. Doing my best to fight them off, I told myself not to let this happen.

As I struggled, I felt myself being shoved and dragged. They were trying to get me into the rear seat of a car they had parked at the curb. I knew I didn't want to go in there, and when I got my arm loose, I clobbered someone's face. But three was too many, and after a minute they finally pushed me onto the backseat. With the rear door still open, one of them jumped in, slammed the car in gear—but it lurched, then stalled. He got the engine going again, backed up, banged against the car behind us. His two partners were holding me down on the rear seat, and one of them produced a roll of duct tape.

The car was out in traffic, but the rear door was still open, banging back and forth.

As his partner held my arms, the one with a hand over his eye reached out to slam the door closed. I tried to shove him out, but he was able to grab the doorframe. Then, using his free hand, he managed to get some duct tape around my wrists. As the other guy held me, he continued to wind the tape. When he was finished, he pointed to his eye. Although I don't understand much Albanian, I knew he was very angry.

As we drove onto the Ring, I felt my head throbbing. My left hand hurt like blazes. As we drove, they talked among themselves. They didn't seem to care that I could hear what they were saying and see where we were going.

I took that as a bad sign.

Then we were on the Leopoldstrasse, and when we turned off, I knew we were headed for the Kalashni Klub. We drove on to the gravel parking lot and with a screech of brakes halted behind the building. They hustled me out of the car, through a door, and tumbled me down some narrow steps. One of them dragged me to my feet, opened the door to a large basement room, and the guy with the hand over his eye pulled me inside. I went in stumbling, lost my balance, and ended up sprawled on the floor. Standing over me, he screeched something in Albanian. I don't think he was saying "Welcome back to Munich."

"Alex, my dear fellow." Kurt Mehling had a pained expression on his elegant, unlined face. "You don't look good." He sighed, dusted a speck of dust from his jacket sleeve. "None of this had to happen, you know. If only you'd listened—"

Wearing a gray ski jacket and a pair of jeans, Mehling had entered the room a few minutes before. I had an idea he'd been awakened from a sound sleep and had dressed hurriedly. I figured the time for around 0400 hours. After a brief conversation with two of his goons, Mehling turned his attention to me. I was seated at the table, my hands taped together and my legs taped so tightly to the chair they ached from lack of circulation. I wasn't going anywhere.

Mehling dropped onto the chair opposite me, sighed again, leaned his arms on the table. "I'm sorry, Alex," he said quietly. "I really am. I had an idea that you and I could work well together." He paused. "Obviously, you had other plans."

"You can't get away with this," I said, giving my voice an authority I didn't feel. "You can't kill me and think the police won't find out." But the truth was, I didn't see why he couldn't.

He smiled indulgently, probably realizing I had to say something along those lines.

"I can forgive a lot of things. Believe me, I really can. But what you did—" His voice broke off.

"Untie me, Kurt. Then we can talk better."

Sighing, he said. "I like you, Alex. I really do. You're saucy and funny, and I like that. You're so typically American. I wondered whether you would accept my generous offer. I hoped you would.

Really. I sensed you were suspicious of me, but you shouldn't have been. I think we could have made a good team."

He lit a cigarette. "What you did, Alex, was really hurtful to me. As I say, it amounted to a betrayal. You returned my kindness with unkindness. Extraordinary unkindness."

"I don't know what you're talking about."

"Well, let me explain it just to eliminate all possibility of misunderstanding—and so that you understand why you are going to have to be—what's the word you people use? Terminated? Treacherous people need to be terminated. In order to make the world a better place. And you, Alex, are a treacherous person."

"You're not making sense. Untie me."

"You remember that at our meeting I offered you a job where you would have every opportunity to utilize your skills and at the same time be well paid."

"Of course I remember."

Mehling removed an object from his jacket pocket. It was my Beretta. Fixing me with a hostile stare, he pointed it at me. "Bang, bang, Alex, you're dead." He lowered the weapon, smiled, obviously amused at his little joke. "You're not dead yet? Soon, Alex, soon." Then, looking at the weapon, he said, "I think it's poetic justice that you should be killed with your own gun."

Although I sat perfectly still, I could feel beads of perspiration on my forehead.

"Do you know how I came into possession of this?" When I only stared, he said, "Would you believe that on the very next day, the day following our little talk, I was personally summoned to police headquarters and that my car was impounded? Well, it's true. But I am a most cautious person, and I had already made a thorough examination of the vehicle, from top to bottom. One of the two gentlemen who aided me found this. It was under the passenger seat."

After a brief pause, he said, "That was not nice." Mehling placed the weapon in his jacket, then zipped up the pocket. "If I hadn't taken the trouble to go over the car, I might have had some difficulty explaining to the police the presence of this weapon in my automobile. Why aren't you saying anything, Alex? Has the cat got your tongue?"

My scheme hadn't worked after all. Looking back, I suppose it wasn't all that brilliant. Max, Irmie, and Buck had all suggested as much. I hoped Irmie hadn't said anything to make Schneider suspicious. I hated to think how I'd involved her in all this.

"I would have expected more from you. Really, did you think I was so careless that I wouldn't look over the car after our conversation? Then the detectives wanted to know where I was on the evening that a murder took place out here." Mehling sighed.

"Where were you?"

"I had the foresight to bribe my mechanic. He provided an airtight alibi. He said my car was in the shop for repairs for two days. It required only a phone call for the police to determine that it couldn't possibly have been at the K Klub on the evening of the murder."

At that moment the door opened and Vickie, wearing a pink cashmere sweater and brown slacks, stepped into the room. She looked very different from the way she had looked in Kosovo, when she was dressed in loose-fitting black cammies.

I wondered whether she mightn't be working her magic on Mehling. Her sweater was tight and emphasized her breasts. As they spoke, keeping their voices low, Mehling placed his hand on her arm. I sensed they were talking about me. I seemed to be on everyone's mind all of a sudden.

Vickie left, and Mehling said, "The whole thing was embarrassing for the detectives, Alex. They kept offering explanations for why they'd called me. Except for one female detective, they were all extremely apologetic. They even played a tape of a telephone message on which some drunk said he'd seen someone being shot in a vehicle. It was so ridiculous—"

"Untie me, Kurt."

Mehling squashed out his cigarette and shook his head. "As I say, this detective, a blonde woman, kept asking unpleasant questions. Making herself obnoxious."

That would have been Irmie.

"After a time, my patience really wore thin. I have a certain amount of influence with the police authorities. I promise you that this female detective, whoever she is, won't be with the police force much longer. And one day she'll just disappear. I'll see to that."

When I didn't say anything, Mehling shrugged. "Balkan gangsters, men like Igor, can be very effective."

"Effective at what?"

"At instilling discipline, Alex. To start with, a sedative to make the woman drowsy. After she's been raped fifteen or twenty times, she has little choice but to become cooperative, wouldn't you agree? Provide some cocaine from time to time, and rape her until she's crying for the drug and telling you she'll do anything for another high. When Igor puts them to work, they'll oblige even the most revolting men." He smiled. "Anything to keep her pimp happy."

I didn't say anything. I'd spent enough time in the Balkans investigating these types of operations to know how they worked. Max had hinted that Mehling's influence extended in every direction. One thing I knew: the trafficking of drugs and women can only exist in countries where the authorities look the other way, and to me it looked as if the countries of Europe, like some of the countries of the Far East, were permitting the traffickers to have free rein.

"Why are you looking at me like that, Alex? The only way to survive in the world is to destroy your enemies—to do what you have to do."

Why had I involved Irmie in this? I felt sick.

"Don't you agree? What's wrong, Alex? Are you squeamish?"

I made an effort to move my legs, but it was no use.

"Relax. You're not going anywhere." Mehling grinned. "This detective seemed to want to connect me to the murder of Ursula Vogt. Now, tell me, where she would get the idea that I would want to murder one of my own employees?"

Mehling might have figured out that I had told Irmie he was behind Ursula Vogt's murder.

"Well?"

"Ursula Vogt wouldn't go along with the sarin gas story. You had to get rid of her." Mehling wanted to talk. He was obviously curious about how much we'd been able to figure out.

"Really?"

"Sure. You had to have her killed if you were going to stay on the good side of Bin Laden and his buddies. They're paying your salary, Kurt. The American government knows that."

"I'm not afraid of your government. I've defied it for a long time. And I'll tell you something else. I'm not the only one, Alex. Some of the most influential and admired people in the West are al-Qaeda agents. Money buys everything in our world, absolutely everything."

Mehling patted his jacket pocket. "I have an idea that this is the weapon that killed the unfortunate Quemal." He smiled. "Alex, I can't tell you what a favor you did me by getting rid of that unpleasant individual. However, I've just been informed that a team of Americans in Kosovo have taken Quemal's commander, Ramush Nadaj, into custody. You remember him, I'm sure."

I assumed that was the news that Vickie had brought to Mehling.

"That should end any thoughts you had about printing stories about the United States using sarin gas in Afghanistan. Nadaj has another story to tell, and he may be telling it at the World Court one of these days. That crumb gassed his own men."

Mehling was probably one of the people behind the decision to gas the KLA soldiers. He didn't like what I'd just told him, and began toying nervously with the zipper on his jacket. He opened the door and stepped outside. When he returned, he had one of his goons with him, the one who now had a bandage over his eye.

"As you know, Alex, Kosovo is a primitive country, by our standards at least. Feuds and rivalries endure for centuries. The rule there is, an eye for an eye. According to Igor here, you have cost him the sight in his left eye. It's a matter of honor with him. He's now demanding that before we kill you he be allowed to return the favor."

Igor had some kind of small curved knife in his hand. As he and Mehling were speaking, Mehling was interrupted by the ringing of his cell phone. This situation was growing worse by the minute. As Mehling spoke, I eyed Igor warily.

With the phone to his ear, Mehling's face suddenly took on a troubled expression. "What? Here?" He shook his head. "Impossible." Since he was speaking English, I had an idea he might be talking with Vickie, who was probably in another part of the building.

I wondered what she might be telling him.

"How many?" Then a pause. "Are you sure?"

Without another word, Mehling clicked off his phone, turned, and removed the automatic from his jacket pocket. With a concerned look still on his face, he stepped toward me.

"Goodbye, Alex. I have to leave. Igor will function as the agent to execute Kosovo justice."

Mehling said something to Igor, then placed the automatic back in his pocket. At the door, he hit the light switch. The only light came from a small lamp in the far corner. Before leaving, Mehling took one last look at me, nodded at Igor, then shut the door behind him. I was in the last place in the world that I wanted to be: alone with Igor.

Chapter 41

Friday, February 15, 2008

The shadowy darkness seemed to suit Igor just fine. He pointed to his bandaged eye and, speaking quietly, said something.

I wondered what it was that had changed Mehling's mood so suddenly.

"Let me loose, Igor."

Igor shook his head, then said something I couldn't understand. Even in the darkness, I could see a strange glint in his good eye, as though he was enjoying the moment.

When the door behind Igor began slowly to open, I wondered whether Mehling was coming back to watch as Igor dispensed his country's justice. Igor was so enraged, he trembled. His entire attention was focused on me. As he waved his knife in a strange circular motion, I couldn't take my eyes from it.

Igor stepped forward, then looking directly at me, said something in Albanian. It had a formal sound to it, as though he was reciting a chant and we both were part of some kind of strange ritual. In the darkness behind Igor something moved—a green shadow. Then it moved again, this time with the silence and speed of a jungle cat. A second later, it was directly behind Igor.

As Igor continued his eerie chant, I recognized the word *"Drejtësi!"* Justice. He said the word twice and raised his knife. But the voice that spoke the word a third time was that of a woman.

Igor's chant ended abruptly, in mid-sentence, with his knife inches from my face.

He stumbled forward, fell to his knees, then as if he'd been struck by a train, dropped to the ground, the last sounds he would ever utter a pathetic, hardly audible gargle. In the darkness, a green figure flitted through the shadows and within seconds slipped back into the corridor. The door closed, and I heard the lock click.

Prostrate in front of me, his left arm extended, lay Igor, the blade of what looked like a bayonet protruding from his back. The force from the blow was so great I could well believe the blade had punctured his heart.

Still held down by the duct tape, I couldn't move. Soaked in sweat and with my heart pounding, I remained alone in the dark, drafty room for maybe five minutes. Then someone started banging on the door.

A second later, two policemen, both wearing green Kevlar helmets and flak jackets and carrying weapons, came crashing into the room. One of them hit the light switch, and the other stuck his Uzi in my face, and asked me who I was.

I said, "My name is Klear." I hoped that was the right answer. It seemed to be because he nodded. When he asked if I was "the American," I said I was. I guess that was the right answer too because he lowered his weapon.

When he asked who Igor was and what had happened, I told him.

"I think we've found the Ami," the cop said into his radio. "We're downstairs, in the cellar." After a pause he added, "But you're not going to believe this. There's a damned body down here."

A minute later, we were joined by two more cops, also in SWAT team regalia.   After they'd cut through the tape, I spent a couple of minutes trying to restore some circulation and regain my sea legs. As I was doing so, Detective Paul Schneider came strolling through the door, hands in the pockets of his leather jacket. When he saw me, he shook his head.

"So this is where you spend your free time, Klear. In the *Poof*."

"You seem to have a dumb remark for every occasion, Detective."

"It's become a habit. I learned it from you."

Looking down at Igor, he said, "Who's this?"

When I told him, he frowned, then shook his head. After giving some orders to the SWAT team guys concerning the body, he turned his attention back to me.

"You had a close call," he said.

"How'd you find me?"

"I'll tell you later." Looking me over, he shook his head unsympathetically. "You're a little banged up."

"I'll be all right."

Schneider then headed out of the room and back up the flight of stone steps. I followed. In the parking area next to the building, which was now lit up by searchlights from police vans, there was a lot going on. Half a dozen men, one of whom was Kurt Mehling, were being frisked while leaning against a pair of police vans. As I watched, one of the policemen removed the Beretta from Mehling's jacket pocket. My gun. The one I used to shoot Quemal.

Then I saw Irmie. She came striding out of the building's side door, and as she walked by me, we exchanged the briefest of glances. She may have smiled, but in the darkness it was hard to tell.

In all, I counted twenty policemen. A minute later, half a dozen women, a couple of whom I remembered from my earlier visit to this place and all with their heads down, emerged from the building and began shuffling across the gravel. Two policemen herded them toward a police van. It was a gut-wrenching sight.

One of the women was Tania, the woman who'd been in the car and who'd escaped after I shot Quemal. When she saw me, she halted for a second, then fixed me with a long stare. As she walked, she continued to look toward me, turning her head as she went. Finally, she stopped, still staring. When one of the policemen tried to urge her along, she brushed away his hand. Then they were moving again.

I watched. Standing on the van's top step, Tania hesitated, again looked toward me—and silently mouthed a word. Even in the darkness and from a distance of fifty feet, I thought I knew what it was. I nodded just as she disappeared inside the police van. Tania, I noticed, was wearing a green jacket and green slacks.

It would only occur to me later that Vickie was not among the women arrested by the police.

"Are you enjoying the show?" I turned to see Schneider and another detective standing next to me.

I said, "This looks likes a full-fledged old-fashioned *Razzia*." A *Razzia* is a police raid.

"That's what it is," Schneider said. "It's been a while since I've been on one."

"Do you intend to close this place?" I asked.

"We'll try." Schneider pulled a pack of cigarettes out of his jacket pocket. When he offered me one, I said I had enough bad habits. After a minute, the other detective drifted off.

"You're still a murder suspect," Schneider said. "One of my theories is that you were sent over here with orders to terminate Sheholi, first name Quemal. Is that right?"

"No way, Detective. You've got an overactive imagination."

"You can't blame me for thinking that. American intelligence agencies have their people all over the world, knocking off the unfriendlies."

I said, "Look at it this way. If they sent me over here for something like that, they'd have me out of here by now, wouldn't they?"

"Maybe. Something else, Klear. The Green Beret who busted out of jail had help."

I said, "Whoever helped spring the Green Beret saved the German government from the embarrassment of convicting an innocent man. Give the guy a medal."

"Fat chance." Schneider blew some smoke.

"What the police should be investigating is Kurt Mehling's connection with the drugs and women being trafficked up here from the Balkans. The traffickers send the money they earn back to the KLA."

"We're the police, Klear. Just investigating the local stuff keeps us busy."

I didn't say anything. I had the feeling that Schneider knew I'd shot Quemal and that he was determined to nail me for it. But I also wondered whether he didn't agree that the Albanian Mafia had too much influence in Europe.

Then I said, "Before you ask me any more questions, let me ask you one: how did you know I was at the K Klub?"

"Before I tell you that," Schneider said, "let me ask you this question. Where have you been the last three days? That apartment you've been staying in has been empty."

"I took a short trip."

"I thought you might be trying to leave the country. We already have the word out. You would have had a tough time flying out of any airport in the EU. If you'd been outside the EU, you'd have been in violation of the law. Where were you?"

"I was staying with a friend."

Schneider fixed me with a skeptical stare. "We staked out your apartment because we were watching you. When we saw these other characters hanging around, we ran the plate number of their vehicle and saw it was registered to someone from Kosovo. They were there for almost two days. Also waiting for you, we figured. You put up one hell of a fight when they jumped you."

"I got banged up a little. Any chance of getting a ride home?"

Schneider nodded and called over a van driver. He looked at me. "If we need to talk with you again, we know where to find you. Right? You won't be making any more trips?"

"Without a passport," I said, "I wouldn't get very far."

Chapter 42

Saturday, February 16, 2008

It was close to 0900 hours when the police van dropped me in front of my building. Although I lost the carry-on with my keys in the scuffle, I had my name and address on the tag, and some thoughtful person had returned the bag to the *Hausmeister*. I'd been gone for only three and-a-half days, but it was good to be back—and the bed looked particularly inviting. But while I felt tired and had slept only one night in the last three, my adrenalin was still churning. After wrapping my hand in ice, I drank a liter of beer for breakfast before finally falling into a troubled sleep.

I dreamed of Irmie, which definitely beats dreaming about coffins.

When I awoke in the early afternoon, I called her extension at police headquarters. I was told she was out, and left a message. Shortly before 1330 she returned my call.

"Are you all right?"

"Were you worried?"

"Maybe a little, Alex. You looked shaken up last night."

"I hurt my hand. Otherwise I'm fine. I'm calling because I'd like to see you."

Even on the phone I could sense her hesitation. "I don't think so."

"Can I ask why?"

"There's an investigation, and you're involved."

Irmie was being diplomatic. She was referring to the investigation of Quemal's murder, and I was not only involved, I was the chief suspect. It would be impossible for us to meet anywhere socially.

I thought for a second, then said, "Kurt Mehling was carrying the murder weapon when he was arrested last night."

"How do you know, Alex?"

"I was watching while they frisked him. During the raid, I saw a policeman remove a gun from his pocket. A Beretta." She knew instantly it was mine, and had been used to kill Quemal. "You might want to bring this to Detective Schneider's attention."

"He'll want to know why Kurt Mehling would want to—"

"—kill Quemal? To shut him up. Quemal murdered Ursula Vogt. He was called the Assassin. Although Miss Vogt worked for Mehling, she was writing an article exposing the conspiracy that he set in motion."

"How do you know it was the murder weapon?"

"We talked. He told me."

"If Mehling was in possession of the murder weapon, that fact really could change things." At that moment I heard voices in the background, and Irmie said hello to someone. And then she said goodbye.

Chapter 43

Sunday, February 17, 2008

The official announcement finally came: Kosovo declared itself independent of Serbia.

The news broadcasts carried pictures of people holding red flags and dancing in the streets of all Kosovo's major cities. It was a foregone conclusion that the United States would recognize Kosovo as an independent nation.

Although the story never hit the newspapers, the United States' rendition of Ramush Nadaj prevented him from taking a place in the president's cabinet, and thereby prevented al-Qaeda from gaining an influential place in Kosovo's fledgling government.

On the following day, Max and I were seated on high stools at the counter in his kitchen drinking coffee and smearing Gruyere cheese on Bavarian rolls. The weather was cold and clear, and beams of late afternoon sun were streaming through the curtains.

"You've seen the news, I guess." I pointed at the headline in the copy of the *Washington Post* I had spread out on the kitchen counter: "Independence Is Proclaimed by Kosovo."

Max nodded. "I saw it on the news yesterday. This is really going to change the situation in the Balkans. United with Kosovo and northern Macedonia, Albania is going to be a rival to Serbia."

I took a sip of coffee, but didn't say anything. It had taken a while, but I could now understand the logic behind the events I'd become tangled up in. Although the Kosovo Liberation Army had played a major role in Kosovo's push for independence, it was largely supported by funds obtained from drug and human trafficking, most of it carried on in Western Europe. And certain murky elements within the KLA were closely allied with both al-Qaeda and the Taliban.

"Your people knew this was coming, Alex. With Nadaj so closely involved with al-Quaeda, they couldn't allow him to have a post in the new government."

"And they couldn't allow the world to believe the United States had gassed forty enemy soldiers in its eagerness to capture Bin Laden."

"You did a helluva good job." I thanked Max for the kind words. But the fact that I'd been able to short-circuit Mehling's publishing plans was overshadowed by the murder charge still hanging over my head.

"I hate to say it, Alex, but you look awfully pale. And you've lost some weight."

"Is it that obvious?"

"I'm afraid it is."

The truth was, I was having trouble thinking about anything besides the murder charge. I'd spent the previous night tossing and turning, and had hardly slept since my return to Munich. I'd also been suffering from headaches that sometimes lasted for hours. Max had sensed that I needed someone to talk to and had asked me to stop by.

"I haven't heard very much," Max said. "Most of the people I know are either out of the loop or are retired."

"How much influence does Irmie have on Schneider's thinking, do you think?"

"Schneider isn't a pushover. He has a reputation for being tough minded and independent." Max bit into his roll. "And I have to tell you, Alex, he's closed every case he's caught."

All of a sudden, the rolls and cheese no longer looked very appetizing, and I pushed away the plate. I left a few minutes later.

Chapter 44

Thursday, February 21, 2008

I had the same nervous feeling I had when, as a high school sopho-
more, I was called into the principal's office. Except on this occasion,
I was in the Munich Police Presidium, and the person who was lec-
turing me was Detective Paul Schneider. Irmie was next to Schneider,
behind her desk and looking on with an expression filled with curiosity. Schneider had a mug of coffee on his desk, but hadn't offered me
any.

In the five days since Kosovo had declared independence, the
United States had formally extended its recognition. I'd spent much of
the time taking long walks around the city, many of them in the English
Garden. I wasn't sleeping well, and my powers of concentration had
dwindled to the point where I was hardly able to even read a newspaper. I'd lost my appetite and had the feeling I'd dropped ten pounds.
I'd stopped by Max's apartment a few times, and although we'd talked,
he hadn't been able to find out much of what was going on downtown.
I took that as a bad sign.

Suddenly, from out of the blue, Irmie called. She said I was wanted
at police headquarters and that I should report to Schneider's office.

"When you first showed up here, Klear," Schneider said, "I took
you for just another wisecracking American." He took a bite out of a
cruller, picked up a napkin, and wiped his mouth.

"And I assume you haven't changed your opinion since."

As he chewed, Schneider cocked his head. "Is there any reason I
should have? Does a leopard ever change its stripes?"

"It's the tiger with the stripes."

"See what I mean? You and I can hardly have a sensible conversation. Now we're talking about animals."

Schneider's expression was noncommittal. I was resigned to the fact that when I left Munich police headquarters I'd be wearing handcuffs.

"I thought that when I indicated you were a suspect in a murder case you'd immediately hightail it out of Munich." He paused. "Flight is a sign of guilt. And we would have caught up with you eventually. Either that, or you would have spent the rest of your life fighting extradition—"

"Filling out forms and consulting with lawyers."

"Which might be a fate even worse than life behind bars."

Schneider was right. In some ways, it would have been. "I never thought of leaving."

"I had to change my opinion of you, Klear. You're a determined guy. And I was watching last week when those goons were trying to get you into their car. You put up some fight. But I also have to say when someone like you turns up these days, the cops in any country are going to be uneasy."

"What do you mean?"

"I'll tell you. Max Peters said that back before the Wall came down you were some kind of intelligence officer. According to Max, you were very good at it too. Max said your MI colleagues told him about you. He said you personally ran a bunch of agents in the East. He says, one way or another, you always squeezed every last drop of information out of them."

"I didn't do it alone. I had a partner." I couldn't help wondering why Schneider wanted to talk about those years.

"Sure. Max mentioned your partner too. What was his name?"

"Romero. Buck Romero."

"He says people like you and Romero did as much to win the Cold War as anyone."

"There were plenty of other people who did a helluva lot more than we did."

"Max says they even gave you guys a nickname—the Gold Dust Twins?"

"Looking back, I'd say Buck and I were very lucky."

"Klear, I have to confess that I asked Max about you because I was curious. He says you were very conscientious, going over the Wall and holding agents' hands when they were having their breakdowns and personal problems—and often putting yourself in real danger when you did. Running agents in those days was a very risky, tricky business, one slipup and you were toast. I'm assuming that's how you became such a cool customer."

"Like I say, it was what they paid us to do."

"Max also says you stayed loyal to your people, making sure the American government delivered on whatever they'd promised."

"That was my job too."

"The Cold War is over now, and sometimes I have to wonder what all the fuss was about. But we've got another war now, and we need people like you—guys who believe in something and aren't afraid to stick their necks out when necessary."

"Are you sure you're not mixing me up with someone else, Detective Schneider?"

"One thing you learn as a cop, Klear. Most people are opportunists. They can't help themselves for the bad things they've done."

I laughed. "And then they go out and do the same thing again."

"That's right, and that's why there are so many crooks in the world. And why they never seem to learn."

"Look at the bright side. As a cop, you'll always have a job."

Schneider grinned. "Personally, I do think you sometimes cut corners, but like they say, no one's perfect. Max is a little older than me, but he and I agree on some things—one of them being that if it wasn't for guys like you, Germany today would be a Russian colony. And so would a few other European countries." Before I could interrupt, Schneider raised his hand. "But the world has really changed in the past couple of years, Klear. Situations have changed, and the way the American government does things has also changed. You send your intelligence and special ops people just about all over. That's what I mean when I say police people begin to worry when someone like you shows up. I've heard stories from MI5 officers in England telling about the problems American intelligence people have caused them."

I couldn't argue. Schneider was accurately describing the way our intelligence agencies operate in the post-9/11 world, often inside the borders of friendly countries and without any official permission from the host government. It was the way we'd handled the rendition operation down in Kosovo. And it was pretty much the way Sylvia and I had operated here in Munich.

Is it any wonder that the governments of other countries are wary? And is it any wonder that so many of our operations officers, people like me, find themselves in hot water?

I looked over at Irmie, who had put on a pair of reading glasses and was pretending to look through a pile of papers on her desk. The glasses gave her a prim look, but didn't in any way detract from her sexiness—not for me, anyway. She was nine years older than she was when I left, but to my mind, just as lovely. In some ways, she seemed even lovelier. Although her expression remained completely noncommittal, I knew she was hanging on every word.

Schneider said, "It's probably inevitable that our countries go their separate ways, but in a sense it's a shame too. I think things were better when we were partners." He reached into his drawer, pulled out my passport, tossed it onto the desk. "You can have this back." He slid a piece of paper across his desk for me to sign. "The murder investigation is going in a different direction. And I agree with what you said the other evening. Whoever broke the Green Beret out of jail did everyone a favor."

I wanted to jump on the desk and shout for joy. Doing my best to stay calm and give the impression my release was a foregone conclusion, I said, "I'm happy to hear that." After signing the form, I said, "I'm wondering—"

"About the different direction?" When I nodded, Schneider said, "I'll tell you this much. Kurt Mehling was arrested carrying a murder weapon—and he hasn't provided a very persuasive account for how he got it. And there's reason to believe he was involved with his reporter's murder. That detective you saw me with at the K Klub was a Balkan specialist from the BND. They've provided information that's shed some new light on things."

At last Mehling's connection to Nadaj had come to light.

"Oh yeah, one other thing. From some of the women we learned that the dead guy in the basement—what was his name?"

"Igor."

"Right, Igor. Some of the women said his specialty was turning young girls onto drugs and then into prostitutes. Anyway, his death was no great loss." He glanced over at Irmie. I wondered what kind of role she'd played in influencing Schneider's thinking.

All I really wanted at that moment was to get out of police head-quarters—and start celebrating.

I stood up. As I glanced at Irmie, I thought I saw in her expression just a trace of the same sparkle that had attracted me on that long-ago evening, at a party in this very building.

I told Schneider thanks. He got to his feet and stuck out his hand.

Before I left, I took one last glance at Irmie, whose expression continued to betray nothing. But I had noticed one thing: she was wearing the silver necklace that I'd given her so many years before.

Back in the apartment, I flung myself down on the bed and was asleep within minutes. For the first time in weeks I slept soundly.

When I awoke, it was late afternoon, and I felt I had to talk to Irmie. She answered on the first ring, and I said, "I have the urge to celebrate, and I don't want to have to do it alone." I thought I heard her laughing.

"Well, I'm sure there are plenty of people around who you—"

"There's only one person who I want to celebrate with."

"Oh, really?"

As we talked, I could hear Irmie's tone begin to soften. I got the feeling she was just as relieved as I was by the way things had worked out.

Chapter 45

Friday, February 22, 2008

For our first date I chose an out-of-the-way café in Schwabing, a dark place with candles on the table and two musicians, on piano and violin, supplying a romantic background. At one point I recognized "Mephisto Walz," a piece that I'd always liked and one which brought back some memories. Years ago, we'd attended a program of romantic composers at the Residenz Theater and that piece had been on the program. I wondered if Irmie remembered. The café was the kind of place she and I used to end up in after one of our long walks in the English Garden.

I was no longer tense, and I really was in the mood to celebrate. Although I supposed the police were in the process of wrapping up the case and had arrested Mehling, I didn't want to talk with Irmie about any of those things.

"I have to thank you, Irmie." Before she could interrupt, I said, "You were taking an awful risk—"

"I had a responsibility to fulfill." Although she continued to look at me with her blue-green eyes, she didn't say anything more.

I was still wondering why Irmie had done it. To whom did she feel a responsibility—to her job? She'd said a number of detectives had doubted Brinkman's guilt, but would that suspicion have led her to do what she did?

Or did she do it for me?

I said, "I don't think a day went by that I didn't think about you. Has it really been nine years?"

"Do you say things like that to all the girls, Alex? That you were always thinking of them?" Irmie began toying with the stem of her wine glass.

"Only to the girls that are special."

"And how many of them are there?" Was there just the trace of a smile at the corner of her mouth? I couldn't tell.

I reached out and took her hand in mine. "Only one."

"And who might she be?"

"Irmie, are you being coy?" When she finally did smile, I said, "I can't reveal her name."

"Now who's being coy?"

"I can say this. She's the only woman I've ever really loved. She's the only woman I ever will love. But it took a long time to realize that."

"My goodness!"

"I know. I'm making all kinds of confessions."

"Why is that, do you think?"

I pointed to the bottle standing on the table next to the flickering candle. "It must be the wine." The musicians were playing "Yours Is My Heart Alone," and I said, "Or maybe it's the music."

Or was it only a guilty conscience?

"I have to admit, Alex. I never thought this evening would become so serious." Irmie looked away, and her hands moved nervously.

"You know how serious I always am."

She shook her head, looked at me with her round eyes, eyes that had suddenly filled with tears. "No, Alex. That's the one thing I don't know. I just think I have a completely different idea about you. I think of you as a person who—only wants to enjoy life."

"Irmie!"

"You're like a grasshopper. Hop from here to there and avoid re-sponsibilities."

"Why do you say that?"

"You know why. Don't play dumb."

I shook my head. "That shows we need to spend more time together. I think you should have the opportunity to get me know better."

"I think it's time to leave, Alex."

Although we continued to talk while waiting for the check, I can't remember anything of what we talked about. But that's the way it always was with us. We could talk endlessly about nearly anything.

That was something that hadn't changed, and I was glad of that.

Although it was a chilly evening, we walked arm in arm down to the Münchner Freiheit, the big square, and then up the Leopoldstrasse. It had begun to snow, we were both chilled, and I hailed a cab. On the ride to Gröbenzell, Irmie seemed lost in thought. When she dabbed at her eyes with a tissue, I didn't say anything.

At her building, she said, "I'll invite you in, but only for a few minutes."

"Make me a cup of tea, and I'll be on my way."

While we were drinking tea on her sofa, I asked her how long she expected to continue working.

For a moment Irmie looked away nervously. Then she reached for her cup and took a sip. "I'm not sure, Alex."

I thought I understood Irmie's hesitation. I wondered whether Irmie would ever trade her career for marriage and a family. At one time, she used to talk about things like that.

As she placed her cup back on the saucer, I took hold of her free hand and placed my lips on hers. Although she pulled her hand free and tried to push me away, I was insistent. After a minute, her resistance melted away, most of it anyway.

"Alex, you promised—"

"That seems so long ago."

"Nevertheless, you—"

"I can't be trusted." When I kissed Irmie a second time, her resistance was fleeting. When I kissed her a third time, it was even more fleeting. I couldn't believe I was holding in my arms the woman whose memory had haunted me for the past nine years.

But when I tried to kiss her again, she pushed me away and got to her feet. Her lipstick was smeared and strands of blonde hair were going in every direction. Naturally, her mild dishevelment only made her look even sexier.

But there was anger in her eyes. I asked her what was wrong.

"I'll tell you what's wrong, Alex. I can't trust you."

"That's not true, Irmie."

She was crying. Tears were running down her cheeks. Mascara was all over her face. As I tried to put my arms around her, she pushed me away.

"You're irresponsible, Alex."

Would I be in Munich working at an impossible job if I wasn't responsible? Would I have hung on here in this city while the police were holding a murder charge over my head if I wasn't responsible? But I couldn't say those things. I wanted to talk about another time—and another kind of responsibility.

She looked at me with her round eyes. "Are you going to break my heart again? Well?"

After learning she was in the hospital, I'd written, but she hadn't answered. But what I should have done was drop everything and fly to Munich. By the time I realized what the right thing was, it was too late. It was a series of heartbreaking misunderstandings.

It hurt to have to acknowledge that I was responsible for all these misunderstandings.

"Good night, Alex. I never should have asked you in."

There were so many things I wanted to say, but I knew this wasn't the moment to try and say them. Instead I said, "I haven't finished my tea, Irmie."

"You can finish it next time."

Irmie clicked the door closed behind me, and I'm not sure she heard my "good night." On the way out of the building, I wondered whether there would be a next time.

"I heard the news," Max said. "Congratulations!"

It was slightly more than an hour after my visit to Irmie's apartment. Max and I were standing in his kitchen, both of us holding a glass of *Weissbier* with a slice of lemon floating on top. He had already gotten the news that the police no longer considered me a murder suspect.

We touched glasses, and I took a long swallow. Then I followed Max into the living room and plunked myself into an easy chair.

He said, "You can start enjoying life again."

My argument with Irmie was still very much on my mind. "I'm not sure I can."

"What's the problem now?"

I told him that I wondered whether Irmie and I would ever get together again, and gave him a brief description of our little spat.

Looking at me with his cold, blue eyes, Max said, "You're overreacting, Alex. Irmie has to sort out her feelings. Since you left, all kinds of things have happened to her."

I said I knew that. "Nevertheless, Max—"

"She's still in love with you. That's all you should be concerned about."

"If that's true, she certainly has a strange way of showing it. She was angry, Max. She all but tossed me out of her apartment this evening."

"Alex, she's wild about you. She really is."

For the next ten seconds, I gazed into the beer glass sitting on the coffee table in front of me. Max's reasoning was impossible to argue against, and I didn't try.

Max grinned. "I didn't know you were so sensitive."

I set the beer glass down on the coffee table. "I didn't know it either. The way you're talking, Max, it seems you know more about what Irmie's thinking than she knows herself."

"I know a great deal." Max paused. "When you showed up, I spoke with Irmie. You remember us talking in the English Garden just after you arrived?"

"Of course."

"That evening, right after I dropped you off, I called her. We had a drink together. When I told her you were back in Munich, she very nearly fainted. I realized later I should have broken the news a little more gently."

I didn't say anything. I knew Max well enough to know he wasn't exaggerating.

"She began shaking, Alex. That's how excited she became. Then she had to go to the ladies' room to compose herself. When she got back, she was pale, and I could see she'd been sick. Then she began talking, a blue streak. About you, Alex. About the times you spent together. About how there hadn't been a day in the last nine years when she hadn't thought about you. About what you were doing and how you were getting along. Some days, she said, she spent the whole day thinking about you, and that the biggest disappointment in her life was that things between the two of you hadn't worked out differently."

The funny thing was, Max was describing almost perfectly my feelings for Irmie. And how I'd spent much of my time during those years.

"She wondered whether it would be possible for you two to get back together."

"Irmie wasn't to blame for what happened, Max. I was."

Max shrugged. "Who's to blame isn't important anymore. Think of the future, not of the past. The woman loves you. And, unless I'm mistaken, you love her."

"I'll never fall in with love another woman. It's taken me nearly nine years to realize that."

"Something worries me, Alex." When I asked Max what it was, he said, "What I think is you're about to make the same mistake you made last time. You're not being decisive enough."

"What do you mean?"

"I mean, don't go wandering off like you did last time. Now is the time, believe me. There can be only one explanation for the tremendous effort she made to keep you out of jail and get this case solved." Max paused, fixed me with an unwavering gaze. "She loves you, she really does. And she'd marry you in a second." Max paused. "Do you know what I'd do in your place?"

"I think I do."

Max raised his glass, and we both finished off our beers with a long swallow. I left a few minutes later.

During the taxi ride home I thought about what Max had said. When I found I couldn't relax, I went for a long walk. But that didn't help. After finally going to bed, I was too wide awake to fall asleep, and spent most of the night tossing and turning. In the course of the evening I made my decision.

On Saturday morning I visited a downtown jewelry shop. The people were very helpful, showing me styles and estimating sizes. They said I could pick up the ring on Monday afternoon. I couldn't wait.

My plan was to call Irmie on Monday, ask for a date, and then pop the question. I went over in my mind just how I would do it and just what I would say. I wondered, first of all, whether I should first ask for her hand and then produce the ring. Or should I just take out the ring, and let her draw her own conclusion. Finally, I decided I'd let events take their course.

I thought that a nice place to go might be the café we visited the previous week. Maybe I could ask the musicians to play an appropriate piece of music, something really romantic.

On Monday, just after noon, I picked up the ring. The people in the shop all offered their congratulations. After lunch, I was so keyed up I needed to relax and took a long walk. After getting home, I put through a call to police headquarters.

Someone else, possibly another detective, picked up. I told him who I was and asked for Detective Nessler.

"Detective Nessler is tied up," the guy said a minute later. "She can't come to the phone right now."

That evening I called Irmie at home. When she didn't answer, I assumed she was out, and left a message.

On Tuesday, I called headquarters again and finally got through to Irmie. But when I asked if she cared to go out that evening, she said, "I'm awfully busy at the moment."

"How about tomorrow? I could come by and—"

"I'm tied up tomorrow evening." Before I could say anything more, she called out to someone, "I'll be right there. I have to run, Alex. Bye."

By now, I was really nervous, like every man, I suppose, before popping the big question.

Although I called twice on Thursday, I was told both times that Irmie was unavailable.

I finally caught up with Irmie late Friday afternoon. When I told her I wanted to see her, hopefully that evening, she said, "I don't think so, Alex."

"But Irmie. I've been calling all week. I was hoping—"

"I know that. I just don't think that it's right."

"That what's not right?"

"I don't know. I'd prefer not to see you tonight—or tomorrow night."

"When then?"

"I don't know, Alex. I have to sort out my feelings."

How dumb am I supposed to be? How much of a doormat? I should have known I was getting the runaround. I'd bought a wedding ring for a woman who not only didn't want the ring; she didn't even want to see me. Maybe I should have made a smart remark—like "go sort out your feelings with someone else"—but managed to show some restraint.

Still holding my cell phone, I began punching in numbers. I was looking for an airline with an available seat on a flight to New York.

Chapter 46

Sunday, March 2, 2008

Late Sunday morning, standing at the curb in front of my building, I tossed my suitcase and carry-on into the trunk of Max's car, then nodded. "That's it." Max slammed the trunk closed. In a couple of hours I'd be in the air. I couldn't wait to be gone. I'd endured too much in this city.

When I phoned Max and said I was leaving, he'd offered to drive me to the airport.

With both hands on the steering wheel, he drove silently. Neither of us made any attempt at small talk. As we drove, I recalled that the Kosovo rendition had taken place the previous March, just one year ago. I looked out at the sights, the Olympic Stadium, the TV tower, and the modern skyline—and realized I was probably seeing them for the last time. I'd first landed here a long time ago, and I winced as I recalled how young and impressionable I was back then.

It was only after we arrived at the airport that Max said, "Are you sure you're doing the right thing?"

"I'm positive."

Max shook his head. "I hope you don't mind me saying this, Alex, but I think you're making the same mistake you made nine years ago."

"Maybe, but I kind of doubt it."

"How do you feel about Irmie?"

"How does she feel about me? I have an idea Irmie is leading a full life. She doesn't need me around."

For some reason Max had the idea that I was the one person who could make Irmie happy.

It was a nice thought.

I'd been busy. I'd called Shenlee in D.C. and spoken with his secretary. I told her to let Jerry know that I was on my way back to the States and would be available for a post-op debriefing within the next week. I was also able to get in touch with Gary Lawson, my partner in the ice business. According to Gary, things were going good, and he was looking forward to having me back.

Max identified himself as a former policeman for the security people and after they'd checked us out, we decided to have a farewell cup of coffee standing at the quiet corner of a lunch bar.

Max again said I was making a mistake except this time he was blunter about it.

"It's no go, Max." I was finding it difficult to forget the humiliation of the past week.

"Now I'm going to tell you something else. You're not admitting to yourself that it was Irmie who kept you out of jail. And she did it because she thinks the world of you. If you killed that character, she knew you had a damned good reason."

I shook my head. I just couldn't shake the memory of this past week. After I'd bought her an engagement ring, she gave me the runaround—and finally told me she'd prefer not to see me.

Max grabbed his mug, emptied it with a long swallow, then slammed it back down on the bar. "I have the feeling I'm talking to a wall."

Just as they were calling my flight, I ordered a coffee refill that I didn't really want. When the woman looked at Max, he shook his head. Neither of us said anything, but I had an idea what Max was thinking. He seemed to think I should get back into the car with him and return to Munich, but that wasn't going to happen.

I guess he was right when he said he was talking to a wall. Other people have told me that. Irmie used to tell me that, and Sylvia said it too. Vickie and her crew in Kosovo were definitely talking to a wall when they tried to get me to say things into their video camera.

Neither of us spoke for a good two minutes. "You better get going, Alex." Max stuck out his hand. "*Auf Wiedersehen.*"

"Auf Wiedersehen, Max."

I drank the coffee slowly, then strolled in a leisurely fashion through the airport. I suppose I was having second thoughts, but I knew I wasn't going to change my mind. Max had been right when he said he was talking to a wall.

The passengers were already boarding when I arrived at the gate. I took my place at the rear of the line, my carry-on slung over my back.

I was standing there perhaps two minutes when I heard someone say my name.

"Alex?"

Because I knew whose voice it was, my heart jumped. Irmie was standing next to me, smiling her fabulous smile, her wide eyes gazing up at me. "I wanted to see you before you left." Around her neck was the silver necklace.

I dropped my carry-on, took her in my arms, and kissed her. Her lips were soft and yielding, and I couldn't let her go. As I held her, I was aware of the last passengers moving by us.

A flight attendant called out something about tickets and boarding. Oblivious to the people around us, I began fumbling through my carry-on, searching feverishly. I had to find it. The loudspeaker announced the final call.

A minute later, I had the small box in my hand. As I removed the ring, I heard Irmie gasp. "Oh, Alex."

I mouthed the words, "I love you," and then I placed the ring on the finger of her left hand. "And I always will," I said.

Out of the corner of my eye I saw one of the attendants standing with her hand on the handle of the door to the boarding tunnel.

"Come back this time, Alex."

I nodded. Words were unnecessary. As I passed through the door, the flight attendant was smiling. She held the door open long enough for me to turn around and blow Irmie a kiss. My last sight of Irmie was of her waving. Her mascara was smudged and there might have been a tear on her right cheek.

Epilogue

American Consulate
Königinstrasse 5
80539 Munich
Germany

Dear Mr. Klear:

Your request concerning Tania Moisiu has been forwarded to me by the deputy secretary in Washington, D.C.

You were correct in saying that Miss Moisiu was under arrest here in Munich. Until two weeks ago, she was being detained in prison prior to going to trial. The German authorities had charged her with a number of criminal violations, some quite serious, among them soliciting and being resident in the Federal Republic without a visa. Subsequent to eventual conviction, she almost certainly would have served some jail time before being deported to her native Kosovo.

I was able to speak with the police president on the phone two weeks ago in connection with your request, and he said he had already spoken with Washington about the matter. He was more than cooperative. It has been arranged to have all the criminal charges against Miss Moisiu dropped, and the consulate has been able to provide living quarters and per diem for her until the paperwork is completed.

I understand that the problems regarding her immigration status to which you referred have been resolved. When I personally interviewed Miss Moisiu, I found her to be personable and determined, but extremely depressed. One can only guess at the hardships people from that part of the world have endured in recent years. Miss Moisiu's mood changed dramatically when I informed her that the criminal charges against her had been dropped and that the possibility existed for her to begin a new life in the United States.

Sincerely yours,
Grant Martinez,
Assistant Legal Attaché

PS. As per your instructions, the fact that you initiated this request is known only to me and the deputy secretary. Be assured that your name will remain outside the formal process and never be mentioned. However, Miss Moisiu said that she had a one-word message to "someone": *Drejëtsi.* It's my understanding that the word is Albanian for "justice." And she also said, *Falemnderit.* Thank you.

Glossary

The following explanations might help to clarify some situations and expressions in common use by military personnel stationed overseas.

Alpha, Bravo, Charlie—The first three letters in the military phonetic alphabet.

Ariana Hotel—In 2002, the CIA took over the Ariana, which is close to the presidential palace and has since had various uses as a hotel for transient personnel, a military command post, and the CIA station in Kabul.

Article 15—A punishment for a minor infraction that will not be entered into a soldier's permanent file.

Balad—In 2007 Joint Base Balad, which is about fifty miles north of Bagdad, was the central hub for airlift and U.S. Air Force operations in Iraq.

Battle of Kosovo—A critical event in Kosovo's history. The battle, which was fought not far from Pristina in 1389, ended with a Turkish victory over Serbia. Kosovo then came under Turkish rule, but with the decline of the Ottoman Empire, Kosovo was annexed by Serbia. Before February 2008, Kosovo had never been an independent nation.

besa—An oath taken by Kosovar soldiers in which they pledge loyalty to their comrades and commit themselves to carrying on the struggles of their ancestors.

BND (Bundesnachrichten Dienst)—Germany's foreign intelligence agency, the BND faced its greatest challenges from the Stasi and the KGB during the Cold War years. It now fights terrorism and other threats to German security in a manner similar to that of the FBI.

BOQ (Bachelor Officer Quarters)—Transient accommodations for military people, often situated in an installation's Officers' Club.

Camp Bondsteel—Established in June 1999, the installation is the largest built by the United States since the end of the Vietnam War. Located in eastern Kosovo not far from the city of Urosevac, it can quarter six thousand, has a hospital, and is also the site of a detention facility.

Class As—Military dress appropriate for formal occasions.

CONUS—A common way for people overseas to refer to the United States.

C-130 (Hercules)—A versatile four-engine turboprop cargo aircraft that, because it can be landed on a relatively short runway, has been widely used in Iraq and Afghanistan.

DI—Military acronym for drill instructor.

DSC (Distinguished Service Cross)—The second highest military decoration that can be awarded to a member of the U.S. Army.

Eagle Base—Located near Tuzla in northern Bosnia, Eagle Base was headquarters for Task Force Eagle, the U.S. component of the sixty thousand soldiers who were deployed to the Balkans in 1996 in order to bring to an end the war between invading Serbs and Bosnian Muslims.

82nd Airborne—The airborne infantry division that has its permanent home at Fort Bragg.

EU—The European Union.

Fayetteville—The North Carolina city adjacent to Fort Bragg, the home of many active duty and retired Special Forces soldiers.

Force Protection—Specially trained contractors with the mission of keeping a military installation secure.

Hirschgarten—One of Munich's largest beer gardens.

intel—Short for intelligence.

Kanun—A centuries-old belief among Kosovars that existence is a life-and-death struggle in which wrongs can only be righted by the shedding of blood, either an individual's own or that of an enemy.

KFOR—A peacekeeping force of fifty thousand troops from thirty-nine NATO nations that entered Kosovo in June 1999.

Kosovo Liberation Army (KLA)—Organized in 1996 in response to Serbian atrocities committed in the homeland, the KLA spearheaded the Kosovo Independence Movement. Although the United States first regarded the KLA as a terrorist group, it officially delisted it from that status in 1998, probably for political reasons. Much of the money raised to buy arms for the KLA came from criminal activities, and at times the KLA was suspected of assassinating political enemies.

Landstuhl Hospital—Located in southern Germany, the Landstuhl Regional Medical Center is the largest military medical facility outside the United States.

Leatherman—A versatile multitool favored by the military.

McGuire Air Force Base—located in south-central New Jersey, it is home to the 87th Air Base Wing.

medevac—Transport for a sick or injured person, often by helicopter, to a medical facility.

MI—Military Intelligence.

MP-5—A submachine gun that fires pistol-caliber cartridges and is favored by SEALs and Special Forces soldiers.

Münchner Freiheit—A major intersection on the Leopoldstrasse in Munich.

National Security Agency (NSA)—A government agency that protects the nation's interests to a large extent through electronic means.

One of NSA's primary missions during the Cold War was the gathering of signals intelligence from East Bloc nations through a network of listening stations, many located in Germany and Turkey.

Northern Alliance—A rebellious force of largely non-Pashtun ethnic groups, mostly from Afghanistan's northern provinces, opposed to the Taliban's control of the Afghan government.

NVGs—Night-vision goggles.

One-Star—A Brigadier General. General officers are often referred to informally by the number of stars indicating their rank.

POTUS—Acronym for the president of the United States.

Pristina—The capital of Kosovo, located in the northeast part of the country, not far from the Goljak Mountains.

Radio Free Europe—A broadcast facility situated until 1995 in Munich's English Garden, originally funded by the CIA to counter Communist propaganda in the countries of Eastern Europe. After moving to Prague, RFE has also begun broadcasting programs to the Middle East, Central Asia, and Russia.

RIAS (Radio in the American Sector)—A West Berlin-based German-language radio station that broadcast news and information to the people of East Germany throughout the Cold War.

S-Bahn—The Munich subway and surface rail system.

Schwabing—A Munich neighborhood of mostly old buildings located near the university, home to many students and young people.

SEA-hut—A temporary five-room wooden structure with a metal roof. Originally designed for military use in Southeast Asia. SEA-huts can house six people per room.

Skopje—The capital of Macedonia, located on the Vardar River.

SOCOM—United States Special Operations Command, headquartered at MacDill Air Force Base in Tampa, synchronizes and directs the activities of Special Operations Forces around the world.

Srebrenica (Silver City)—The Bosnian city outside of which, in July

1995, eight thousand male Muslims were rounded up and killed by the VRS, a Serbian paramilitary unit. A memorial ceremony is held there every year.

Stasi (Staatsicherheitsdienst)—The East German secret police and espionage agency.

SOF stamp—A stamp in a passport that indicates the holder is subject to the Status of Forces treaty between the United States and Germany.

Space A—The available seating on a military aircraft after personnel flying with orders have been accommodated.

S-2—A unit's security office.

Task Force Dagger—A 5th Special Forces Group operation begun in 2001 tasked with making contact with Northern Alliance commanders and enlisting their support to drive the Taliban out of Afghanistan.

TDY—A temporary duty assignment.

Teufelsberg—One of the National Security Agency's listening stations, which was built on a mountain of rubble in West Berlin. It was one of a network of stations that until the end of the Cold War overheard transmissions in the East Bloc countries.

UNMIK—The United Nations Interim Administration in Kosovo, which in 1999 was appointed by the UN Security Council to administer Kosovo on a temporary basis. The soldiers wore easily recognizable blue uniforms.

Viktualienmarkt—The old Munich food market, which is now occupied by food stores and cafes.

Volkspolizei—The East German police force.

VOPO—A shortening of *Volkspolizei.*

Warsaw Pact—An alliance of Eastern European nations organized in 1955 as a counterweight to NATO.